LIVES BEYOND BAKER STREET

A Biographical Dictionary of Sherlock Holmes's Contemporaries

Christopher Redmond

2016

Paperback ISBN 978-1-78092-906-4
ePub ISBN 978-1-78092-907-1
PDF ISBN 978-1-78092-908-8

Published in the UK by MX Publishing
335 Princess Park Manor, Royal Drive,
London, N11 3GX
www.mxpublishing.co.uk

Cover design by www.staunch.com

Introduction

Herein are a baron with colossal schemes, the aristocrat who owned the land beneath the houses of Baker Street, the man who designed Arthur Conan Doyle's house, the woman who invented the brake linings for Von Herling's powerful car, and the art editor who hired Sidney Paget to draw Sherlock Holmes. Herein, in short, are the people of the Victorian and Edwardian era, the contemporaries of Sherlock Holmes, Dr. John H. Watson, and Arthur Conan Doyle.

As the stories of Holmes and Watson amble past their happy reader, one who is familiar enough with the tales yet always finding new pleasures in them, there is a moment every so often when someone mentions a person known not just to the imagination but to the encyclopaedia. "The prospect of an interview with Lord Roberts would not have excited greater wonder and pleasure in a raw subaltern than was now reflected upon the face of Mr. Kent," says Holmes in "The Blanched Soldier". "His broad black hat, his baggy trousers, his white tie, his sympathetic smile, and general look of peering and benevolent curiosity were such as Mr. John Hare alone could have equalled," says Watson in "A Scandal in Bohemia". Lord Roberts was a real person, commander-in-chief of the army; Mr. John Hare was a hugely popular character actor. But not every reader knows that, at least without the benefit of an annotated text.

This work of reference was born out of the realization that there are many such people in the Sherlockian canon. Its scope grew with the realization that there are historical persons not specifically named in the canon, but clearly reflected in it. Charles Augustus Milverton, in the story that bears his name, is almost certainly a portrait (in part) of con man and petty blackmailer Charles Augustus Howell. Thaddeus Sholto in *The Sign of the Four* is generally acknowledged to be based on Oscar Wilde. And then there is the mysterious Illustrious Client.

Other historical persons give their names, though not their characters, to figures in the canon: the Reverend Fitzroy Macpherson, for example. Many people of this kind were first identified in the research done by my father, Donald A. Redmond, into canonical sources, published as *Sherlock Holmes: A Study in Sources*, and I have not scrupled in making use of his findings.

At some early stage, the project expanded well beyond these one-to-one correspondences between historical persons and names or specifics to be found in the published stories. One of the great delights of reading Sherlock Holmes, after all, is the window his adventures provide into the society of late Victorian (and early Edwardian) Britain, with its clichéd aristocrats and governesses and street arabs illuminated by gas-lamps in the yellow fog. In the stories themselves, the emphasis is on crime (though there is never a mention of Jack the Ripper) or at least, in Holmes's phrase, "whimsical little incidents".

But the era of Sherlock Holmes also experienced social change (such as the "board-schools" he mentions in one story, created after elementary education was made compulsory in 1870), technological innovation (Violet Smith's young gentleman is an electrical engineer), art (of which Holmes had "the crudest ideas", in Watson's estimation), and of course public affairs. When Watson reads the newspaper in "The Bruce-Partington Plans", he encounters "news of a revolution, of a possible war, and of an impending change of government". When a telegram comes to Baker Street or there is a ring at the street-door, neither Holmes nor Watson can be sure which of these worlds they may be about to enter; their clients are politicians, hydraulic engineers, makers of artists' materials, conservative but sociable bachelors of a certain sexuality who have unwittingly become entangled with a Central American junta.

In the end I decided that the most useful book for Sherlockians would gather up all these people, from all these worlds, and tell just enough of their facts and stories to be a starting point for further reading. With a little help from my friends, I developed a list of 800 people to include, whether they impinged directly on the lives and work of Doyle and Holmes and Watson, or moved in other spheres but nevertheless formed part of the society of which Baker Street was at the centre. These are the people about whom Watson read in the newspaper, the people Holmes might have encountered in the Marylebone Road, the people who made 1895 (and the surrounding years) what it was.

Of course millions of people were alive at that date, including five million in London alone (Watson says so somewhere) and another 25 million in the rest of England. The people I have selected for attention in these pages are, by and large, the prominent ones — the ones who represent trends, the ones who might have been the subject of conversation in the clubs (except the Diogenes), the ones whose names and dates have been preserved and so were available to me. There is no doubt that these pages are dominated by barons, knights and tycoons. Still, I want to note that I have tried hard to include some people of humbler backgrounds, among them a dead baker, a street prostitute and a Swiss shopkeeper. I have also mentioned as many women as possible, a difficult endeavour since the Victorians were inclined to subsume women's lives into those of their husbands or fathers. (Mrs. Beeton is an easy exception to note, and I am proud to have found some other cases in which I could redress that wrong a little.)

The scope of these biographies extends well beyond Britain, particularly to the United States but as far afield as Brazil and Siam, and some of them have no discernible connection to Sherlock Holmes. There is a reason for that: London was the crossroads of the world, where one might encounter lascars, American miners, Andaman Islanders and Peruvian beauties. It seemed to me that acknowledging what was happening on many parts of the world stage in 1895 might provide some perspective on the lives Holmes and Watson were living in Baker Street.

Writers are perhaps over-represented in this listing, again for what I thought was a good reason: the stories of Sherlock Holmes are, above all, literature, published between 1887 and 1927, and there is something to be learned from seeing what other literature was appearing at the same time. I have made a particular point of including some authors who were friends of ACD himself, or whose work he read and admired. The entries do not include ACD's immediate family, but a few of his in-laws have found their way in.

The time period I have tried to keep in mind is the years when Sherlock Holmes is said to have been in professional practice, that is, from about 1880 to 1903. Most of the people noted in these capsule biographies were active, or at least well known, during that period. I have extended the dates forward for some years here and there, to include more of Arthur Conan Doyle's associates, a few early figures in the popularization of Sherlock Holmes and detective fiction, and some individuals who are notable because of World War I, an important period in ACD's life and thought. And I have extended the dates backward to include some people who clearly cast a shadow onto the 1880s, though they were no longer living. In this category are Winwood Reade, whose iconoclastic book Sherlock Holmes recommended to Watson, and the novelist Thackeray, who dandled the infant ACD on his knee. Besides, I wanted to write about Lola Montez. With some regret I have omitted Edgar Allan Poe (but there are plenty of other places to read about him) and Henry Bradshaw, who invented the railway timetable, but regrettably died before Sherlock Holmes was born. From Holmes's ostentatious little speech in "The Illustrious Client" about talented criminals of the past, I have included Charlie Peace (who lived to 1879) but omitted Thomas Griffiths Wainewright (died 1847).

The original idea was to keep each biography to no more than 100 words. That restriction immediately proved to be laughable. About nearly every one of these people, so much is known, and so much is interesting, that I had to write far more, no matter how desperately I pruned. And still each of the 800 biographies is a mere placeholder for a full life story — just enough, I hope, to help the reader place that individual chronologically and geographically and within the complicated matrix of Victorian life. There's an Internet and a library waiting to tell you much more.

I have given each individual's most familiar name and, where relevant, other names such as birth names, pseudonyms and titles of nobility. I have tried to be as clear as possible, but it's an uphill battle. When it comes to titles, the one I have shown is generally the one the individual had at the end of his or her life, reflecting an accumulation of honours. Some public figures — the 8th Duke of Devonshire is a striking example — lived practically a whole career under another name, a "courtesy title" that was eventually outgrown.

Entries are listed according to the individual's year of birth. As much as possible, people with multiple names have multiple entries in the index, which is the primary approach to this book other than simple browsing (although I hope there will be plenty of that). Within an individual entry, names of other people are shown in *bold italics* for those who also have a full entry at the appropriate place, and in bold type only for those who do not.

Deliberately, I have given no exact dates for births, deaths, or events, not even the Ripper murders or the sinking of the *Titanic*. My intention is to give a narrative in broad strokes, avoiding too much detail. This rule also saves space and improves consistency, since in many cases specific dates simply are not available.

Basic public-domain information about public figures has frequently been derived from reference websites, most importantly Wikipedia and Biography.com. I have quoted directly from Wikipedia — with credit, of course — in a number of instances where I found its phrasing particularly admirable and pithy. Other factual information has been extracted from, as Sherlock Holmes put it, "several trustworthy books of reference". I need not list the general books I have consulted, but I should like to acknowledge the most important Sherlockian books that I have used with gratitude:

• Jack Tracy's *Encyclopaedia Sherlockiana*
• *A Bibliography of A. Conan Doyle*, by Richard Lancelyn Green and John Michael Gibson
• Leslie Klinger's *Sherlock Holmes Reference Library*
• *A Chronology of the Life of Sir Arthur Conan Doyle*, by Brian W. Pugh

• Andrew Lycett's *Conan Doyle: The Man Who Created Sherlock Holmes*
• *The Films of Sherlock Holmes*, by Chris Steinbrunner and Norman Michaels
• Donald A. Redmond's *Sherlock Holmes: A Study in Sources*, already mentioned
• *A Sherlock Holmes Almanac*, originally compiled by Svend Petersen, in its expanded 2003 edition

I have also benefited enormously from the Sherlock Holmes Pastiche Characters listing maintained online (www.schoolandholmes.com).

The illustrations are all engravings and photographs dating from the late 19th century or the first few years of the 20th, and I believe them all to be in the public domain.

I want to express enormous gratitude to Sherlockian friends who have helped and encouraged along the way, and particularly to Leah Cummins Guinn, who made her formidable research skills lavishly available to help me with several otherwise evasive minor figures of history, and Mattias Böstrom, who apparently knows everything and is generous in sharing it. Other Sherlockian friends — John Sherwood, Susan Dahlinger, Barbara Rusch — have kindly helped with particular points.

And I am most grateful to my wife, Susan, who not only refrained from complaining at the amount of time I was spending over my keyboard as this book took shape, but allowed me to tell her about many of the more interesting figures I turned up, and asked questions that improved the way the stories are told.

George Wombwell (1777-1850) was the owner of a highly successful travelling menagerie. His show's fame earned him a mention in "The Veiled Lodger", as Sherlock Holmes comments that the showman Ronder "was the rival of Wombwell, and of *[George] Sanger*, one of the greatest showmen of his day". Wombwell was no rival, being long dead, but his name survived in the Bostock & Wombwell Menagerie, operated by **Edward Bostock** (1858-1940), whose mother had been Wombwell's niece, **Emma Wombwell**. George Wombwell's original menagerie dated from 1810, and at its height it included everything from elephants to ostriches. Wallace, one of the stars of the show, was the first lion to be bred in captivity in Britain. Wombwell was noted for his ingenuity in attracting customers; when his elephant died en route to London's annual Bartholomew Fair, he exhibited it anyway with a notice promising "The Only Dead Elephant in the Fair", something Londoners would rarely get to see.

Sir **Moses Montefiore** (1784-1885) was a London businessman who became a prominent figure in Jewish political and charitable activities, and president of the Board of Deputies of British Jews for thirty years. He began as a grocer's apprentice, later was a stockbroker, and eventually had interests in insurance, railways, gas and other businesses; his wife, **Judith Cohen**, was a relative of the *Rothschild* family. He settled in Ramsgate, Kent, where he built a synagogue and a yeshiva (religious college). Montefiore tried to influence the treatment of Jews in Russia, Morocco and Romania, and poured money as well as time into projects in Palestine, as it was then generally called. A windmill that he built in Mishkenot Sha'ananim, just outside Jerusalem, remains a landmark.

Sir **Samuel Cunard** (1787-1865) was the founder of the Cunard Steamship Company. Born in Nova Scotia, he was a success in business there (notably with the Halifax-Dartmouth ferry), then went to England to bid for a contract to carry mail internationally. Cunard's transAtlantic service began in 1840, and after the firm was reorganized as a stock corporation in 1879 it entered an era of frantic competition with the White Star Line and German steamship companies for speed on the Atlantic crossing. Famous ships included RMS *Etruria* (1885; Arthur Conan Doyle travelled on it in 1894) and RMS *Carpathia* (1901). "The Illustrious Client" speaks of "the Cunard boat *Ruritania*, starting from Liverpool on Friday". There was no such ship, and the Cunarders left Liverpool for New York on Saturdays and for Boston on Tuesdays.

Horace Vernet (1789-1863) may be the man to whom Sherlock Holmes refers in "The Green Interpreter: "my grandmother… was the sister of Vernet, the French artist." But there were other artists in the family, notably **Claude-Joseph Vernet** (1714-1789), and the dates are awkward. Horace Vernet specialized in broad scenes of sports and battles, particularly from the era of the Emperor **Napoleon**; some of them are a major tourist attraction at Versailles. His 1835 "Self-Portrait with Pipe" is sometimes cited as showing a remarkable resemblance to Holmes. He was actually born in the Louvre, and lived in Paris most of his life, through travelling to see the sites of battles, and accompanying the French army during the Crimean War.

Sir **George Sartorius** (1790-1885) entered the Royal Navy at age 11, and reached the rank of Admiral of the Fleet at 79. His experience at sea ranged from the Napoleonic Wars to an incident off Gibraltar in 1843 in which he helped to save USS *Missouri*, which had caught fire; the Congress of the United States voted him its thanks. (His Royal Navy career had a break in the 1830s when he went to assist the winning side in a small war over the Portuguese crown.) He was a naval aide-de-camp to Queen *Victoria* as of 1846, and was then promoted to successively higher levels of admiral. As a strategist he argued that the navy should build "ram ships" for brute-force attacks, and he was also interested in submarine artillery.

Charles Babbage (1791-1871) was an engineer and thinker who designed, but was unable to build, the "difference engine", a machine that would have been the world's first programmable computer. He studied mathematics at the University of Cambridge, became a Fellow of the Royal Society, developed actuarial tables, helped found the As-tronomical Society, published work on what would now be called industrial engineering, collaborated with **Ada Lovelace** on mathematical formulas, promoted novel theological ideas and campaigned against street noise. For 11 years he was Lucasian Professor of Mathematics at Cambridge.

Colin Campbell, born **Macliver**, 1st Baron **Clyde** (1792-1863), was a military officer, eventually a field marshal. He fought in Britain's major wars from the Peninsula (opposing Napoleon in Spain, 1807-1814) to the Crimea (opposing Russia, 1853-1856) and was appointed comman-der-in-chief of British forces in India just as the Mutiny of 1857 was gathering steam. Battling the rebels, he captured Lucknow not once but twice and won a significant victory at Cawnpore (Kanpur). With the mutiny at an end, he returned to Britain in 1860. He is referred to (only as "Sir Colin") in *The Sign of the Four*.

Thomas Charles Druce (1793?-1864) was the proprietor of the Baker Street Bazaar, an establishment on the west side of Baker Street, between King Street and Dorset Street, that sold heavy furniture, carriages and equipment for horses, and other goods. The same property was home to the Portman Rooms entertainment hall, Madame *Tussaud*'s waxworks (until 1884), and an artificial ice rink. Druce's origins were obscure and his habits eccentric, facts that added some credibility when his daughter-in-law, **Anna Maria Druce**, went to law in 1898 claiming that Druce had been a secret identity the **5th Duke of Portland**, making her son the rightful duke. There were other claimants as well, as Druce proved to have had two marriages and seve-ral children. The Bazaar was operated after Druce's death by a son, **Herbert Druce**, who learned late in his life that he had been born illegitimate.

Sir **Rowland Hill** (1795-1879) was the inventor of the postage stamp, as well as other aspects of the modern postal system. The "sheet of stamps" Watson kept in his desk (*The Sign of the Four*) were pre-sumably the Penny Lilac variety, each worth 1d (about 40 cents in today's money), that had succeeded the Penny Blacks introduced by Hill in 1840. Hill was a teacher, holding no official position, when he proposed an overhaul of the post office, and was hired to implement his ideas despite initial ridicule. In the course of his career he also pre-sented ideas for educational reform, promoted the colonization of South Australia, and for a time managed the London and Brighton Railway.

Thomas Carlyle (1795-1881) was apparently unknown to Sherlock Holmes at the time of *A Study in Scarlet*, but he speaks patronizingly to Watson about him in *The Sign of the Four*. The website Victorian Web identifies him as "Scottish historian, critic, and sociological writer", who realized he was unsuited for Christian ministry. "In June 1821, in Leith Walk, Edinburgh," it goes on, "he experienced a striking spiritual rebirth which is related in *Sartor Resartus*," his master-work, published in 1833-1834. "No coherent body of philosophy can be extracted from his teachings," says the website. "His central tenet was the worship of strength." He translated German texts and wrote a life of **Friedrich**

Schiller, as well as a history of the French Revolution, and articles about **Jean Paul Richter**, whom Holmes refers to airily as "Jean Paul".

Jean-Baptiste-Camille Corot (1796-1875) was a French artist whose landscape painting hung in the "little sanctum" of aesthete Thaddeus Sholto in *The Sign of the Four*. Corot first sent paintings to the Paris Salon in 1827, and was still travelling in the 1870s to locations where he would identify scenes and sketch them, completing the paintings in his studio in the winter. "In his late studio landscapes, which were often peopled with bathers, bacchantes and allegorical figures," says the National Gallery website, "he employed a small range of colours, often using soft coloured greys and blue-greens, with spots of colour confined to the clothing of the figures." Sholto's reference to "a genuine Corot" reflects the prevalence of forgeries and doubtful Corots on the market.

Sir **Robert Christison** (1797-1882) was a medical graduate of the University of Edinburgh, and joined its faculty in 1822 as professor of forensic medicine, later becoming professor of materia medica and therapeutics. "In his role as an expert on toxicology and physiology," says an Edinburgh web site, "he was a key witness in many criminal trials, notably that of serial killer **William Burke** (1792-1829), where he used as evidence the distinctive differences between injuries inflicted before and after death, which had not been previously commented upon in trials." (Sherlock Holmes was caught beating corpses to study exactly the same question.) Also: "He was well known for his ferocious opposition to the admission of women to the medical faculty." He was president of the British Medical Association in 1875-1876, just before Arthur Conan Doyle began medical studies at Edinburgh.

Wilhelm I (1797-1888) was the first Emperor of Germany, adding that title to his previous status as King of Prussia when the German states were united. He was the son of Prussian King **Friedrich Wilhelm III**, and had a military career before taking on the responsibilities of government as Regent when his brother, King **Friedrich Wilhelm IV**, suffered a stroke in 1857. He became King in his own right in 1861. The North German Confederation, established in 1867, became the German Empire with Wilhelm's crowning as Emperor in 1871, while the Franco-Prussian War was still in progress. He had limited taste for politics and for the most part, in Prussia and then in the affairs of the Empire, allowed himself to be led by his chancellor, ***Otto von Bis-***

marck. His Queen, and then Empress, was **Augusta of Saxe-Weimar-Eisenach**, from the ruling family of one of the German states.

Edward Pusey (1800-1882) was a theologian and Oxford professor who was probably the most influential figure in the Church of England for a quarter of a century, and who stirred debate on topics that even devout church folk might now find tedious. His 1843 sermon "The Holy Eucharist, a Comfort to the Penitent" got him suspended from preaching for two years, and sold 18,000 copies. He was based at Oriel College, Oxford, from 1823 to his death, as a theologian, preacher, and Regius Professor of Hebrew. In company with *John Henry Newman*, **John Keble** and others, he was a central figure of the "Oxford Movement", aimed at purifying and reviving the Church, a re-thinking that led many of its members (but not Pusey) to become Roman Catholic. He wrote some of the famous tracts that gave the movement the name Tractarianism; at other times it took his name specifically and was called Puseyism.

George Hudson (1800-1871) was "the Railway King" as Britain went from a few short railways in the 1830s to a network of 7,000 miles of track in 1852. Hudson controlled a large share of the system, including the York and North Midland Railway, the key link connecting London to the north (1840). He also built and bought other lines, in an atmosphere of frantic competition and ambition leading to a stock bubble. About 1849 it became clear that Hudson was running a Ponzi scheme, paying and collecting dividends where there were no profits. He was forced out and had to leave England for a time. But the railways remained, as did the Railway Clearing House, a bookkeeping agency created by Hudson to facilitate travels over multiple companies' lines.

William Calcraft (1800-1879) was one of Britain's hangmen, and is thought to have performed the last public execution and the first private execution when laws on the matter changed in 1868. It is estimated that he hanged a total of 450 people between 1829 and 1874, among them the poisoner *Edward Pritchard*. He was a devotee of the "short drop" method of hanging, by which the victim slowly strangled, rather than the quick-death "long drop" introduced later by *William Marwood*. He would frequently jump onto the victim's shoulders, or pull on his legs, to bring about death, whether out of incompetence or showmanship is not clear. *W. S. Gilbert* mentions him in the *Bab Ballads*: "In busy times he laboured at his gentle craft all day — 'No doubt you mean his Cal-craft you amusingly will say."

William Cavendish-Scott-Bentinck, 5th Duke of **Portland** (1800-1879), served in the army and in Parliament, advanced to the honorary title **Marquess of Titchfield** when his older brother died in 1824, and became Duke on his father's death in 1854. He played almost no role in public life, but became a recluse at his country house, Welbeck Abbey in Nottinghamshire, and his London house in Cavendish Square, where he built 80-foot garden walls. At Welbeck he built a network of tunnels and large underground rooms, and lived furtively in a small suite, leaving the rest of the Abbey unfurnished. He had a large correspond-ence, like the Duke of Holdernesse in "The Priory School", but almost never spoke in person with anyone. Almost two decades after his death, a series of lawsuits — the "Druce-Portland Case" — alleged that he had led a secret life as *Thomas Charles Druce* of the Baker Street Bazaar.

Brigham Young (1801-1877) was the leader of the Latter-Day Saints or Mormons, after the death of their Prophet, **Joseph Smith**; he is also the only historical figure who has a speak-ing role in any of the Sherlock Holmes stories (*A Study in Scarlet*). Born in Vermont, he joined the developing LDS church in 1832, and became one of its leaders (in the Quorum of the Twelve Apostles) in 1835. When Smith was murdered in Carthage, Illinois, in 1844, there was uncertainty about who should head the church; Young attracted the most follow-ers, though other parts of the church followed other men. In 1846-1847 he led the Mormons

on the long trek (described not very accurately in *A Study in Scarlet*) from Nauvoo, Illinois, to what is now Utah. There he built Salt Lake City and other communities, supervised settlements, and was named both president of the LDS church and governor of the Utah Territory. He taught and exemplified the doctrine of polygamy, and by one count married 55 wives.

Heber C. Kimball (1801-1868) was a potter by trade, and a major figure in the early hsitory of the Latter-Day Saints (Mormon) church, under the Prophet, **Joseph Smith**, and then under *Brigham Young*. He and Young, with their wives, joined the church in its early days, in 1832 in New York state, and moved with it to Ohio, Missouri, and Illinois. In 1847, during the Mormons' long trek to what became Salt Lake City, led by Young, he was named First Counselor in the First Presidency of the church, a position he held for the rest of his life. He is mentioned, misspelled as "Kemball", in *A Study in Scarlet* as one of "the four principal elders" along with Young and two fictional characters, Drebber and Stangerson. A footnote in the story refers to "his hundred wives"; historical sources say he had 43.

John Henry Newman (1801-1890) was "the most illustrious of English converts" to the Roman Catholic Church, the *Catholic Encyclopedia* says. He was a member of the Church of England for almost half his life, and from 1824 until his conversion in 1845 he was a clergyman, serving in the religious hothouse of Oxford University, where the "Oxford movement" was rediscovering the Catholic roots of Anglicanism. After converting, he was quickly ordained again, and served Roman Catholic establishments in London and, for most of his life, Birmingham. He was asked to establish a Catholic university in Ireland, which was not a success, but his book *The Idea of a University* (1858) remains a classic. His voluminous other writings included a spiritual autobiography, *Apologia pro Vita Sua* (1864). Newman never worked as a bishop, but was made a Cardinal in 1879. He was beatified (designated "Blessed", a step short of sainthood) in 2010.

Dorothea Dix (1802-1887) was superintendent of army nurses for the United States during the Civil War, and before and after that time a crusader for social reforms, particularly in the care and treatment of mentally ill people. A teacher from the age of 14, she became aware of terrible conditions at institutions in Massachusetts and then elsewhere, and lobbied across the United States and elsewhere for improvements and the opening of new, better asylums. She was unsuccessful and unpopular as an administrator, but effective in swaying public opinion, legislators, and leaders such as Pope **Pius IX**, and her efforts led to the passage of the Lunacy (Scotland) Act of 1857.

John Cadbury (1802-1889) built one of the world's best-known brands as a chocolate maker. At the age of 22 he opened a shop next door to his father's drapery business in Birmingham, selling tea, coffee, and a recently introduced luxury, cocoa. Seven years later he opened a factory, which expanded as a brother joined the business. In 1853, with a reduction in import duties on cocoa, chocolate came into reach for a larger share of the population. However, the company went through a difficult period; Cadbury retired in 1861 and two of his sons rebuilt the firm with the introduction of a new unadulterated, "absolutely pure" product. An emulsification process also made solid chocolates tempting for the first time. The Cadbury family were devout Quakers, supporters of temperance (cocoa was presented as a healthy alternative to alcohol) and interested in social improvement, such as the creation of the Bournville model suburb where the Cadbury factory employed 2,600 people by 1899.

Sir **Edwin Landseer** (1802-1873) painted enormously popular pictures of animals, the most popular of all being "The Monarch of the Glen" (1853) showing a red stag in a Scots landscape. Originally intended for the refreshment-room at the House of Lords, it was instead sold to a private collector and eventually was bought by Pears Soap for an advertising image. Reproductions were sold by the thousand. A member of the Royal Academy before he was 30, Landseer was also responsible for the lions at the base of the Nelson Column in Trafalgar Square (installed 1867), and painted many royal portraits. He suffered from life-long depression and ill health, and was formally declared insane in 1872.

Edward **Bulwer-Lytton, Lord Lytton** (1803-1873), is mocked by posterity for the novel he wrote that begins "It was a dark and stormy night." But he wrote many other things, from historical fiction (notably *The Last Days of Pompeii*, 1834) to science fiction. The "dark and stormy" line is from *Paul Clifford* (1830); the trope of a hollow earth, used by many authors ever since, originates in *Vril: The Power of the Coming Race* (1871). Apart from his writing, which brought him a generous income, Lytton (who adopted the hyphenated surname only in 1844) served in Parliament in the 1830s and was elected again from 1852 to 1866, when he was raised to the peerage as a baron and thus gained a seat in the House of Lords. In 1862, when the King of Greece abdicated, he was offered the throne, but turned it down.

Joseph Hansom (1803-1882) was the inventor of the hansom cab (or just "hansom"), the one-horse, two-wheeled, two-passenger vehicle that Holmes and Watson hail with a whistle over and over again during their adventures. A hansom was smaller than a four-wheeler (clarence cab or growler). Born in York, Hansom apprenticed as an architect and settled in the Yorkshire town of Halifax. His professional work included many Roman Catholic churches and schools, as well as Birmingham Town Hall; he was also founder of the professional journal *The Builder*. The patent for his "safety cab", with a lower centre of gravity than existing vehicles, was issued in 1834.

Nathan Marcus Adler (1803-1890) was Chief Rabbi of the British Empire from 1845 to his death; his son **Hermann Adler** acted in his place after 1879 because of his poor health, and himself was Chief Rabbi 1891-1911. The position represents the Orthodox Ashkenazi tradition, which was dominant in British Judaism. Born in Hanover, Germany, Adler represented his religion during the period of legal "emancipation" of British Jews, allowing them to attend the universities and hold public office. He (or his son) has been suggested as the "Hebrew rabbi" mentioned in "A Scandal in Bohemia".

Sir **Archdale Wilson** (1803-1874) was, from the British point of view, a hero of the Indian Mutiny, briefly referred to in *The Sign of the Four*: "Wilson took Delhi." He had been serving in India since he was 16, initially in the Bengal Artillery, seeing action in various places and working his way up the ranks. When the Mutiny ("the First Indian War of Independence") broke out in 1857 he was at Meerut in north central India, and during the first few weeks of operations was promoted to major-general. There was political pressure to recapture the capital city, Delhi, and Wilson began a siege, forcing his way into the city only six days later. He was dubious about whether he could hold it, but subordinates told him there was no alternative. "After much hard fighting the capture of the city was triumphantly completed," says the *Oxford Dictionary of National Biography*, "and the first decisive blow struck at the mutiny."

Sir **Titus Salt** (1803-1876) was a wealthy Yorkshire manufacturer who built the model village of Saltaire beside a large textile mill. As a young man he built up his father's wool business to be the largest employer in the industrial city of Bradford; among his innovations was the invention of alpaca cloth. When expansion was necessary, he bought land outside Bradford, and in 1851 began construction of the mill followed by houses, churches and public buildings for the new village. His motives, according to the *Dictionary of National Biography*: "a mixture of sound economics, Christian duty, and a desire to have effective control over his workforce". Salt held a succession of civic offices and served in Parliament for two years.

Benjamin Disraeli, Lord Beaconsfield (1804-1881), was twice Conservative prime minister of Britain, rival of the Liberal *William Ewart Gladstone*. Born into a middle-class Jewish family in London (though the family converted to the Church of England), Disraeli was a successful novelist and then entered politics, making a mark quickly through flamboyant style, reformist policies and adroit diplomacy. He served as prime minister for a few months in 1868, and then 1874-1880. Major issues of his time included grain tariffs, education reform, the Suez Canal and the politics of eastern Europe. Disraeli's policies were based on "Tory democracy", a traditional England in which all classes would share the benefits. He was an enthusiastic supporter of the monarchy, and a genius at flattering the elderly Queen **Victoria** and attracting her affection.

Edward Vickers (1804-1897) was a tycoon whose company was a forerunner of several important firms in the history of British industry, involved in steel production, armaments, ships, aircraft, railways and automobiles. Associated companies range from Rolls-Royce to the John Brown and Company shipyard near Glasgow. Vickers himself was initially a miller, who invested in his father-in-law's steel business, reestablishing it as Naylor Vickers & Co. in 1828. He was also involved in the construction of several railways during the boom of the 1840s. Vickers lived most of his life in Sheffield and served as mayor of the city in 1847.

George Sand, born **Amantine-Lucile-Aurore Dupin** (1804-1876), was a French author known to Sherlock Holmes, since he referred to her (and her friendship with *Gustave Flaubert*) in "The Red-Headed League". She had a brief marriage and a long series of affairs with artists of various sorts, including **Frédéric Chopin**, and she scandalized society with her bohemian ways, male clothing (something Irene Adler also favoured), and public smoking. Sand's writing career began with pastoral novels and moved on to essays, literary criticism, and socialist journalism, particularly at the time of France's 1848 revolution.

James Clay (1804-1873) had all the skills society admires, said his friend *Benjamin Disraeli*: he excelled at cards, at racquet sports, at billiards, at social encounters. He was also "an object of dread to families with daughters of marriageable age", the *Oxford Dictionary of National Biography* adds. Though a life-long Londoner, he was elected to Parliament for the northern city of Hull, and actively promoted Hull's business interests. On broader issues he had radical opinions, proposing "a test of literacy and numeracy" for voters, rather than the property qualification then in effect. But his greatest contribution was not to national laws but to the laws of whist, one of the card games most played by gentlemen (and possibly by Sherlock Holmes, judging from "The Red-Headed League"). He chaired a committee to revise the rules of the game after the shift in popularity from 18th-century "long whist" to the new "short whist", and his *Treatise on the Game of Whist* was published in 1864.

Ferdinand de Lesseps (1805-1894) built the Suez Canal, which cut many days off the voyage from Britain or Europe to India and the far east. The Emperor **Napoleon** had envisioned such a project almost a century earlier. As a French diplomat, posted to Egypt, he made friends with **Said Pasha**, son of the Viceroy and later Viceroy himself. After retirement, de Lesseps negotiated with his friend, got permission to go ahead, and rounded up financial and political backing, some of it from Emperor **Napoleon III**. Work began in 1859 and the 100-mile Suez Canal opened in November 1869. In 1875 Egypt sold its share of the hold-ing company to Britain, which thus effectively controlled the canal. Late in life, de Lesseps was appointed to take charge of building a canal in Panama, and work began in 1881, but the project foundered, and the Panama Canal did not become a reality until 1914.

Jérôme Napoléon Bonaparte (1805-1870) was a nephew of **Napoléon I,** the son of the Emperor's brother **Jérôme** and his wife, who came from a wealthy Maryland family. He grew up partly in the United States (he graduated from Harvard University) and partly in Europe, where he made connections with the royal branches of the family but did not make a royal marriage, choosing a Maryland wife instead. "He was regarded as one of the wealthiest and most worthy citizens of Baltimore," says a volume on *The Bonapartes in America*. He formed closer links with France when his cousin became Emperor *Napoleon III* in 1852;

one of his sons, also named **Jérôme Napoléon Bonaparte**, served as a colonel in the Franco-Prussian War.

Mary Seacole, née **Grant** (1805-1881), overcame racial prejudice to become a self-taught nurse and establish a convalescent "hotel" for sick and injured British officers during the Crimean War. A poll in 2004 voted her the greatest black Briton of all time, and comparisons are sometimes made with *Florence Nightingale*. Seacole was born in Kingston, Jamaica, daughter of a Scots soldier and a mother who kept a hotel and ministered to ailing soldiers. She learned traditional medicine from her mother, but travelled to Britain and elsewhere learning modern science as well. In 1854, with the advent of the war, she came to Britain again and asked to be sent to the Crimea as an army nurse, since medical facilities for soldiers were notoriously bad. She was turned down, but went anyway, paying for her own travel and establishing the British

Hotel near Balaclava to provide "a mess-table and comfortable quarters for sick and convalescent officers". She also acted as a sutler bringing provisions to British troops.

Giuseppe Garibaldi (1807-1882) was the best-known hero of the Risorgimento, the series of conflicts that led to the unification and independence of Italy in 1861. At various times he led troops or guerrillas against Austria-Hungary, France, Naples, the Papal States, and Prussia. For the most part he fought in the name of **Victor Emmanuel II**, King of Piedmont-Sardinia, of the ancient House of Savoy, who eventually became the first King of Italy. But neither Victor Emmanuel nor anyone else could control him: he was a charismatic leader, not exactly a socialist but certainly a nationalist before anyone except revolutionary thinker **Giuseppe Mazzini** could see a nation. Garibaldi had been born in Nice, now in France but then part of Piedmont-Sardinia. He worked as a sailor, was involved in an 1834 naval mutiny, and spent a dozen years in South America, where he gained military and naval experience in several local wars. He wore Argentinian gaucho costume for the rest of his life.

Henry Wadsworth Longfellow (1807-1882) was the American poet who wrote "Evangeline" (1847), "The Song of Hiawatha" (1855), and "The Courtship of Miles Standish" (1858), as well as much other poetry. The contemporary of *Alfred Tennyson*, he held a similar position in popular esteem: "I should have to think long if I were ask'd to name the man who has done more and in more valuable directions, for America," **Walt Whitman** wrote. Longfellow studied and then taught at Bowdoin College in Maine and (1836-1854) at Harvard, before abandoning teaching to write full-time. His work was popular rather than elitist — it found many publishers across the English-speaking world, and was also widely translated; his 75th birthday, a few months before he died, was celebrate across the United States. He adhered to European styles rather than breaking new ground that would be peculiarly American; indeed, he was accused of imitating Tennyson.

Robert E. Lee (1807-1870) was the commander of the Army of Northern Virginia who surrendered to *Ulysses S. Grant* in 1865, ending the United States Civil War. He is one of several Confederate generals mentioned in "The Five Orange Pips", which has its background in the politics of the Reconstruction era that followed the Civil War in the American south. Lee had served in the United States Army for most of his career, with combat experience in the Mexican War and administrative experience as superintendent of the United States Military Academy at West Point, but when war broke out his first loyalty was to his home state, Virginia, which joined the Confederacy. He was initially a military advisor, but from 1862 was commander of the principal army. His battles against the Union included Manassas, Antietam, Fredericksburg, Chancellorsville, Gettysburg (July 1863), and finally Appomatox. After the war Lee was president of Washington College, now Washington and Lee University.

Henry Edward Manning (1808-1892) was Archbishop of Westminster, the head of the Roman Catholic Church in England, and the second Catholic bishop in England in modern times to become a Cardinal. He was ordained a Church of England priest in 1833, but "went over to Rome", like other prominent members of the High Church movement, in 1851. In 1865 he succeeded the first Cardinal, **Nicholas Wiseman**, as Archbishop, and in 1875 Pope **Pius IX** named him a Cardinal. Manning was an influential figure in developing Roman Catholic policy about social justice, and became well known and admired in England, even among non-Catholics, for his role in settling the London dock strike of 1889.

Thomas Cook (1808-1892), was the first large-scale travel agent. As a young man he was a Baptist clergyman and temperance campaigner, and in 1841 he organized a trip for more than 500 temperance advocates from Leicester to Loughborough on the Midland Counties Railway, which had been in operation for about a year. More excursions followed, and Cook's great success was a trip to the Exhibition of 1851 in London. Five years later he was sending customers on "grand tours" of Europe. In the 1870s, with his son **John Cook** increasingly operating the business, Thomas Cook & Son was based in Fleet Street, London, and a decade later there were offices around the world, including the one in Lausanne which Watson reports visiting in "Lady Frances Carfax".

Georges-Eugène Haussmann (1809-1891) was the government official who redesigned Paris under the authority of Emperor **Napoleon III**. After serving in civil service posts in several parts of France, he was called to Paris in 1853 as prefect of the Seine *dèpartement*, and began twenty years of work, which included annexing large areas outside the existing city, demolishing neighbourhoods, and creating new boulevards, parks and waterworks. Haussmann's crew — at times one-fifth of the city's workforce — built 50 miles of wide streets, as well as two main railway stations, the Bois de Boulogne park, and *Charles Garnier*'s opera house. Under criticism from legislators, Haussmann was finally removed from office in 1871.

Frances (Fanny) Kemble (1809-1893) was born into a theatrical family, her father **Charles Kemble** being an actor and the manager of the Covent Garden Theatre, where Fanny first appeared on stage in 1829 as Juliet. She was immediately a star in London, and then in the United States when she and her father went on tour in 1832. Two years later she retired to marry **Pierce Mease Butler**, heir to huge estates in Georgia. When Kemble visited there for the first time in 1838-1839, she was horrified by what she saw of slavery. The experience put strains on the marriage, and she and Butler separated permanently in 1845. Kemble

returned to the American stage for a time in 1847. Her book *Journal of a Residence on a Georgian Plantation* (1863) was a controversial exposé of American slavery, although other authors including one of her own daughters denied her account. Her other daughter, **Sarah Butler**, married the author *Owen Wister*. By the 1870s, Kemble was a notable figure in London society, and is said to have told *Henry James* the story that forms the basis of his 1880 novel *Washington Square*.

William Ewart Gladstone (1809-1898) was known as "the Grand Old Man" by the end of his long career as Prime Minister. The son of a Liverpool merchant, he had begun as a Conservative, but helped to form the Liberals (successor to the Whigs) in 1859, when he had already been in Parliament 27 years. He spent time both in government and in opposition, serving as a tax-cutting Chancellor of the Exchequer (finance minister) for a time and earning a reputation as an orator. He became leader of the Liberals in 1867 and was Prime Minister 1868-1874, 1880-1885, 1886, 1892-1894. The social reforms introduced by his first government, including the secret ballot, were not equalled by later accomplishments, and he was eventually trapped in the quagmire of Irish Home Rule, which he could not get Parliament to approve. His party split over this issue in 1886, some of its members becoming Liberal Unionists, under whose banner Arthur Conan Doyle twice ran for Parliament. One reference work describes Gladstone as "a good classical scholar and an earnest high churchman". His moral uprightness, coupled with personal quirks, gave him a keen interest in the rehabilitation of prostitutes, and he sometimes walked London's streets seeking soiled doves to rescue. Two future kings were pallbearers at his state funeral in Westminster Abbey.

Charles Darwin (1809-1882) is generally known as the discoverer of the principle of evolution, although ***Alfred Russel Wallace***, ***Thomas Huxley***, and others also played a part. After studies at Edinburgh and Cambridge, he was chosen to be a naturalist aboard HMS *Beagle*, which in 1831 began a five-year trip around the world under the command of captain **Robert FitzRoy**. He collected fossils, plants and bird specimens from many regions including, famously, the Galapagos Islands off South America, and noticed variations that led him to believe in "natural selection" as the mechanism behind changes in species. He introduced his theory in a presentation to the Linnaean Society in 1858, and in his book *On the Origin of Species by Means of Natural Selection* the following year. For the rest of his life he was the object of mockery for his supposed belief that humanity are descended from monkeys, but Darwin continued his laboratory work and responded to critics as knowledge developed.

Alfred Tennyson, 1st Baron **Tennyson** (1809-1892), was the marquee poet of the Victorian era. He wrote formally sentimental verse such as "In Memoriam" (1850), mourning a friend, **Arthur Hallam**, who had died as a young man, but also more accessible work such as "The Charge of the Light Brigade" (1854), commemorating a disastrous British defeat in the Crimean War and pointing the finger at incompetent military leadership. His long blank verse poems of King Arthur and his knights and associates shaped traditions and earlier writings into a coherent narrative that has largely been the default ever since; the complete collection of *Idylls of the King* was completed in 1885. Tennyson was named Poet Laureate of England in 1850, and continued to write into old age: "Crossing the Bar", a poem about death that is still much anthologized, appeared in 1889.

Edward Fitzgerald, born **Purcell** (1809-1883), met active and future poets during his university years at Cambridge, settled near his family in Suffolk, and quietly wrote poetry. He had an affinity for "Oriental studies", or what would now be called the culture of the Middle East, and in 1859 he published the work for which he would always be best known, a free translation of the "Rubaiyat" of 11th century Persian poet **Omar Khayyam**. (The Persians are a poetic people: 300 years after Omar came **Hafiz**, the writer whom Sherlock Holmes quotes in "A Case of Identity".) Later editions were hugely popular, more so than Fitzgerald's other translations and original work. In *The Hound of the Baskervilles*, Holmes practically quotes from Fitzgerald's *Rubaiyat* when he speaks of "a loaf of bread and a clean collar. What does man want more?"

John Hill Burton (1809-1881) was a Scots historian, and in all likelihood the inspiration for the name of "Dr. Hill Barton" in "The Illustrious Client". He started out as a lawyer, and in 1839 published a *Manual of the Law of Scotland*. His most important book was a *Life of David Hume*, a central figure in the 18th-century Scottish Enlightenment. Also of interest are *Narratives from Criminal Trials in Scotland* (1852) and a two-volume *History of Scotland* (1853, 1870); the *Encyclopaedia Britannica* credits him with being "the first to introduce the principles of historical research into the history of Scotland", and with "a fund of dry humour exceedingly effective in its proper place".

Oliver Wendell Holmes (1809-1894) was a medical professor at Harvard University for most of his life, and the author of such humane volumes as *The Autocrat of the Breakfast-Table* (1858) and its sequels, as well as poetry ("Old Ironsides", "The Deacon's Masterpiece") and novels. He was much admired by Arthur Conan Doyle, who visited his fresh grave when he came to Boston late in 1894, and who repeatedly praised him in his writings about literature. Whether he took the genial doctor's surname for that of his great detective seems an unanswerable question. The doctor's son, **Oliver Wendell Holmes Jr.** (1841-1935), became a justice of the United States Supreme Court.

James Neill (1810-1857) is mentioned in "The Crooked Man" as "General Neill", whose column of troops was "moving up-country", and on a historical website as "the most controversial of the senior British officers who took part in the suppression of the 1857 Indian Mutiny". He is credited with rescuing British forces and civilians from the mutineers at Allahabad, Cawnpore (Kanpur), and Lucknow, where he was killed by a sharpshooter at the moment of victory. He is also noted for insubordination and abuse of other generals, and for atrocities including random killings and deliberate attempts to degrade prisoners before executing them. Born in Scotland, he had been a military officer in the army of the British East India Company for three decades before the 1857 conflict began.

Leo XIII, born **Gioacchino Vincenzo Pecci** (1810-1903), was Pope, the head of the Roman Catholic Church worldwide, from 1878 to his death. He is mentioned (as "His Holiness the Pope") as one of Sherlock Holmes's clients, in the story "Black Peter", and there is a reference to "the Vatican cameos" in *The Hound of the Baskervilles*. Pecci, who came from an Italian noble family, was ordained a priest in 1837, already marked for administrative work in the church's bureaucracy. He served for a time as governor of Benevento and then Perugia, Italian cities that were under the Vatican's control. In 1843 he became a bishop, and served at Perugia for 32 years. Pope **Pius IX** made him a cardinal in 1853; in 1878 he was elected Pope on the third ballot. His papacy was largely occupied by negotiations with various European powers about the status of the church, and with Italy about the independence of the Vatican, which still had extensive territory. In 1896 he issued an encyclical stressing that Church of England priests were not, from the Catholic point of view, validly ordained.

Phineas T. Barnum (1810-1891), who declared "I am a showman by profession," founded the Barnum & Bailey Circus after ventures in theatre, museums, lotteries and politics. He established a museum of freaks and sideshows in New York in 1841, stocking it with frauds like "the Feejee mermaid" (a product of taxidermy) and human oddities such as the midget **"General" Tom Thumb (Charles Stratton)**. He brought *Jenny Lind* to sing in America in 1850, acquired the elephant **Jumbo** from the London Zoo, and promoted the original Siamese Twins **Chang and Eng Bunker**. The Barnum & Bailey partnership, which began in 1881, also involved the circus of *George Sanger*, and was billed as "The Greatest Show on Earth".

Robert Napier, 1st Baron **Napier** (1810-1890), not to be confused with the Scots engineer and shipbuilder of the same name, was born in Colombo, son of a military man, and joined the Bengal Engineers himself at the age of 16. He fought in a number of Britain's countless frontier wars, being wounded twice in the Anglo-Sikh Wars and a third time at Lucknow during the Indian Mutiny. He subsequently fought in China in what was called the Second Opium War, taking part in the destruction of the Summer Palace at Peking in 1860, an action ordered by Lord *Elgin*. Napier followed Elgin back to India, and served as acting Governor-General of India for a few weeks in 1863 after Elgin's sudden death. Finally in 1868 he was sent to Abyssinia (Ethiopia), where he defeated the troops of Emperor **Tewodros II** at the Battle of Magdala. He subsequently served as commander-in-chief for India, then Governor of Gibraltar, and at the end of his life Constable of the Tower of London.

Franz Liszt (1811-1886) was one of the great musicians of the Romantic movement, renowned as a pianist but now remembered as a composer, particularly of symphonic poems and piano solos including his 19 Hungarian Rhapsodies. Born in Hungary, he was a child prodigy and a protegé of **Antonio Salieri**, who had been the rival of **Wolfgang Amadeus Mozart** in Vienna. A life crisis at the age of 15 introduced him to artistic and religious ideas that would influence his music ever afterwards. Two long-running romantic relationships also had an important effect on him. The mother of his children was **Marie de Fla-**

vigny, Countess **d'Agoult**, and he had hoped to marry Princess **Carolyne Sayn-Wittgenstein**; his mistresses included *Lola Montez*. From 1848 he lived in Weimar, Germany, composing and teaching, but in 1863 he entered a monastery outside Rome, subsequently taking religious orders. However, he continued to compose, and travelled to perform; his last concert was given in Luxembourg in July 1886.

William Makepeace Thackeray (1811-1863) was one of the giants of English literature, and Arthur Conan Doyle treasured a vague memory from early childhood of having once sat on his knee. That must have been during Thackeray's brief tenure as editor of the newly-founded *Cornhill* magazine, in which ACD would later be published. A young man of wealth, Thackeray attended Cambridge, studied law, but found his métier in journalism, particularly for *Punch*, and then in a long series of novels. His greatest work, the social satire *Vanity Fair*, appeared in 1848. By the time *Pendennis* was being serialized (1849-1850) he was seen as a rival of **Charles Dickens**, whose *David Copperfield* was appearing at exactly the same time. The two had a personal quarrel that was mended almost at the end of Thackeray's life.

Sir **John Hawkshaw** (1811-1891) was a civil engineer who began his career working on railroads in Yorkshire, moved to Liverpool and then London, and eventually was involved in projects all over the world. He had a great influence on the early construction of railways as they were being introduced in the 1840s, from the Lancashire and Yorkshire to London's Charing Cross Station. Hawkshaw also worked on two Thames bridges, parts of the Underground (the London subway system), canals (his consulting report tipped the decision in favour of building the Suez Canal), and  the port of Buenos Aires. He was involved for a time in a project, ultimately unsuccessful, to build a tunnel to France under the English Channel.

Harriet Beecher Stowe (1811-1896) was the author of about 30 books, the most influential by far being *Uncle Tom's Cabin* (1852). A powerful, sentimental story of what it meant to be a slave in the United States, it did much to stir up abolitionist sentiment and, **Abraham Lincoln** once said, to start the Civil War. *Uncle Tom's Cabin* was commissioned by **Gamaliel Bailey**, editor of the anti-slavery newspaper *The National*

Era. Stowe's other works included textbooks, homemaking manuals, and biographies, as well as more novels. Her father, **Lyman Beecher**, and her husband, **Calvin Stowe**, were both professors of theology; her brother *Henry Ward Beecher* was an influential clergyman.

Charles Lewis Tiffany (1812-1902) was the founder of the renowned New York jewellery store Tiffany & Co. — "the premier source for the luxuries and unlimited extravagance that defined the Gilded Age", as the firm's website puts it today. He opened a shop on Broadway in 1837 selling "stationery and fancy goods", became known as "the king of diamonds" in the 1840s, and began winning international awards for its silverware with the Paris world's fair of 1867. The Tiffany Diamond came from the mines of Kimberley, South Africa, in 1877. His son **Louis Comfort Tiffany** (1848-1933), who became design director at Tiffany's after his father's death, was an influential Art Nouveau designer in jewellery and stained glass.

Edward Greathed (1812-1881) was a British commander during the Indian Mutiny of 1857-1858. He bought his commission (as one did in those days) in the 8th Regiment of Foot, and worked his way up through the officer corps in the same way, with postings to the West Indies, Canada, and (as of 1846) India. His unit — including his brother **William Greathed**, of the Royal Engineers — was part of the forces led by *Archdale Wilson* that recaptured Delhi in September 1857. He then was sent to chase mutineers into Oudh and then to relieve the besieged city of Lucknow. Along the way his troops fought an impromptu  battle at Agra, near the famous fort ("A flying column under Colonel Greathed came round to Agra and cleared the Pandies away from it," says *The Sign of the Four*). He subsequently served under Sir *Colin Campbell* at Cawnpore before returning to Britain for medals, new commands, and eventually a promotion to general.

Edward Lear (1812-1888) was hired as a youth to draw birds, but ended up playing with words. His first book of tricks, published 1846, is still highly valued by nerds. In addition to limericks ("There was an old man with a beard..." is slightly autobiographical) he created "The Dong with the Luminous Nose" and "The Owl and the Pussycat". He also painted landscapes, using the same artistic talent for which the

London Zoological Society had once employed him as an illustrator, and he wrote volumes about his travels. His *Nonsense Botany* was published in the year of his death. Lear suffered all his life from seizures and depression, and was deeply awkward in personal relationships, especially a long-lasting homosexual crush that was not reciprocated. His cat, who figures in his nonsense verses, was named Foss.

Alfred Krupp (1812-1887) inherited a small steel business in the German town of Essen when his father died in 1826. Over six decades he built it into Friedrich Krupp AG, an industrial giant, specializing in armaments, that employed 75,000 people and sold its products worldwide. (The abbreviation AG, for Aktiongesellschaft, is the successor of the "Gt" that Sherlock Holmes refers to in "A Scandal in Bohemia".) Alfred Krupp's contributions included new technology for cast steel, making it possible to build breech-loading cannon that were powerfully effective in the Franco-Prussian War (1870-1871). He also developed a program of social services, housing and insurance for employees, and made Essen largely a company town. His son **Friederich Alfred Krupp** headed the company from 1887 until his suicide in 1902 amid a scandal about his relationships with young boys. Under succeeding generations the company became the major source of weaponry for Germany in two world wars.

Robert Browning (1812-1889) was one of the major English poets, noted for his dramatic monologues such as "Porphyria's Lover" and "My Last Duchess". His single most important work is thought to be "The Ring and the Book" (1869), dramatic narratives based on a 17th-century murder case in Rome. Born in Surrey on the fringes of London, and never much employed except as a writer, he was a master of languages and a student of history. After a brief courtship mostly through letters, retold in the 1930 play "The Barretts of Wimpole Street", he married poet **Elizabeth Barrett** in 1846, and lived with her in Italy, returning to England after her death in 1861. He was so prominent in his lifetime that a Robert Browning Society was formed in 1881.

Andrew Peterson (1813-1906) had been a lawyer in India until he retired, came home to England and bought a country house near Sway, Hampshire, which he remodelled and expanded. He also became a convert to Spiritualism, and fell under the influence of a medium named **William Lawrence**, undeterred by Lawrence's record of a prison term for fraud. Many prominent people of the past spoke to Peterson through Lawrence's séances, including Sir **Christopher Wren**, the 17th century architect, who told him to build a concrete tower on his property. Work began in 1879, and the tower was completed in 1886. At 218 feet, it is still the world's tallest non-reinforced concrete structure. In 1885, Peterson published a volume of *Essays from the Unseen*, taken from the messages Lawrence had delivered to him.

David Livingstone (1813-1873) was a medical missionary and explorer, best remembered for the dramatic incident in which journalist ***Henry Stanley*** found him near Lake Tanganyika in 1871. Born in South Lanarkshire, Livingstone followed his medical studies (in Glasgow) with training from the London Missionary Society, and went to Africa for the first time in 1841. His travels took him across the Kalahari Desert; he was the first European to see the Zambezi River, and gave Victoria Falls its name. Returning to Britain, he wrote *Missionary Travels and Researches in South Africa* (1857) and prepared for a second trip, during which he made more geographical discoveries and learned much about East African slavery, becoming a vocal abolitionist. His third trip began at Zanzibar in 1866. When he had not been heard of by 1871, two energetic newspapers, the *London Daily Telegraph* and the *New York Herald*, commissioned Stanley to find him and write about it. He succeeded, but Livingstone chose to stay in Africa, where he died of dysentery and malaria.

Giuseppe Verdi (1813-1901) composed his first opera, "Oberto", when he was 26; it was performed at La Scala in Milan, before Irene Adler, who later sang at the same historic venue (built 1778), was even born. He struggled professionally for a time, but, as Biography.com says, "He became known for his skill in creating melody and his profound use of theatrical effect. His rejection of the traditional Italian opera for integrated scenes and unified acts only added to his fame." "Rigoletto", "Il Trovatore", "Aida" and "Otello" are among his most important works. His last opera was "Falstaff" (1893). Verdi also played a role in the politics of Italian reunification in the 1860s, significant since Milan was at that time within the Austrian empire.

Henry Ward Beecher (1813-1887), whose picture hung on Dr. Watson's wall at Baker Street, discarded the Presbyterian beliefs of his Connecticut upbringing and became a more broad-minded preacher and activist. He was minister from 1847 to his death of the Plymouth Congregational Church in Brooklyn, and a prominent religious and political figure across the United States. Beecher played a part in smuggling rifles ("Beecher's Bibles") to anti-slavery partisans in Kansas, pressed president **Abraham Lincoln** to emancipate slaves during the Civil War, and endorsed scientific belief in evolution as well as a form of social Darwinism. He was embroiled in a sex scandal, 1872-1875, over a relationship with **Elizabeth Tilton**, wife of his friend **Theodore Tilton**. Beecher was the brother of *Harriet Beecher Stowe*.

Richard Wagner (1813-1883) was one of the great composers, primarily of opera. Sherlock Holmes enjoyed his work at any rate: "It is a Wagner night at Covent Garden!" he says eagerly at the end of "The Red Circle". Wagner was born in Leipzig but is most associated with the Bavarian town of Bayreuth, where he moved in his later years and had an opera house built. His "romantic" operas such as *Tannhäuser* (1845, first performed in London in 1876) are classical standards, but he is remembered most of all for the "Ring cycle" of four operas based on German mythology, completed between 1854 and 1874. Wagner has become controversial for the use to which his political and nationalist views were put by Nazi Germany, in part through the influence of *Houston Stewart Chamberlain*.

Sir **Henry Bessemer** (1813-1898) was the inventor of the Bessemer converter, which made the manufacture of steel simpler, faster and more economical, and led to the development of Sheffield, in Yorkshire, as a manufacturing city. Bessemer took after his father, a successful inventor, and was first commercially successful with improvements in paint and glass production. Several years' research led to an 1855 patent for his process of removing the impurities by blowing air through pig iron. Suddenly steel, far stronger than cast iron, would be available for bridge construction and other projects. When technical problems arose,  Bessemer went into the steel business himself, solved them and became wealthy. Into old age he continued developing more than 100 other inventions.

Sir **Isaac Pitman** (1813-1897) was a member of a religious group that was considered somewhat eccentric, the Swedenborgians or "New Church", and published books and tracts about its founder and teachings. He was a total abstainer and vegetarian (indeed, vice-president of the Vegetarian Society). He campaigned for reform of the notoriously inconsistent spelling of English, with which, as a teacher, he was all too familiar. And, in 1837, he produced a pamphlet titled *Sound-Hand* explaining a method for writing down the words that people speak. This "phonotypy" was later known as Pitman shorthand and remains, with revisions, the most common form of shorthand in Britain, although Gregg is more used in the United States. Several shorthand editions of *The Sign of the Four* were published beginning in the 1890s.

Angela **Burdett-Coutts, Baroness Burdett-Coutts** (1814-1906), gave much of her enormous wealth to charity, including a home for women escaping "a life of immorality", church schools, projects to relieve suffering in Africa and Borneo, and social housing. She was president of both the British Goat Society and the British Beekeepers' Association, was a founder of the National Society for the Prevention of Cruelty to Children, and paid for Edinburgh's landmark fountain and statue of the dog Greyfriars Bobby. Her money came from her maternal grandfather, banker **Thomas Coutts**. In 1871 she was made a baroness, becoming the first woman in modern times to receive a peerage in her own right. At age 67 she married **William Bartlett**, her American-born secretary, who was 29.

Ellen Wood (Mrs. Henry Wood), née **Price** (1814-1887), was the best-selling author of some thirty novels, and from 1867 to her death the editor of *Argosy* magazine and its principal author. Born in Worcester, she was always a voracious reader. A childhood curvature of the spine left her small (less than five feet tall) and so weak she could hardly lift anything. She did much of her writing in a reclining chair. For some 20 years she lived in France with her husband, **Henry Wood**; in 1851 she began sending short stories to the *New Monthly Magazine* edited by novelist **Harrison Ainsworth**. In 1859 her first novel, *Danesbury House*, won first prize in a competition. Her most successful work, the melodramatic *East Lynne*, was serialized in the magazine in 1860-1861 and then published in three volumes. Other novels followed, two of them involving a Scotland Yard detective. Many of her short stories narrated by "Johnny Ludlow", an orphan living with a wealthy family in Worcestershire, are also mysteries.

Sheridan Le Fanu (1814-1873) was the most important ghost story writer of the 19th century. Born in Dublin, he studied law at Trinity College there, and was called to the bar but never seriously practised law; instead, from 1838 he was writing stories and becoming a successful newspaper proprietor. In 1861 he became editor of the *Dublin University Magazine*, an important periodical in Ireland's small literary and cultural circles, and a number of his stories were first published in its pages. His work ranges from historical novels to ghost tales and the so-called "sensation fiction". "He specialised in tone and effect rather than 'shock horror'," Wikipedia says of his work, "and liked to leave important details unexplained and mysterious." His important works include *The Purcell Papers*, a set of short stories based on Irish folklore; *Uncle Silas* (1864), a gothic horror novel; and *The Watcher and Other Weird Stories* (posthumous, 1894).

William Claridge (1814?-1882) was a butler turned hotel-keeper and "by all accounts, the walking embodiment of a bow and scrape, a one-man lexicon of servilities," says the author of a 2012 feature in the *Independent* newspaper. In 1854 he and his wife, **Marianne Maloney**, bought the long-established Mivart's Hotel at 51 Brook Street in London's Mayfair district. They already operated an adjacent boarding-house, and knocked several buildings together to create Claridge's Hotel. It became known as the leading hotel for royalty, aristocracy and sophisticates — and, according to "His Last Bow", once for Sherlock Holmes, though that was after *Richard D'Oyly Carte* bought it in 1894 and rebuilt it. The theme is now art deco; Marianne's portrait continues to hang in the lobby.

Thomas Chambers (1814-1891) was, at the summit of his career, Recorder of London, the chief judge at the Central Criminal Court or "Old Bailey". He held that post from 1878 to his death, after two decades in the next most senior position, Common Serjeant of London. Chambers became a barrister in 1840 and was a Liberal Member of Parliament 1852-1857 and 1865-1885, in an environment when there was not thought to be a conflict between legislating and judging. When Spy (**Leslie Ward**) caricatured Chambers for *Vanity Fair* magazine in 1884, the caption was "The deceased wife's sister", reflecting his interest in the long-running controversy over whether the law should be changed so that a man whose wife died could then marry his sister-in-law.

Sir **John A. Macdonald** (1815-1891) was responsible more than any other person for the creation of what is now Canada, and became its first prime minister. Born in Scotland and raised in Kingston, he practised law, entered municipal and then territorial politics, and worked with fellow Conservative **George-Étienne Cartier**, Liberal rival **George Brown**, and others to negotiate "confederation" among Québec, Ontario, Nova Scotia and New Brunswick, with the creation of a federal Parliament and government, in 1867. Major issues during his leadership included construction of transcontinental railroads and relationships, especially tariffs, with the United States. Macdonald had a reputation as a reckless drinker, and was touched by a bribery scandal over railway construction, but he served six terms as prime minister, serving 1867 to 1873 and 1878 to 1891.

Henry Highland Garnet (1815-1882) was the United States minister to the African nation of Liberia when Arthur Conan Doyle met him, weeks before Garnet's death. Indeed, he may have examined Garnet during his final illness. The young ACD was the ship's doctor on SS *Mayumba*, trading along the west coast of Africa, and he notes in his autobiography that Garnet came aboard for three days at Monrovia and they talked at length about literature and travel. He does not use Garnet's name, but notes that he "had possibly been a slave himself". Indeed, Garnet was born into slavery in Maryland. His family escaped to New York, and Garnet acquired an education, became a clergyman (serving at churches in Troy, Washington, and New York), and was a leading abolitionist, noted for his call to rebellion at the 1843 National Negro Convention.

Julia Margaret Cameron, née **Pattie** (1815-1879), was the wife of a legal official stationed in Calcutta until he retired and the family came home to England, settling in the Isle of Wight. When she was 48, her daughter gave her a camera as a gift; within a year she was a member of the Photographic Society and was taking pictures, selling them to the Victoria and Albert Museum and having prints made and sold. Her most important specialty was portraits, in which she preferred a soft focus and close cropping, a style that has influenced photographers more than a century later. Through family connections she had access to such figures as **Charles Darwin**, **Robert Browning**, and actor **Ellen Terry**, who posed for her. She also photographed allegorical figures arranged in what is recognizably a Pre-Raphaelite style. In 1875 the family returned to India, settling in Ceylon, and Cameron took comparatively few pictures in her final years.

Sir **William Jenner,** 1st Baronet (1815-1898), was still a young doctor at the London Fever Hospital, then located in Gray's Inn Road, when he began studying two diseases that looked strikingly similar. His resulting book, *On the Identity or Non-Identity of Typhoid and Typhus Fever*, was published in 1850. His career led him to a professorship at University College, London, and an appointment at its hospital, presidency of the Royal College of Physicians 1881-1888, and the rank of "physician in ordinary" to both Queen *Victoria* and the Prince of Wales, later *Edward VII*. He was not a descendant of the more famous physician **Edward Jenner**, the inventor of smallpox inoculation.

Anthony Trollope (1815-1882) was the author of dozens of novels, including several about life in the mythical county of Barsetshire and several more about the political career of Plantagenet Palliser, Duke of Omnium, who even has an opportunity to serve as prime minister. His first success was *The Warden* (1855), the first of the Barsetshire novels, and he was still at it in the final years of his life with such books as *Doctor Wortle's School* (1881). His books in general deal with politics, money, social conflicts and sex roles; *The Eustace Diamonds* (1871) is, in addition, a mystery. Trollope also wrote more than a dozen books of non-fiction. He produced much of his work while employed full-time at the post office, initially as a clerk, eventually as a senior administrator. He is thought to have invented the pillar-box (mailbox). After taking early retirement he made one disastrous attempt to be elected to Parliament, and then concentrated full-time on his writing.

Sir **Bartle Frere**, 1st Baronet (1815-1884), was one of those who took up (in the language of the day) the white man's burden, spending a long career in the Indian civil service after his graduation from the East India Company's college at Haileybury, Hertfordshire. He spent the 1850s as chief commissioner of the Sindh district, which was little affected by the 1857 Mutiny, so that he was able to send troops to the Punjab where the conflict was hotter. Later he was governor of Bombay (now Mumbai) for five years. Eventually he returned to Britain and worked in the India Office, housed in its new building in King Charles Street, Whitehall, with the magnificent Durbar Court at its centre. In 1877 he was sent to South Africa to be governor of the Cape Colony and implement a confederation of several colonies there. The project foundered, and Frere was largely blamed for instigating the Zulu War, which ended in British victory only after a disastrous battle at Isandhlwana in January 1879.

Otto von Bismarck (1815-1898) was the "Iron Chancellor" who united 39 fractious German states into one nation and made it a world power. He came from a Junker (aristocratic land-owning) family in Prussia, where he served in Parliament as a young man and then held a series of diplomatic posts, learning much about European realities. Prussian king **Wilhelm I** appointed Bismarck chief minister in 1861; by 1871 he was bringing the Franco-Prussian War to a triumphant end, absorbing Alsace and Lorraine from France and seeing Wilhelm crowned Emperor of Germany. He built up domestic support with reforms and a social safety net (old age pensions were introduced in 1889), and left office shortly after Wilhelm was succeeded by his son *Frederick III*.

William **Brett,** Viscount **Esher** (1815-1899), was a Conservative politician, then a judge, rising to be Master of the Rolls, one of the most senior positions in the judiciary, 1883-1897. A barrister since 1840, he was elected to Parliament in 1866, and briefly held the government post of solicitor-general. He was a judge, initially in the court called Common Pleas, in time to be affected when the Supreme Court of Judicature Act, passed in 1873, reorganized the complex system of courts. Master of the Rolls was his final career rung; it brought appointment to a peerage. Among the cases Lord Esher judged was Filburn v. People's Palace and Aquarium Co. Ltd., in 1890, in which a man who had been injured by an elephant won damages from the beast's owners.

James Donnelly (1816-1880) was the patriarch of a family of Roman Catholic Irish immigrants who were massacred by other settlers, probably also Irish and Catholic, near Lucan, Ontario, in February 1880. The family had come to Canada about 1844, settling eventually on the "Roman Line" outside Lucan. Feuds, land disputes, arson, business competition, and a murder charge culminated in a night attack on the homestead and another family house. James Donnelly was killed along with his wife **Johannah Donnelly**, sons **John** and **Tom**, and a niece, **Bridget**. No one was ever convicted of the killings. The "Black Donnelly" conflict, which grows out of similar Irish ethnic and class conflicts to those reflected in *The Valley of Fear*, has become enshrined in Canadian folklore.

Manuel Murillo Toro (1816-1880) was president of Colombia 1864-1866 and 1872-1874, and has been suggested as the original of Don Murillo, the evil president of San Pedro who figures in "Wisteria Lodge". Colombia's Murillo seems not to have been evil throughout his career as journalist, legislator, Secretary of the Treasury and president. He was associated with such causes as the abolition of slavery (1851), freedom of the press, law reform, the first project to produce maps of the country, and the end of capital punishment for political crimes. During Murillo's lifetime the "United States of Colombia"  included what is now Panama, the presumed homeland of the Panama hat mentioned in "The Dancing Men".

Paul Julius Baron von **Reuter**, born **Israel Beer Josaphat** (1816-1899), founded the Reuters news agency, which is mentioned in "The Final Problem". As a young man he was interested in the new technology of the telegraph, and when he moved from Germany to Paris in 1848, just as revolutions across Europe were generating a demand for up-to-date news, he began translating French news reports and sending them back to Germany using carrier pigeons to fill the gap between the two nations' telegraph lines. In 1850 he moved on to London, opening a telegraph office near the Stock Exchange and at first specializing in fast financial data. General news followed. After a few years, Reuter made a working arrangement with two rival agencies, Havas of France and Wolff of Germany, and the three dominated worldwide news transmission for many years.

Sir **William Gull** (1816-1890) studied medicine at Guy's Hospital and the University of London, and spent most of his career at Guy's, a major institution in Southwark just south of London Bridge. A researcher as well as a practising physician, he coined the term "anorexia nervosa" and worked on paraplegia and Bright's disease. In 1871, the same year he became president of the Clinical Society of London, he treated the Prince of Wales (the future *Edward VII*) for an attack of typhoid fever. The prince's recovery, and Gull's role in it, were national news, and Gull was made a baronet ("the Baronetcy of Brook Street", noting a London street where many doctors practised, including Dr. Percy Trevelyan of "The Resident Patient"). Various writers, without much evidence, have associated Gull with the Jack the Ripper murders, either as the killer or as someone involved in a conspiracy to protect a high-born individual, such as the *Duke of Clarence*.

Bahá'u'lláh, born **Mírzá Husayn-Alí Núrí** (1817-1892), was the founder of the Bahá'i religion and, according to its teachings, a Manifestation of God. Born in Tehran, he was a young man when he heard the teachings of **Siyyid Mírzá Alí-Muhammad** ("the Báb", or "gate") heralding a new prophet. He became a believer, then a leader, and in 1863 in Baghdad he declared that he was himself that "messenger" of God. In the ensuing years he wrote to believers and to the world's leaders, calling for justice and peace. He spent his final years as a prisoner of the Ottoman Empire at Acre in Palestine, where he received visitors and wrote extensively, and described himself as the messiah awaited by many religions.

Benjamin Jowett (1817-1893) was Master of Balliol College, Oxford, and a renowned polymath. As they said behind his back: "Here come I, my name is Jowett. All there is to know I know it. I am Master of this College. What I don't know isn't knowledge!" He studied at Balliol and spent his life there as a professor of Greek (though his real field was theology), master of the college and for a time vice-chancellor (president) of the university. He pressed for a change in the law so that students who were not of the Church of England could attend the great universities (approved in 1871), and he took advanced positions in his theological writings, which earned him opposition from conservative churchmen. But generations of students were loyal to him, and Balliol became a major influence in the country thanks to, as the *Encyclopaedia Britannica* put it in 1911, "his precept and example, his penetrative sympathy, his insistent criticism, and his unwearying friendship".

Charles-Édouard Brown-Séquard (1817-1894) was born to French and American parents in Mauritius, the Indian Ocean island where Alice Rucastle and her bridegroom ended up according to "The Copper Beeches". He studied medicine in France, and served as a professor of neurology at various institutions in France, the United States and Britain. He was the first researcher to describe a syndrome, the result of spinal cord injury or lesion, that now bears his name. He was a pioneer in the study of hormones, and in 1889, when he was 72, delivered a paper (based on self-experimentation) reporting that injection of an extract from the testicles of dogs and guinea pigs produced rejuvenation in human males. This finding, though possibly explained by nothing more than a placebo effect, is an obvious source for the use of langur serum in "The Creeping Man".

Sir **Joseph Dalton Hooker** (1817-1911) was a prominent botanist in an age when gentlemen collectors, like Holmes and Watson in "Wisteria Lodge", were becoming scientists. A friend and collaborator of *Charles Darwin*, he collected specimens in New Zealand, India, and the United States, finding evidence for Darwin's theory of evolution. He took part in the famous 1860 debate over evolution that pitted *Thomas Henry Huxley* against **Samuel Wilberforce**. Hooker succeeded his father, **William Hooker**, as director of the Royal Botanic Gardens at Kew, along the Thames west of London, and served there 1865-1885. With collaborator **George Bentham** he published *The Genera Plantarum*, listing some 100,000 species in a definitive classification, in 1883.

William III (1817-1890) was King of the Netherlands from 1849, when his father **William II** died, to his death; he was succeeded by his daughter (by his second wife), *Wilhelmina*. During his father's reign he held the traditional title Prince of Orange, often associated with a previous holder who happened to have the same name, **William III** of the United Kingdom more than a century earlier. In addition, he was Grand Duke of Luxembourg, which became an independent country after his reign. In general, the 19th century William was conservative, militaristic, erratic, violent, and debauched. "Most people around him agreed that he was, to some degree, insane," Wikipedia says blandly.

Alexander II (1818-1881) was Czar (emperor) of Russia from the death of his father **Nicholas I** in 1855. Although he continued to rely on secret police, suppress minorities, and send dissidents to Siberia (presumably including "Anna", who figures in "The Golden Pince-Nez"), he was responsible for many reforms, including the abolition of serfdom and a proposal for an elected parliament. Such progressive measures were far from satisfying the revolutionaries (loosely called Anarchists or Nihilists) who opposed the royal family and government, and he was assassinated near the Winter Palace in St. Petersburg.

Karl Marx (1818-1883) was the author of *Das Kapital* (English, "Capital") and the *Communist Manifesto*, and the economist and philosopher who gave his name to Marxism. His central principle was that class struggle has been the main agency of historical change; Communism and socialism are seen as elaborations of Marx's ideas. Born in Germany, he was expelled at the age of 30 and spent the rest of his life in Paris (where he met **Friedrich Engels**), Brussels, and finally London, doing journalistic work and talking with other leaders of the Communist League about the prospects for revolution. He did much of his research and writing in the circular Reading Room of the British Museum, and he is buried among the Gothic tombs of Highgate Cemetery.

John **Walter** (1818-1894) was born at Printing-house Square in the City of London, where his father, also named John Walter, published *The Times*. His grandfather, yet another John Walter, had founded it in 1785, initially as *The Daily Universal Register*. The third-generation Walter attended Oxford and became a barrister, but was involved with the newspaper as well. He became its manager when his father died in 1847, and ran it for more than forty years. "He was a man of scholarly tastes and serious religious views," said the 1911 *Encyclopaedia Britannica*, "and his conscientious character had a marked influence on the tone of the paper." Walter was also a member of Parliament, sitting as a Liberal, for most of the years 1847-1885. After his death his son **Arthur F. Walter** was proprietor of *The Times* until Lord *Northcliffe* acquired it in 1908.

Richard Gatling (1818-1903) became wealthy through many inventions, including some that improved agricultural productivity, but is chiefly remembered for the Gatling gun. He developed it during the United States Civil War, ostensibly to permit armies to be smaller, and to make nations "see the futility of war". The hand-cranked Gatling gun, which could shoot 200 rounds per minute, saw very little use in the 1861-1865 war, but was widely used later — by the Royal Navy in Egypt in 1882, for example. Gatling's other inventions included devices for planting rice and wheat, improved toilets and bicycles, and steam ploughs. Born in North Carolina, he spent most of his life in Missouri and Indiana; he earned a medical degree but never practised as a physician.

Christian IX (1818-1906), King of Denmark, was the grandfather of Europe just as Queen *Victoria* was the grandmother. He and his queen, **Louise of Hesse-Kassel** (married 1842), were parents of two kings and two queens, and ancestors of countless more. Born in Schleswig, he came to the Danish throne in 1863 because the old king, **Frederick VII**, died childless and he was at least a cousin by marriage. He survived war with Germany over Schleswig-Holstein and spent most of his reign resisting pressures for democratic government. The King was closely associated with authoritarian prime minister **Jacob Estrup** (in power 1875-1894), and democracy was not fully instituted until 1901, although Christian's government did introduce old age pensions and other reforms, and give partial independence to Iceland. He was succeeded as King by his son **Frederick VIII**; a daughter became Britain's Queen *Alexandra* and a son became *George I* of Greece.

James Joule (1818-1889) inherited his father's brewing business in Salford, Lancashire, but is remembered by history for his scientific work about heat and energy, which grew out of experiments to make the brewery more efficient. He concluded among other things that the newly developed electric motor would not be as efficient as his existing steam engines. Expertise from brewing also helped him measure temperatures and other units far more accurately than scientific contemporaries thought possible. "His efforts had a profound influence on the theory of conversion of energy (the First Law of Thermodynamics)," says FamousScientists.org. "He collaborated with Lord **Kelvin** on the formulation of the absolute scale of temperature.... He established the relationship between the flow of current through a resistance and the heat dissipated, which was later termed as Joule's law." His gravestone is inscribed with the number 772.55 — his calculation of the amount of energy (in foot-pounds) required to heat one pound of water by one degree Fahrenheit.

Albert, Prince Consort (1819-1861), was the husband of Queen *Victoria* and the father of her nine children. Born into German nobility (the house of Saxe-Coburg-Saalfeld), though not royalty, he was introduced to the Queen by an uncle and married her in 1840. It was notoriously a love match, and Victoria was to mourn him extravagantly through her 40 years of widowhood. Albert took on the management of royal estates and administration, nudged the Queen in the direction of non-partisanship (vital in a constitutional monarchy), and advocated for progressive causes and the advancement of science. He served as president of the Great Exhibition of 1851, promoting the industry of Britain and the Empire.

Allan Pinkerton (1819-1884) founded the Pinkerton National Detective Agency, which figures in *The Valley of Fear* in a thinly disguised retelling of the exploits of agent *James McParland*. Born in Scotland, Pinkerton ended up in Chicago in the 1850s doing a little of this and a little of that, including assisting the sheriff's office. His agency, formed in 1855, did much of its work on behalf of railroads and the post office, in the absence of effective law enforcement in most rural areas. Pinkerton's gained a reputation for persistence and accurate, detailed work, but also sometimes for entrapment, violence, and oppression of unions and workers in the interest of corporate bosses. Pinkerton wrote several books, including *The Molly Maguires and the Detectives* (1877), by way of publicizing his experiences and his company.

Jacques Offenbach (1819-1880) was a musician who made a significant contribution to the development of operetta, though his own master-work, "Les Contes d'Hoffmann" ("The Tales of Hoffmann"), was unfinished at his death. It tells three stories of a poet's love affairs, including one with the mechanical doll Olympia. Born in Germany, but based in Paris for most of his life, Offenbach was a noted cellist before taking up composition and, for a while, theatre management. His work is known for sexy humour and romantic melody, and influenced composers including Sir *Arthur Sullivan* and *Johann Strauss*.

John Ruskin (1819-1900) was, according to a 2014 commentary in the *Guardian*, "a critic who could out-paint most painters, a great educator who reinvented how we see art". Formed by evangelical Christianity and the romantic art of the early 19th century, he began his career as a critic defending the work of **J. M. W. Turner**. In a succession of books including *Modern Painters* (1843-1860), *The Stones of Venice* (1851-1853), and *Sesame and Lilies* (1865), he praised ancient, particularly Gothic, buildings, and supported the Pre-Raphaelite Brotherhood in their efforts to return to the purer roots of art. In 1877 he wrote that a painting by *James McNeill Whistler* amounted to "flinging a pot of paint in the public's face"; Whistler sued for libel and won, but was awarded only a farthing in damages. Ruskin married **Effie Gray**; the marriage was annulled after six years on grounds of non-consummation, allegedly because Ruskin was repelled at the sight of her pubic hair; she then married *John Everett Millais*. He was founder of a utopian society called the Guild of St. George, the exact name used for a charitable group mentioned in "The Crooked Man".

Sir **Charles Hallé** (1819-1895) was already a successful musician in Germany and France before coming to England when the revolutions of 1848 made Continental life uncomfortable. His piano recitals, held first in his own house and then in public halls, became fashionable, and in 1857 he formed his own orchestra. He was also the first principal of the Royal Manchester College of Music. He remained best known as a pianist, however, and was recognized, in the words of Wikipedia, "for crystal clearness rather than for warmth". His second wife (they married in 1888) was violinist *Wilma Neruda*, formerly **Norman**. In *A Study in Scarlet*, Holmes remarks that "I want to go to Hallé's concert to hear Norman Neruda this afternoon."

Prince **George, Duke of Cambridge** (1819-1904), was a cousin of Queen *Victoria* (his father was brother to the Queen's father, Prince **Edward, Duke of Kent**). Born in Germany, where the British royal family still had close connections, he began his military career with the forces of Hanover, then was commissioned in the British army and by 1845 was a major-general. In 1856 he became the army's "general commanding-in-chief", and with changes of title he remained the senior military officer for 39 years. Wikipedia says the duke "earned a reputation for being resistant to doctrinal change and for making promotions based upon an officer's social standing, rather than merit. Under his command, the British Army became a moribund and stagnant institution, lagging far behind its continental counterparts." Politicians from *William Ewart Gladstone* to Sir *Henry Campbell-Bannerman* pushed for reform; the duke eventually resigned in 1895 and was succeeded by *Garnet Wolseley*, 1st Viscount **Wolseley**.

Sir **Joseph Bazalgette** (1819-1891) was the primary creator of London's sewer system. An engineer who worked first on railroads, he became interested in drainage and sewers, and in 1856 became chief engineer for the Metropolitan Board of Works, just in time for the "Great Stink" scandal of 1858. To replace the drainage of London's excrement directly into the Thames, Bazalgette proposed and supervised construction of more than 1,000 miles of sewers to carry it downstream away from the city. (Actual treatment of sewage did not begin until 1900.) The project largely eliminated cholera in London, and the main sewers were designed with such generous capacity that many are still in use. Bazalgette also designed a number of bridges and other projects.

Sir **Monier Monier-Williams** (1819-1899), previously just **Williams**, coined the name "Hinduism" for the polytheistic religions of India, and introduced it to westerners. He had been born in India and educated at Oxford, and for a time taught eastern languages to young men about to go out to work for the East India Company. When the Company's rule ended after the Indian Mutiny of 1857, he tried for the professorship of Sanskrit at Oxford, emphasizing the importance of language training for Christian evangelism, and won a bitter, hard-fought election. He held the post until 1887. His book *Hinduism* (1877) framed various South Asian cults as a single religion; other works included a grammar and dictionary of Sanskrit, and translations.

William Perry (1819-1880) was a boxer known as the Tipton Slasher, who was heavyweight champion of England 1850-1857. He came from a family that operated boats on the complex network of canals in the Midlands around Birmingham, and it was said that he learned to fight by brawling with other boat operators for priority in getting through the locks. Perry, whose fighting weight was 186 pounds, once went 70 rounds — each a minute long, in the days before the *Queensberry* rules — against an American rival, with no decision. After losing his championship he operated a pub in Wolverhampton.

Victoria (1819-1901) was Queen of the United Kingdom from 1837, when her uncle, **William IV**, died, to her own death 64 years later. She wore the crown longer than any other British sovereign and gave her name to an age that lasted from the end of the Napoleonic wars in 1815 until the opening of World War I in 1914. Social and economic changes during her reign were accompanied by the development of a constitutional monarchy, made possible by her long stable reign. She was stubborn, eccentric, and middle-class in habit, but well aware of her role as mother of her far-flung peoples. She came to be much loved (and by Sherlockians is frequently alluded to as "A Certain Gracious Lady", a phrase from "The Bruce-Partington Plans"). Through the royal marriages of her nine children, Victoria was also mother of most of Europe's rulers. **Albert**, Prince of Saxe-Coburg and Gotha, became Prince Consort when he married Victoria in 1840. The Queen never recovered from his death, living in seclusion as "the Widow of Windsor" for most of her last four decades. A Golden Jubilee in 1887 and Diamond Jubilee in 1897 celebrated the fiftieth and sixtieth anniversaries of her accession to the throne.

David Henry Friston (1820-1906) was a well-known and experienced illustrator by the time he was hired to do four drawings for the first publication of *A Study in Scarlet*, in *Beeton's Christmas Annual* for 1887. He thus became the first artist to give visual form to Sherlock Holmes, who appears in the first of the four with a somewhat odd hat and what may or may not be an Inverness cape. Bibliographers think his drawings were engraved (prepared for the printer) by **William M. R. Quick**, whose initials appear on one of them. The cover illustration on *Beeton's* is not thought to represent Holmes or anybody else in *A Study in Scarlet*. Friston was also a painter, who showed one of his paintings at the Royal Academy some 14 times in the 1850s and 1860s. He drew for the *Illustrated London News*, for an edition of *Pilgrim's Progress*, and for reviews of the original productions of the *Gilbert* and *Sullivan* operettas, among many other projects.

Donald Smith, 1st Baron **Strathcona and Mount Royal** (1820-1914), was one of the Scottish entrepreneurs and philanthropists who built Canada. In particular he was co-founder of the Canadian Pacific Railway, an institution that figures in "Black Peter", and it fell to him to drive the famous last spike at Craigellachie, British Columbia, that completed the CPR in November 1885. He was also president of the Bank of Montreal, governor of the Hudson's Bay Company, a member of the House of Commons of Canada, the provider of funds to raise Lord Strathcona's Horse for service in the South African War, and a donor to higher education. His partner in many of these ventures was his cousin, **George Stephen,** 1st Baron **Mount Stephen** (1829-1921).

 **Florence Nightingale** (1820-1910) was a pioneer of nursing, who became famous for her work looking after wounded British soldiers during the Crimean War (1853-1856). Feeling called by God to be a nurse, she trained in Germany, gained experience at London's Institution for Sick Gentlewomen in Distressed Circumstances, and during the war was invited to go to Turkey with a party of 38 women to assist in British hospitals. "Nightingale found conditions filthy, supplies inadequate, staff uncooperative, and overcrowding severe," says the *Encyclopaedia Britannica*. Her leadership helped improve food, cleanliness and basic care, and individual soldiers spoke of her comforting presence: "the lady with the lamp". She returned to Britain a heroine, and used her prominence to press for

reforms of the army medical system. She also founded a school of nursing based at St. Thomas's Hospital in south London. Her book *Notes on Nursing* (1859) is still in print.

Friedrich Engels (1820-1895) was the philosopher who originated Marxism as later generations knew it, every bit as much as ***Karl Marx*** himself. Born in Germany, he moved away from his prosperous upbringing as soon as he could, returning to take part in uprisings during the exciting revolutionary year of 1848, but meanwhile studying and working in Belgium, Switzerland, Britain, and France. He met Marx for the first time in 1842, and Marx published a number of his essays which were collected as *The Condition of the Working Class in England* (1845). They then collaborated on what became the *Communist Manifesto*, published early in 1848. By the early 1880s they were concentrating their attention on Russia as the likely first country to experience a Communist revolution. Engels was known as an enthusiast of music, art and jollity, as well as sexual relationships unfettered by bourgeois requirements; his book *The Origin of the Family, Private Property and the State* was published in 1884.

Herbert Spencer (1820-1903) trained as an engineer in the days when railway construction was a major industry, turned to journalism, and by 1851 was writing philosophy, with the publication of *Social Statics, or the Conditions Essential to Human Happiness*. That was followed by *The Principles of Psychology* (1855) and then the nine-volume *A System of Synthetic Philosophy*, which took thirty years to complete. He was an early believer in ***Charles Darwin***'s theory of evolution, and in fact coined the phrase "survival of the fittest"; he spoke of an evolution in human nature, and interpreted society as an organism that could also evolve. "For human beings to flourish and develop," says the *Internet Encyclopedia of Philosophy*, "Spencer held that there must be as few artificial restrictions as possible, and it is primarily freedom that he... saw as promoting human happiness."

Johanna (Jenny) Lind, later **Lind-Goldschmidt** (1820-1887), was "the Swedish nightingale", an operatic soprano who quickly became an international star after her debut in 1838 at the Royal Swedish Opera. She performed across Europe, and for two seasons in London, then announced her retirement, but was instead persuaded by ***P. T. Barnum*** to tour the United States. In 1852, as the tour ended, she married conductor and pianist **Otto Goldschmidt**, and the two settled in London in 1855. After that date Lind gave only occasional concerts; she sang in public for the last time at a chariaty concert in 1883. Beginning in 1882 she served as a teacher at the Royal College of Music. Lind can be seen as a possible original of Irene Adler, except that she was not a contralto, not born in New Jersey, not associated with Warsaw, not the mistress of a king, and not the wife of a barrister.

Sir **Henry Yule** (1820-1889) was an orientalist, someone interested in the lands to the east of Europe. He had gone there as a young military man, assigned to the Calcutta district as an engineer; he promptly wrote a report for the *Journal of the Bengal Asiatic Society*. He worked on the Delhi Canal, and on a study of whether canals helped spread sickness; he surveyed passes in the mountains between India and Burma. During the Mutiny of 1857 he supervised defensive works at Allahabad, and afterwards he designed a memorial for the British victims of the Cawnpore Well massacre. He left India in 1862 and became a writer, living mostly in Italy, where he translated old books about travels in the east, including Marco Polo's 14th century writings about China, and wrote articles for geographical and engineering journals and for the *Encyclopaedia Britannica*. In 1886 he produced *Hobson-Jobson: A Glossary of Anglo-Indian Words*. Two days before his death he received an invitation to join one of the scholarly Paris académies; he telegraphed his acceptance in Latin.

Joseph Whitaker (1820-1895) was, from 1869 onwards, the publisher of *Whitaker's Almanack*, which is suggested but not named in the opening passage of *The Valley of Fear*. By the 1890s the *Almanack* was a substantial volume with more than 700 pages of information, displayed in blindingly tiny type, and another 100 or more pages of advertising. In almanac tradition, it began with astronomical information, but went on to address government, events, silver marks, sports records and far more. A copy of the 1878 edition was buried in the time capsule under Cleopatra's Needle on the Embankment in London. Whitaker, born in London, was a bookseller from the age of 14 and then a publisher, responsible for the *Reference Catalogue of Current Literature* (from 1874) and other titles. His son, Sir **Cuthbert Whitaker**, edited the *Almanack* from 1895 to 1950.

Sir **Henry Thompson**, 1st Baronet (1820-1904), was a physician in London, the leading authority on urological surgery. He had gone to

Brussels in 1863 to treat King **Léopold I** for bladder stones, and he wrote papers and textbooks with titles such as *The Diseases of the Prostate* (1883). In 1874 he startled the public with an article in the *Contemporary Review* advocating cremation, rather than burial, of human bodies, calling it "a necessary sanitary precaution against the propagation of disease". That same year he became the first president of the Cremation Society of Great Britain; the country's first crematorium, in Woking, began operation in 1884. Thompson was also an astronomer, artist, and novelist, and a collector of Chinese porcelain (rather like Baron Gruner of "The Illustrious Client"), specializing in blue and white pieces.

Sir **William Howard Russell** (1820-1907) was a war correspondent, though he did not like the term. He reported, between 1850 and his retirement in 1882, from India (during the 1857-1858 Mutiny), the United States (the Civil War), continental Europe during various conflicts, and most important, the Crimea. His reports from that war in 1854-1855, telegraphed home and published in the *Times*, were shocking in their immediacy and detail, and led to public anger at the quality of medical care for the sick and wounded troops. One dispatch referred to the 93rd Highlanders at Balaclava as "that thin red streak topped with a line of steel", a phrase that found its way into the language. In 1860 he was asked to be editor of a new publication, the weekly *Army and Navy Gazette*, and he continued in that role for four decades, so that his own reporting became more intermittent. He was not on hand for the 1896 expedition from Egypt to Sudan, led by ***Herbert Kitchener***, which gave Arthur Conan Doyle his own brief experience as a war correspondent.

Susan **B. Anthony** (1820-1906) was president of the National Woman Suffrage Association, campaigning for women's right to vote in the United States while her counterparts, including ***Emmeline Pankhurst***, were making the same case in Britain. From a Quaker background, she had earlier been involved in the movement to abolish slavery, and through abolitionist organizations she met **Elizabeth Cady Stanton**, with whom she also fought for another cause — "temperance", the opposition to alcoholic drinks. The two founded the New York State Woman's Rights Committee and, in 1869, the NWSA. Famously, Anthony cast a vote illegally in the 1872 presidential election (she was fined $100 but never paid the fine). The suffrage campaign continued to her life's end; votes for women at the national level in the US came with a constitutional amendment in 1920.

Thomas Beecham (1820-1907) learned about herbal medicine as a shepherd boy, and by 1847 was in business selling the nostrum that made him famous, Beecham's Pills, a laxative made chiefly from aloe, ginger and soap. "No matter what may be your bodily ills," wrote *William Topaz McGonagall*, "the safest and quickest cure is Beecham's Pills." In 1880 Beecham opened his own factory in St. Helens, Lancashire, which was already a significant industrial centre. Beecham's Pills were manufactured until 1988, and the business is now a part of pharmaceutical giant GlaxoSmithKline. Beecham's grandson, Sir **Thomas Beecham** (1879-1961), was an orchestra conductor and founder of the London Philharmonic and Royal Philharmonic.

William Marwood (1820-1883) was the British hangman who introduced the "long drop", producing instant death through a broken neck, rather than the traditional "short drop" that led to slow death by strangulation. Marwood, a cobbler based in Horncastle, Lincolnshire, conducted his first execution in 1872, and became a celebrity, travelling by rail to wherever he was required and distributing business cards inscribed "William Marwood, Public Executioner". He hanged 179 people in 11 years. After the 1874 retirement of **William Calcraft**, who had received a salary and hanged more than 400 men and women over a 45-year period, a hangman was paid on a fee-for service basis; Marwood received £10, for example, for hanging *Charles Peace* in 1879.

Elizabeth Blackwell (1821-1910) was the first woman to receive a medical degree in the United States, and one of the pioneering women in British medicine as well. Her family, originally British though living in New York and later Cincinnati, was involved in liberal and reform causes, and Blackwell became a teacher as a step towards entering medicine in the hope of advancing social reform. Eventually she was accepted by the Geneva Medical College, predecessor of Hobart College in Geneva, New York, and graduated in 1849. She did further study in Paris, opened a medical practice and infirmary in New York, and eventually helped create a school of medicine in London, working with *Sophia Jex-Blake*; she was also associated with *Elizabeth Garrett Anderson*, who had followed another path to medical qualifications. In her later years she was interested in a broad range of reform movements. Blackwell must be one of the figures behind Arthur Conan

Doyle's short story about women entering medicine, "The Doctors of Hoyland".

Ford Madox Brown (1821-1893) spent 13 years, on and off, creating a painting more than six feet wide and four feet high, depicting labourers digging for the expansion of London's sewer system. Titled "Work", it now hangs in the Manchester Art Gallery. Brown, who explained his works of art at length, said it was intended among other things to demonstrate that British urban workers were as suitable a subject for art as Italian crowds. Much influenced by 18th century artist and satirist **William Hogarth**, Brown was an associate of Pre-Raphaelite artists such as *Edward Burne-Jones* and *William Morris*. His other works include a major series of murals for the Manchester Town Hall, and the often reproduced round painting "The Last of England".

Frederick Temple (1821-1902) was Archbishop of Canterbury, the head of the Church of England, for the last six years of his life. It fell to him to officiate at the coronation of King *Edward VII* and Queen *Alexandra* in August 1902, although he was so short-sighted the text of the ceremony had to be printed for him on huge rolls of paper, and so feeble he was unable to stand up unaided after kneeling to pay homage to the King. Although Temple had been ordained in 1847, much of his career had been in education, as a school inspector, headmaster of Rugby School and a member of a government inquiry commission. He was widely seen as an exemplary figure of "muscular Christianity". He was chosen Bishop of Exeter in 1869, Bishop of London in 1885 and Archbishop in 1896. His son, **William Temple**, was Archbishop of Canterbury 1942-1944.

Fyodor Dostoevsky (1821-1881) was the author of *Crime and Punishment*, *The Brothers Karamazov*, and other Russian novels as well as short stories, journalism and philosophy. "Many of his works," says Wikipedia, "contain a strong emphasis on Christianity, and its message of absolute love, forgiveness and charity, explored within the realm of the individual, confronted with all of life's hardships and beauty." *Crime and Punishment*, for example, is not a mystery novel but a study of morality. Dostoevsky served five years' imprisonment in Siberia in his youth, and suffered financial difficulties later in life, but grew in popularity and eventually received Russian and international honours.

Sir **Richard Burton** (1821-1890) did in 1853 what Sherlock Holmes claimed to have done circa 1892: visit Mecca, the Muslim holy city where westerners were not welcome. His skill in passing as a Muslim began when, as a young army officer in India, he was asked to gather intelligence in the bazaars, and eventually in the homosexual brothels of Karachi. He was a master of languages (European tongues in his teens; Arabic, Punjabi and Telugu, among others, in his military days) and eventually published about 30 volumes of translations. Most famous is an uncensored multi-volume version of the *Arabian Nights* with commentary about homosexuality, pornography and cultures. He also wrote dozens of anthropological volumes, and memoirs of his explorations in Africa and the Arab lands.

Gustave Flaubert (1821-1880) was the author of *Madame Bovary*, a tale of adultery that shocked French readers when it first appeared in 1857, but that is now considered a pioneering masterpiece of realist writing. His books also include *Salammbô* (1862) and the unfinished work he considered his masterpiece, *Bouvard et Pécuchet*, published posthumously. He completed less work than many other writers — probably because of his punctilious insistence on finding *le mot juste*, the perfect word — and spent most of his life in provincial Rouen. He had a close friendship and long correspondence with **George Sand**, which was known to Sherlock Holmes, since he quotes from it (albeit not quite accurately) in "The Red-Headed League".

Sir **Edmund Henderson** (1821-1896) had a military career, mostly in Canada, then in 1850 accompanied the first consignment of convicts to be sent to Western Australia. He served in administrative posts there until 1863, building Fremantle Prison and introducing reforms to the penal system. Returning to England, he was Surveyor of Prisons for the Home Office, then in 1869 was named the second Commissioner of the Metropolitan Police. In that role he achieved various reforms — including an end to the rule that constables could not grow facial hair — but got sloppy in administration after a few years, and resigned when the Trafalgar Square riot of 1886 revealed how unprepared the police had been.

William Henry Vanderbilt (1821-1885), of the notoriously wealthy Vanderbilt family of New York, is said to have been the richest man in the United States. He was the eldest son of "Commodore" **Cornelius Vanderbilt** (1794-1877), who had built the family fortune on ferries and later railways. The son expanded the business, building the New York Central system and extending control to other parts of the country. His mansion at Fifth Avenue and 51st Street contained, according to the *Encyclopaedia Britannica*, "what was claimed to be the finest private collection of paintings and sculpture in the world". It is not clear whether, as hinted in "The Sussex Vampire", he ever encountered a yeggman.

Lola Montez, born **Eliza Rosanna Gilbert** (1821-1861), lived a generation or more too early to be the original of Irene Adler, but could well have inspired her. Irish-born, she married at 16, left her husband at 21, reinvented herself as a "Spanish" dancer in London, had an affair with *Franz Liszt*, and captivated King **Ludwig I** of Bavaria, who had a taste for pretty women. She is said to have nudged him towards liberal policies, but was resented by the populace and driven out of the state during the revolution of 1848. After a brief stay and dubious marriage in England, she made herself a star for a time in the United States and Australia. Along the way she wrote *The Arts of Beauty, Or, Secrets of a Lady's Toilet: With Hints to Gentlemen on the Art of Fascinating.*

Matthew Arnold (1822-1888) was a literary critic, advocate of modernization in the Church of England, and author of much poetry, including a mainstay of English classes, "Dover Beach", which concludes with the lines "We are here as on a darkling plain Swept with confused alarms of struggle and flight, Where ignorant armies clash by night." He was the son of **Thomas Arnold**, the almost legendary headmaster of Rugby School 1828-1841, and spent much of his life as an inspector of schools, though he also held a professorship of poetry at Oxford for ten years. Arnold argued for "culture" in the face of the "Barbarians" and "Philistines" among his contemporaries, and spoke in one 1865 essay of "the note of provinciality" in English literature.

Heinrich Schliemann (1822-1890) found Troy, or at least persuaded his contemporaries that he had, though modern scholars are more sceptical. Born in Germany, a self-made businessman, he went to Greece in 1868, living off the fortune he had amassed and looking for sites that corresponded to the narratives in Homer's *Iliad*, a text well known to all educated people in the Europe of his day. He identified Troy as Hisarlik on the northwest coast of what is now Turkey — not an entirely new idea but one that he advocated fiercely and demonstrated through pioneering work in archaeological excavation. In 1875, with *Troy and Its Remains*, he let it be known that he had found Priam's treasure at the lowest level of his site at Hisarlik, cutting through upper levels (later cities) with dynamite. Other digs followed through the 1880s.

Juan Carlos de Borbón, Count of **Montizón** (1822-1887), was claimant to the throne of Spain at one point in his life, to the throne of France at another, but never got to reign in either kingdom. His father claimed the title of King **Carlos V** of Spain in 1833 following the death of his brother, **Ferdinand VII**, but there was another claimant, the infant **Isabella II**, whose partisans were successful both in war and in politics. Another rising in favour of the "Carlists" in 1860 was equally unsuccessful. After 1868, Juan Carlos lived mostly in England, in the town of Worthing, using the name **Charles Monfort**. In 1883, with the death of a distant kinsman in Austria, he became head of the House of Bourbon and thus, according to one faction, a claimant to the French throne, as a descendant of 18th century King **Louis XIV**. He made no active attempt to press the claim, France being a republic at the time.

Louis Pasteur (1822-1895) was the scientist behind two important public health innovations, vaccination and pasteurization. As a young professor at the University of Strasbourg, he studied molecular asymmetry; at the University of Lille, he investigated fermentation, including the compounds that cause milk to sour, and developed the theory that specific organisms, or germs, some of them anaerobic, are associated with each kind of fermentation. The process that now bears his name, pasteurization, was first developed for wine but is now used for milk and other foods. Later in life he moved to the Sorbonne, in Paris, where his bacteriological work led to vaccines for anthrax and rabies. His native France awarded him the Légion d'honneur (a distinction also held by Sherlock Holmes, according to "The Golden Pince-Nez").

Gregor Johann Mendel (1822-1884) did research that established the rules of heredity that are the basis of the science of genetics and that are now known by his name. His research, between 1856 and 1863, involved pea plants in the garden of St. Thomas's Abbey at Brno, Moravia (now in the Czech Republic). He was a Roman Catholic priest and a largely unsuccessful teacher, and had to abandon his scientific research for administrative work after he became abbot of St. Thomas's in 1864. From work on some 29,000 plants, Mendel developed the concept of dominant and recessive genes, and the principle of one dominant, one recessive, and two hybrid plants following a cross-pollination. His work remained obscure until about 1900, and was not available to the author of "The Yellow Face" or, apparently, to most of its readers.

Prince **Napoléon Bonaparte** (1822-1891) was a nephew of the Emperor **Napoléon I**, and a central figure in the on-again, off-again fortunes of his family, the Bonapartes. The great Emperor had remade France in little more than a decade at the beginning of the 19th century, and also placed family members on various thrones, his brother **Jérôme** becoming King of Westphalia. The younger Napoléon Bonaparte was Jérôme's son, born at Trieste after the Emperor had been defeated and his father had lost his kingship. But the family still moved in noble circles and in French politics. When a cousin became president of France in 1848, and then Emperor in 1852 as *Napoleon III*, the Prince became a close advisor, and was called on to play diplomatic and military roles.

Rutherford B. Hayes (1822-1893) was a one-term president of the United States (1877-1891), a Republican from Ohio. The White House web site notes that he "oversaw the end of Reconstruction, began the efforts that led to civil service reform, and attempted to reconcile the divisions left over from the Civil War. Beneficiary of the most fiercely disputed election in American history [which saw him defeat the Democrats' **Samuel Tilden** by one electoral vote amid conflict over the legitimacy of votes in several southern states], Rutherford B. Hayes brought to the Executive Mansion dignity, honesty, and moderate reform."

Sir **Francis Galton** (1822-1911) is described by a website dedicated to his work as a "Victorian polymath: geographer, meteorologist, tropical explorer, founder of differential psychology, inventor of fingerprint identification, pioneer of statistical correlation and regression, convinced hereditarian, eugenicist, proto-geneticist, half-cousin of *Charles Darwin* and best-selling author." Born in Birmingham, he travelled widely (his book *The Art of Travel*, 1855, went through many editions and is still in print) and was associated with many scientific institutions in London. In 1888 he established a laboratory in the science galleries of the South Kensington Museum. His work, presented in hundreds of papers and in books such as *Natural Inheritance* (1889), will have been of interest to Dr. Mortimer (*The Hound of the Baskervilles*) and to Sherlock Holmes himself, who often spoke with interest about heredity.

Ulysses S. Grant (1822-1885) was the commander who won the Civil War and then served as President of the United States. A graduate of the US Military Academy at West Point, he spent a decade in the army (with combat experience in the Mexican-American War), failed at several ventures in civilian life, and returned to military service when the Civil War began in 1861. He held commands in Tennessee, Mississippi and finally Virginia, at last accepting surrender from the Confederate commander, *Robert E. Lee*, in April 1865. Four years later he was elected President on the Republican ticket. His presidency (1868-1876) was dogged by scandal and saw his efforts to establish stability and civil rights in the former Confederate states largely thwarted. In retirement he lost everything through unsuccessful investments, but wrote a popular book of war memoirs which restored his finances. Grant's Tomb in New York City was dedicated in 1897.

Coventry Patmore (1823-1896) published his first book, simply called *Poems*, when he was 21, and kept on writing poetry as well as art criticism. The website Poetryfoundation.org notes that *The Angel in the House*, published in four volumes over a decade, "presented a portrait of married life that became a Victorian ideal of domestic bliss. The work was inspired by Patmore's first wife, Emily Augusta Andrews. Andrews was an author of children's stories and the mother of six of Patmore's children." She died in 1860, and Patmore had two further marriages. He worked for two decades as an assistant librarian at the British Museum and was

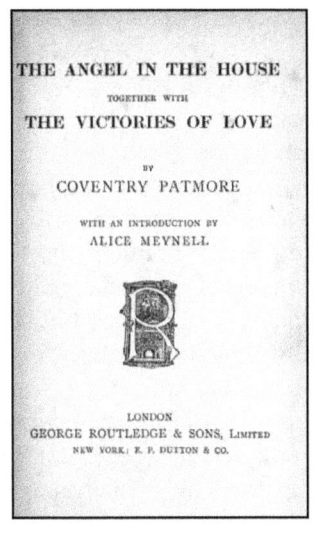

friends with **Dante Gabriel Rossetti** and others of the Pre-Raphaelites.

Sir **Penrose Charles Penrose** (1822-1902) entered the Royal Marines at the age of 15 and ended up as a general, commanding the Plymouth division, and a Knight Commander of the Order of the Bath. His obituary in the *London Standard* noted that "He served with the Royal Marine Battalion on the North Coast of Spain, in 1838, and three years later he took part in the operations on the Yang-tse-kiang. In 1858 he landed with a force to protect British property in Canton, and for his gallantry at the storming of the wall of that city he was mentioned in Despatches and awarded the medal with clasp." His unusual name, coupled with that of Admiral **John 'Jacky' Fisher**, could have provided that of Penrose Fisher in "The Dying Detective".

Alfred Russel Wallace (1823-1913) was "known for his courageous views on scientific, social, and spiritualist subjects", says the *Encyclopaedia Britannica*. He was an important contributor to the theory of evolution. Wallace got most of his education from a London mechanics' institute, trained and worked as a surveyor, and read widely in scientific fields. An important influence was **Robert Chambers**'s 1844 book about evolution, *Vestiges of the Natural History of Creation*. He travelled to South America with naturalist **Henry Walter Bates**, and then for eight years by himself to Malaya. His observations led to theories about how evolution produces new species, presented in 1858 under the joint names of Wallace and **Charles Darwin**. As his work continued, however, Wallace maintained, unlike some other naturalists, that evolution could not account for humanity's "higher faculties". He wrote a total of 21 books, including *Island Life* (1880).

Goldwin Smith (1823-1910) and Arthur Conan Doyle shared an enthusiasm for an "Anglo-Saxon federation" based on the historic relationship between Britain and America. (Sherlock Holmes speaks in similar terms in "The Noble Bachelor".) Smith was first a journalist, then (1858) professor of modern history at Oxford. His writings were stronger on opinion (the "natural theology" argument that creation demonstrates God; the belief that God favours a free market) than on modern history. In 1869 he crossed the Atlantic, first teaching at Cornell University, then settling in Toronto, where he married the heiress to the opulent house The Grange. The *Dictionary of Canadian Biography*: "From his 'English mansion,' this talented and acerbic political and literary critic would hurl his jeremiads at a world that irritatingly deviated from the Manchester liberal faith in which he was steeped.... His output was prodigious, the writing crisp and often epigrammatic." He disliked Jews and maintained that Anglo-American world leadership should start with Canada's assimilation into the United States.

Hardinge Giffard, Earl of **Halsbury** (1823-1921), served three times as Lord Chancellor, the senior legal official in the British government. A barrister from 1850, he played a role in prominent cases in the London courts, including the litigation over whether *Arthur Orton* was really Sir *Roger Tichborne*. He was elected to Parliament as a Conservative in 1877. In 1885 he received his earlship and moved to the House of Lords, serving as Lord Chancellor 1885-1886, 1886-1892, and 1895-1905, in the governments of Lord *Salisbury* and *Arthur Balfour*. He edited a definitive compilation of the *Laws of England*, published 1905-1916, and other legal reference works.

Sir **Mackenzie Bowell** (1823-1917) was Prime Minister of Canada during 1895 and the first part of 1896, having taken on the job when Sir *John Thompson* died in office. A newspaper editor, school trustee and militia colonel, he was sent to Parliament in Canada's first national election (1867) and served as minister of customs, an important role since most of the government's revenue came from that source, 1878-1892. Historians find him conscientious in detail work, but somewhat out of his depth as a political strategist, which explains a sentence in "The Bruce-Partington Plans", set in November 1895. Watson speaks of newspaper reports about "an impending change of government", which almost certainly refers to the disarray in Bowell's cabinet because of the national crisis over funding Roman Catholic schools in Manitoba. In the event, he staved off resigning for a few months, but in June 1896 *Wilfrid Laurier*'s Liberals defeated his Conservatives in a general election.

Charles Blondin, real name **Jean François Gravelet** (1824-1897), was the best known of the 19th century funambulists. It was Blondin, not the **Great Farini**, who came to Sherlock Holmes's mind when he was about to walk on the roof of Pondicherry Lodge in *The Sign of the Four*. Blondin had walked in the air from the time he was four years old in France. When he decided to cross Niagara Falls one day in 1859, bystanders wagered on whether he would succeed or die. In spangled pink tights, carrying a 26-foot balancing pole, he made the crossing and went back again. In the end he did it some 300 times with increasingly eye-catching handicaps. He died of diabetes at age 72.

Sir **George Jessel** (1824-1883) was, like so many influential figures, a lawyer who went into politics. He was called to the bar in 1847, elected to Parliament in 1868, and appointed Solicitor-General, one of the government's minor ministerial positions, in 1871. "Jessel's reputation at this time stood high in the chancery courts," said the 1911 *Encyclopaedia Britannica*. "His forceful and direct method of bringing his arguments home to the bench was not modified in his subsequent practice." In 1873 he was appointed a judge — the first Jewish judge in Britain — and became Master of the Rolls, the third highest position in the judiciary. The encyclopaedia observes that "Never during the 19th century was the business of any court performed so rapidly, punctually, and satisfactorily as it was when Jessel presided," and adds that the reorganization of the judicial system which began in 1873 "would have been impossible without him".

Nana Sahib, birth name **Dhondu Pant** (1824-1857?), was the adopted son of a prince at Bithur, part of the Maratha empire in India, but on his father's death in 1852 the British East India Company cancelled his rights on the ground that he was not a legitimate heir. When the Mutiny (First War of Independence) broke out in 1857, he enthusiastically joined in. His most important military engagement was at Cawnpore (Kanpur) in June: a siege led to the surrender of General Sir **Hugh Wheeler** in return for a promise of safe-conduct. In the confusion as the column was leaving, shooting began and most of the British were killed. Some 120 women and children were taken to Nana's headquarters and killed with machetes three weeks later, their bodies thrown into a well. Cawnpore was recaptured by British forces shortly afterwards, and Nana was not seen again, though rumours of his whereabouts continued for decades. As Jonathan Small says in *The Sign of the Four*, "Fresh troops came pouring in, and Nana Sahib made himself scarce over the frontier." His troops (sepoys) were finally defeated in December 1857 by the forces of Sir *Colin Campbell*.

Samuel Plimsoll (1824-1898) was called in his obituaries "the Sailors' Friend" for his work in improving safety on merchant ships. Markings on a ship's hull, indicating the maximum depth to which it can be loaded, are now known as the Plimsoll line. He started out in the coal business, eventually prospered, and became knowledgeable about the dangerous conditions on coal ships. To press for reforms that would outlaw unseaworthy ships he managed to get elected to Parliament in 1868, serving there, as a Liberal, until 1880. In 1875 a Merchant Shipping Act was introduced, then withdrawn by prime minister *Benjamin Disraeli* because of objections by the many ship-owning members of Parliament. A revised law was finally passed in 1876.

Alexandre Dumas (1824-1895) is often called "Dumas fils" by literary historians to distinguish him from his father, **Alexandre Dumas père**, the author of *The Three Musketeers* and other successful novels. The younger Dumas — born out of wedlock but later legitimized by his father — wrote many novels but even more plays, becoming the dominant French dramatist of his era. His best-known work was the 1848 novel *La Dame aux camélias*, which became the play "The Lady of the Camellias" in 1852. The play, generally known in English as "Camille", was the basis for **Giuseppe Verdi**'s opera "La Traviata". Its heroine is based on Dumas's lover, **Marie Duplessis**, and is one of the many suffering and tragic women in Dumas's work.

Thomas J. 'Stonewall' Jackson (1824-1863) was a general in the Confederate armies during the United States Civil War. He is one of three southern commanders mentioned in the story "The Five Orange Pips", which deals with incidents during and after the Civil War. Jackson graduated from the United States Military Academy (West Point) in 1842, served in the Mexican War, taught at Virginia Military Academy, and was a colonel in the early months after the Confederate army was organized. Soon promoted to general, he fought a series of actions against the United States in Virginia, under the command of **Robert E. Lee**. He was judged to be a first-rate military strategist, as well as stubborn, eccentric, and religious man. He was killed by friendly fire during the Battle of Chancellorsville in northeastern Virginia in May 1863; his last words, spoken in delirium, were, "Let us cross over the river, and rest under the shade of the trees."

Sir **John Charles Robinson** (1824-1913) was an artist himself, trained in Paris, but primarily he was a critic, curator and collector. In a seventeen-year term (1852-1869) he built up the collection of the South Kensington Museum to where it was one of Europe's leading institutions; in 1899 it was renamed the Victoria and Albert Museum. He later worked on behalf of wealthy collectors, and acquired paintings, drawings, gems, porcelain, furniture, and fabrics on his own account — all this in an era when prices were a tiny fraction of what they later became. He was Surveyor of the Queen's Pictures 1882-1901.

William Palmer (1824-1856) was the physician and murderer Holmes mentions in "The Speckled Band": "Palmer and *[Edward] Pritchard* were among the heads of their profession." A website devoted to *Charles Dickens* tells the story: "Palmer poisoned his friend John Cook for money and showed little remorse;... several other deaths were linked to Palmer, including his own children, but also the death of one **George Abley**.... Dickens himself reported on the sensational and much-discussed case... in his article 'The Demeanour of Murderers' for *Household Words* in which he called Palmer 'the greatest villain that ever stood in the Old Bailey dock'." Palmer's motivation in most of the cases was money, needed to feed his gambling habit. He was hanged.

William Thomson, 1st Baron **Kelvin** (1824-1907), wrote a scientific essay at the age of 15, when he was already a student at the University of Glasgow, and used it as the basis for much of his life's scientific work, still consulting it when he was past the age of 80. "His contributions to science," says the *Encyclopaedia Britannica*, "included a major role in the development of the second law of thermodynamics; the absolute temperature scale (measured in kelvins); the dynamical theory of heat; the mathematical analysis of electricity and magnetism, including the basic ideas for  the electromagnetic theory of light; the geophysical determination of the age of the Earth; and fundamental work in hydrodynamics." He was also involved in practical work, including the laying of the first transAtlantic telegraph cable in 1858. A professor at Glasgow for 53 years, he is seen as one of the great synthesizers, seeking a unified theory of energy; he was a mentor to *James Clerk Maxwell*, who carried that project forward.

William Wilkie Collins (1824-1889) was a novelist, a close friend of **Charles Dickens**. He was most famously the author of *The Woman in White* (1859) and *The Moonstone* (1868), the latter being considered the first detective novel in English. Sergeant Cuff, the detective in *The Moonstone*, is said to have been based on the actual Scotland Yard inspector **Jonathan Whicher**. Many of the book's themes can be detected in the work of Arthur Conan Doyle, particularly in the plot of *The Sign of the Four*. Collins was trained in law, an expertise that is evident in many of his plots, and is considered a master of the suspense structure in serialized "sensation novels" that kept readers returning week by week for the next episode.

Charles Frederick Worth (1825-1895) was an Englishman, born in Lincolnshire, but made himself famous in Paris as the creator of *haute couture* clothes for ladies. He initially learned about fabrics as a bookkeeper at the London firm of Swan and Edgar, and began to design clothes while working for Maison Gagelin in Paris. He opened his own shop in 1858 in the rue de la Paix. It was the era of Second Empire conspicuous consumption — soon in Britain and America as well as in France — and as Worth attracted the attention of the French aristocracy, he became the best-known and most expensive dressmaker of them all. Among his products was the dress worn by the Empress *Elisabeth* for her coronation in 1867. He produced several thousand dresses each year, nearly all of them sold through individual fittings at his salon, and he is credited with inventing the bustle, the princess silhouette, the walking-dress, and many of the customs and routines that have become the basis of the fashion industry. By 1871 his shop employed 1,200 people.

Charles Garnier (1825-1898), not to be confused with the saint of the same name, was the architect of the building that houses the Paris Opéra and its phantom. The structure, in the Rue des Capucines on the right bank, is formally called the Palais Garnier. Its designer was 35 when the authorities held a contest for a new opera house, as part of the Second Empire rebuilding of Paris supervised by *Georges-Eugène Haussmann*. Drawing on what he had seen during architectural studies in Italy and Greece, Garnier proposed a massive neo-baroque building supported on a framework of metal girders. The jury selected his plan from among 170 entries; construction began in 1861 and took until 1875, being delayed by everything from the Franco-Prussian War to the discovery of an underground stream that had to be diverted. Garnier also designed other major buildings in Paris, Monte Carlo, Bordighera and elsewhere.

George Sanger (1825-1911) was a circus proprietor, as a casual mention in "The Veiled Lodger" makes clear: "He was the rival of [*George*] *Wombwell*, and of Sanger, one of the greatest showmen of his day." Following his father into show business, he trained small animals to do tricks, operated a travelling conjuring show with his two brothers, and married a lion tamer in 1850. Their show grew gradually, and settled into a purpose-built Amphitheatre in Ramsgate, a seaside town in Kent, in 1883. Sanger sold off his animals and retired in 1905; in 1911 a former employee attacked him with a hatchet, killing him, in an incident that could well have echoes in "The Veiled Lodger".

Edward William Pritchard (1825-1865) was coupled with *William Palmer* in Sherlock Holmes's estimation: "Palmer and Pritchard were among the heads of their profession." They were murderers both, but not really among the heads of anything. Pritchard had briefly been a navy surgeon, then worked as a general practitioner in Yorkshire, and wrote books about his travels and about the water cure available at Hunmanby, near the coast in Yorkshire's East Riding. He got away from his debts by moving to Glasgow, where in due course a servant girl, his mother-in-law, and his wife, **Mary Jane Taylor**, died in mysterious circumstances. In the latter two cases, poisoning by antimony was proved. Pritchard became the last person to be publicly hanged in Scotland.

Henry Walter Bates (1825-1892) was a pioneering naturalist (biologist), one of the early theorists of evolution. He is well known for bringing home specimens of 14,000 species of insects from an 11-year sojourn in the Amazon basin of South America, a trip made in company with *Alfred Russel Wallace*, and for developing the principle of "mimicry" as a part of the workings of evolution. From 1864 to his death he was assistant secretary (chief executive) of the Royal Geographical Society, and influential in supporting British explorers around the world. "A pin, a cork, and a card, and we add him to the Baker Street collection!" said Sherlock Holmes about Stapleton the entomologist in *The Hound of the Baskervilles.*

Jean-Martin Charcot (1825-1893) is described as "the father of neurology" for his research achievements, as well as the vast number of patients treated at his Paris hospital, the Salpêtrière. He developed clinical descriptions for many neurological diseases — first distinguishing multiple sclerosis from Parkinson's, and epilepsy from hysteria — and described the vascular system of the brain. His work on spinal lesions resulting from syphilis overlaps with Arthur Conan Doyle's 1885 MD thesis and with the work of Dr. Percy Trevelyan in "The Resident Patient". As a professor of pathological anatomy, Charcot taught *Sigmund Freud* and **Gilles de la Tourette**, among others. The Salpêtrière had some 3,000 patients under his supervision by the 1860s, and his work became internationally known when he travelled to London for an International Medical Congress in 1881.

Johann Strauss (1825-1899) was the son of **Joseph Strauss** "the Elder" (1804-1849) and is thought to have surpassed his father as a composer. Strauss "the Younger" left more than 500 musical compositions including 150 waltzes, among them "The Blue Danube" (1867) and "Tales from the Vienna Woods". In his early years as a musician he was overtly in competition with his father in the active musical world of Vienna. Things were no easier for him when he took the revolutionary side in the political unrest of 1848, but composing several patriotic marches dedicated to the new King, **Franz Joseph I**, helped restore his respectability. He led a popular orchestra for a few years, then turned it over to his two brothers in order to concentrate on composing — chiefly dances and operettas such as "Die Fledermaus" (1874).

William Topaz McGonagall (1825-1902) was a terrible poet, but he apparently didn't know it. Poems about current events, such as "The Tay Bridge Disaster", only demonstrated that he was an unrivalled master of lame word selection and hackneyed rhyme; he had no sense of rhythm or time. Originally a weaver in Dundee, he took up poetry in 1877, apparently thinking he had a gift from heaven. McGonagall recited his poetry in pubs and theatres and halls, persevering despite laughter and catcalls. In 1890 a collection of his verses, *Poetic Gems*, was published with the support of his friends. He also distributed copies of individual poems (for sale, not free) but nevertheless died in poverty.

Sir **Geoffrey Hornby** (1825-1895) was, according to Sir *John Fisher*, "the finest admiral afloat since **[Horatio] Nelson**". He joined the Royal Navy at the age of 12 —his father, Sir **Phipps Hornby**, also became an admiral — and saw action (at Acre, Palestine) when he was 15. As a captain he served in various parts of the world, notably at Vancouver Island during the "Pig War" dispute of 1859. As commander-in-chief of the West Africa Squadron he denounced the involvement of African rulers in the continuing slave trade. In 1869, promoted to rear admiral, he sailed around the world in HMS *Liverpool*. In 1882 he became commander-in-chief at Portsmouth, the city and harbour on England's south coast that is the navy's home, and in 1888 he became Admiral of the Fleet.

Sultan **Hashim Jalilul Alam Aqamaddin** (1825-1906) was the ruler of Brunei, on the north coast of Borneo, from 1885 until his death. Brunei is now, by some measures, the richest nation in the world; in the 1890s it was noted as an exporter of "sago, beeswax, edible birds' nests, camphor, hides, rattans", according to *Whitaker's Almanack*. The sultans' power was in decline, with much of the territory already ceded to **Charles Brooke**, the "White Rajah of Sarawak", and other rulers. Desperate for help after inheriting a weakened realm from his father, Sultan

Omar Ali Saifuddin, Hashim agreed in 1888 to make Brunei a British protectorate, an arrangement that lasted until 1984. A British "resident" was installed in 1906, further diminishing the Sultan's power.

Stephanus Johannes Paulus (Paul) Kruger (1825-1904) was for 17 years president of the South African Republic (Zuid-Afrikaansche Republiek), the region the British called Transvaal. Of Dutch (Boer) ancestry and born in the British-ruled Cape Colony, he was both a farmer and a soldier, and held a fierce and simple Calvinist religious faith. He took part in Boer battles against indigenous Africans in the 1850s and was among the leaders of the Transvaal region from the time of its independence in 1852, through a British attempt at annexation in 1877 and the First Boer War of 1880-1881. He was elected president in 1883 and 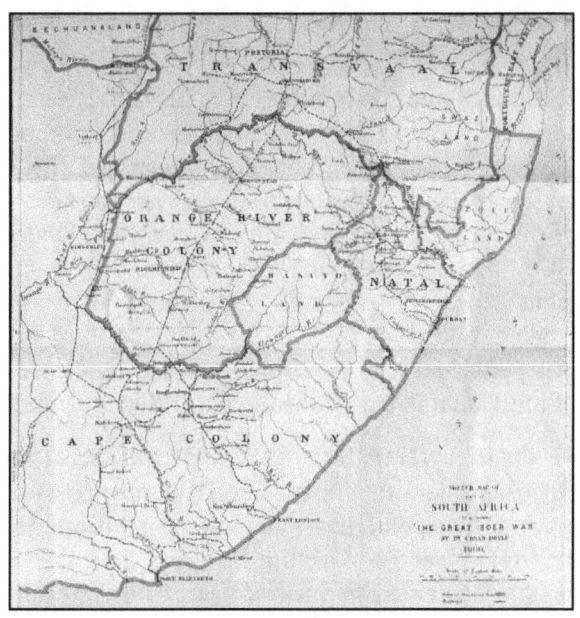 reelected three times; it fell to him to deal with the tension between long-time Boer settlers and British newcomers ("uitlanders"), the provocative military raid in 1895 led by *Leander Starr Jameson*, and eventually the Second Boer War (Second South African War), 1899-1902. As British victory seemed likely, Kruger left South Africa for a life in exile, and died in Switzerland.

Julia Martha Thomas (1825?-1879) was the victim in the "Richmond Murder" committed by **Katherine Webster** in March 1879. Thomas was a widow and former schoolteacher who lived in a semi-detached villa in Richmond, southwest of London and was, by all accounts, a difficult employer. Webster, who had served several prison terms for theft, was her housemaid for a few weeks. In a quarrel one Sunday evening, Webster killed Thomas by choking her and throwing her down the stairs. She dismembered the body, boiled and burned parts of it, dumped some of the remains into the Thames, and buried the head under a nearby stable. (It was unearthed by chance in 2010.) After a sensational trial in July, Webster was found guilty and hanged.

Pedro II (1825-1891) was the second and last Emperor of Brazil, gaining the throne at the age of 5 when his father, **Pedro I**, abdicated, and losing it in a coup in 1889. Dedicated to improving the life of Brazilians (whose numbers doubled from 7 million to 14 million during his reign), he promoted civil rights and economic growth, maintained a democratic constitutional monarchy, and abolished slavery. He was in touch with leading thinkers worldwide, corresponding with the likes of *Alexander Graham Bell* and *Henry Wadsworth Longfellow*, and became a member of learned academies, as well as visiting Europe and North America. He died in exile in Paris, but was mourned extravagantly by Brazilians living under the newly created republic.

Thomas Huxley (1825-1895) was known as "Darwin's bulldog" for his advocacy of the theory of evolution by natural selection as developed by *Charles Darwin*. First a navy surgeon, he became a lecturer at the School of Mines in London, and was "a great biologist in his own right, who did original research in zoology and paleontology," a Berkeley website notes. "Nor did he slavishly and uncritically swallow Darwin's theory; he criticized several aspects of it, pointing out a number of problems." He argued that evolution need not be gradual, but might make rapid jumps, or "saltations". His own book *Evidence on Man's Place in Nature* (1863) was the first attempt to apply evolution to humanity. Huxley famously debated evolution with bishop and scientist **Samuel Wilberforce** at Oxford in 1860.

William H. Smith (1825-1891) was not the founder of the bookseller W. H. Smith — that was his grandfather, **Henry Walton Smith** — but he threw himself into the family business with the idea of setting up bookstalls at railway stations, just as a vast middle class was adopting the habits of taking trains and reading books and papers. The first such bookstall opened at Euston Station in northwest London in 1848. A generation later, W. H. Smith would be a major retailer of the *Strand* magazine with its cargo of Sherlock Holmes tales. Smith built on commercial success to enter politics, serving in Parliament (as a Conservative) 1868-1891. He held several government positions while the Conservatives were in power, including First Lord of the Admiralty 1877-1880. He is caricatured as Sir Joseph Porter in the comic opera "HMS Pinafore".

William-Adolphe Bouguereau (1825-1905) painted, according to a historians' inventory, 822 pictures, one of which was owned by Thaddeus Sholto of *The Sign of the Four*. "There cannot be the least question about the Bouguereau," he tells Holmes and Watson. "I am partial to the modern French school." Trained in Bordeaux and Paris, Bouguereau painted mostly classical scenes in a highly realistic style and with much emphasis on shapely, mostly naked women. "Les Deux Baigneuses" (1884) is frequently reproduced. His work was much in demand, and brought him wealth. "You have to follow public taste," he observed in 1891. But his style went out of fashion as Impressionism came in at the turn of the century.

Andrew Jackson Davis (1826-1910) was "a miracle man", according to Arthur Conan Doyle in his *History of Spiritualism*. He "was able to enter into a higher sphere of consciousness and access higher spiritual and physical knowledge", according to a web site in his memory. As a profoundly uneducated teenager in New York's Hudson Valley, he became interested in mesmerism, then "found that he was clairvoyant and could understand incredible truths". His book reporting on this knowledge, *Principles of Nature*, was published in 1847. He predicted a "coming age" of Spiritualism, a year before the "spirit rappings" heard by **Margaret** and **Kate Fox** in Hydesville, New York, that are usually considered the beginning of the Spiritualist movement. In later years Davis studied medicine and went into practice in Boston specializing in herbal remedies.

Frederick   Hamilton-Temple-Blackwood, Marquess of **Dufferin and Ava** (1826-1902), was a diplomat whose career took him to the lofty posts of Governor General of Canada (1872-1878) and Viceroy of India (1884-1888). His father was a baron and Royal Navy captain, his mother the daughter of a literary family. As a young man he explored the Arctic regions in his own ship, and wrote the successful travelogue *Letters from High Latitudes* (1856). By 1860 he was in government work, sent to investigate a civil war in Syria and Lebanon. Other positions followed. He was in Canada as Governor General  during the Canadian Pacific Railway scandal of 1873, which saw *John A. Macdonald* lose the post of prime minister, at a time before the CPR was the kind of blue-chip investment suggested in "Black Peter". He was in India as Viceroy at the time the Indian National Congress was founded. His career also included postings as British ambassador to Russia, the Ottoman Empire, Italy, and (1891-1896) France.

Henrik Ibsen (1826-1906) was an important dramatist, "the father of realism" and an influential modernizer of what happened on the theatre stage. Born in Norway, he lived for much of his career in other parts of Europe; his plays were written in Danish, but produced almost immediately in German, English and other languages. His major plays, including "A Doll's House" (1879), "Hedda Gabler" (1890), and "John Gabriel Borkman" (1896), deal with such themes as feminism (Nora in "A Doll's House", famously, slams the door on her marriage), psychological conflicts and family secrets. The author of dark, controversial works, Ibsen himself seems to have had a happy personal life. He married **Suzannah Daae Thoresen** in 1858, and she is thought to have provided support for his work as well as inspiration for his female characters.

John Beddoe (1826-1911) was an Edinburgh-educated physician who pioneered in studies of ethnology (anthropology). His 1862 book *The Races of Britain: A Contribution to the Anthropology of Western Europe* introduced an "Index of Negrescence" which drew a sharp distinction between the racial identity and physiognomy of Celts and those of Anglo-Saxons. Dr. Mortimer in *The Hound of the Baskervilles* was keenly interested in such matters: "Sir Charles's head was of a very rare type, half Gaelic, half Ivernian in its characteristics." "It is hard to imagine any one of such a sweet nature as Dr. Beddoe ever making an enemy," said his obituary in the *British Medical Journal*.

John Brown (1826-1883) was Queen *Victoria*'s "Highland servant" for the last two decades of his life. Innuendo about the nature of his relationship with the Queen — sex? marriage? — circulated at the time and underlies the 1997 film "Mrs. Brown". Previously a ghillie at Balmoral Castle in Aberdeenshire, Scotland, which Victoria and Prince *Albert* bought in 1851, Brown moved from being a loyal servant to being a personal support for the Queen after the Prince's death in 1861, then an intimate. **Edward Stanley, Earl of Derby**, is said to have noted in his diary that it was "contrary to etiquette and even decency" that Brown and the Queen slept in adjoining rooms. She mourned him passionately after his death from a chill, but subsequently focused her affections on another servant, ***Abdul Karim***.

Walter Bagehot (1826-1877) was a lawyer, journalist and essayist who edited *The Economist* for 17 years. He developed Bagehot's Dictum about what should be done in times of economic crisis, summarized by a later writer thus: "To avert panic, central banks should lend early and freely (i.e. without limit), to solvent firms, against good collateral, and at 'high rates'." Bagehot also wrote *The English Constitution*, an 1867 analysis of how British government (constitutional monarchy) works. It distinguishes the "dignified" or symbolic parts of government from the "efficient" parts, by which action is taken, and it summarizes the prerogatives of the Queen or King: "the right to be consulted, the right to encourage, the right to warn".

Frederic Thesiger, 2nd Baron **Chelmsford** (1827-1905), was the commander of the British forces defeated at the Battle of Isandhlwana in eastern South Africa in January 1879. More than 1,300 of about 1,800 British troops were killed by a force of 20,000 Zulu warriors armed mostly with assegais (iron spears). Thesiger, who had begun his military career with the Grenadier Guards in 1845, was by this time a major-general, with combat experience in the Crimean War and the Indian Mutiny. He survived the debacle and managed to engineer a victory over the Zulu at Ulundi,  using far more troops and armament, before being relieved of his command in favour of Sir *Garnet Wolseley*. At the war's end, the Zulu Kingdom came under British control, and its king, **Cetshwayo**, was imprisoned at Robben Island for a time.

Edward Stanford (1827-1904) went to work as a young man in a London stationery shop that sold maps and charts — this in an era when there were few highways and few railroads. What was becoming available were the one-inch-to-the-mile Ordnance Survey maps of Britain; the so-called Old Series for all of England but the most northern regions was completed in 1844, and work at still larger scales was being done. Stanford took over the stationery business in 1853 and established himself at 7-8 Charing Cross Road as essentially London's only map dealer and printer. His Library Map of London was published in 1862. The founder's son, **Edward Stanford II**, took over from his father in 1885 and consolidated the business in Long Acre, near Leicester Square. Sherlock Holmes ordered a map of Dartmoor from this shop (slightly misnamed), according to *The Hound of the Baskervilles*.

Alfred **Drayson** (1827-1901) was a military officer and scientific amateur who greatly influenced Arthur Conan Doyle when they were friends in Portsmouth. When ACD joined the Portsmouth Literary and Scientific Society in 1883, Drayson had retired as a major-general (after a career in the Royal Artillery and teaching at the Royal Military Academy) and was president of the society. Already the author of *The Art of Practical Whist* and books about travel and military surveying, he was devoting his efforts to astronomy, Spiritualism and other passions. He had a pet theory that the earth rotates twice a day, not just once, and liked to talk about the obliquity of the ecliptic (as Holmes does in "The Greek Interpreter") and the movements of asteroids (on which Moriarty wrote).

Frederick Somner Merryweather (1827-1900) was at various times a newspaperman, a bookseller, a historian and an author. His most prominent book was *Bibliomania in the Middle Ages, Sketches of Bookworms, Collectors, Bible Students, Scribes and Illuminators* (1849). At that time he was in the book business himself in London's Holborn neighbourhood. He also wrote *Lives and Anecdotes of Misers*, which is mentioned in **Charles Dickens**'s *Our Mutual Friend*, and from 1878 to his death he was editor of the weekly *Surrey Comet*, published in Kingston-upon-Thames in southwest London. Mr. Merryweather of "The Red-Headed League" may well be named for him.

George Burrows (1827-1917) was the brigadier-general commanding British forces at what Watson (in *A Study in Scarlet*) calls "the fatal battle of Maiwand", during the Second Afghan War (1878-1881). Burrows, an officer since 1844, had seen little action until he found himself, on a hot August day in 1880 near Kandahar, heading about 2,500 British and Indian soldiers against possibly 15,000 Afghan troops. British losses in the disaster were 969 killed, 175 wounded; the 66th (Berkshire) Regiment of Foot and two regiments of Bombay Native Infantry were particularly hard hit. "His performance left much to be desired," historian Edmund Yorke says of Burrows, "notably his delay of the advance to Maiwand to intercept **Ayub Khan**, his poor logistical arrangements, his decision to fight on an open plain rather than behind more protected village buildings and his overall lack of tactical flexibility."

John George Wood (1827-1889) was the naturalist whose book *Out of Doors*, published in 1874, provides the clue by which Sherlock Holmes solves the mystery of "The Lion's Mane". Wood was born in London, son of a surgeon and his wife, and educated at Oxford, after which he was ordained and served in various church positions. For a time (1856-1862) he was chaplain at St. Bartholomew's Hospital in London, where Holmes and Watson are reported to have met, and from 1878 to his death he lived at Upper Norwood, not far from what would be Arthur Conan Doyle's home 1891-1894. Like some other clerics of his time, he became more interested in nature than in church work, and he lectured widely, as well as writing several books, including the best-sellers *Common Objects of the Country* and *Common Objects of the Seashore*.  His audience was the general public, and his work delivers popular interest rather than scientific rigour.

Joseph Lister, 1st Baron **Lister** (1827-1912), was the pioneer of antisepsis (sterilization) in surgery. Trained as a doctor at University College, London, he worked and taught surgery at Glasgow, at Edinburgh (where Arthur Conan Doyle would become a medical student in 1877), and then at King's College, London. In 1865, as ***Louis Pasteur***'s work on bacteria became better known, Lister experimented with disinfecting a wound using carbolic acid (phenol), a compound then produced from coal tars. (Carbolic acid is mentioned in "The Cardboard Box" and coal-tar derivatives in "The Empty House".) Thereafter, his articles and lectures advocated the use of a 5 per cent solution of carbolic acid to wash surgical instruments and the surgeons' hands. ACD's mentor, ***Joseph Bell***, studied under Lister and believed in antiseptics, but not everyone did. "The wards of the infirmary," ACD wrote later, "were divided between the antiseptic people and the cold-water school, the latter regarding the whole germ theory as an enormous fad."

Sir **Sandford Fleming** (1827-1915) was the inventor of Universal Time and time zones, which replaced a vast patchwork of local time standards across North America and then elsewhere. The new system was made necessary by long-distance railways; Fleming was at various times chief engineer for the Intercolonial Railway, a surveyor developing a route for the Canadian Pacific (mentioned in "Black Peter"), and chief engineer for the Northern Railway of Canada. He was the author of a proposal (1862) for a railway line across Canada, Atlantic to Pacific, which eventually came to pass. Among other projects he advocated construction of a round-the-world British-owned undersea cable ("the All Red Line"), finally completed in 1902.

Mary Ann Girling (1827-1886) was a farmer's daughter, then a sailor's wife, in a village in Suffolk, who in 1864 received a message from God. She preached revelations, and followers gathered, calling themselves the Children of God. At first they were in London, but in 1872 a wealthy sympathizer provided a house and farm in the New Forest in Hampshire. True believers would live forever, Girling told them, and she herself was the incarnation of God: "I am the second appearing of Jesus, the Christ of God, the Bride." She demanded celibacy of the "New Forest Shakers", and forbade commercial transactions, which led to an eviction from their farmstead, so that they lived in cold and poverty. The sect dwindled, although tourists continued to visit, drawn by rumours of hypnosis and naked dancing.

Valentine Baker (1827-1887) served in South Africa and the Crimea, explored central Asia to collect intelligence about Russian moves on the frontier of British India, and by 1874 was a colonel with a staff position at Aldershot, Hampshire. In 1875 he was sentenced to a year in prison for assault — kissing, at the very least, 22-year-old **Rebecca Dickinson** in a train between Woking and London. *Encyclopaedia Britannica*, 1911: "His dismissal from the service was an inevitable consequence; it must be stated, however, that the view taken of the circumstances by good authorities was that Baker's conduct, when judged by conventional standards, admitted of considerable extenuation." "The Bruce-Partington Plans" owes something to this incident. Leaving England, he entered the service of the Ottoman Empire, serving in military action (some of it against *Muhammad Ahmad*, the Mahdi) and heading the Egyptian police.

William Holman Hunt (1827-1910) was a member of the Pre-Raphaelite Brotherhood of artists, and is particularly remembered for his dramatic religious painting "The Light of the World" (1854). It shows a figure representing Jesus, with crown and halo, about to knock on a symbolic door; reproductions of the painting are still frequently seen. Religion in a broad sense was important to Hunt, *Dante Gabriel Rossetti* and the other Pre-Raphaelites, who looked to mediaeval art for inspiration. Hunt also travelled to Palestine to soak up the atmosphere, and lived in Jerusalem for a time. He placed great emphasis on symbolism and repeatedly wrote explanations of what he had meant in his works of art.

Dante Gabriel Rossetti (1828-1882) was one of the founders of the Pre-Raphaelite Brotherhood, along with *William Holman Hunt* and Sir *John Millais*. He was a close friend of *Ford Madox Brown* and the brother of *Christina Rossetti*, and the great personal drama of his life was a love triangle involving *William Morris* and Morris's wife, *Jane Burden*. He was, however, married to **Elizabeth Siddal**; at her death in 1862, he buried a manuscript of his poetry with her, but later arranged with *Charles Augustus Howell* to retrieve it for him. All his life Rossetti divided his attention between poetry ("fleshly" sonnets were a specialty; a final edition of his collected work appeared in 1881) and painting, not to mention alcohol, drugs and paranoia. His best-known paintings include "Beata Beatrix" (1864-1870) and "The Blessed Damozel" (1875-1878).

George Meredith (1828-1909) is one of the most respected, if not necessarily most read, of English novelists. "Your mind is in a state of tension the whole time you are reading him," Arthur Conan Doyle wrote in *Through the Magic Door*, who admired him greatly, despite acknowledging that his style is difficult for many readers. His major books include *The Ordeal of Richard Feverel* (1859 — "how wise and how witty!" ACD called it) and *Diana of the Crossways* (1885). Meredith began his career as a journalist, and later was a publisher's reader; he wrote much poetry as well as his novels and stories.

Ignatius Pollaky (1828-1918) was a private detective. Indeed, he was a "private consulting detective", as he told a sceptical magistrate in an 1882 trial at Worship Street Police Court. He opened Pollaky's Private Inquiry Office in 1862, and by 1865 was located at 13 Paddington Green; as a result he was well known as "Paddington Pollaky", a nickname mentioned in the 1881 comic opera "Patience". He famously made use of the agony column (personal advertisements) in *The Times*, sending messages about his cases or perhaps for publicity. In 1867 he was appointed a special constable of the Metropolitan Police, providing information about alien residents in Britain. He retired in 1882, so that Sherlock Holmes's claim to be "the only unofficial consulting detective" at the time of *The Sign of the Four* (1887 or 1888) may be strictly true.

Jules Verne (1828-1905) wrote in French, but his novels of science fiction and adventure are beloved in English also. Wikipedia has a useful insight: "Verne is generally considered a major literary author in France and most of Europe, where he has had a wide influence on the literary avant-garde and on surrealism. His reputation is markedly different in Anglophone regions, where he has often been labeled a writer of genre fiction or children's books, not least because of the highly abridged and altered translations in which his novels are often reprinted." Major titles include *Twenty Thousand Leagues Under the Sea* (1869) and *Around the World in Eighty Days* (1872). From 1888 to 1903 Verne was a city councillor in Amiens, where he lived for most of his adult life.

Leo Nikolayevich Count **Tolstoy** (1828-1910) was one of the greatest novelists of all time, known particularly for *War and Peace* (1865-1869) and *Anna Karenina* (1875-1877). "Especially during his last three decades," says the *Encyclopaedia Britannica*, "Tolstoy also achieved world renown as a moral and religious teacher." It cites his doctrine of "nonresistance to evil" in particular, and calls him "a living symbol of the search for life's meaning". Tolstoy lived most of his life at the family estate south of Moscow. He studied law, enjoyed the fast life, served in the army, and began publishing stories in 1852. Much of Tolstoy's work includes unconventional forms (*War and Peace*, for example, incorporates a series of essays) and all of it emphasizes the importance of the individual and ordinary as opposed to grand systems. His writings after about 1880 largely present his own pared-down version of Christianity.

Sir **Joseph Swan** (1828-1914) was the inventor of the electric light bulb, developing something in 1860 (and patenting it in 1878) that looked much like ***Thomas Edison***'s later design. He surmounted his difficulties, such as problems maintaining a vacuum, and the Swan

Electric Light Company went into business in 1881. Within a year, London's Savoy Theatre was lit by Swan incandescent bulbs. In 1883, following a legal dispute, it merged with Edison's enterprise to form the Edison & Swan United Electric Light Company — referred to by Sir Henry Baskerville when he promises to install "a thousand candle-power Swan and Edison" at the entrance to Baskerville Hall. Earlier, Swan, working for a firm of manufacturing chemists in Newcastle, had developed the dry photographic plate, a huge step forward in making photography practical on a broad scale. He received a patent for bromide paper, still widely used, in 1879. His other inventions included a miners' safety lamp and a process for squeezing nitrocellulose through holes to form fibres.

Chester A. Arthur (1829-1886) was elected vice-president of the United States in 1880, but ended up serving most of a four-year term as President following the assassination of **James Garfield**. Originally from Vermont, he had been a stalwart of political patronage for the Republican party during a seven-year tenure as Collector of the Port of New York, managing more than 1,000 staff in the customs service. "But when Arthur succeeded to the Presidency, he was eager to prove himself above machine politics," says the White House website. He promoted government reform and the creation of the Civil Service Commission, and introduced new policies on tariffs and immigration (including a measure to ban paupers, criminals, lunatics and Chinese). He did not run for re-election in 1884.

Edward White Benson (1829-1896) was Archbishop of Canterbury for 13 years. His church career had involved teaching and administration until in 1877 he was named the first Bishop of Truro, in Cornwall, one of 18 new dioceses created during the 19th century. Prime minister *William Ewart Gladstone* tapped him for Canterbury in 1883, and in that role, the most senior position in the Church of England, he worked to reform the patronage system. "Benson facilitated a reconciliation among the various factions within the English church," says the *Encyclopaedia Britannica*, "and virtually brought to an end the prosecutions relating to ritualism that had plagued Anglicanism during the 19th century." He is also remembered as the author of the "Nine Lessons and Carols" service now widely used at Christmas.

Geronimo, real name **Goyathla** (1829-1909), was a leader of the Apache nation or tribe as they fought in defence of their territory in what is now Arizona. Initially the enemy were Mexican troops, as well as neighbouring Navajo and Comanche tribes. After the war of 1848 in which Mexico lost much of its territory to the United States, says the website Biography.com, "settlers and miners streamed into their lands. The Apaches stepped up their attacks, which included brutal ambushes on stagecoaches and wagon trains." It adds that Geronimo's followers "viewed him as the last great defender of the Native American way of life. But others, including fellow Apaches, saw him as a stubborn hold-out, violently driven by revenge." He surrendered in 1886 and spent the rest of his life as a prisoner.

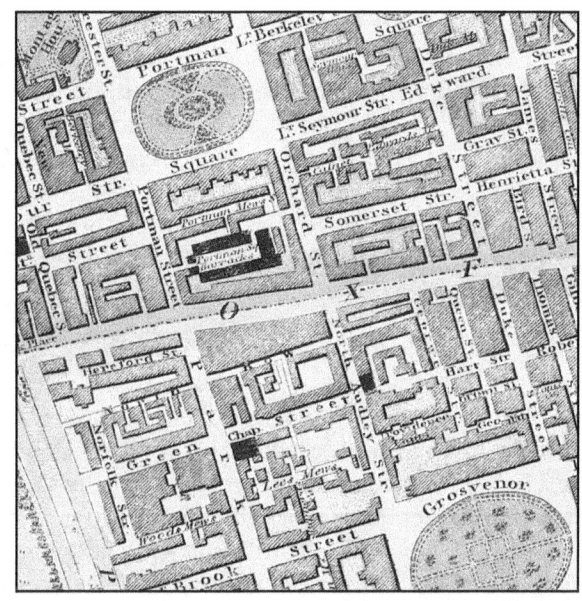

Henry Portman, 2nd Viscount **Portman** (1829-1919), might have been Mrs. Hudson's land-lord. As well as a Liberal member of Parliament 1852-1885, he was heir to the Portman Estate. The property of the Portman family since the 16th century, the Estate amounted to 270 acres (almost half a square mile) in London's Mary-lebone district, in-cluding much of Baker Street. The streets there, including Portman Square near the south end of Baker Street, were developed by the Estate beginning in the 1750s. In modern times the holdings have dwindled to 110 acres and 2 million square feet of floor space. Many of the traditional 99-year leases were expiring in the late 19th century, generating a vast income for the Viscount, who succeeded to the title on his father's death in 1888. He invested the money in a mansion at the family's country estate in Dorset, designed by architect *Norman Shaw*, which passed out of the family's hands a generation later.

Laura Bell (1829-1894) was one of the "pretty horse-breakers" who provide the social background to the possibility of an Irene Adler. This particular courtesan, born in Ireland, could be noticed driving her fashionable carriage in the park every day, as one did. The prime minister of Nepal, **Jung Bahadur Rana**, was said to have spent £250,000 on her while in London on an 1850-1851 world tour. It was also said that he had given her a ring, promising that if she ever sent it to him he would do anything she asked, and that she sent it to him at Katmandu during the Indian Mutiny of 1857 to ask that Nepal take the British side, or at least stay neutral. In 1852 Bell married a rambunctious army captain, **Augustus Thistlewayte**, and for a time joined the Plymouth Brethren and became an amateur preacher.

Margaret Oliphant, née **Wilson** (1829-1897), wrote best-selling novels for half a century and was reputed to be Queen *Victoria*'s favourite author. Born near Edinburgh, though her family later lived in Liverpool, she presents many Scots characters and settings in her books, which began in 1849 and continued until her death. Always financially harried, she wrote fast and prolifically, with much of her output being published in the Edinburgh-based *Blackwood's Magazine*, where a few of Arthur Conan Doyle's stories also appeared. Many of Oliphant's tales, notably the Chronicles of Carlingford, deal with local and religious politics, gender and class. She also wrote a series of supernatural short stories.

Oscar II (1829-1907) was King of both Sweden and Norway during the late Victorian era — in other words, the King of Scandinavia referred to in two Sherlock Holmes stories. ("What! Had he lost his wife?") In 1872 he succeeded his brother, **Charles XV**, as King, and was recognized as a judicious diplomat, to say nothing of a talented poet and an enthusiast for Arctic exploration. As the years progressed he realized the difficulty of one King reigning for two countries, a system that dated from 1814, and he helped to negotiate a separation in 1905 under which he remained King of Sweden while a Danish prince became King **Haakon VII** of Norway. Oscar's queen was **Sophia of Nassau**.

Silas **Weir Mitchell** (1829-1914) was both a physician — a pioneer in neurology — and an author. His medical work led to the discovery of what is now called "complex regional pain syndrome", the coining of the phrase "phantom limb", and writings such as *Injuries of Nerves and Their Consequences* (1872). At the same time he wrote novels, children's stories and poetry, one successful book being *The Autobiography of a Quack and Other Stories* (1903). He spent his life in Philadelphia, and attended a dinner party with Arthur Conan Doyle when ACD visited that city in November 1894.

Sir **James Fitzjames Stephen**, 1st Baronet (1829-1894), wrote *A General View of the Criminal Law of England* as a young barrister (1863). A Cambridge graduate (and the brother of Sir *Leslie Stephen*), he had been called to the bar in 1854. In 1869 he went to India as an advisor on revised legal procedures; the Indian Evidence Act 1872 was largely his work and is still in place. He came back to Britain keen to see English law, a muddle of precedent and complication, codified in a similar way, but was largely unsuccessful. The Criminal Code of Canada is largely based on his work, however, and he wrote *A History of the Criminal Law of England* (1883). Stephen was named a judge of the High Court in 1879; by 1891 he was in decline to the point that there were comments in the newspapers about his abilities, and he resigned. He was father to *James Leslie Stephen*.

Katharina (Katti) Lanner (1829-1908) was born in Vienna, where her father was director of ballet music at the Imperial court, and trained at the court opera. She married **Johann Geraldini**, director of the Vienna Ballet Company, and toured Europe and America with that company. She finally settled in London in 1875, initially performing at the Theatre Royal, Drury Lane, for impresario **James Mapleson**. Later she became a teacher and choreographer, and works that she choreographed for the 2,000-seat Empire Theatre in Leicester Square at the turn of the century did much to revive and popularize ballet as an art in Britain.

Sir **John Watson** (1829-1919) was a career soldier, who joined the army of the British East India Company at the age of 19 and got himself transferred as soon as possible to Bombay, on India's west coast, where the excitement seemed to be. He saw action at least twice before 1857 when, as Henry Wood says in "The Crooked Man", "the Mutiny broke out, and all hell was loose in the country." Watson, by now a lieutenant in the 1st Bengal Cavalry, came face to face with a detachment of rebels, headed by, as the official report later said, "a fine specimen of the Hindustani Mussalman… Lieutenant Watson ran the man through with his sword and dismounted him." He was awarded the Victoria Cross. He saw further action at Cawnpore and Lucknow. A decade later, he was responsible for organizing the 4th Sikh Irregular Cavalry, otherwise known as Watson's Horse, and after holding various commands was promoted to general in 1891.

Sir **John Everett Millais** (1829-1896) was a founder of the Pre-Raphaelite Brotherhood of artists and the creator of dramatic paintings in the pre-Raphaelite style, such as "Ophelia" (1852). He later turned to a less distinctive style including many landscapes. His 1886 painting "Bubbles" is an icon, largely because it was long used in advertising for Pears Soap. Millais received high honours for his work, including a baronetcy and the presidency of the Royal Academy. His personal life included a romance with **Effie Gray**, the wife of *John Ruskin*, whose marriage was famously annulled when it became known that it had never been consummated. Millais married Effie in 1855.

William Booth (1829-1912) founded the Salvation Army in partnership with his wife **Catherine Booth**, née **Mumford** (1829-1890). Both were passionate Christians of the Methodist persuasion — Catherine from childhood, William after a conversion in his teens. He was an amateur evangelist, then a full-time preacher, and founded the Christian Revival Society in London's sordid east end in 1865. The "Salvation Army" name followed in 1878, with uniforms, marching bands and military metaphors; Booth became a General. The Army quickly spread to the United States, Europe and the Empire, preaching a traditional Christian theology of sin and salvation, as well as providing social services where needed, and battling vice and liquor. Booth's book *In Darkest England and the Way Out* (1890) was a best-seller.

Christina Rossetti (1830-1894) was the rival of **Elizabeth Barrett Browning**, at least in public acclaim, as the greatest woman poet of the Victorian era. Born in London of a mostly Italian family, she had periods of bad health and apparent depression most of her life. Her brother was *Dante Gabriel Rossetti*, who made her his model for some of his early Pre-Raphaelite paintings. The majority of her work expresses her Anglo-Catholic religious beliefs; her best-known poem is the Christmas hymn "In the Bleak Midwinter". Often anthologized is "Goblin Market", an 1862 poem that can be interpreted as Christian, lesbian or political. In later years she moved away from poetry to devotional writing, including *Time Flies: A Reading Diary* (1885).

James Payn (1830-1898) "was not a man of genius, not a great novelist, not even a considerable litterateur, but he interested and amused an entire generation," the *Spectator* said in his obituary. "He was a born teller of stories." The story "Lost Sir Massingberd", published in *Chambers's Journal* in 1864, established him as a writer, as novels (about a hundred in all), short stories and essays poured out. His specialties were gentle humour, anecdote, digression, and the not-terribly-villainous villain. He was editor of the *Cornhill Magazine* 1883-1896. Arthur Conan Doyle tells a little about his friendship in *Memories and Adventures*.

Emily Davies (1830-1921) was a founder of Girton College, Cambridge, the first college at either of the ancient universities to provide education and degrees for women. She was also a campaigner for women's suffrage, editor of the *English Woman's Journal*, and a member of the London School Board, where she helped open school examinations to girls as well as boys. Girton College was founded in 1869, initially in Hertfordshire; it was moved to Cambridge in 1873, and Davies was its Mistress (corresponding to the Master of many men's colleges) 1873-1875. Women could study at Girton, and at Newnham College (founded 1871), but were not officially part of the university until 1948.

Isma'il Pasha (1830-1895) was Khedive, or viceroy, of Egypt, in an era when that country (including Sudan to the south) was nominally part of the Ottoman Empire, but in fact increasingly under British influence. He succeeded his father, **Ibrahim Pasha**, as ruler in 1863, and was an energetic advocate of modernization and urban development. But such activities, as well as an unsuccessful war with Ethiopia, led to heavy debt, which the Egyptian government could pay off only by selling its share of the Suez Canal Company to Britain. (The canal, largely owned by French investors, opened in 1869.) The Ottoman Sultan, **Abdulaziz I**, granted increasing autonomy and titles to the Khedive, but finally deposed him in 1879 in response to Egyptian unrest over Isma'il's financial submission to Britain. Three years later a British "protectorate" over Egypt was established.

Franz Joseph I (1830-1916) was monarch of one of Europe's great powers, in the dual role of Emperor of Austria and King of Hungary. He reached the Austrian throne when his uncle, Emperor **Ferdinand I**, abdicated in 1848, Europe's year of revolutions. He began as an absolutist ruler, failed to hold Austria's Italian possessions, stumbled into a war with Prussia, and finally settled on a policy of alliance with Germany (of which Prussia was the leading component). The "dual monarchy" system, established in 1867, favoured Hungarians and German-speaking Austrians at the expense of other nationalities within the empire, and particularly alienated Serbia. Franz Joseph signed up for ***Otto von Bismarck***'s "League of Three Emperors" (Germany, Austria-Hungary, Russia), but it did not last. His final mistake was issuing the ultimatum to Serbia, after the assassination of his heir Archduke *Franz Ferdinand*, that led to World War I. In domestic matters he headed a conscientious, efficient, and even progressive administration. His marriage to Empress *Elisabeth* was a long-running drama; their son and heir, Crown Prince *Rudolf*, committed suicide.

Eadweard Muybridge, born **Muggeridge** (1830-1904), took photographs of animals, more than 100,000 of them, to document their motion in a time before "moving pictures" were possible. Strips of his black-and-white photos, including moose, buffalo, and clothed and nude men and women, remain a common meme. He began his "animal locomotion" work in 1872 at the behest of former California governor **Leland Stanford**, a horse-owner who wanted evidence about racing gaits. Muybridge's photographic work also included scenic and anthropological studies. He was born and died at Kingston-upon-Thames in

England, but spent much of his career in the United States (including 1883-1886 at the University of Pennsylvania). In 1874 he was tried for murder in Napa, California, after shooting his wife's lover; he was acquitted on the grounds of justifiable homicide.

Samore Touré (1830-1900) was a military and political leader of the Mandinka (Mandingo) ethnic group in west Africa during a period when conflict among indigenous groups was being complicated by the arrival of European imperial powers determined to draw borders and take control. He was a Muslim, a member of an economic and cultural elite that dominated the traditionally animist population following the disruption caused by massive eighteenth-century slave raiding. By 1880 Samore's troops controlled an empire across the present-day countries of Guinea, Mali, Burkina Faso and Ivory Coast, and he established a government on Islamic principles. Conflict with French forces beginning in 1891 led him to withdraw eastward. France's capture of Timbuktu in 1894 was a landmark event in the colonial warfare.

Robert Gascoyne-Cecil, 3rd **Marquess of Salisbury** (1830-1903), might or might not be the statesman disguised as "Lord Bellinger" in "The Second Stain". Salisbury came from a family that had been involved in statecraft for centuries, and was elected to Parliament for the first time at the age of 23. In 1868 he acquired the title on the death of his father, the 2nd Marquess. His career in government was conducted from the House of Lords, something no prime minister since then has attempted. Salisbury held positions in ***Benjamin Disraeli***'s last government, and succeeded him as Conservative leader on his death in 1881. He was prime minister for a short time in 1885, then 1886-1892 and 1895-1902. Issues in his era included local government reform and the organization of British colonies in Africa.

Sir **Charles Wyville Thomson** (1830-1882) was chief scientist for the 1872-1876 expedition of HMS *Challenger*, which gathered data and samples from all parts of the world, provided the basis for theoretical advances by ***Charles Darwin*** and others, and incidentally gave a name to Arthur Conan Doyle's character Professor George Challenger. A specialist in marine life, Thomson had just arrived at the University of Edinburgh as professor of natural history, after 20 years in other academic institutions. His early findings, which dramatically changed the field of oceanography, were published in *The Depths of the Sea* (1873). He wrote a two-volume summary of the *Challenger* findings (published 1880) and started issuing some 50 volumes of illustration and scientific information, though other hands had to finish the job.

Sir **Eyre Massey Shaw** (1830-1908) was London's fire chief from 1861 to 1891 — captain of the London Fire Engine Establishment and then superintendent of the Metropolitan Fire Brigade when it was created in 1865. The website for today's MFB recalls that "He established a new rank system; introduced a new uniform that consisted of a brass or silver helmet and woollen tunic; built new fire stations and introduced advanced technology to improve the service. He brought in steam fire engines that could pump, on average, 300 gallons of water a minute." Shaw moved in high society; famously, he had a box  for the first performance of the **Gilbert** and **Sullivan** operetta "Iolanthe" in 1882, and was singled out for attention in a stanza of one of the Fairy Queen's songs.

Sir **George Chesney** (1830-1895) wrote the short story "The Battle of Dorking", published in *Blackwood's Magazine* in 1871, pioneering the so-called "invasion literature" of stories about European powers threatening Britain. Arthur Conan Doyle would contribute to it much later with his 1914 story "Danger!" Like many other writers in the genre, Chesney had a military background. He saw action (and was severely wounded) in the Indian Mutiny (1857), then spent the 1860s working on "public works accounts", rather like Mycroft Holmes. He was president of the Royal Indian Civil Engineering College for a decade, then in the 1880s was back in India, rising to be commandant of the Royal Engineers and a full general, and urging that native Indians be allowed to serve as officers in the Indian Army.

Anna **Leonowens**, née **Edwards** (1831-1915), was an Englishwoman, born in India, who served 1862-1867 as governess at the court of the King of Siam. The musical "The King and I" is based on her 1870 book *The English Governess at the Siamese Court*, which may have included a grain of truth, and she may have had some influence on the Crown Prince, later King **Chulalong-**

korn. Their paths crossed again in 1897 when the King visited London (and reported expressed dismay at the inaccuracy in Leonowens's writings about Siam). In later years Leonowens lived in the United States as a writer, lecturer, and teacher, and eventually moved to Halifax and then Montréal; she was a founder of the Nova Scotia College of Art and Design.

Anthony Ashley-Cooper, 8th Earl of **Shaftesbury** (1831-1886), waited most of his life to inherit his title, which ran in a long-established family of the Irish nobility (though he was born in London). He became earl only on the death of his father in 1885. Meanwhile, he served in the Royal Navy during the Crimean War; under his temporary title of **Lord Ashley** he was a "Liberal-Conservative" Member of Parliament for a few years and was active in the Society for the Suppression of the Opium Trade. His wife was Lady **Harriet Chichester**, who would be a cousin once removed to the future **Edward Donald Chichester, 6th Marquess of Donegall** (1903-1975), editor of the *Sherlock Holmes Journal* for many years. The earl was known to be "despondent" and hypochondriac, and his family sent him to doctors and instructed the servants to keep an eye on him. One Tuesday afternoon he bought a revolver at a shop in Piccadilly, then hailed **Samuel Wakeland**'s cab in Regent Street, had him drive back and forth a few times, and shot himself in the head. He died at the Middlesex Hospital.

Frederick III (1831-1888) was King of Prussia and Emperor of Germany for a few weeks — from the death of his father, *Wilhelm I*, to his own death from throat cancer. He was then succeeded by his son, *Wilhelm II*. He was married to Princess *Victoria*, daughter of Britain's Queen *Victoria* and *Albert*, the Prince Consort, and was known to be a great admirer of his father-in-law and an advocate of a government conducted in the British fashion based on the advice of ministers. However, his 99-day reign gave no opportunity for taming the conservative Chancellor, *Otto von Bismarck*, and his son did not follow his intended liberal path.

Helena Blavatsky (1831-1891) was the central figure in the cult of Theosophy, which had a vogue in the late 19th century, and remains "the pioneer esotericist of our age" according to a website celebrating and promoting her work. She maintained that Theosophy had rediscovered an Ancient Wisdom which underlay all religions. She was one of three founders of the Theosophical Society in 1875 (formed in New York, it soon moved its headquarters to Madras) and her massive 1888 book *The Secret Doctrine* remains the most important Theosophical work. Born in Ukraine, she travelled the world for two decades, encountering many adventures, before settling down to write and proselytize. From 1887 she lived in London, where her path crossed with those of *Mabel Collins, Annie Besant* and others.

Isabella Bishop, née **Bird** (1831-1904), was told by her doctor that she should travel, as a way of coping with her insomnia and depression, and in 1854 she went to North America on the strength of a £100 gift from her father. The letters she wrote to her sister over several months made the basis of a book, *The Englishwoman in America* (1856). Later in life she travelled to Hawaii (a trip that produced *Six Months in the Sandwich Islands*, 1875) and the American west (*A Lady's Life in the Rocky Mountains*, 1879). During her American adventures she met **"Rocky Mountain Jim" Nugent**, describing him as "a man any woman might love but no sane woman would marry"; the man she married instead was Scots physician **John Bishop**, but he died in 1886 after just five years of marriage, and Isabella resumed her travels: Japan, India, Persia, Korea, and Tibet (*The Yangtze Valley and Beyond*, 1900).

Henry Labouchère (1831-1912) inherited a fortune, but sat in Parliament as a Radical for 26 years (1880-1906). He was best known, however, as a journalist, particularly for his reports from Paris during the 1870-1871 siege by German troops. His despatches were sent out by balloon over the besieging army, and published first in the *Daily News*, of which he happened to be part owner, and then in a book, *Letters of a Besieged Resident*. In the political arena, he sided with *Charles Stewart Parnell* and opposed the expansionism that led to the South African War of 1899-1901. He was also responsible for the notorious "section 11" of the Criminal Law Amendment Act 1885, a last-minute addition to the bill (previously intended to protect underage girls against sexual abuse) which made any form of male homosexual activity a crime.

James A. Garfield (1831-1881) was President of the United States for six months in 1881, his four-year term cut short by assassination at the hands of a man bitter at not getting a government job. A Republican, he had been a college president, then served 18 years in the United States House of Representatives before being nominated as a dark-horse candidate and narrowly elected. His brief presidency was dominated by a struggle with Senator **Roscoe Conkling**, also a Republican, over who would control government patronage in New York; the president was victorious. He proposed, but was not able to implement, federal funding for a "universal" education system, considering it the best way to guarantee civil rights for Blacks who had been freed from slavery.

James Clerk Maxwell (1831-1879) was the scientist who developed the theory of electromagnetic radiation. "He is rightly acclaimed as the father of modern physics," says the foundation that now exists in his name. "He also made fundamental contributions to mathematics, astronomy and engineering." Said *Albert Einstein*: "This change in the conception of reality is the most profound and the most fruitful that physics has experienced since the time of Newton." Educated at Edinburgh (a generation before Arthur Conan Doyle) and Cambridge, Maxwell taught at Aberdeen and at King's College, London, then in 1871 became a professor and head of the new Cavendish Laboratory at Cambridge.

John Bell Hood (1831-1879) was a general for the Confederacy during the American Civil War. "The Five Orange Pips" notes that the late Elias Openshaw "fought in *[Stonewall] Jackson*'s army, and afterwards under Hood". A first lieutenant in the United States Army when the war began, Hood chose to fight for the South, and had initial success leading what became known as Hood's Texas Brigade. Known for his derring-do, he was wounded several times. He eventually rose beyond his level of competence as commander of the Army of Tennessee, failing to defend Atlanta and being defeated at Nashville in 1864. He died in a yellow fever epidemic at New Orleans, rather like the one mentioned in "The Yellow Face". Fort Hood, Texas, is named for him.

Naser al-Din Shah Qajar (1831-1896) was Shah, or King, of Persia (now Iran) from 1848 until his assassination by an Islamic activist. He was responsible for many innovations in Persia — roads, schools, telegraphs, a newspaper — but resisted political reforms, and is famous for an ill-conceived plan to give foreign interests a long-term monopoly on tobacco, an incident that led to lasting unrest. He was also troubled by religious dissent in the chiefly Muslim country. Early in his reign he ordered the execution, by firing squad, of the prophet **Siyyid Alí Muhammad Shírází**, known as the **Báb**. Two years later **Mírzá Husayn-Alí Núrí**, who as *Baha'u'llah* would be the founder of the Baha'i faith, was accused of trying to assassinate the Shah, and was exiled. The Shah fought an unsuccessful war with Britain over territory in 1856, but all was forgiven by 1873 when he visited Britain and was presented with the Order of the Garter.

Prince **Christian of Schleswig-Holstein** (1831-1917) was the husband of Princess *Helena*, and thus a son-in-law of Queen *Victoria*. His family was a minor branch of Danish royalty, but politically associated with the German side of the continuing conflict over Schleswig-Holstein, and he served briefly in a Schleswig-Holstein army as war began in the region in 1848. Denmark prevailed for the time being, Christian went on to university in Bonn (where he became friends with the future Emperor *Frederick III*), and he met and became engaged to Helena. The couple, married in 1866, settled in Britain; Christian held a series of military ranks including honorary colonel of a battalion of the Berkshires, the regiment with which Watson served at the Battle of Maiwand.

Sitting Bull, Sioux name **Thathanka Iyotake** (1831-1890), was a chief of the Lakota Sioux tribe whose career battling the United States Army was curiously interrupted by a season performing in *Buffalo Bill Cody*'s wild west show. His military struggle to keep White interlopers out of Sioux territory in what is now North Dakota began in 1863 and reached a climax with his victory at the Battle of the Little Big Horn (Battle of Greasy Grass), often known as Custer's Last Stand, in 1876. He and his band escaped to Canada for a time, but surrendered to American authorities in 1881. He was allowed to go east in 1885 as one of Cody's celebrity performers, but stayed only for a four-month season. In 1890 Sitting Bull briefly returned to a leadership role as the Ghost Dance religious and political revival swept through the Sioux, and was killed during a botched attempt to arrest him.

Arminius Vámbéry (1832-1913), described as "one of the Jewish Orientalists", may have been the international figure whose name suggested that of "Vamberry, the wine merchant" ("The Musgrave Ritual"). Born into a poor family in what is now Slovakia, he had a remarkable ability with languages, and began his life-long travels by going to Constantinople, capital of the Ottoman Empire, as a young tutor. In 1861-1864 he visited Trebizond, Mecca, and Samarkand in disguise, as Europeans were not welcome there, and subsequently wrote a book about his travels, as well as volumes about language, especially about the roots of Hungarian. He was widely recognized for promoting British interests, as against Russian, in southwestern Asia.

Charles Peace (1832-1879), or "my old friend Charlie Peace" as Holmes calls him in "The Illustrious Client", was primarily a burglar, but also committed two murders and was executed by the hangman of the day, *William Marwood*. Peace's life of crime began after he was crippled in an industrial accident at age 14. He made his living by burglaries at Sheffield and Manchester (and, at intervals, from a picture-framing business) but eventually, in 1876, killed a police officer who interrupted his work. Later the same year he shot a neighbour dead following a dispute over the man's wife. He moved his burglary practice to London, where he was identified in 1878 and brought to justice. As Holmes says, Peace was a violinist, if not a "virtuoso".

Émile Gaboriau (1832-1873) was an author known to Sherlock Holmes, who describes his fictional detective, Monsieur Lecoq, as "a miserable bungler" in *A Study in Scarlet*. Arthur Conan Doyle was more respectful, as he had every reason to be: Gaboriau was a master of suspense, intrigue and logical reasoning, and was one of the authors, along with **Edgar Allan Poe**, who had laid the foundations of detective stories on which ACD then built. Originally from the little town of Saujon in southwestern France, he learned much about prisons, morgues and police courts through years working as a journalist in Paris. He had written several novels before his big success with *L'Affaire Lerouge* (1866) and four more volumes of Lecoq. Another dozen books followed with other characters. Lecoq is thought to be based on the real-life **Eugène François Vidocq**, a Paris criminal turned policeman.

Frederick Roberts, Earl **Roberts** (1832-1914), was an awesome figure indeed by the time Sherlock Holmes dropped his name in "The Blanched Soldier", set in 1903 (though not published until long after Roberts's death). He was Commander-in-Chief of the Forces by that time, having reached the rank of Field Marshal in 1895, even before the South African War (1899-1901) that was his greatest triumph. As a lieutenant during the Indian Mutiny (1857) he was awarded the Victoria Cross, he was a general during the Second Afghan War (Watson might have glimpsed him in Kandahar), and he commanded forces in India

1885-1893 and then at home in Ireland. He was sent to South Africa to replace the luckless Sir **Redvers Buller**, where he was triumphant in battle but can be blamed for logistical confusion and the creation of squalid concentration camps for Boer civilians. Arthur Conan Doyle had dinner with him once at headquarters in Bloemfontein. Roberts was Commander-in-Chief 1901-1904, when the position was abolished.

Gustave Eiffel, born **Bönickhausen** (1832-1923), was a French engineer who mostly built bridges, but was involved with two of the world's most iconic metal structures. Born in Dijon, he was educated in Paris and worked designing such projects as an iron railway bridge over the Garonne at Bordeaux, now a landmark. In 1866 he set up his own company. In 1879, when the engineer responsible for building the Statue of Liberty (a gift to the United States from France) died suddenly, Eiffel was appointed to take over. And in 1887 he began work on the world's tallest structure, intended to be a focal point for the 1889 Paris International Exposition. The Eiffel Tower, as it became known, is 1,063 feet tall. An important factor in its stability was wind resistance; his work in that respect led Eiffel to an interest in aerodynamics, and he set up a laboratory that included the world's first wind tunnel.

Gustave Doré (1832-1883) was "arguably the most renowned illustrator of all time", according to one art catalogue. He worked in oil painting and sculpture, but specialized in wood engraving for book illustrations. His homeland was France, but much of his work was done for English publications, including an 1866 edition of the Bible, and for several years he was paid £10,000 a year, the equivalent of a seven-figure sum in modern terms, to spend three months a year in London working on *London: A Pilgrimage*, published in 1872. His last such work involved 26 steel engravings for an edition of **Edgar Allan Poe**'s "The Raven", which appeared after his death.

Herbert Vaughan (1832-1903) was Archbishop of Westminster — the head of the Roman Catholic Church in England — from 1892 to his death, and a Cardinal from 1893. He had five brothers who were also priests (including **Bernard Vaughan**, 1847-1922, a Jesuit especially known for his 1906 sermon series "The Sins of Society") and five sisters who were nuns. He was a protegé of his predecessor as Archbishop, *Henry Manning*, but less interested in social issues. As a theological conservative he induced Pope *Leo XIII* to issue a papal Bull in 1896 declaring that Church of England ordination was null and void. (He is, however, remembered for visiting the United States in 1871 to help establish a mission to freed slaves in the southern states.) He was largely responsible for the building of Westminster Cathedral.

Lewis Carroll, properly **Charles Lutwidge Dodgson** (1832-1898), wrote *Alice's Adventures in Wonderland* (1865) and *Through the Look-ing-Glass* (1871) in the intervals of his mathematical work as a lecturer at Christ Church, Oxford. He wrote extensively in his field, particularly geometry and linear algebra, but is remembered for the two children's books that he wrote for *Alice Liddell*, the daughter of an academic col-league. They were illustrated by Sir **John Tenniel**. Dodgson also wrote a satirical novel, *Sylvie and Bruno*, invented several gadgets, and was an early master of photography. He did not marry, and some bio-graphers have hinted at paedophilia, though the evidence is against it.

Sir **Leslie Stephen** (1832-1904) was a prominent writer, editor and bio-grapher, the brother of Sir *James Fitzjames Stephen*. He taught briefly at Cambridge before entering the London literary world, rather as an editor and critic than as an author. He edited the *Cornhill* magazine 1871-1882 (it would later publish some of Doyle's early fiction), and wrote works such as *History of English Thought in the Eighteenth Century* (1876). Stephen was creator and editor of the *Dictionary of National Biography*, a landmark of British historical scholarship and self-awareness, from 1882 to 1891, in that time producing its first 26 volumes for Smith, Elder & Co. His first wife, Harriet, was the daugh-ter of the novelist *William Makepeace Thackeray*; his daughters by his second marriage were author **Virginia Woolf** and artist **Vanessa Bell**.

Louisa **May Alcott** (1832-1888) was an American author, best known for *Little Women* (1868) and its sequels although she wrote many other novels and stories for both children and adults, as well as plays. Transcendentalist thinkers such as **Ralph Waldo Emerson** and **Henry David Thoreau**, friends of the Massa-chusetts family in which she grew up, taught and influenced her, and she campaigned against slavery and for women's suffrage. She worked as a domestic servant, teacher and nurse before becoming a full-time writer and editor, eventually drawing a substantial income from her work.

Patrick Heron Watson (1832-1907) was an 1853 graduate of the University of Edinburgh and probably the greatest surgeon of his generation. In the era before anaesthetics, speed was the essential; Watson planned his operations meticulously and was said to be able to do an amputation at the hip in 9.5 seconds. He performed operations no one in Edinburgh had done before, such as ovariotomy and laryngectomy, although he was slow in accepting new antiseptic techniques. During the Crimean War he spent several months at a filthy and ill-equipped military hospital, where he came down with typhus and then dysentery.
Returning to Edinburgh in 1858, he was appointed surgeon at several of the city's hospitals, including Chalmers Hospital, where he was on staff from 1865 to 1904. He also was appointed lecturer (though never professor) in surgery, and was an advocate for women's medical education. *Joseph Bell*, who was Arthur Conan Doyle's mentor and, supposedly, model for Sherlock Holmes, was his assistant and later his colleague.

Sir **William Crookes** (1832-1919) was the discoverer of the element thallium, the inventor of the Crookes tube (a form of vacuum tube or cathode ray tube), and a researcher in chemistry, physics, meteorology, and even psychiatry. Though briefly a teacher, he did much of his research independently, in a laboratory in his London home. He used the recently developed techniques of spectroscopy to identify thallium in 1861; identified the fourth state of matter, now called plasma, in 1879; and by 1903 was studying radioactive decay in uranium. Crookes had a life-long interest in Spiritualism, served as president of the Society for Psychical Research, and joined Theosophical and other occult societies. He is mentioned repeatedly in Arthur Conan Doyle's *History of Spiritualism*.

Alfred Nobel (1833-1896) invented dynamite, and left his immense fortune to provide annual prizes for scientific advancement, literature, and peace. Born in Stockholm and raised partly in St. Petersburg, then the capital of Russia, he was a chemist with a keen interest in explosives. His work on nitroglycerin, punctuated by disasters, led to the 1867 invention of dynamite (nitroglycerin dissolved in diatomaceous earth), followed in 1875 by gelignite. He eventually earned some 350 patents, and by his life's end owned 90 armaments factories, although a major use of dynamite was in construction and mining rather than in weaponry. His will, written in 1895, established the prizes in physical science; chemistry; medicine or physiology; literature; and peace ("fraternity between nations").

Benjamin Harrison (1833-1901) was the 23rd president of the United States, serving 1889-1893 and being both preceded and followed by *Grover Cleveland*. A lawyer from Ohio, he fought in the Civil War, then entered politics as a member of the new Republican Party and served in the United States Senate. He was elected over Cleveland, a Democrat running for a second term, who actually won the popular vote in November 1888 but lost in the Electoral College. Major issues during Harrison's presidency included civil service reform, Civil War pensions, tariffs, and the "bimetallic question" (referred to in "The Bruce-Partington Plans") of whether silver as well as gold should be the basis for currency. The Sherman Antitrust Act was passed during his term. He sought reelection in 1892, but was defeated by Cleveland.

Charles George Gordon (1833-1885) served in the army in several parts of the Empire, earning the nickname "Chinese" for his role in leading British troops that helped the Manchu emperor suppress the

Taiping rebellion in China. One of the most destructive wars in history, it ended in 1864 with an estimated 20 million dead. Gordon subsequently went to Egypt to join the staff of the Khedive or governor, *Isma'il Pasha*, then served as Governor-General of the Sudan. He became a general in 1882. In 1885 he was sent to Khartoum, Sudan, to deal with the latest rebellion, led by *Muhammad Ahmad*, "the Mahdi". He succeeded in evacuating more than 2,000 British civilians, but wound up trapped in a prolonged siege, and was killed by the forces of the Mahdi before British relief arrived. His death outraged Britain and made an impression on Dr. Watson, who subsequently displayed his portrait in the Baker Street rooms, as noted in "The Cardboard Box".

Charles Bradlaugh (1833-1891) was, famously, an atheist; elected to Parliament in 1880, he refused to take an oath of office that involved God, and only in 1886 was he permitted to "affirm" and take his seat as a member. From about 1860 he had been writing articles and pamphlets as a "freethinker", editing the *National Reformer* and working with social activist ***Annie Besant***. Their 1877 book *The Fruits of Philosophy*, advocating contraception, led to charges of "obscene libel" and a conviction that was, however, thrown out on appeal. Bradlaugh advocated Irish home rule, land reform, republicanism and British military involvement overseas, and opposed socialism.

Constantine Alexander Ionides (1833-1900) was an art collector like his father. The older man, **Alexander Constantine Ionides**, had come to Britain in 1827 with his own father, an import-export businessman, and became a patron of the arts. His children carried on in that tradition, and Constantine in particular built up the family collection to the point that in his will he was able to leave 1,138 pictures and prints, including 82 oil paintings, to London's Victoria and Albert Museum. Artist **Alphonse Legros** was his advisor, helping him acquire works by the likes of **Eugène Delacroix** and **Edgar Degas**. His surname of "Ionides", said to mean simply "the Greek", may have inspired the reference to "Ionides of Alexandria" in "The Golden Pince-Nez".

Daniel Dunglas Home (1833-1886) was a prominent medium who did not accept payment, but enjoyed the hospitality of the wealthy and famous. Arthur Conan Doyle's *The History of Spiritualism* devotes an entire chapter to him, noting his unusual "range of mediumship", including healing powers. Born in Scotland, he grew up in Connecticut; as a child he was associated with poltergeist activity, and as a young man he gave séances at which tables moved and messages arrived from the dead. In 1854 he moved to London, where the manifestations continued. During one session in 1868 he reportedly levitated, floated out a third-storey window, and floated back in through a different window. He was accused of creating his effects through conjuring tricks, but many of them remain unexplained.

Garnet Wolseley, 1st Viscount **Wolseley** (1833-1913), was commander-in-chief of Britain's armed forces from 1895 to 1900, at the end of a military career in which he saw action throughout the world-wide empire. His father was a major in the 25th Regiment of Foot, and the son, born in Dublin, joined the 12th Foot at the age of 19. His first experience of combat was in Burma in 1853; the Crimean War followed, then the Indian Mutiny, then the Second Opium War in China, then the Fenian raids and the Red River Rebellion in Canada (1870), and then a series of actions in Africa, climaxed by the 1884 action to rescue General *George Gordon* from Khartoum. (Wolseley's forces arrived just too late.) He held a series of administrative offices, was promoted to field-marshal, and was named commander-in-chief as successor to the dithering old Duke of *Cambridge* in 1895.

Hortense Schneider (1833-1920) had some resemblances to Irene Adler, being both an opera star (though a soprano, where Adler was allegedly a contralto) and the companion of princes (in Schneider's case, reputedly a mistress of *Edward VII*). Born in Bordeaux, she based her career in Paris, not Warsaw, and was particularly known for her performances in *Jacques Offenbach*'s operettas. She became the toast of the Second Empire (the period 1852-1870 in France), admired for her vivacity and feared by theatre managers for her inclination to stamp off stage demanding a salary increase. She retired at the age of 45 rather than give up the star repertoire to play secondary roles.

Margaret (Maggie) Fox, later **Kane** (1833-1893), was, with her younger sister **Catherine (Kate) Fox**, later **Jencken** (1837-1892), the accidental founder of Spiritualism, the belief to which Arthur Conan Doyle adhered in the last fifteen years of his life. Early in 1848, as young teenagers, they produced rapping noises in their house in Hydesville, New York, purporting to be messages from spirits. Under the supervision of their older sister, **Leah Fox Fish**, they became popular mediums in New York and elsewhere. The phenomena were widely considered to be fraudulent, made by the girls cracking their toes. Margaret confessed as much in October 1888, but inevitably later recanted the confession. The Fox sisters' later lives were a welter of alcoholism, bad company and conflicting allegations. Arthur Conan Doyle in his *History of Spiritualism* admits of no doubt whatever that the spirit phenomena were genuine.

Sir **Edward Burne-Jones** (1833-1898) was one of the important Pre-Raphaelite painters, a student of ***Dante Gabriel Rossetti*** and co-founder of ***William Morris***'s studio. "His paintings, inspired by medieval, classical, and biblical themes, are noted for their sentimentality and dream-like romanticized style," a website says. Another site counters: "Under increasing Renaissance influence, the rich primary colors of medieval glass gave way to anemic, stylized figures in pallid colors." He also did book illustration, created jewellery, and designed stained glass, mosaics, and tapestries, particularly for churches. His best-known painting is "King Cophetua and the Beggar Maid" (1884). He was an uncle by marriage of both ***Rudyard Kipling*** and **Stanley Baldwin**.

Sir **George Lewis**, 1st Baronet (1833-1911), was a solicitor so noted for his negotiating skills and society connections that his name is casually dropped in the story "The Illustrious Client" as someone who was involved in "the Hammerford Will case". Educated at University College, London, he got his law training as an apprentice to his father, and at first was largely in criminal practice. He represented *Valentine Baker* (1875); **Virginia Crawford** (1885, in her divorce case involving Sir *Charles Dilke*); and the defendants in the ***William Gordon-Cumming*** libel case (1890). Said his obituary in *The Times*: "Sir George Lewis was perhaps not so much a lawyer as a shrewd private inquiry agent; audacious, playing the game often in defiance of the rules, and relying on his audacity to carry him through. He was the confidential adviser of many prominent people. He was probably right in priding himself most upon his peculiar success in keeping his clients from coming before the public eye at all." He relied on his "encyclopaedic memory", the obituary added, rarely making notes.

William Orange (1833-1916), not related to William of Orange, King **William III**, was superintendent of the Broadmoor Criminal Lunatic Asylum 1870-1886, and in that position earned an international reputation as an authority on how criminals with mental illness could be handled and treated. He trained as a physician at St. Thomas' Hospital in Lambeth and worked at an asylum in Surrey and then for eight years at Broadmoor before becoming superintendent. The institution, which is located in Berkshire west of London, is now called Broadmoor Psychiatric Hospital. On behalf of the

Home Office, which is responsible for law enforcement in England, Orange conducted a number of enquiries into notable cases of condemned criminals whose sanity was in question.

Sir **Richard Tangye** (1833-1906) was "the most prominent of the five brothers who founded the well-known engineering firm of Messrs. Tangye, Ltd., of the Cornwall Works, Birmingham," said a tribute in the journal *Nature* on the centenary of his birth. "From the humblest beginnings, the business, begun in one small workroom in Birmingham in 1855, grew into a great concern employing 2,500 persons supplying machinery to all parts of the world. Success first came to the firm when it supplied hydraulic jacks to **[Isambard Kingdom] Brunel** for the purpose of pushing the *Great Eastern* into the Thames." The brothers helped found the Birmingham Museum and Art Gallery in 1885.

Spencer Cavendish, 8th Duke of Devonshire, formerly **Marquess of Hartington** (1833-1908), was a figure right out of ***Anthony Trollope***'s political novels. "He declined to become Prime Minister on three occasions," says Wikipedia, "not because he was not a serious politician but because the circumstances were never right." He has been suggested as the original of the Duke of Holdernesse who figures in "The Priory School". He was a Member of Parliament from 1857 (as a Liberal and later a Liberal Unionist, the party to which Arthur Conan Doyle adhered), and held a succession of government posts including Secretary of State for India (1880-1882). For a brief period he was leader of the Liberal Party. He succeeded to the dukedom only in 1891, and married only in 1892; for many years his mistress was the courtesan *Catherine Walters*. His younger brother was Lord *Frederick Cavendish*, assassinated 1882.

Aimé Guerlain (1834-1910) was a master perfumer, son of the founder of what is still the House of Guerlain. With the father's death in 1864, Aimé took responsibility for creating scents, and his brother **Gabriel**

Guerlain became the business manager. His creations included Fleur d'Italie (1864) and the internationally famous Jicky (1889), the latter offering notes of lemon, mandarin, bergamot, and rosewood. Guerlain's scents undoubtedly were among the "seventy-five perfumes, which it is very necessary that a criminal expert should be able to distinguish from each other", as Sherlock Holmes asserts in *The Hound of the Basker-villes*.

Alexander Pollock Watt (1834-1914) was the founder of what his suc-cessors at A. P. Watt now call "the oldest literary agency in the world". Son of a bookseller in Edinburgh, he married into **Alexander Strachan**'s publishing business, worked there for a time, and branched out into representing authors, possibly starting with fantasy author **George MacDonald**. That was his full-time business by 1891, when he represented Arthur Conan Doyle in the sale of the first "Adventures of Sherlock Holmes" to the *Strand* magazine. Watt's correspondence file, now in the New York Public Library, indicates that he identified the *Strand* as the right magazine, helped ACD get a contract for six stories, negotiated the price (£4 per thousand words, as much as more pro-minent authors were already getting), and sold American rights for an additional sum, all for a fee of 15 per cent on the first story and 6 per cent afterwards. "No one was so intimately in the heart of the whole mystery of the art and craft of publishing," said **W. Robertson Nicoll** in Watt's obituary.

Charles Spurgeon (1834-1892) was a Baptist minister from the age of 20, preaching to growing crowds in London — first in an exist-ing church, then in larger halls, finally in the purpose-built Metropolitan Tabernacle. It opened in 1861 in the Elephant and Castle neighbourhood of south London, and had room for congregations of as many as 10,000 people who came to hear Spurgeon. Unapolo-getically, he preached Christianity of a conser-vative kind that was popular with 19th-century Protestants: "the divinity of Jesus and the real-ity of vicarious expiation", as one of his eulo-
gists put it. His weekly sermons were transcribed as he preached, printed and sold for a penny, and also collected in a series that reached 63 volumes. He was also the author of dozens of other books, and many hymns; his magnum opus is the seven-volume *The Treasury of David*, explicating the Psalms.

Arthur Orton (1834-1898) was a butcher, originally from London and later in Australia, where he also took up various other occupations. In 1865 he saw advertisements asking for information about the fate of Sir **Roger Tichborne** (born 1829), who had possibly been lost at sea in 1854. He put himself forward as the missing man, returned to England, and claimed the position (and the wealth that would go with it). Sir Roger's mother, Lady **[Henriette] Tichborne**, insisted that she recognized her son, but other family members disagreed, and evidence such as Orton's apparent level of education told against him. Litigation began in 1871; in 1874 "the Claimant" was sentenced to 14 years' imprisonment for perjury. He died in poverty, maintaining his claim, and historians concede that much about the Tichborne case remains unclear.

George du Maurier (1834-1896) was the author of *Trilby*, one of the most popular and influential novels of the 19th century. He was born in Paris of a French father and English mother, and came to London with his English fiancée. A cartoonist as well as a writer, he joined the staff of *Punch*, the noted humour magazine, in 1865, and was the creator of the 1895 cartoon in which a fawning curate assures a pompous bishop over breakfast that his boiled egg is not in fact bad: "My Lord, I assure you that parts of it are excellent!" *Trilby* (1894) was much the most successful of his three novels. It tells the story of artists' model Trilby O'Ferrall as she becomes a musical sensation under the hypnotic guidance of the evil Svengali (a story that is said to have inspired *Gaston Leroux*'s *The Phantom of the Opera*).

Gottlieb Daimler (1834-1900) was one of the several engineers and entrepreneurs who collectively invented the modern automobile. Daimler's contribution was the development of a gasoline-powered engine in 1885, at the machine shop in Stuttgart (in Baden-Württemburg in southwestern Germany) that he operated jointly with long-time partner **Wilhelm Maybach**. Other engineers were at work at the same time, notably *Karl Benz* sixty miles away. Daimler and Maybach successively attached the so-called "grandfather clock engine" to a bicycle (producing the earliest motorcycle), a stagecoach, and a boat. Gasoline ("petrol") was unusual at the time, as the usual products of raw petroleum were kerosene, lubricating oil and benzene. The first recognizable Daimler-Maybach automobile was built in 1889; a high-speed Daimler motor was displayed at the Paris exhibition of 1900.

James McNeill Whistler (1834-1903) was the creator of the iconic picture "Arrangement in Grey and Black No.1: Portrait of the Artist's Mother", painted in London in 1871. Other important paintings include

"The White Girl" (1862) and "Nocturne in Black and Gold: The Falling Rocket" (1874). He has been credited with developing "a version of Post-Impressionism" when most of the art world was still realist or impressionist; his book *Ten O'Clock Lecture* (1885) articulated his belief in "art for art's sake". American-born, he spent most of his career in London and Paris and had many artistic friends in both cities, though he was often at odds with the art establishment and had his own ideas, seeing his paintings as "arrangements" or "nocturnes" in the musical sense. In 1878 the critic *John Ruskin* accused him of "flinging a pot of paint in the public's face", an incident that prompted a celebrated lawsuit. But his reputation rose in the 1890s, a highlight being the purchase of "Whistler's Mother" by the French government for its museums.

Sabine Baring-Gould (1834-1924) was a clergyman and scholar who served most of his career as rector of Lew Trenchard, Devonshire, where he owned an estate. He collected Devon and Cornwall folklore, emphasizing folk songs (but also spectral hounds), carried out archaeological digs on Dartmoor, wrote fiction and hymns (including "Onward Christian Soldiers"), and begat 15 children. He appears in Sherlockian writing including Laurie R. King's *The Moor*. A grandson, **William S. Baring-Gould**, who edited the original *Annotated Sherlock Holmes*, adapted elements of his grandfather's early life for the childhood of his central character in *Sherlock Holmes of Baker Street* (1967).

William Chester Minor (1834-1920) was trained in medicine at Yale and served as a surgeon with the Union Army during the United States Civil War. His postwar behaviour became increasingly erratic, likely from post-traumatic stress disorder following the appalling 1864 Battle of the Wilderness. He spent some time in St. Elizabeth's Hospital, a mental institution in Washington, before going to Britain in 1871. Delusions led him to kill a man, **George Merrett**, and he was found not guilty by reason of insanity and sent to Broadmoor Asylum in Berkshire (an institution mentioned in "The Retired Colourman"). He read extensively, corresponded with booksellers, and became a volunteer collecting words and quotations for the *Oxford English Dictionary*. His vast work for the *OED* and his correspondence with its editor, *James Murray*, are described in the 1998 book *The Professor and the Madman* by Simon Winchester.

William Morris (1834-1896) is the central figure of the "Arts and Crafts Movement", which in turn is closely associated with the Pre-Raphaelite artists including his friends *Edward Burne-Jones* and *Dante Gabriel Rossetti*. For his interior design firm, founded 1861, he created furniture, wallpaper, stained glass and textiles that became widely popular. He famously advised the public to "have nothing in your houses that you do not know to be useful, or believe to be beautiful." Morris was also the proprietor of the Kelmscott Press, the author of the utopian novel *News from Nowhere* (1890) and other books that influenced fantasy writers of later generations, the founder of the Society for the Protection of Ancient Buildings (the "anti-scrape" movement opposing the damage caused by restoration), and an activist in socialist causes. His wife, **Jane Burden**, was the model for Rossetti's painting "Beatrice" (1869). The name "William Morris" is used as an alias in "The Red-Headed League".

Andrew Carnegie (1835-1919) made millions — in modern terms, billions — in the steel industry and gave most of the money away, primarily to build 2,500 Carnegie libraries. Born in Scotland, he worked his way up from nothing in the Pittsburgh area, becoming a telegraph operator for the Pennsylvania Railroad and then an investor. He managed railways for the Union Army during the Civil War, and afterwards built an iron and steel empire, finally selling his interests to *J. Pierpont Morgan* in 1901 to create United States Steel. He continued some business activity, but became busiest as a philanthropist, donating funds not only for libraries but for universities in the United States and Scotland, thousands of church organs, and Carnegie Hall.

Cesare Lombroso (1835-1909) was one of the pioneers of criminology, whose theories focused on the relationship between physical characteristics and criminal behaviour. Born in Verona, he spent his career at two Italian universities — Pavia and then Turin — as a professor of psychiatry, forensic medicine, hygiene, and anthropology. He proposed, says the "Brain & Mind" website, "that certain criminals had physical evidence of an 'atavistic' or hereditary sort, reminiscent of earlier, more primitive stages of human evolution. These anomalies, named as *stigmata* by Lombroso, could be expressed in terms of abnormal forms or dimensions of the skull and jaw, assymmetries in the face, etc, but also of other parts of the body." (Sherlock Holmes and Dr. Mortimer discuss atavistic tendencies in *The Hound of the Baskervilles*, and similar ideas are alluded to in other stories.) Lombroso's books include *Le Crime, Causes et Remèdes* ("Crime, Its Causes and Cures", 1899).

Cora Pearl, born **Emma Elizabeth Crouch** (1835-1886), was one of the great courtesans, the grandes horizontales, the women who ran with wealthy and noble men as long as their wiles lasted. She is, like the others, a possible inspiration for Irene Adler of "A Scandal in Bohemia". Convent-educated and originally trained as a milliner, she discovered that a night of her company was worth £5 to a gentleman, and worked her way up the social ladder until **Victor Masséna, Duc du Rivoli**, was buying her jewels and horses. She entertained lavishly, once famously having herself brought to the dinner table, naked, on a silver platter. There were other patrons as well, including Prince *Napoléon Joseph Bonaparte*, and **Alexandre Duval**, who attempted suicide at her house, launching a scandal that ended her reign in fast society.

Benjamin Briggs (1835-1872?) was the captain of the *Mary Celeste*, which was found adrift near Gibraltar in 1872. The entire crew was missing, along with Briggs, his wife **Sarah** and their young daughter **Sarah Matilda**. Briggs was a life-long mariner from a seafaring Massachusetts family; the *Mary Celeste* was the fourth ship he had captained. The incident, never explained, has become a part of folklore and literature, notably Arthur Conan Doyle's 1884 story "J. Habakuk Jephson's Statement", which some readers took as truth. And Holmes says in "The Sussex Vampire": "Matilda Briggs was not the name of a young woman, Watson. It was a ship which is associated with the giant rat of Sumatra, a story for which the world is not yet prepared." References to the *Sophy Anderson* in "The Five Orange Pips" and the *Alicia* in "Thor Bridge" are also suggestive.

George Monro Grant (1835-1902) was a Presbyterian minister and educator, born in Nova Scotia and educated at Glasgow, who probably invented the term "British Commonwealth". He was principal of Queen's University, Kingston, 1877-1902, building it up as a leading Canadian educational institution, but also played an influntial role as a moderate and peacemaker in the fractious Presbyterian Church in Canada, and spoke out on national issues. He argued for aboriginal rights and Roman Catholic schools, opposed restrictions on Chinese immigration, and called for justice and morality in public policy. In 1872 and 1883 he travelled across Canada with his friend *Sandford Fleming*, surveying a route for the Canadian Pacific Railway; in 1888 he took a world tour, returning with the conviction that the British Empire should mature into a Commonwealth of independent but related nations.

J. Gelson Gregson (1835-1909) went to India to preach temperance to the army, and had some success at it, partly because the officers found that sober soldiers worked harder and got into less trouble. Apparently born to a Church of England family (he was baptized at St. Luke's, Finsbury), he became a Baptist, was ordained to the ministry, and headed for India in 1858, immediately after the Mutiny. He founded the Soldiers' Total Abstinence Association at Agra in 1862, and by 1886 it had 134 branches across India. Gelson came home to England for the last time in 1887, leading a church in Bradford for a time, then retiring to Southsea, where he already had a home, and where the Baptist chapel was in Elm Grove, yards away from Arthur Conan Doyle's house. Gregson's published work included *Through the Khyber Pass to Sherpore Camp, Cabul. An Account of Temperance Work Among Our Soldiers in the Cabul Field Force* (1883).

Jayajirao Scindia, born **Bhagirath Rao** (1835-1886), ruled from 1843 until his death as Maharajah of Gwalior, a powerful region in north central India (now part of the state of Madhya Bharat). Born into another branch of the Scindia dynasty, he was adopted by the widow of the previous ruler and named maharajah at the age of 8, with a regent wielding the actual authority. When one official ousted another as regent, the British East India Company's "resident" called in British forces to restore order. A transfer of more power from Indian rulers to Britain followed. When the Mutiny broke out in 1857, Jayajirao sided with Britain, but most of his troops defected, and he and his bodyguard fled the 80 miles to Agra; they might well have been there at the time of the events narrated in *The Sign of the Four*. Jayajirao was restored to power and is noted for extensive spending on railways, fortifications and other infrastructure, in cooperation with British authorities.

John Spencer, 5th Earl **Spencer** (1835-1910), was a close friend, both personal and political, of Liberal Prime Minister *William Ewart Gladstone*. He held various government positions over a long career, but primarily was involved with the affairs of Ireland. He served as Lord Lieutenant of Ireland 1868-1874 and again 1882-1885, and was responsible for putting various reforms into effect, notably the Irish Land Act of 1870. The 1882 assassination of *Lord Frederick Cavendish* made the Irish situation still trickier. Spencer was converted to the cause of Home Rule, a policy which Parliament could not be persuaded to implement. On Gladstone's retirement in 1894, Spencer was considered a strong candidate for Prime Minister, but Queen *Victoria* chose *Lord Rosebery* instead. The 5th Earl was succeeded by his half-brother, **Charles Spencer**, also a Liberal politician, who became 6th Earl.

Léopold II (1835-1909) was King of the Belgians (the official title) for 44 years, and probably the most rapacious of all colonial exploiters. Belgium had come into existence in 1830, with the break-up of the United Kingdom of the Netherlands along religious and linguistic lines, and **Léopold I of Saxe-Coburg and Gotha** had become its first king. His death in 1865 brought his son Léopold II to the throne. The younger Léopold, always pressed for money, was eager to establish lucrative Belgian colonies in Africa, and commissioned explorer *Henry Stanley* to negotiate treaties with local chiefs along the Congo River. Léopold established the "Congo Free State" as his personal property, and exploited it energetically, first for ivory and later for rubber. By the 1890s, his private army, the Force Publique, was using techniques such as holding women hostage to force the men to work harder. As torture, mutilation and starvation became widely known,

Arthur Conan Doyle was among those who joined a campaign to expose "the crime of the Congo"; his book by that title was published in 1909. At home, Léopold's popularity was sapped by his taste for high living and teenage girls, as well as reports of what was happening in the Congo; the government took it away from him in 1908.

Simon Newcomb (1835-1909) was the first president of the American Astronomical Society and is remembered for his work in making new, accurate calculations of the movements of the Moon and the planets. He has been suggested as an original of Professor Moriarty not only for his scientific achievements (although Moriarty specialized in asteroids) but for his success, over decades, in hampering the career of philosopher *Charles Sanders Peirce*. Born in Nova Scotia, Newcomb obtained a post at the United States Naval Observatory in 1861; he later headed the Nautical Almanac Office and held a professorship at the Johns Hopkins University.  Newcomb also did research in statistics and economics. *Newcomb's Tables of the Sun* (1895) was an international standard reference work for almost a century.

Mark Twain, real name **Samuel Clemens** (1835-1910), was the iconic American writer, author of *The Adventures of Tom Sawyer* (1876) and *The Adventures of Huckleberry Finn* (1884), as well as much more. "Twain began his career writing light, humorous verse, but evolved into a chronicler of the vanities, hypocrisies and murderous acts of mankind," says Wikipedia. Born in Missouri and raised along the Mississippi River, he worked as a river pilot, prospected for silver in California, and took up newspaper writing and then fiction. His first book was *The Innocents Abroad* (1869); another great success was *A Connecticut Yankee in King Arthur's Court* (1889). His comic 1896 book *Tom Sawyer, Detective* is told in the voice of Huck Finn and is a send-up of the detective literature of the period, no doubt including the stories of Sherlock Holmes.

Paul Du Chaillu (1835-1903) was born in New Orleans and spent his youth accompanying his father on trading expeditions to west Africa. In 1856 he began a three-year exploration trip in what are now Gabon and Congo, coming home with scores of animal specimens, as well as enough anthropological information to fill a book (*Explorations and*

Adventures in Equatorial Africa, 1861). "I suffered fifty attacks of the African fever," he wrote, "taking, to cure myself, more than fourteen ounces of quinine." He made a second, less successful, expedition in 1863-1865, and wrote several more books, including a series of adventure stories for young people. Much of the rest of his life was spent in explorations of far northern Europe; he is thought to have coined the phrase "land of the midnight sun". At a festive dinner in Chicago in 1894, attended by Arthur Conan Doyle, the explorer claimed in a speech that various African chiefs had offered him a total of 22,000 potential wives; however, he remained single.

Sir **William Grantham** (1835-1911) was a Conservative member of Parliament (1874-1886) and, it appeared, a Conservative judge after that. He was appointed to the Queen's Bench, an appeals court that had been created in an 1873 reorganization of the judicial system. Says the *Encyclopaedia Britannica* edition published in the year of his death: "He was never at pains to conceal his own views on politics, and after 1906, when he was on the rota of judges for election petitions, his decisions were sharply criticized as biassed against the Liberal party, notably in the Great Yarmouth case, which led to a motion of censure in the House of Commons in July 1906. But in certain criminal cases he gained considerable credit, and in the ***Adolf Beck*** trial he was one of the first to suspect the mistake as to the prisoner's identity."

Thomas Cadell (1835-1919) was one of 182 British soldiers to receive the Victoria Cross for actions during the Indian Mutiny (First Indian War of Independence), 1857-1859. The VC had been created just the preceding year, as the Crimean War was winding down, to recognize "most conspicuous bravery, or some daring or pre-eminent act of valour or self-sacrifice, or extreme devotion to duty in the presence of the enemy". Cadell, a lieutenant in the  2nd Bengal European Fusiliers, was honoured for actions at Delhi on June 12, 1857, when he rescued two seriously wounded men "who would otherwise have been cut up by the rebels". Cadell rose to be a colonel and then held administrative jobs in India. He was Governor of the Andaman and Nicobar Islands 1879-1892, in which role he might well have come across Jonathan Small of *The Sign of the Four*.

Walter Potter (1835-1918) was a taxidermist with a difference. He established his own hugely popular museum at Bramber, Sussex, showing off not just stuffed specimens, not just freaks of nature such as a two-headed kitten, but also tableaux picturing animals and birds in elaborate anthropomorphic scenes. There was a little classroom with 48 rabbit pupils hunched over their books; there was "The Death and Burial of Cock Robin" with almost 100 British birds; there was a kittens' tea party, and a gentlemen's club with 18 squirrels enjoying champagne and playing cards. Potter, whose family ran the White Lion pub, learned taxidermy as a teenager (first trying to preserve his own canary), and opened his first display in 1861, with later additions. His final creation was "The Kittens' Wedding" (1890).

William Palmer (1835?-1888) was a Scotland Yard inspector who went bad. Born in Surrey, he was a police sergeant by 1861, promoted to inspector in 1869 and chief inspector in 1870. He worked on such cases as the Fenian conspiracy of the mid-1860s, prosecutions of illegal betting in 1869 and the Regent's Canal murders of 1872. But when the "Great Turf Fraud" of 1876 was cleared up, it was found that Palmer, with police colleagues who were also friends through a Masonic lodge, had been involved, at least to the extent of warning the chief fraudsters to get out of town in time. He was convicted of corruption and served two years at hard labour, as did Inspector **John Meiklejohn** and Chief Inspector *Nathaniel Druscovich*. Palmer later operated a pub in Lambeth.

Bret Harte (1836-1902) was a prolific author, best known for his stories of the "forty-niners" who rushed to California, 1848-1855, in search of gold. Born in Albany, he was part of that rush himself, reaching California in 1853 and working as a miner for a time before ending up a journalist. His story "The Luck of Roaring Camp" (1868) established his reputation for fiction. In 1878 he was appointed a United States consul in Germany; he moved to London in 1885 and spent the rest of his life writing more stories as well as poetry. "The Stolen Cigar-Case" (1902), featuring Hemlock Jones, is one of the earliest Sherlock Holmes parodies.

Elizabeth Garrett Anderson (1836-1917) was Britain's first female physician, and later the first woman mayor. London-born, she grew up in Aldeburgh, Suffolk, and set her mind to medicine after meeting

Elizabeth Blackwell in 1859. She studied privately and through the Society of Apothecaries, and went into practice just in time to help cope with the cholera epidemic of 1865. She was the only female member of the British Medical Association from 1873 to 1892. Garrett Anderson served briefly on the London School Board, worked beside her sister **Millicent Fawcett** to promote women's suffrage, and was elected mayor of Aldeburgh in 1908. She married businessman **James Anderson** in 1871 and had three children.

Franklin B. Gowen (1836-1889) was a lawyer who became president of the Philadelphia and Reading Railroad, undoubtedly one of the "two railroads" that hired detectives to destroy the Scowrers in *The Valley of Fear*. In sober fact, the Reading, under his leadership, was a major owner of Pennsylvania coalfields by the time of the economic depression that began in 1873. He brought in **James McParland** of the Pinkertons to investigate a series of 1875 murders, and a number of what would now be called labour leaders were among the "Mollie Maguires" who were hanged as a result. Gowen himself acted as special prosecutor at the trial of **Jack Kehoe**. He went on to deal harshly with a major railroad strike in 1877, but the financially precarious company went bankrupt twice, and Gowen was forced out by stockholder **J. Pierpont Morgan**. His death, by gunshot to the head, was ruled a suicide.

George Sigerson (1836-1925) was an Irish writer, scholar, scientist and patriot who traced his ancestry to Vikings and may have lent his Norse surname to "the remarkable explorations of a Norwegian named Sigerson", mentioned in "The Empty House". He studied medicine at University College, Cork, and in Paris under **Jean-Martin Charcot**. He spent much of his career at the National University in Dublin, where he was professor of zoology and botany, as well as his real specialty, neurology. His other enthusiasms included Irish literature and language, which enjoyed something of a resurgence in parallel with the pressures for Irish independence from Britain. He presided over the first meeting of the Senate of the Irish Free State (1922), and was involved in choosing Ireland's national symbol, the harp. His writings ranged from "Celtic Influence on the Evolution of Rimed Hymns" to "Cannabiculture in Ireland, Its Profit and Possibility".

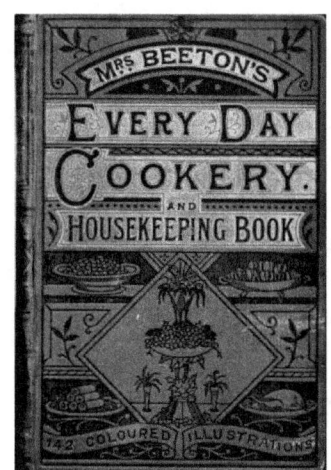

Isabella Beeton (1836-1865), née **Mayson**, was the author of *Mrs. Beeton's Book of Household Management*. Its compiler, who tested the recipes personally and had learned the knack of housekeeping from helping to raise 20 brothers and sisters, married publisher **Samuel Orchart Beeton** (1830-1877) when she was 20. She contributed much to his business, initially by writing articles about cookery and housekeeping. The famous *Mrs. Beeton's Book* went through many editions starting in 1861, selling millions of copies, and included hundreds of recipes as well as information about everything from laundry and budgeting to public affairs. In 1860 the duo founded *Beeton's Christmas Annual*, where *A Study in Scarlet* would appear in 1887. The business suffered after Isabella's death, and Samuel Beeton was forced to sell the brand name to Ward, Lock & Co.

James Macleod (1836-1894) was the second commissioner of the North West Mounted Police — now the Royal Canadian Mounted Police — and founder of Calgary. Initially a soldier, he joined the NWMP in 1873, and the following year led an expedition to the western Canadian territories aimed at establishing law and order, suppressing the illegal whiskey trade, opening negotiations with the Native inhabitants, and bringing to justice those responsible for the previous year's Cypress Hills massacre, which he eventually did. His forces established the early outpost of Fort Macleod, followed by Fort Calgary. Macleod served for several years as both NWMP commissioner and magistrate in the Territories, and in 1887 became a judge.

Jan Bloch (1836-1902) was born in what is now Poland, and became wealthy in finance and the development of a railway between Warsaw and St. Petersburg. In Poland, which was essentially a puppet state of Russia, he came to hold government positions as well as having a huge commercial influence, and he published extensive economic studies. His most influential book, however, was a seven-volume analysis published in 1898, English title *The Future of War in Its Technical, Economic, and Political Relations*. His predictions of the horrors that technology would bring to war were a major reason for the convening of the Hague conference of 1899 (and a sequel in 1907), which produced the *Con-*

vention with Respect to the Laws and Customs of War on Land and other international agreements about the laws of warfare.

Joseph Chamberlain (1836-1914) was a shopkeeper's son who made a fortune in manufacturing and entered municipal politics. In three years (1873-1876) as mayor of Birmingham — a large Midland city, grown quickly on the proceeds of the textile industry — he built parks, roads, courts, markets, gas lines, sewers and water pipes, adopting policies of activism unlike anything Britain had previously seen, including extensive slum clearance. He then became the first of the prominent Liberal Party "radicals" sent to Parliament from the Midlands, though he later also worked well with Conservatives, particularly in Empire affairs. He served in important Cabinet posts in the governments of **William Ewart Gladstone** and **Arthur Balfour**. **Neville Chamberlain**, prime minister in the 1930's, was his son.

Jane Ellice Hopkins (1836-1904) was a social reformer from her early days in Cambridge, and more prominently so after she fell under the influence of physician and writer **James Hinton** (1822-1875) in 1872. As the *Dictionary of National Biography* puts it, "she embarked on her lifework — the endeavour to raise the moral standard of the community, and to secure the legal protection of the young from ill-usage.... She arduously wrote and lectured through the three kingdoms on the theme of pure living.... Although personally frail and insignificant, she exerted over her audiences an instantaneous influence." Her work helped lead to the Criminal Law Amendment Act 1885, which strengthened the penalties for sexual abuse of women, but also made homosexuality an offence.

Jason (Jay) Gould (1836-1892) owned the Erie Railroad, the Union Pacific, and eventually (from 1881) the Western Union Telegraph Company, making millions through ruthless and frequently illegal business manoeuvres. He was blamed for the "Black Friday" panic of 1869, worked out quid pro quo arrangements with New York political boss **William M. Tweed**, issued bogus stock and persuaded legislators to legalize it, once kidnapped an investor who had cheated him and then fled to Canada, and boasted during the great railway strike of 1886 that "I can hire one-half of the working class to kill the other half." History calls him one of the greatest of the American industrial robber barons; the man who began his working life as a bookkeeper left an estate of $72 million. Lyndhurst, his mansion in Tarrytown, New York, has been designated a historic site.

Leopold von Sacher-Masoch (1836-1895) gave his name to masochism as the *Marquis de Sade* gave his to sadism. But he was not institutionalized for mental illness until late in his life, and earned a respectable living as journalist and author in Lviv, then in Austria but now in Ukraine. Early in his career he worked as a professor and wrote about Austrian history; later he turned to fiction and used the traditional stories of Galicia, the region surrounding Lviv, in many of his books. However, his best-known work is the short novel *Venus in Furs* (1869), which articulates a fur fetish and a series of male submissive fantasies. In 1869-1870 Sacher-Masoch actually lived out a six-month slave contract with Baroness **Fanny Pistor**. The term "masochism" was coined by *Richard von Krafft-Ebing* in 1886.

Lord **Frederick Cavendish** (1836-1882) was the younger brother of the eighth *Duke of Devonshire* and a Liberal member of Parliament from 1865 to his death. As a protegé of prime minister *William Ewart Gladstone* he held a series of government posts, leading to his appointment in 1882 as chief secretary to the Lord-Lieutenant of Ireland. On the day he arrived in Dublin and took his oath of office, he was stabbed to death in a city park along with his deputy, **Thomas Burke**, who was walking with him. Five members of a nationalist group called the Irish National Invincibles were hanged the following year for the "Phoenix Park murders".

Piet Cronjé (1836-1911) was a general commanding Boer forces against Britain in the Second South African War. After British annexation of the Transvaal region (officially the South African Republic) in 1877, he started a rebellion which became the First South African War, 1880-1881. The Republic regained a measure of independence, but the 1896 raid from Rhodesia led by *Leander Starr Jameson* demonstrated British intentions. It was Cronjé who captured Jameson after the failed raid. When full-scale war began again in 1899, Cronjé led Boer armies in the western region, where action included the siege of Mafeking (defended by British colonel *Robert Baden-Powell*). Cronjé was defeated and captured by Lord *Roberts* in early 1900, shortly before Arthur Conan Doyle's arrival in South Africa to work with a field hospital.

Ramakrishna, born **Gadadhar Chatterji** (1836-1886), "represents the very core of the spiritual realizations of the seers and sages of India", according to a web site honouring him and his work. "Sri Ramakrishna proved that the revelation of God takes place at all times and that God-realization is not the monopoly of any particular age, country, or people." Born in a village outside Calcutta, he became a priest at a temple to the goddess Kali at Dakshineswar, pursued tantric meditation, made a study of other religions, and attracted a swarm of followers. He wrote nothing himself about his teachings of God's presence, but a follower, **Mahendranath Gupta**, made notes for *The Gospel of Sri Ramakrishna*, published only in 1942. Another follower, **Vivekananda** (born **Narendra Nath Datta**), was largely responsible for introducing vedanta and yoga to the western world.

Sir **Edward Bradford** (1836-1911) was one in the series of former military men who took a turn as Commissioner of the Metropolitan Police. He had been with the 14th The King's Light Dragoons during the Indian Mutiny, and despite losing his left arm to a tiger during a hunt in 1863, he stayed in India, holding administrative positions including superintendent of the Thuggee and Dacoity Department, aimed at stamping out gangs. Returning to England, he held more administrative posts, and in 1890 was named Commissioner, serving until 1903. "His years in control of the Met were generally peaceful and stable," says Wikipedia, "with the police's standing in public opinion rising steadily. In 1899, crime in London fell to its lowest point in recorded history."

Sir **Henry Campbell-Bannerman** (1836-1908) was the first person to be officially titled "prime minister" of the United Kingdom, though the chain of prime ministers goes back to the 18th century. He held that office from the resignation of Conservative prime minister *Arthur Balfour* in 1905 to the onset of his own fatal illness early in 1908. In the meantime his Liberal Party won a landslide victory in the general election of January 1906. He had been a Member of Parliament since 1868, and in 1899 became leader of the badly divided Liberals. Campbell-Bannerman's policies included home rule for Ireland, free school meals, and protection for unions against claims for damages during strikes. Arthur Conan Doyle, calling himself a Liberal Unionist, had longed to run against him in his district, Stirling Burghs, in the 1900 election, but party officials steered him elsewhere (and he still lost).

Sir **William Schwenck Gilbert** (1836-1911) wrote the words for the classic "Gilbert and Sullivan" operettas, as well as a large number of plays and a volume of comic verse, *Bab Ballads*. His collaboration with composer Sir *Arthur Sullivan* began with "Thespis" (1871) and continued with "HMS Pinafore" (1878), "The Mikado" (1885) and other hits, fourteen shows in all. Twelve of them were produced at the Savoy Theatre managed by *Richard D'Oyly Carte* and so are called "Savoy operas". The last, "The Grand Duke" (1896), was a flop, as Gilbert and Sullivan were feuding and inspiration was running out. Gilbert was known for verbal wit as well as social satire ("Iolanthe", for example, mocking the pomposity of aristocrats and making the Lord Chancellor a comic figure).

Thomas Crapper (1836-1910) did not, in fact, give his name as a slang term for household plumbing, as the word was in use (according to the *Oxford English Dictionary*) by the time he was 10 years old. He did, however, enter the perfect line of work for someone of his name, being a plumber and manufacturer of plumbing fixtures; he operated the world's first showroom for bathroom fittings. Crapper took out several patents related to toilets, including one for the floating ballcock. He installed plumbing fixtures at Sandringham House for *Edward VII*; it is not clear whether he did the same at 221B for Mrs. Hudson, although Watson speaks of "a bath at Baker Street" as early as *The Sign of the Four*.

Algernon Charles Swinburne (1837-1909) was a fin-de-siècle poet, associated with the Pre-Raphaelite artists, including *Aubrey Beardsley*, and authors such as *Oscar Wilde* — the whole decadent set, in fact. "He perhaps professed to more vice than he actually indulged in," says Wikipedia, though noting that he was both an alcoholic and an algolagniac, that is, someone who derives sexual pleasure from physical pain. Among his most notorious poems is "Dolores" (1866), with its refrain about "Our Lady of Pain" and its memorable lines about "the lilies and languours of virtue" and "the raptures and roses of vice". But his large body of work includes more conventional poetry, from ballads to political enthusiasms, and critics give him high praise for technical skill. He grew up mostly in the Isle of Wight, though he considered Northumberland his home, and in later years lived respectably in London.

Elisabeth, Empress of Austria (1837-1898), was the wife of Emperor *Franz Joseph I*, a sad, beautiful woman who disliked court life but was obsessed with her hair, her figure and her diet. She was born into the Bavarian aristocracy, but had no experience of the constraints she encountered in Vienna, and from early in her marriage preferred to travel in other regions. She formed a special attachment to Hungary (she was also, as the empire was structured, Queen of Hungary, Croatia and Bohemia). She gave the Emperor two daughters, one of whom died in infancy, and a son and heir, *Rudolf,* whose 1889 suicide was the final blow to her stability. Elisabeth exercised compulsively, suffered from eating disorders, wore her chestnut hair long and so elaborately that it required three hours' care daily, and experimented endlessly with beauty oils; she may have been hyperactive. She was assassinated by an anarchist while holidaying in Switzerland.

Anne Blunt, née **King**, later Baroness **Wentworth** (1837-1917), was the daughter of programmer **Ada Lovelace** and the wife of poet **Wilfred Scawen Blunt**. She was also an important figure in the breeding of thoroughbred horses, which had begun in the previous century with the importing of three "Arabian" stallions. From 1877, Blunt and her husband made trips to Egypt and elsewhere, buying horses for their stud farm at Crabbet Park, Sussex. Portions of Blunt's journals were published as *Bedouin Tribes of the Euphrates* and *A Pilgrimage to Nejd*. Husband and wife differed about how to raise the horses, and many beasts died from mistreatment, but nearly all thoroughbreds today can trace their ancestry to at least one Crabbet horse. Isonomy, however, the champion horse mentioned in "Silver Blaze", was born in 1875, before Crabbet was founded.

Amelia Dyer (1837-1896) was a baby-farmer and serial killer. She was hanged for the murder of an infant from Cheltenham named **Doris Marmon**, but guesses are that she may have killed as many as 400 babies over some two decades. Dyer initially trained to be a nurse, but after being widowed in 1869 she offered lodging to expectant mothers and undertook to look after unwanted babies, or see to their adoption, for a fee, a practice known as baby-farming. She lived in a succession of towns and used a succession of aliases; her habit was to accept the agreed fee (£10 in the case of Doris Marmon) from the mother, take the baby, and as soon as convenient strangle it with white sewing tape, then dispose of the body. Arrested at her home in Reading, she offered insanity as a defence; she was also a heavy user of alcohol and laudanum. The jury found her guilty in four and a half minutes.

Farrer Herschell, Lord **Herschell** (1837-1899), was a prominent lawyer who twice served as Lord Chancellor. He "was called to the bar" (became a barrister) in 1860, was elected to Parliament in 1874, and in 1880 was appointed solicitor-general in the Liberal government of *William Ewart Gladstone*. Despite political reverses, he was offered the post of Lord Chancellor in 1886; he served briefly that year and again 1892-1895 in another Gladstone administration. The Lord Chancellor at that time was the head of the legal system, presiding judge in the Chancery Division, and the presiding officer of the House of Lords, as well as a cabinet member. Herschell died in Washington, DC, while serving there as a member of a commission on the disputed boundary between Alaska and Canada.

Grover **Cleveland** (1837-1908) was both the 22nd and 24th President of the United States, as he served 1885-1889 and 1893-1897. He was the first Democrat elected after a generation of Republicans who won the Civil War and attempted to consolidate its achievements in freeing Black slaves and equipping them with civil rights. Formerly mayor of Buffalo and governor of New York, he battled rumours and scandals about his love life, but stood for integrity and impartiality in public matters. It was the depression of the 1890s that put an end to his career; his attempt to put the United States back on the gold standard (saying no to the "bimetallic question" mentioned in "The Bruce-Partington Plans") was too little too late.

J. Pierpont Morgan (1837-1913) was a fabulously wealthy financier whose library, stocked with rare books and manuscripts by the likes of Milton, Mozart and Byron, remains a major tourist attraction in New York. Morgan began his financial career in his father's small banking house, but in 1860 he established J. Pierpont Morgan & Company, and specialized in corporate financing and restructuring. General Electric, American Telephone and Telegraph, and United States Steel are among the companies he brought into existence. He also helped to found the

Metropolitan Museum of Art, bought yachts, drawings, and gemstones, and in 1902 commissioned the design and construction of the library attached to his Madison Avenue home.

John (Black Jack) Kehoe (1837-1878) was a prosperous tavern-owner in Girardville, Pennsylvania, and reputedly the leader of the Molly Maguires, the secret society on which the Scowrers of *The Valley of Fear* are modelled. He is thus the original of the "bodymaster" in that tale, Jack McGinty. Born in Ireland's County Wicklow, he came to the United States as a boy with his family to escape the devastating potato famine of 1845-1849. He worked as a miner for several years before opening his tavern, the Hibernian House, which is still in business. Kehoe was county delegate for the Ancient Order of Hibernians, and was twice elected high constable of the village. Historians continue to argue about how closely the Order was related to the Mollies and how murderous they were in the context of labour conflict in the Pennsylvania anthracite coal mining region. But on the evidence of secret agent *James McParland*, Kehoe was hanged at Pottsville; 18 other Mollies or union members were also executed. Kehoe received a posthumous pardon in 1979.

John **Ellor Taylor** (1837-1895) was a product of the Mechanics' Institute system, by which working people acquired both theoretical and practical learning, and devoted his life to spreading scientific knowledge. His writings began with a book (1864) on the geology of the Manchester area and continued through *Our Island Continent: A Naturalist's Holiday in Australia* (1886). He also wrote many articles, both popular and scholarly. As a boy he started work in a locomotive factory in Longsight, an inner-city area of Manchester. Encouraged by the factory manager, he attended evening classes at the city's Mechanics' Institute (founded 1824, and preparing to move into its new building, now a historic site, in 1855). From 1863 he worked in the newspaper business, and he became a popular lecturer all over England and in Australia. He also served for twenty years as curator of the town museum in Ipswich, Suffolk, which still boasts a geology gallery.

Louis (Ludwig) IV, Grand Duke of **Hesse** (1837-1892), was a German nobleman and the husband of Princess *Alice*, a daughter of Queen *Victoria*. They were married in 1862 and had seven children, one of whom, **Alexandra Feodorovna**, eventually became the Tsarina (Empress) of Russia as wife of *Nicholas II*. In 1877, Louis succeeded an uncle to the hereditary title rendered in English as "Grand Duke of

Hesse and by Rhine", making him ruler of one of the states in the recently created German Empire.

Joseph Bell (1837-1911) was professor of surgery at the University of Edinburgh, and a mentor to Arthur Conan Doyle when he studied medicine there. As clerk for Bell's clinics at the Royal Infirmary, he heard the great man assess patients with rapid perceptions that he would later put into Sherlock Holmes's mouth, along with Bell's compassion and his thirst for justice. ACD dedicated *The Adventures of Sherlock Holmes* to "my told teacher, Joseph Bell, M.D., &c." and wrote in *Memories and Adventures* that when he came to create the detective, "I thought... of his eagle face, of his curious ways, of his eerie trick of spotting details." Bell was editor of the *Edinburgh Medical Journal* from 1873, and a teacher from 1878, as well as an expert consulted by the police in forensic matters, but it was as a practising surgeon that he was best known, in an age before anaesthetics or antibiotics. His textbook *A Manual of the Operations of Surgery* first appeared in 1866.

Marie François Sadi Carnot (1837-1894) served six years as president of France before being assassinated in June 1894. He was thus president at the time Sherlock Holmes investigated a "matter of supreme importance" on behalf of the French government, mentioned in "The Final Problem". A civil engineer from Limoges, Carnot held a series of posts in local and then national government, winding up as minister of finance in 1885. The National Assembly elected him president of the Third Republic in December 1887. He served through a tumultuous period, as though there were any other sort of period in French politics. He was stabbed to death by an Italian anarchist after a speech in Lyon (the assassin was guillotined seven weeks later).

Paul Morphy (1837-1884) excelled at chess — "one mark, Watson, of a scheming mind," as Holmes put it in "The Retired Colourman". He was recognized as an excellent player in childhood, won a tournament in New York at 20, and was quickly recognized as America's, and then the world's, best player. Morphy typically played fast, and often in an "open" style not much used by modern grandmasters. He never faced the European champion, **Howard Staunton**, but most observers felt Morphy would have defeated him. Within two years of his initial success, he announced that he was retiring from chess to practise law, although he was never successful in that pursuit.

Richard Norman Shaw (1837-1912) was an Edinburgh-born architect, known for his designs for large country and suburban houses. Among them is Grim's Dyke, built 1870-1872 in northwest London as a home for Sir *William S. Gilbert*. Now a hotel, it has been much used as a film location. Shaw also designed churches, commercial buildings, and public buildings, including New Scotland Yard, opened 1890 as the headquarters of the Metropolitan Police, which moved from its previous site in Great Scotland Yard (Whitehall Place). Shaw's building, on the Victoria Embankment, is distinctive for its horizontal bands of red and white stone. An adjoining building was added in 1906 as the police needed more space. The two structures are now known as the Norman Shaw Buildings and provide office space for Parliament. The police moved to a new New Scotland Yard in 1967.

Sir **James Murray** (1837-1915) was the original editor of the *Oxford English Dictionary*, although two men had served as editors of the proposed "new English dictionary" before the Oxford University Press took on the project in 1879. The image of Murray working in his "scriptorium", a shed lined with pigeonholes in which millions of slips of paper bearing words and quotations were sorted, is familiar from the book *Caught in the Web of Words*, by granddaughter **Elizabeth Murray**. The dictionary emerged one "fascicle" at a time beginning with "A to Ant" in 1884 and concluding only in 1928. Murray was a teacher from the age of 17, although he also held a bank job in London for a time. His book *The Dialect of the Southern Counties of Scotland*, dealing with his home region, was among his credentials as a language specialist that earned him the job of dictionary editor.

Washington Roebling (1837-1926) built the Brooklyn Bridge, which his father **John A. Roebling** had designed. As a young man he had worked on the Allegheny Bridge in Pittsburgh, also designed by his father. After service in the Civil War (including air reconnaissance using balloons) he joined his father in building the Cincinnati-Covington Bridge and then the Brooklyn project. It connects what were then separate cities, Brooklyn at the east end and New York (Manhattan) at the west end. The elder Roebling died in 1869, and Washington was named chief engineer. He was the designer of the pneumatic caissons on which the two large towers of the bridge were built, and despite health problems he carried the project through to completion in 1883 with the assistance of his wife, **Emily Warren Roebling**. The pedestrian and traffic link over the East River helped to unite New York and Brooklyn, which were organized into a single New York City in 1898.

William Dean Howells (1837-1920) was editor of the *Atlantic Monthly* 1871-1881 and author of many stories and novels. His father was a printer in Ohio — an occupation associated with both literary and political activity because printers had to be able to read — and Howells followed all those pursuits; he is said to have written **Abraham Lincoln**'s campaign biography in 1860. Eventually he settled in Cambridge, Massachusetts, working for the magazine and writing extensively. His realist novels *A Modern Instance* (1882) and *The Rise of Silas Lapham* (1885) were particularly successful. His reputation was enhanced by his reviews and criticism of both American and foreign writers, again championing realism; he also wrote on public issues from a Christian socialist viewpoint.

Yohannes IV, birth name **Lij Kassay Mercha**, also called King John (1837-1889), was Emperor of Ethiopia (Abyssinia). Born into a noble family, he could, like other Ethiopian aristocracy, trace his ancestry to the Biblical King Solomon. He was a protegé of the nobleman who made himself Emperor **Tekle Gyorgis II** after the suicide of Emperor **Tewodros II** in 1868, but by a combination of political manoeuvres and military force claimed the throne for himself, and was crowned in early 1872. His reign featured continuing skirmishes on the northern border, in which he was unable to persuade Britain to restrain its Egyptian allies. He also organized a general synod of the Ethopian (Coptic) church and strengthened the church's political position; there is no evidence that this process involved two Coptic patriarchs ("The Retired Colourman"). He was killed in battle against **Muhammad Ahmad**, "the Mahdi", after which factions of relatives contended for his throne.

James B. Pond (1838-1903) was an abolitionist newspaperman, then an officer in the 3rd Wisconsin Volunteer Cavalry Regiment during the United States Civil War, ending his military career as a major. He then embarked on a career organizing lecture tours and providing speakers on what was known as "the lyceum circuit". He began by sending ex-Mormons and anti-Mormons on the lecture trail, and from 1879 headed a lecture bureau in New York, with clients incuding literary figures, explorers, humorists and social reformers. He presented **Henry Ward Beecher**, **James Whitcomb Riley**, and for two months in the fall of 1894, with lectures from Massachusetts to Wisconsin, Arthur Conan Doyle. ACD reported him to be "a quaint character… the very personification of his country, huge, loose limbed, straggling, with a goat's beard and a nasal voice".

James **Monro** (1838-1920) was Commissioner of London's Metropolitan Police from 1888 (after the resignation of Sir **Charles Warren**) to 1890. He had been inspector-general of police in the Bombay Presidency, a large region of British India, before coming to London to manage Scotland Yard's Criminal Investigation Department as Assistant Commissioner in charge of crime, during a period of behind-the-scenes political manoeuvring. In that role he dealt with Fenian espionage, the Jack the Ripper case, and an attempted bombing of Queen **Victoria**'s Golden Jubilee. His time as Commissioner involved more politics, over budgets and discipline; after resigning, he served for a decade as a missionary in India.

Liliuokalani, born **Lydia Kamakaeha** (1838-1917), was Queen of Hawaii for just two years, from the death of her brother, King **Kalakaua**, in 1891 until she was deposed in an 1893 coup. The Hawaiian kingdom and the Kamehameha dynasty dated from 1810, but much of its power had trickled away to industrialists and (American) landowners by the 1890s, and the Queen's overthrow, organized by **Sanford Dole** and other businessmen, was carried out with the support of

United States Marines. Once the monarchy was abolished, the US annexed Hawaii in 1898. Well educated, initially by missionaries, Lydia married **John Owen Dominus** in 1862. She acquired her royal name, Liliuokalani, when she became Crown Princess in 1877; she served as regent in 1881 when the King went on a world tour, and in 1887 she represented Hawaii at the Golden Jubilee of Queen *Victoria* in London. She wrote a large number of songs including "Aloha Oe", Hawaii's best-known melody.

Prince **Philippe d'Orléans, Count of Paris** (1838-1894), was a claimant to the throne of France beginning in 1848, when his grandfather King **Louis Philippe** was deposed. His descendants, the Counts of Paris, continue to make the claim, though a restoration of the monarchy is now unlikely. The young Philippe was heir to the throne even in his grandfather's time, as his father, Prince **Ferdinand-Philippe**, was killed in an 1842 carriage accident. After Louis Philippe's abdication, the young prince and his mother fled France and a republic was proclaimed (soon to be interrupted by the Second Empire, 1852-1870, still with no acknowledgement of the House of Orléans). Philippe served as an officer in the United States Army in the first year of the Civil War, and later lived in exile in England, where he rented historic Stowe House in Buckinghamshire.

Sir **Arthur Moseley Channell** (1838-1928) was a judge, and the son of a judge, **William Fry Channell**. The father served in the Court of Exchequer; the son, in the High Court, from 1897 to his retirement in 1914 (and after that took a hand in the work of the Judicial Committee of the Privy Council, the nearest thing Britain had to a supreme court before 2009). Channell clearly had an affinity for water, being a champion rower in his youth and a yachtsman in later years, making his home at the port of Falmouth in Cornwall.

Sir **Evelyn Wood** (1838-1919) had a military career of almost comic intensity, seeing action in many nations and three separate continents over half a century. He persuaded a surgeon not to amputate his arm after he was shot in the Crimea, then removed bone fragments from his elbow with his pen-knife a year later. He won a Victoria Cross at the age of 20, rescuing a civilian during the Indian Mutiny, with the aid of the irregular cavalry regiment he was leading. He read the funeral liturgy under enemy fire during the Zulu War in South Africa, ensuring that the British dead had a proper burial. He defeated a force of 23,000 Zulus at Khambula Hill. He was assigned to organize a new army for Egypt under British command; he was injured trying to ride a giraffe;

he took a lucky shot to the pericardium during the Ashanti War in west Africa, rested for three days, then left the hospital and marched all night to be in at the victory. A midshipman at the beginning of his military career, before he switched from navy to army, he reached the rank of field marshal in 1903. Wood was the brother of *Katharine O'Shea*.

Sir **Henry Irving**, born **John Henry Brod-ribb** (1838-1905), was the first British actor to be both so successful and so respectable that he received a knighthood (in 1895). He found his way into amateur, then professional, the-atre, and is said to have played 400 parts in three years with a travelling company. "In 1871," says the *Encyclopaedia Britannica*, "Irving emerged as one of the leading actors of his day with his performance in 'The Bells'." He played that spooky part intermittently for the rest of his career. In 1878 he took over management of the Lyceum Theatre, just off the Strand, a London landmark that figures in *The Sign of the Four*, and hired **Bram Stoker** as manager. With lavish spending and an emphasis on the popular genre of historical romance, Irving made the Lyceum a mighty success for more than two decades. He played lead roles opposite actress **Ellen Terry** for 22 years in London and on tour.

William Leonard Hunt (1838-1929) crossed Niagara Falls on a wire but, unlike *Charles Blondin*, did not get a mention from Sherlock Holmes in *The Sign of the Four*. Born in Lockport, New York, and raised near Port Hope, Ontario, Hunt was always a daredevil, and after seeing a circus decided to become a showman himself. At the age of 21 he gave his first wire-walking performance, over the Ganaraska River, calling himself "Signor Farini" (later **The Great Farini**). In 1860 he crossed Niagara repeatedly on a wire, doing stunts on the way such as turning somersaults. He performed in the United States and Britain for the next several years, then retired to train performers and devise new stunts; he is credited with inventing the "human cannonball".

Wilma Neruda, **Lady Hallé**, formerly **Norman** (1838-1911), was a violinist whose work appealed to Sherlock Holmes, judging by his eagerness to get to her concert and his rhapsodies afterwards (*A Study in Scarlet*). Born in Brno, Moravia, where her father was the cathedral organist, she gave her first public performance at the age of 7, and when she was 20 was playing first violin in a quartet of her siblings. She performed across Europe, becoming the first woman violinist to play chamber music professionally with men, and did much to make the violin fashionable as an instrument for girls. She was married to Swedish conductor and composer **Ludwig Norman** (giving her the name Holmes uses for her, Norman-Neruda) and, after his death, to pianist *Charles Hallé*, in the year (1888) when he was knighted.

William Winwood Reade (1838-1875) was the author of *The Martyrdom of Man*, which according to Sherlock Holmes in *The Sign of the Four* was "one of the most remarkable [books] ever penned". Published in 1872, it is a history of the world under the headings of War, Religion, Liberty, and Intellect, all from a secular, liberal, social Darwinist viewpoint. It gives more attention to African history than European writers generally did; Reade knew more about Africa, or "Negroland" as he frequently called it, than many of his contemporaries because he had travelled in the then very dark continent as a young man, writing to **Charles Darwin** with his anthropological observations. "Reade never seems to be sure whether he is writing a philosophical meditation on Africa or a universal key to all known historical facts," an essay on the *Princeton Independent* website comments. Reade also wrote several novels as well as non-fiction works including an 1861 book about Druidism.

Bernard Marius Cazeneuve (1839-1913) was a stage magician from Toulouse, France, as well as an accomplished mathematician and astronomer and, during the Franco-Prussian War, an army captain. He was sent to Madagascar in 1886 by the French authorities in hopes of cultivating France's influence there. Says the MagicPedia website: "He became an expert in mind-reading experiments and card tricks. In the early 1880s, he and his wife performed their Second Sight trick at the Court of Russia. He was also known for performing a number of popular tricks with fruits including Card in Orange. Cazeneuve performed for royalty in Belgium, Greece, France, Italy, Russia, Spain and Persia. Prior to [*Harry Houdini*] making Metamorphosis famous, Cazeneuve presented his 'Double Indian Mail' illusion."

Arthur H. Stanton (1839-1913) was a Church of England priest —
"priest" rather than some other title because he was emphatically of the
Anglo-Catholic persuasion — whose name may well have been
borrowed for "Arthur H. Staunton, the rising young forger", mentioned
in "The Missing Three-Quarter". He served 51 years, 1861-1912, at St.
Alban's Church, Holborn, which even now is a bastion of high-church
Anglicanism, and he was frequently involved in controversy, sometimes in litigation, over the legality of using Catholic liturgy and traditions in an Anglican church. "Stanton was an indefatigable champion
of the poor, staunch champion of ritual and exuberant preacher," says
Wikipedia. "He attracted devoted supporters and horrified critics in
equal measure."

Catherine Walters (1839-1920) was born into poverty in Liverpool,
and slept her way to fame and riches in London and sometimes Paris.
One nobleman was supporting her when she was 16; at 19 she was the
mistress of Lord **Hartington** (later the 8th Duke of *Devonshire*). She
was one of the fashionable "pretty horsebreakers" — a euphemism for
"whores" — who rode their mounts in Hyde Park, catching the eye of
gentlemen who could afford her company. In 1861 *Edwin Landseer*
used her as the model for his painting of woman and horse, "The Shrew
Tamed". Men who made gifts to "Skittles" (the nickname came from a
job she had briefly held in a bowling-alley) included the Prince of
Wales (later *Edward VII*) and French Emperor **Napoleon III**. She had,
of course, nothing in common with Irene Adler.

Charles Sanders Peirce (1839-1914) was a philosopher who
contributed to mathematics, logic, and semiotics while working
desultorily for the United States Coast and Geodetic Survey. He
endured difficult personal relationships and poverty, as well as the professional enmity of *Simon Newcomb*, to leave more than 100,000 pages
of manuscripts. In contrast to traditional deduction, a moving from
cause to effect, Peirce spoke of induction as moving from case and
result to rule: "These beans are from this bag. These beans are white.
All the beans from this bag are white." He also offered a third form of
logic, abduction: "All the beans from this bag are white. These beans
are white. These beans are from this bag." (Sherlock Holmes in "The
Second Stain": "The odds are enormous against its being coincidence.
No, my dear Watson, the two events are connected.")

Ira Davenport (1839-1911) was an early Spiritualist medium, along
with his younger brother, **William Davenport** (1841-1877). The duo
were fraudulent, historians think, but so talented with their effects that

they taught some of them to *Harry Houdini*. (However, Arthur Conan Doyle in his *History of Spiritualism* makes clear that he believed the brothers genuine mediums.) They began performing as teenagers in Buffalo, first with table-rapping and other manifestations like those introduced by **Margaret** and **Kate Fox**, then with more elaborate stunts such as floating musical instruments. Within months they were performing in New York and had introduced miraculous escapes from rope bondage as their most dramatic effect. The brothers did not actually claim to be spirit mediums, but they were interpreted as such, and their "spirit guide", John King, became well known.

John Nevil Maskelyne (1839-1917) was one of the greatest of stage magicians, whose show occupied the landmark Egyptian Hall in Piccadilly 1873-1904, making it "England's Home of Mystery". Maskelyne invented levitation as it is now practised in the magical world, and revealed many of the secrets of card tricks in his 1894 book *Sharps and Flats: A Complete Revelation of the Secrets of Cheating at Games of Chance and Skill*. He also campaigned against Spiritualism and any belief in occult powers, founding a committee of the Magic Circle "to investigate claims to supernatural power and to expose fraud". His son and grandson followed him in becoming magicians.

Ouida, born **Maria Louise Ramé** (1839-1908), was an English novelist of French ancestry. Says the *Oxford Companion to English Literature*: "Her forty-five novels deal chiefly with fashionable life and show a spirit of rebellion against the moral ideas reflected in much of the fiction of the time. She incurred a good deal of ridicule on acount of the languid guardsmen, miracles of strength, courage, and beauty, whom she frequently presented as her heroes, and of her amusing mistakes in matters of men's sports and occupations. But these faults were redeemed by her gift for stirring narrative and other merits." She lived in London's Langham Hotel for some time, and in the 1870s moved to Italy.

Paul Cézanne (1839-1906) "has inspired generations of modern artists," says the Metropolitan Museum of Art website. "Generally categorized as a Post-Impressionist, his unique method of building form with color and his analytical approach to nature influenced the art of Cubists, Fauvists, and successive generations of avant-garde artists." The site gives much credit to **Camille Pissarro** for influencing Cézanne's shift from dark, thick layers of paint in his early work to the lighter touch typical of the Impressionists. But he moved beyond that style in his later work, experimenting with perspective, geometric rhythm and subtle colour distinctions. He was born in Aix-en-Provence, spent years in Paris, but returned to Provence after about 1880 and painted many of its scenes.

Robert Armitage Sterndale (1839-1902) went to work for the finance department of the East India Company at the age of 17, and progressed both in administrative work and in knowledge of the natural world. His most important book is *Natural History of the Mammalia of India and Ceylon* (1884), in which he reported significant observations about the behaviour of gibbons, cheetahs and other species. Another book, *Seonee, or Camp Life on the Satpura Range* (1877), is said to have been the inspiration for **Rudyard Kipling**'s *Jungle Book*. After his retirement from finance in 1890, he became involved in a campaign to "save" the tiny South Atlantic territory of Saint Helena, which was in economic difficulty because ships were now using the Suez Canal rather than the traditional southern route to the east. He ended up as the island's governor from 1895 to his death.

Sir **John Robinson** (1839-1903) was the first Prime Minister of Natal, one of the colonies that would later (1910) form the Union of South Africa. It was an era when British possessions around the world were gradually acquiring "responsible government" with local, elected rule, rather than being ruled chiefly by governors sent out from London. Robinson had begun as a journalist, taking over the fledgling *Natal Mercury* from his father, but in 1863 he was elected to the legislative council, such as it was, and campaigned over the years for a greater degree of self-government. He was a member of a delegation that came to London in 1892 to press the cause; it was successful, and when the new legislature met in 1893 he became prime minister, serving four years before retiring.

Walter Pater (1839-1894) "survives chiefly as a kind of literary aroma punctuated by a handful of famous phrases", reviewer Roger Kimball wrote in 1995. "Few serious modern writers indulged themselves in prose so effulgently purple as did Pater." He was known for painstaking writing and rewriting in an attempt to structure sentences and paragraphs perfectly, and expressed an aspiration "to burn always with this hard, gemlike flame". Pater wrote fiction, including *Marius the Epicurean* (1885), but chiefly, in a career based at Oxford University and in London, he produced art criticism and philosophy. Sometimes called an aesthete, he influenced such younger writers as **Gerard Manley Hopkins** and **Oscar Wilde**, to say nothing of his effect on fiction of the early 20th century.

Sir **Redvers Buller** (1839-1908) "has become a byword for military stupidity and out-dated attitudes to changing 19th century society", according to the Britishempire.co.uk website. As an officer in the King's Royal Rifle Corps he saw action in the Red River expedition in Canada (1870) and the Zulu War (1879), in which he won a Victoria Cross for his rescue of three men at Inhlobana. Later he held desk jobs, becoming Adjutant-General of the Army 1890-1897. ("He was virtually running the army himself since the Duke of *Cambridge* was increasingly incapacitated," the same website notes.) He was commander-in-chief  during the second Boer War (1899), and developed tactics now considered standard for ground war, but a series of defeats and blunders led to his removal in favour of Lord *Roberts*.

William A. Clark (1839-1925) had much in common with Neil Gibson of "The Problem of Thor Bridge", although he was known as the Copper King rather than the Gold King. To quote Sherlock Holmes, "he was once Senator for some Western state," namely Montana, where he had begun as a miner during the gold rush of 1862. He moved on to selling supplies, then to banking and foreclosing on bankrupt mines, and eventually railroads, utilities and newspapers. Las Vegas was founded as a maintenance stop for one of his railroads. He dabbled in territorial politics as Montana prepared for statehood in 1889, and then tried to buy support in the state legislature for an appointment to the United States Senate. He finally served a Senate term 1901-1907. *Mark Twain* called him "a shame to the American nation" for his business practices, but he died in a mansion on New York's Fifth Avenue.

William **Rutherford** (1839-1899) was a professor of physiology in the University of Edinburgh medical school, known for, in Daniel Stashower's phrase, "his booming voice and Old Testament beard". Though born in Roxburghshire, he was not an Edinburgh graduate himself, but came to the medical school as an assistant after studying in Europe. He left for London for a few years, then held a professorship at Edinburgh 1874-1899, during which time Arthur Conan Doyle was among his students. ACD based his character Professor Challenger on Rutherford, going so far as to look at photographs of a statue of Rutherford when he was writing the first Challenger novel (*The Lost World*) in 1911. A number of Rutherford's lectures were published; his *Syllabus of Lectures on Physiology* dates from 1887.

Edward Stanley Gibbons (1840-1913) founded the firm of Stanley Gibbons Ltd., the major British dealer in postage stamps and publisher of stamp catalogues. His father was a chemist (retail pharmacist) in Plymouth, and when Edward took over the business in 1867 he quickly converted it to a stamp dealership, less than thirty years after Sir ***Rowland Hill*** had introduced the world's first postage stamps. He issued his first catalogue in 1865 and moved to London in 1874. Shortly after his death, his firm received a royal warrant ("by appointment to His Majesty the King") from *George V*, himself a stamp collector. Gibbons was married five times; four of his wives predeceased him.

George Cadogan, 5th Earl Cadogan (1840-1915), served briefly in the army before entering politics. From the death of his father in 1873 he was an earl and thus a member of the House of Lords, in an era when government ministers could routinely be in the Lords. He served as an under-secretary briefly in the government of Conservative prime minister ***Benjamin Disraeli***, then as Lord Privy Seal for six years under Lord ***Salisbury***, and from 1895 to 1902 as Lord Lieutenant of Ireland. His work in that role included support for the 1896 Land Act that allowed tenants to buy their farms from their landlords' estates, and  promotion of economic development in Ireland. He gets a mention in **James Joyce**'s *Ulysses*: "The cabby read out of the paper he had got hold of that the former viceroy, earl Cadogan, had presided at the cab-drivers' association dinner in London somewhere." Such a dinner did take place, in 1904.

Émile Zola (1840-1902) was a French writer, remembered for the scandalous novel *Nana* (1880) and for his intervention in the long-running miscarriage of justice that sent military officer ***Alfred Dreyfus*** to Devil's Island. His major literary legacy is the 20-volume sequence of novels known as *Les Rougon-Macquart*. Zola grew up in Aix-en-Provence, a classmate of ***Paul Cézanne***, who later introduced him to the artistic coteries of Paris. He began his Paris life in poverty, however, eventually managing to get a menial job at the Hachette publishing company and work up to more stable positions. He took up magazine journalism and then fiction, including the murder story *Thérèse Raquin* (1867). He also wrote several books expounding his "naturalist" theories of art. His famous open letter "J'accuse", telling truths about the Dreyfus case, appeared in *L'Aurore* in January 1898.

James Watson (1840-1926) was a physician who lived near Arthur Conan Doyle in Southsea in the 1880s and was a member with him of the Portsmouth Literary and Scientific Society. In all likelihood his name was borrowed for that of Sherlock Holmes's colleague Dr. John (or, once, James) Watson. He graduated from the University of Edinburgh medical school in 1863 — a generation before ACD — with a thesis about four new drugs. Only one of the four, he concluded, was likely to be useful: carbolic acid (mentioned in "The Cardboard Box") as a disinfectant. He was quickly hired by the Imperial Chinese Maritime Customs Service, which was just setting up a medical unit, and served in the obscure seaport of Newchwang, Manchuria, from 1865 to 1884. The work mostly involved treating foreign officials and visiting sailors, but his reports also said much about local living conditions and hygiene. Returning to England, he spent the rest of his career practising at the Portsmouth Royal Infirmary; he joined the PLSS and gave an early lecture, which ACD surely heard, on "China and Its People".

Charles Augustus Howell (1840-1890) was a confidence trickster, perhaps a blackmailer, and the original of Charles Augustus Milverton. Born in Portugal, where a considerable tribe of people who consider themselves English still exist, he came to England as a young man, spent a while in Italy, and then was back in England getting involved in the business affairs of *John Ruskin, James McNeill Whistler* and others, to his own benefit. In 1869 Howell arranged the exhumation of *Dante Gabriel Rosseti*'s wife, **Elizabeth Siddal**, for the sake of the poems he had buried with her. Whistler called him "the genius, the superb liar... the creature of topboots and plumes, splendidly flamboyant". Historians are divided about whether blackmail was really one of his activities. He was found dead one morning outside a pub, his throat slit.

John Boyd Dunlop (1840-1921) was a veterinarian, in Edinburgh and then Belfast, who found his long rounds in a carriage over rough roads to be uncomfortable. He experimented with ways of making a less rigid, inflatable rubber tyre, receiving a patent for his design in 1887 and not realizing that another man from Scotland, **Robert William Thomson**, had patented a similar invention 40 years earlier. A legal battle ensued between Thomson and the company formed by Dunlop and a partner. Dunlop was ultimately successful, but sold his interest in the business in 1895. His name remained with the Dunlop Rubber Company, which was chiefly associated with tyres for bicycles; Sherlock Holmes refers to Dunlop tyres and their rival, Palmer's, in "The Priory School".

Sir **Charles Warren** (1840-1927) was a military officer, an archaeologist in Palestine, and for three years (1886-1888) Commissioner of the Metropolitan Police. His police career was notable for bureaucratic conflict with the Home Secretary (the cabinet minister responsible for policing) and with his subordinates, the Bloody Sunday conflict in Trafalgar Square in 1887, and the unsuccessful Jack the Ripper investigation in the fall of 1888. Before and after that period, military service took him to various parts of the world with the Royal Engineers. For a time he was chief instructor in surveying at the School of Military Engineering. His archaeological work  involved surveying and excavation at Temple Mount in Jerusalem (1867-1870). During the South African War he commanded forces attempting a relief of Ladysmith; his management was blamed for the disastrous defeat at Spion Kop in January 1900.

John Dixon Mann (1840-1912) was a leading researcher on poisons, a field in which Sherlock Holmes was said to be "well up". He began as a physician in Manchester and then taught at the University of Manchester, holding a professorship in "forensic medicine and toxicology" from 1892. "His classes on the identification of poisons were especially useful," said his obituary in the *British Medical Journal*. He was "much sought as an expert witness in the law courts", but less than popular with lawyers because he was "impatient" with legal arguments and cross-examination. His book *Forensic Medicine and Toxicology* appeared in 1893; three more editions followed. He also wrote a book about urine, and other publications included a 1908 article on the effects of excessive smoking.

Max Shinburn, born **Maximilliam Schoenbein** (1840-1917), came to the United States from Germany about 1860 and carried out a long series of bank robberies, collaborating (according to lawmen of the time) with such known criminals as **George White**, **George Bliss**, and **Andrew "Fairy" McGuire**. It was the golden age of safe-cracking, and Shinburn was an expert, specializing in Lilly safes. He actually took a job with the company to learn its secrets and, it was said, finally drove the manufacturer right out of business. Leaving the country in 1869 with a rumoured $1,000,000 in assets, he settled in Belgium, prospered in business, gambled his money away, returned to the United States and picked up where he left off. He was eventually arrested in midtown New York in June 1895, carrying everything from skeleton keys and nitroglycerin to firearms, and served four years in New York's Dannemora penitentiary and eight in the New Hampshire pen.

Nathan Rothschild, 1st Baron **Rothschild** (1840-1915), was a scion of the Rothschild dynasty whose appointment to the House of Lords in 1885 finally confirmed that Jewish bankers were welcome in the British upper classes. (An uncle, Sir **Anthony de Rothschild**, had been a baronet since 1847, almost as good.) Nathan was a great-grandson of **Mayer Amschel Rothschild**, founder of the business, and grandson of another **Nathan Rothschild**, who brought it to Britain in 1798. Although Jews were not eligible for degrees at Cambridge, he studied there (and made a friend of the Prince of Wales, the future *Edward VII*). He also could not sit in Parliament, despite being repeatedly elected, until reforms took effect in 1865; he then represented a Buckinghamshire district for 20 years. Meanwhile he was a partner in the family bank in London, N. M. Rothschild & Sons, and its head after his father, **Lionel de Rothschild**, died in 1879. The enterprise helped to finance the Suez Canal and the British South Africa Company. Rothschild was a prominent philanthropist with a particular interest in model housing for impoverished Jewish neighbourhoods.

Victoria, Princess Royal (1840-1901), was the first child of Queen *Victoria* and Prince *Albert*. She was heir to the throne until the birth of her brother, the future *Edward VII*, less than a year after her own birth.

She was engaged at age 14, and married at 17, to Prince **Frederick William of Prussia**, the future Emperor *Frederick III*. "The marriage was both a love match and a dynastic alliance," says Wikipedia. "The Queen and Prince Albert hoped that Victoria's marriage to the future king of Prussia would cement close ties between London and Berlin." Frederick became crown prince in 1861 and Emperor in 1888, but he was already dying of cancer, and Victoria lived 13 years as a widow much like her mother. Their son became Emperor *Wilhelm II*.

Richard Freiherr **von Krafft-Ebing** (1840-1902) was a psychiatrist who worked at several asylums and three universities in Germany and Austria, and was the author of the seminal work *Psychopathia Sexualis*. First published in 1886 (English translation 1892), and written partly in German and partly in Latin, it was a reference book, packed with case histories, providing a classification and analysis of sexual aberrations. Successive editions saw it expand from 45 case histories to, at last, 238. Krafft-Ebing was influential in bringing sexual variations into the realm of science rather than of crime or religion. In particular, he argued for the repeal of Germany's 1871 law against homosexuality on the grounds that it should be considered an illness. He wrote, however, that homosexuality was ipso facto an aberration since it was a form of sexual drive not consistent with reproduction. Krafft-Ebing also wrote several other books including an 1894 study of general paralysis, a consequence of syphilis related to the Tabes Dorsalis about which Arthur Conan Doyle wrote his MD thesis.

Sophia Jex-Blake (1840-1912) was one of Britain's first female physicians, the pioneers Arthur Conan Doyle wrote about in "The Doctors of Hoyland". She initially trained as a teacher, and during her student days developed a close relationship with **Octavia Hill**, later a prominent social reformer. She travelled to Germany and America, and became interested in medicine as a field of study. Harvard would not admit her; in 1869 the University of Edinburgh first allowed her to enrol, then reversed the decision. After a publicity campaign, she and four other women were allowed to attend classes, but it took a riot, a lawsuit,  and action in Parliament before the issue was settled. Jex-Blake qualified as a physician in 1877, just as ACD was beginning his medical studies. She maintained a private medical practice in Edinburgh for about 20 years, and with *Elizabeth Garrett Anderson* founded the London School of Medicine.

Thomas Hardy (1840-1928) was "the greatest author that England possesses at present", in the words of Arthur Conan Doyle: the author of *Far from the Madding Crowd* (1874), *Tess of the D'Urbervilles* (1891), *Jude the Obscure* (1895), and other classics. Born in Dorset, and resident there for most of his life (though he spent some time in London working as an architect), he set his stories in rural "Wessex", the southern and western part of England. Some of his work was strong meat for contemporary readers, as he took a realistic view of sex and social class, and gave more attention to the grim hand of fate than to God. After 1900 his published work shifted from novels to poetry. He is considered a major influence on writers of the 20th century, most of all **D. H. Lawrence**.

Adolf **Beck** (1841-1909) was the victim of a miscarriage of justice that eventually led to the general legal rule that convictions cannot be based on eyewitness identification alone. Beck was a Norwegian businessman, once successful, but living in poverty in London by 1895 when a woman accused him of having defrauded her. Several other women identified him as having cheated them also, and he served five years in prison. Supporters including Arthur Conan Doyle demanded that the authorities re-examine the case and compare the 1895 incidents with a series of frauds in 1877 for which another man, **John Smith** (an alias), had been convicted. Beck was charged and convicted again in 1904, but before his sentencing, Smith was by chance found and identified. Beck was given compensation for false imprisonment in the immense amount of £5,000.

Annie Chapman, born **Annie Eliza Smith** (1841-1888), was the second of the five women definitely thought to have been killed by Jack the Ripper in the fall of 1888 in London's east end. Her body was found at 29 Hanbury Street in Spitalfields, with her throat cut and her abdomen grotesquely mutilated. Annie had married **John Chapman** in 1869 and they had a stable life for some time, with three children, but both became heavy drinkers and they separated in 1884. She did not become a prostitute until support payments from her husband stopped arriving with his death in 1886. She had some relationships with other men, and supported herself by crochet work and flower-selling as well as prostitution.

Charles Penrose-Fitzgerald, later **Uniacke-Penrose-Fitzgerald** (1841-1921), was a Royal Navy officer with a knack for controversy. He joined the navy in 1854 and was a captain by 1880; for five years starting in 1884 he headed the Royal Naval College at Greenwich. He became a rear admiral in 1895, despite damaging his reputation by supporting a proposed new system of signal flags which led to the drowning death of Vice-Admiral Sir **George Tryon** during testing in 1893. After retirement in 1901, he wrote an article about naval policy for a German publication which was interpreted as calling for war quickly, before the German fleet could be expanded. Early in World War I, he organized women to hand out white feathers to men not in uniform, portraying them as cowards; the white feather campaign spread across the country. The same year, when Arthur Conan Doyle's story "Danger!" about submarine warfare appeared, he commented that "I do not myself think that any civilized nation will torpedo unarmed and defenceless merchant ships."

Félix Faure (1841-1899) was elected president of France unexpectedly: there were stronger candidates, but they had enemies, whereas none of the "moderate republicans" had anything much against this minor politician who had been serving as minister of the navy. (Before entering politics, he had been a prosperous businessman.) He took office in January 1895, succeeding **Jean Casimir-Perier**, who had been president for six months following the assassination of *Sadi Carnot*. Later that year Faure extended amnesty to members of France's anarchist movements, allowing several exiles to come from Britain, including **Émile Pouget**, who had found France too hot to hold him after the presidential assassination. He died suddenly during a tête-à-tête in his office with his mistress, **Marguerite Steinheil**.

Georges Clémenceau (1841-1929) was involved in French politics from his days as a medical student in Paris, when he joined groups agitating for the overthrow of Emperor **Napoleon III** (reigned 1852-1870). He developed his ideas about democracy during a four-year stay in the United States, but was back in France in time to see the Emperor dethroned and the Third Republic formed in 1871 after the disaster of the Franco-Prussian War. He soon found himself mayor of the Montmartre district of Paris, and a member of the National Assembly, holding fast for republican principles. Out of office 1893-1902, he turned his attention to political journalism, but returned to public life and served as prime minister 1906-1909 and 1917-1920, representing France at the peace conference that concluded the Treaty of Versailles after World War I.

Henry Stanley (1841-1904) was a journalist, Welsh-born but working for the New York *Herald*, when he went to Africa in 1869 to search for missionary and explorer *David Livingstone*. It took him years; in November 1871, near Lake Tanganyika, he found the missing Briton and famously greeted him, "Dr. Livingstone, I presume?" After Livingstone's death, Stanley continued exploring Africa, tracing the length of the Congo river and telling his tale in *Through the Dark Continent* (1878). He attempted to interest British authorities in developing the central African  region, but got more response from Belgium's King *Léopold II*. Stanley eventually returned to Britain, made a worldwide lecture tour, and served in Parliament 1895-1900.

Evelyn Baring, Earl of **Cromer** (1841-1917), was a British colonial administrator best known for his firm hand in Egypt before and after the revolt led by *Muhammad Ahmad*. Son of Sir **Francis Baring**, founder of Barings Bank, he began a military career but, in India and later in Egypt, found government administration more to his taste. Wikipedia: "Baring came to believe that local rule and autonomy were not the answer, and that only the firm, direct guidance of a British colonial government could bring order and prosperity. Later in Egypt, he became further convinced that native rulers were hopelessly corrupt and oppressive." His 1910 book *Ancient and Modern Imperialism* was a comparison of the Roman and British empires.

Henry H. Gorringe (1841-1885) was a United States naval officer, born in Barbados, who served in the Civil War and later was assigned to exploration projects; in 1875 the government published his book about the Rio Plata, the estuary between Argentina and Uruguay. While on leave from the US Navy as a lieutenant commander, he received a contract in 1879 to transport a massive stone obelisk from Egypt to New York and see it erected in Central Park. He surmounted bureaucratic and practical difficulties and earned great public acclaim for the achievement, which was financed by industrialist *William Henry Vanderbilt*. The 69-foot granite tower, popularly called Cleopatra's Needle, in fact was a memorial to Pharaoh Thutmose III, who lived centuries before Cleopatra. It has a twin on London's Embankment, which was given to Britain by Egyptian officials in 1819 but not transported to London until 1878, also at the expense of a private sponsor, physician Sir **Erasmus Wilson**.

Nicholas I (1841-1921) was the ruler of Montenegro from 1860 to 1918. His little Balkan state, with a coastline on the Adriatic Sea, holds a place in Sherlockian tradition because of the fancy that Sherlock Holmes dallied with Irene Adler there during his Great Hiatus. At that period Montenegro had just (1878) become independent of the tottering Ottoman Empire. Nicholas had become its Prince following the assassination of his uncle, and presided over a period of reform and internal calm, with support from Russia in building up the army. He expanded Montenegro's territory through a series of small wars against Turkey; nevertheless, after independence he managed to maintain good relations with Sultan *Abdul Hamid II*. A constitution was approved in 1905, and Nicholas was proclaimed King in 1910. Always a believer in Serbian leadership, he lost his throne when Austria-Hungary defeated Serbia in World War I, and Montenegro was absorbed with Serbia into the new Yugoslavia.

King **Edward VII**, previously **Albert Edward**, Prince of **Wales** (1841-1910), was the oldest son of Queen *Victoria* and *Albert*, the Prince Consort. Although he became a dignified, popular, and successful king, particularly effective as "Edward the Peacemaker" in managing the squabbles among European nations, his reputation as Prince of Wales (heir to the throne) was for spendthrift luxury, gambling, and womanizing. Occasionally, as in the Tranby Croft scandal of 1891, he came close to serious trouble. His most prominent mistress was **Lillie Langtry**; there were numerous others, probably including the sensational actress *Sarah Bernhardt*. As host or guest at weekend house-parties he also had many opportunities for dalliance with society ladies. The Prince has been plausibly seen as the "illustrious client" who employs Holmes in the story of that title, and his career has echoes in the events of "A Scandal in Bohemia". He succeeded to the throne on his mother's death in January 1901; he was married to Princess *Alexandra* of Denmark, and their son *George V* succeeded him.

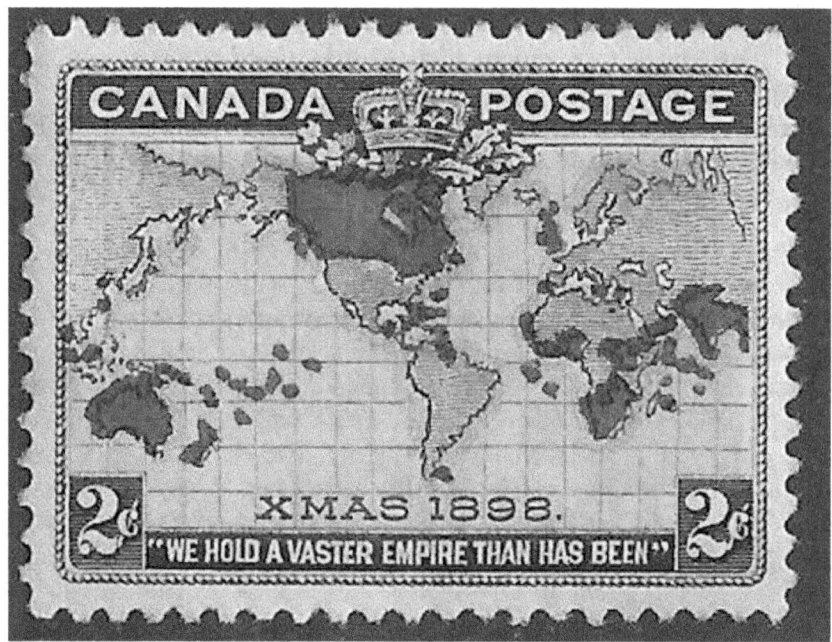

Sir **Wilfrid Laurier** (1841-1919) was prime minister of Canada 1896-1911, a nation-builder after he overcame early suspicions that English would overcome French in a united country. A law graduate of McGill University and then a journalist, he was elected to the national Parliament in 1874, quickly becoming a cabinet minister. In 1887 he was chosen leader of the Liberal Party, then in opposition. He led the Liberals to four consecutive election wins, 1896 through 1908, on policies of compromise over French and Roman Catholic rights; "Imperial preference" in trade (though earlier and later in his career he favoured "reciprocity" with the United States); construction of a second transcontinental railway to complement the existing Canadian Pacific Railway (mentioned in "Black Peter"); admission of Alberta and Saskatchewan as provinces; and progress toward eventual Canadian independence.

John Arbuthnot (Jacky) Fisher, Baron **Fisher** (1841-1920), spent 60 years in the Royal Navy, eventually becoming First Sea Lord 1904-1910 and 1914-1915. (The position should not be confused with First Lord of the Admiralty, a political office.) Born of a British family in Ceylon, he joined the navy in 1854, serving first on HMS *Victory*, which had been **Lord Nelson**'s flagship. He was on the fringes of the Crimean War, fought in China, was promoted to captain in 1874, and became a gunnery expert. In senior positions (admiral, Controller of the Navy, Second Sea Lord) he did much to build up the fleet with modern ironclad ships and armaments, a vast difference from the wooden ships and muzzle-loading cannon of his youth. (Sherlock Holmes and Von Bork speak of such matters in "His Last Bow".) He had a reputation as a difficult man to work with, and is said to have coined the colloquial abbreviation OMG. Jacky of "The Sussex Vampire", who gets sent off to sea, may well be a tribute to his nickname.

Pierre-Auguste Renoir (1841-1919) was a leader of the Impressionist movement of artists, and lived long enough to see one of his works purchased for the Louvre, France's leading art museum. He was born in Limoges, a town famous for its porcelain, and first earned his living decorating porcelain. He practised copying works that hung in the Louvre, studied at the noted École des Arts, and became friends with promising young artists including **Claude Monet**. By 1864 he was seeking portrait commissions; in 1874 he, Monet, *Paul Cézanne* and other "Impressionists" had their first exhibition. "As he aged," says Biography.com, "Renoir continued to use his trademark feathery brush-strokes to depict primarily rural and domestic scenes." His most familiar paintings include "Dance at Bougival" (1882-1883) and "After the Bath" (1910), one of his many female nudes.

Sir **Edward George Clarke** (1841-1931) was a barrister whose cases included some of the celebrated scandals of the 19th century: he represented *Oscar Wilde* in his ill-fated suit against the *Marquess of Queensberry*, and Sir *William Gordon-Cumming* in his suit against those who had accused him of cheating at cards. Clarke was called to the bar (became a lawyer) in 1864, and made his reputation in two high-profile criminal cases in 1877, followed by his successful defence of an accused murderess in the "Pimlico Mystery" of 1886. He entered Parliament as a Conservative and served in government as Solicitor-General 1886-1892, but preferred to go back into private practice; his high-profile clients in later years included *Leander Starr Jameson*. His writings included a *Treatise on the Law of Extradition* (1903).

Abdul Hamid II (1842-1918) was the last effective sultan or emperor of the Ottoman (Turkish) Empire, ruling territories that stretched from the Balkans to the Caucasus and into Africa. He suspended an existing parliamentary system early in his reign, and ruled from the Sublime Porte in Constantinople (Istanbul) as an absolute monarch with the support of secret police. Massacres and starvation of Armenians under Turkish rule extended through much of his reign. He was deposed in the "Young Turk Revolution" of 1908, a precursor of the Turkish Revolution of 1923. Sherlock Holmes had a "commission" from the sultan in 1903, according to a brief sentence in "The Blanched Soldier".

Ambrose Bierce (1842-1904?) wrote realistic war fiction and eventually disappeared into another war. After fighting with the 9th Indiana Infantry during the American Civil War, he took up journalism in San Francisco, becoming a valuable writer on *William Randolph Hearst*'s staff, and also began literary writing. Stories like "An Occurrence at Owl Creek Bridge" drew on his war experience and were acclaimed by veterans as realistically dreadful. In a different genre he compiled *The Devil's Dictionary* (1906): "Selfish, *adj.* Devoid of consideration for the selfishness of others." Late in 1913 Bierce headed for Mexico to take a look at the revolution that was in progress. He accompanied the army of **Pancho Villa** as far as Chihuahua, and was never heard from again.

Camille Flammarion (1842-1925) was the brother of **Ernest Flammarion**, founder of the publishing company that still bears his name, but his interests led him instead to astronomy, psychic beliefs, and science fiction. He was the first president of the French Astronomical Society, and author of more than a dozen books, including novels and works of popular science. His novel *La Fin du Monde* ("The End of the World", 1893) tells the story of a comet colliding with earth. He apparently was genuinely concerned that Halley's Comet, due in 1910, would bring with it gases that would extinguish all life on earth — an idea possibly reflected in Arthur Conan Doyle's 1913 novel *The Poison Belt*. He was sceptical of most Spiritualist mediums but did believe in life after death. Indeed he maintained that human souls are reincarnated on successive planets, gradually becoming more refined.

Catherine Eddowes, also known as **Kate Kelly** (1842-1888), was a victim of the murderer Jack the Ripper in September 1888. Originally from Wolverhampton, she had at one time worked as a tinplate stamper. She had had a long relationship with an ex-soldier, **Thomas Conway**, and had his initials tattooed on her left arm. They had three children, who were grown by 1888, when Eddowes was living in a squalid lodging-house in London and involved with **John Kelly**, a fruit salesman. The two had been hop-picking in Kent, returning to London on a Friday and spending Saturday desperately trying to raise money from relatives and pawn-brokers. Eddowes spent some of the Saturday night at Bishopsgate police station, having been brought in drunk, and was probably killed within minutes after the police released her about 1 a.m. on the Sunday. Her body, extensively mutilated, was found in

Mitre Square, east London. *Elizabeth Stride* was killed on the same night.

Joseph Breuer (1842-1925) was "the 'grandfather' of psychoanalysis," says a *Sigmund Freud* website, noting that it was Breuer who brought to Freud the famous "Anna O" case now known to involve feminist and author **Bertha Pappenheim**. Her treatment, carried on in the 1880s and reported in *Studies in Hysteria* in 1895, is considered the beginning of psychoanalysis as Freud developed it, with the "talking cure" aimed at making unconscious processes conscious and thus alleviating their symptoms. Breuer received his medical training in Vienna and gave up a teaching career to go into private practice, though he also did some research. He was a mentor to the young Freud, but they later parted ways.

Jeremiah Simpson, known as **Sockless Jerry Simpson** (1842-1905), was a United States Congressman from Kansas for six years (1891-1895 and 1897-1899) and one of the most memorable representatives of the rural populism of his era. Born in Prince Edward Island, he was raised in New York, served with an Illinois regiment during the Civil War, worked on ships steaming the Great Lakes from Indiana, and finally settled on a Kansas farm. During hard times in 1883-1884 he joined a locally organized political movement. Things got worse in 1889, to the point that farmers were burning their main crop, corn, for fuel. In the 1890 election Simpson faced a Republican candidate, a wealthy attorney who, he charged, even wore "fine silk hosiery". Silk socks were better than none at all, the Republican unwisely shot back, and "Sockless Jerry" was elected in a landslide.

Prince **Pyotr (Peter) Alexeyevich Kropotkin** (1842-1921) was a prominent scientist and outspoken anarchist. His birth into the high levels of Russian aristocracy did not deter him from advocating communism in his books, or prevent him from being imprisoned in both Russia and France. As a young soldier, he was assigned to geographical explorations in Manchuria, at the far edge of Siberia; subsequent work for the Russian Geographical Society led to new understandings of the physical features of Asia. His first radical step, after much reading, was to join the International Workingmen's Association in 1872, and other affiliations followed. His efforts as a propagandist for anarchism landed him in the Peter and Paul Fortress in St. Petersburg for a time. He visited many countries of Europe, spending a year in London (1881) and then settling in Britain from 1886 to 1914. He returned to Russia after the 1917 revolution but was deeply disappointed when the Bolshevik faction took power at the expense of anarchism.

Lady **Florence Paget** (1842-1907) was the daughter of Sir **Henry Paget, Marquess of Anglesey**, and a society beauty known popularly, if not respectfully, as "the Pocket Venus". She gained notoriety in 1864 when, a few days before her scheduled wedding to **Henry Chaplin**, she slipped out the rear door of an Oxford Street shop and rode off with **Henry Rawdon-Hastings, Marquess of Hastings**, who was a close friend of Chaplin. Within an hour they were married at St. George's, Hanover Square. Hastings, an uncontrolled gambler and drink-er, died in 1868, and two years later Florence married Sir **George Chetwynd**. The jilted Chaplin recovered from the scandal; he served in Parliament for 30 years, and in 1916 became a Viscount.

Nathaniel Druscovich (1842-1881) was considered a great asset to Scotland Yard because of the languages he spoke, although one colleague sniffed that "there was a good deal of the foreigner in him." He was born in east London but raised partly in his father's homeland of Moldavia (now in Romania). He joined the Metropolitan Police at 21, and by 28 was a Chief Inspector. In multicultural London, there was much opportunity for him to investigate cases with a European background, including the 1876 mutiny and murder aboard the *Lennie*, which led to the hanging of four Greeks and Turks. Later the same year he led the investigation of the "Turf Fraud" case, but in 1877 it became clear that two inspectors, *William Palmer* and **John Meiklejohn**, had been taking bribes from the fraudsters; Druscovich, implicated in the cover-up, went to prison for two years.

Roswell L. Cofran (1842-1932) was a businessman, Freemason and Shriner, and the real mayor of Topeka, the capital of Kansas, for four terms, 1885-87, 1889-93 and 1913-1915. Sherlock Holmes tricked

"Killer" Evans in "The Three Garridebs" by referring to an imaginary Topekan, "old Dr. Lysander Starr, who was mayor in 1890", and Evans pretended to recognize the name. Born in Vermont, Cofran served with the Sixth Vermont Infantry in the Civil War, later became a machinist, came to Kansas in 1870, worked for the Topeka (later Western) Foundry and Machine Works, and became its owner. The business closed in 2000 when his grandson retired.

Thomas F. Byrnes (1842-1910) was head of the detective department at the New York police department 1880-1895. He could thus be the original of "my friend, Wilson Hargreave, of the New York Police Bureau", mentioned in "The Dancing Men". Irish-born, Byrnes was a soldier and a firefighter before joining the police force in 1863 and working up through the ranks. He was known as an energetic and ruthless detective, and may have invented the phrase "the third degree" to describe police abuse of suspects under questioning. After being forced out of office by police commissioner *Theodore Roosevelt* in his campaign against corruption, Byrnes opened his own detective agency.

Sir **Robert Warburton** (1842-1899) was a colonel, but he was not mad; the reference in "The Engineer's Thumb" is surely no more than a coincidence. He was born in Afghanistan — his mother Afghan, his father an officer in the Royal Artillery — and educated in England. In 1862 he was sent back to "India" and (with an interlude of combat experience in Abyssinia, now Ethiopia) he remained there in military and then civilian roles; by 1870 he was an assistant commissioner based at Peshawar. The army asked for him back during the Second Afghan War, the one that brought Watson to Peshawar, but civilian authorities declined. "He obtained a remarkable influence over the hill tribes, perhaps in part due to his Afghan blood," the *Dictionary of National Biography* said in 1901. "He was accustomed to travel with no weapon but a walking-stick."

William James (1842-1910) was, according to the *Internet Encyclopedia of Philosophy*, "the second of the three great pragmatists (the middle link between **Charles Sanders Peirce** and **John Dewey**). As a professor of psychology and of philosophy at Harvard University, he became the most famous living American psychologist and later the most famous living American philosopher of his time." He is credited with "pragmatic epistemology", which assesses ideas not theoretically but in terms of their practical implications. James, who was the brother of novelist **Henry James**, was trained as a physician (and had many medical problems himself) and was first appointed to Harvard as an instructor in physiology (1873); by 1889 he held an endowed chair in psychology. His massive book *The Principles of Psychology* was published in 1890.

Sir **Arthur Sullivan** (1842-1900) was a composer who sought to rise above his most popular work, the "Gilbert and Sullivan" operettas, much as Arthur Conan Doyle sought in vain to rise above his most popular creation. But his serious work, such as the 1891 opera "Ivanhoe", was eclipsed by the lighter fare he created in partnership with Sir *W. S. Gilbert*, famously including "HMS Pinafore" (1878) and "The Mikado" (1885). Their first collaboration, "Thespis" (1871), was not considered a success, but theatre manager *Richard D'Oyly Carte* brought them together again, mediated their conflicts (particularly over Sullivan's distaste for Gilbert's silly plots), and brought almost a dozen money-making productions to the stage. The Sullivan tune that has been heard the most often, however, is the melody for the hymn "Onward Christian Soldiers" (words by *Sabine Baring-Gould*).

Adelina Patti (1843-1919) sang in public from early childhood, and made her operatic debut in New York in 1859 in the coloratura role of Lucia di Lammermoor. Two years later she first came to London, where she was a star of the Royal Opera House, Covent Garden, for a quarter of a century. (Her repertoire did not include Wagner, which Sherlock Holmes heard at Covent Garden according to "The Red Circle".) "Her voice was considered small," says the *Encyclopaedia Britannica*, "but was remarkable for its wide range, evenness of pro- duction, and purity of quality." Officially French, she grew up in Spain and then New York, and became a world traveller, singing popular songs as well as operatic mainstays. She had three marriages.

Alice Maud Mary, Princess of Hesse (1843-1878), was the third child of Queen *Victoria*. From the time she visited a military hospital as a child, during the Crimean War, she was interested in medical matters and nursing. She nursed her father Prince *Albert* through his final illness in 1861, and the next year married Prince **Louis of Hesse**, a principality in the Rhine region of Germany; he became Grand Duke there, and she Grand Duchess, in 1877. Her relationship with Victoria was difficult, and they even argued about Alice's determination to breastfeed her daughter. Her death came after a period of nursing family members in Hesse during a diphtheria epidemic. *SS Princess Alice*, which sank in the Thames in 1878 killing more than 650 people, was named in her honour.

Elizabeth Stride, née **Gustafsdotter** (1843-1888), was a victim of the Jack the Ripper murderer, killed early on a Sunday morning off Berner Street in London's Whitechapel district. *Catherine Eddowes* was killed on the same night. She was born on a farm in Sweden, registered in that country as a prostitute (1865), and came to London in 1866. Some records suggest she was initially a domestic servant, and after her marriage to **John Stride** in 1869 the couple operated a coffee shop for several years. She later claimed to have lost her husband, and suffered facial injury herself, in the *Princess Alice* steamship disaster of 1878, but historians doubt her story. From 1882 she lived sometimes at a lodging-house in Flower and Dean Street and sometimes at other locations with **Michael Kidney**, a dock labourer. She was arrested several times as drunk and disorderly, and repeatedly got financial help from the Swedish Church in Princes Square, Wapping. On the night of her death she was seen on the streets with several men. She was found dead about 1 a.m. with a packet of breath fresheners clutched in her hand.

Frederick Abberline (1843-1929) became a constable in the Metropolitan Police in 1863, was promoted to sergeant and then inspector, and was made Inspector First Class just in time to be placed in charge of the detectives investigating the "Jack the Ripper" murders in the fall of 1888. Books and films about those unsolved murders in the Whitechapel district of London have frequently used Abberline as a character, often attributing to him alcoholism, addiction or other traits he is not known to have had. He left the police force in 1892 and headed the European branch of the Pinkerton Detective Agency for twelve years.

Frederic W. H. Myers (1843-1901) was the author of the book *Human Personality and Its Survival of Bodily Death*, published posthumously in 1903. Arthur Conan Doyle called its "the finest expression" of the belief that scientific evidence supports belief in the resurrection of Jesus Christ, and in Spiritualism generally. Myers was a poet, literary critic, lecturer, and schools inspector, and was a founding member (1883) of the Society for Psychical Research, later serving as its president. He wrote at length about the "subliminal self", also described as the collective unconscious, which he considered a source of "supernormal" phenomena. He was active in the exposure of the fraudulent medium **Eusapia Palladino** in 1894, but seems to have been credulous about many of the incidents described in his 1886 book *Phantasms of the Living*.

Henry Faulds (1843-1930) is one claimant to the title of having invented fingerprinting, to the extent that his partisans say his ideas were stolen by *Francis Galton*. Faulds was, as one website says, "one of those delightfully eccentric characters who enlivened Victorian science, brimming with original ideas, a talent for scientific observation, diverse interests and peculiar personality traits". He was a Presbyterian medical missionary to Japan (supervisor of a hospital in Tokyo) who noticed the fingerprints left by potters in their work, wrote to Galton about the phenomenon, and in 1880 had a letter in the journal *Nature* with the title "On the Skin-furrows of the Hand". *William Herschel* responded to *Nature* noting that he had been using fingerprints for police purposes in India for some twenty years. Faulds played no role when fingerprinting was subsequently developed into a practical system, but — now back in Britain and working as a police surgeon — claimed for many years that he deserved the credit.

Henry James (1843-1916) was the author of *The Portrait of a Lady* (1881), *The Turn of the Screw* (1898), *The Ambassadors* (1903), and other novels known for elaborate, not to say tedious, detail. His work, with its long complex sentences and psychological insights, has been compared to Impressionist painting. Much of it deals with the interaction of Americans and British society, a reflection of James's own life: born in New York, he lived mostly in England after 1869. He did not marry, and analysis of his works frequently considers the likelihood that he was homosexual. He was the brother of psychological researcher *William James* and hysterical invalid **Alice James**.

James Addison Reavis (1843-1914) fought on both sides in the United States Civil War, then decided to become the Baron of Arizona, with schemes as colossal as those of Baron Maupertuis ("The Reigate Squires"). Over a period of years, he forged and altered documents in Spanish and Mexican archives, creating an ancient land grant to the fictitious Peralta family for a huge rectangle of the Arizona Territory, which had been part of Mexico until 1848. He also created stone markers and placed them to define the supposed Peralta holdings. In 1883 he showed up asserting his claim to 18,750 square miles, and for 11 years he collected rent from ranches, mines and railways, including the huge Southern Pacific. He made an impression with eastern financiers, and visited London in 1887, where he attended Queen *Victoria*'s Golden Jubilee celebrations as a nobleman. The glory came crashing down when a lawsuit was filed, followed by a criminal trial for fraud in 1896. Reavis spent two years in penitentiary.

James McParland (1843-1919) was a Pinkerton agent and the original of Birdy Edwards, the hero of the second half of *The Valley of Fear*. Born in Ireland, he worked in New York and Chicago, joining the Pinkerton National Detective Agency in 1871. McParland was sent to the Pennsylvania coal region to investigate labour unrest that had reached the stage of violence and murders. Under the alias of **James McKenna** he infiltrated the so-called Molly Maguires and eventually provided the evidence on which ten men were convicted and hanged. Historians, noting abuses and exploitation by management, suggest that the rebellious miners do not carry all the blame. McParland subsequently did other undercover jobs for Pinkerton, mostly involving suppression of unions.

Robert Koch (1843-1910) was a German physician and researcher, winner of the 1905 Nobel Prize in "physiology or medicine" for his research about bacteria as the agent by which many illnesses are spread. Working in private practice, at the University of Berlin, and then at the Imperial Health Office, he turned his attention at various times to anthrax, cholera, conjunctivitis, malaria, typhus, plague, and other diseases. In November 1890, as word spread that Koch had developed a treatment for tuberculosis, Arthur Conan Doyle raced from his Southsea home to Berlin to investigate first-hand. He stayed only a few days, quickly concluding that although the "tubercle bacillus" Koch had discovered in 1882 was the cause of the infection, his proposed cure was a failure (as indeed proved to be the case). His greatest research contributions were the principle that a specific germ is associated with a specific disease, and techniques for growing bacteria *in vitro* and subsequently testing.

Sir **Charles Dilke** (1843-1911) was a prominent figure in the "radical" wing of the Liberal party who could well have become prime minister of Britain, changing the course of history by averting the decline of the Liberals in the early 20th century. A baronet after his father's death in 1869, he entered politics, was in government by 1880 and helped get several reform measures through Parliament. But in 1885 he found himself accused of dalliance in the bed of young **Virginia Crawford**, the daughter of a family friend. The resulting scandal and divorce case largely destroyed his career. Dilke was married to author and feminist **Emilia Francis Strong**.

Sir **Arthur Lasenby Liberty** (1843-1917) was the founder of Liberty & Co., London's internationally known fabric shop. He was born in a town in Buckinghamshire, the son of a draper, and was apprenticed at a draper's shop in London's Baker Street. In 1875 he borrowed money from his fiancée's family to lease space in Regent Street, where he specialized in selling imported goods, especially from Japan. Within 18 months the loan was paid off, he was buying adjacent space, and Liberty's was prospering. It became well known in the 1890s for its Art Nouveau fabric prints, still considered typical of Liberty's. The store's iconic half-timbered building, with its main entrance on Great Marlborough Street and its back to Regent Street, dates from 1924. The founder remained majority owner of the company when it was incorporated in 1890, but moved home to the Chilterns area, where he bought a manor and did much to expand it and improve the district.

Sir **Charles Hall** (1843-1900) worked his way up in the legal profession — after his years at Cambridge, of course, and study of the law at Lincoln's Inn — with a specialty in the Admiralty court. He was attorney-general to the Prince of Wales (later *Edward VII*) from 1877 to 1892; along the way he was elected to Parliament in 1885. In 1889 he represented Britain at the International Marine Congress as to Uniform Rules to Secure Life and Property at Sea, held in Washington. In 1892 he was appointed Recorder of London, the senior judge at the Central Criminal Court (Old Bailey).

William McKinley (1843-1901) was the 25th president of the United States, serving at the time of the Spanish-American War. He had been a lawyer, a Congressman, and governor of Ohio before receiving the Republican nomination in the 1896 election, in which a principal issue was the bimetallic question (the coinage of money in silver as well as gold, a topic mentioned in "The Bruce-Partington Plans"). He defeated **William Jennings Bryan** of the Democrats, the advocate of "free silver", for the presidency, and persuaded Congress to impose high tariffs in support of American industry. In the 1900 election he won a second term, again defeating Bryan. He was assassinated in Buffalo in September 1901 by anarchist *Leon Czolgosz*, and was succeeded as president by *Theodore Roosevelt*.

Alexandra of Denmark (1844-1925) married Albert Edward, Prince of Wales, in 1863 when she was 17 and he 21. She became **Queen Alexandra** when he became King *Edward VII* in 1901. She was daughter of the future King *Christian IX* of Denmark, and maintained anti-German attitudes all her life. The marriage, which resulted in six children including Prince *Albert Victor* and the future *George V*, is said to have been happy despite the Prince's many affairs; famously, Alexandra welcomed one of his mistresses, *Alice Keppel*, to be present at his deathbed. Alexandra suffered from deafness, a limp resulting from a difficult pregnancy, and other physical problems. She was much involved in charitable work, particularly hospitals.

Alfred, Duke of Edinburgh, later **Duke of Saxe-Coburg and Gotha** (1844-1900), was the fourth child of Queen *Victoria*. He entered the Royal Navy as a 14-year-old midshipman and advanced through the ranks, winding up an Admiral of the Fleet. He was injured in an assassination attempt while visiting Australia aboard *HMS Galatea*. At one point he was offered the throne of Greece, but his parents had in mind the duchy of Saxe-Coburg and Gotha in southern Germany, which he would inherit through his father Prince *Albert*. In 1893 the ruling Duke, his uncle, died; he accepted the succession and cut most of his ties with Britain. He married Grand Duchess *Maria Alexandrovna*, daughter of *Alexander II*.

Adam Worth (1844-1902) was "the Napoleon of the criminal world", according to an adversary in Scotland Yard. Whether the detective was quoting Holmes's sobriquet for Professor Moriarty, "the Napoleon of crime", or providing a source for it is not entirely clear. Worth, born in Germany, was raised in the United States and developed his career from bounty jumping and pickpocketing to theft and bank robbery. After the 1869 robbery of Boston's Boylston National Bank, he moved his business to Liverpool, Paris, and eventually London, where he developed a sizeable criminal network and acquired an antagonist, Inspector **John Shore**. In 1876, in his most famous caper, Worth stole a well-known painting from the gallery where it was on display: **Thomas Gainsborough**'s 1785 portrait of **Georgiana, Duchess of Devonshire**, remembered for her coquettish hats as mentioned in "A Case of Identity".  Wealthy on the proceeds of a gambling operation, Worth kept the painting for his own pleasure, returning it for a ransom payment only in 1901. A robbery in Liège, Belgium, in 1892 went wrong, and he served five years in prison.

Andrew Lang (1844-1912) retold the world's legends, from Little Red Riding-Hood to Australia's Bunyip, in a series of twelve "Fairy Books". From the original *Blue Fairy Book* in 1889 to the *Lilac* book in 1910, they included a total of 437 stories, many of which had not appeared in English before. The books were hugely popular and brought fairy tales into the mainstream of children's literature (and no doubt opened the way for Arthur Conan Doyle's *The Coming of the Fairies* in 1922). His wife, **Leonora Alleyne**, did much of the translating, editing, and in some cases original writing of the tales. Lang, born in Selkirk, Scotland, was a prolific writer of poetry, Scottish history, fiction, and scholarship; among his books is *Myth, Ritual and Religion* (1887). He was president of the Societ for Psychical Research in 1911.

Anthony Comstock (1844-1915) was the founder of the New York Society for the Suppression of Vice and the lobbyist behind the 1873 Comstock Law, which barred "obscene, lewd or lascivious" materials from the mail in the United States — rather to the amusement of more sophisticated Europeans. Comstock became a "special agent" of the US Post Office in charge of enforcing the law, which was used at times to restrict information about abortion, contraception, and venereal disease.

He also expressed suspicion of stories about crime and detectives as potentially an immoral influence. The young **J. Edgar Hoover** was an admirer of Comstock, and studied his methods of enforcement and prosecution.

Blanche Warre-Cornish, née **Ritchie** (1844-1922), grew up in, as her grand-daughter put it, "one of those now old-fashioned families with uncles and cousins meting out justice in India, who spent their lives in carefully weighing in the scales Queen *Victoria* against millions of natives". She married **Francis Warre-Cornish**, a master (teacher) at Eton College whose work included a history of the Church of England, and many Eton schoolboys (and others) remembered the unexpected things she said to them. On the day her 1873 novel *Alcestis* was published, she was lunching in Cambridge, and told a startled undergraduate, "My baby was born this morning!" She wrote a second novel, as well as literary articles and some reminiscences of **William Makepeace Thackeray**, a distant cousin. Their large house at Eton was often full of literary folk. One of them, **A. C. Benson**, recorded and eventually published what he called *Cornishiana*. "In all disagreeable circumstances," she once said, "remember the three things which I always say to myself: I am an Englishwoman. I was born in wedlock. I am on dry land."

George Washington Cable (1844-1925) has been called "the first modern Southern writer", decades before **William Faulkner**. His work is deeply rooted in the southern United States and particularly New Orleans, where he lived for the first four decades of his life. He then moved to Massachusetts, where Arthur Conan Doyle visited him in Northampton during his 1894 American tour (and planted a maple tree in his garden). Cable fits awkwardly with any of the stereotypes of southern writing. His essays take a stand against racism: they "embody the spirit of reform and the New  South", says the *Encyclopedia of Southern Culture*. His fiction, beginning with *Old Creole Days* (1879) and *The Grandissimes* (1880), mixes romance with social criticism, and makes clear his belief that the decline of the Creole aristocracy was the result of its unjustified racial pride.

Constance Emily Kent, later **Emilie Kaye** (1844-1944), was a murderer and later a nurse. At the age of 16 she used a razor to kill her three-year-old half-brother, **Francis Kent**, apparently out of resentment at her father's second wife. The crime, at the family house in the village of Road, Wiltshire, became a *cause celèbre*, investigated by **Jonathan Whicher** of the recently established detective branch at Scotland Yard. Constance was a suspect, as were other family members, but no one was charged until Constance, having experienced a religious conversion, confessed the crime to a clergyman and came forward for trial in 1865. She was convicted, although much doubt about the details of the killing remained, and still remains. She served 20 years in prison, and on her release in 1885 emigrated to Australia. She changed her name, trained as a nurse in Melbourne, and worked in hospitals and other institutions, retiring in 1932 as matron of the Pierce Memorial Nurses' Home at East Maitland.

Francis J. Dickens (1844-1886) was the third son of novelist **Charles Dickens** (1812-1870), the author of *Oliver Twist*, *A Tale of Two Cities* and the rest, to whom Arthur Conan Doyle gives remarkably short shrift in *Through the Magic Door*. Francis served seven years with the Bengal Mounted Police and later joined Canada's North-West Mounted Police, which in 1873 was just being organized. He spent 12 years with the NWMP at posts in Canada's western territories. During the North West Rebellion of 1885, a brief uprising of Métis (mixed-race) people led by **Louis Riel**, Dickens was in charge of the defence of Fort Pitt, a trading post on the North Saskatchewan River. With the fort surrounded by a Cree force led by **Big Bear**, Dickens's police escaped to Battleford by the river; Big Bear kept the civilian occupants as hostages. In 1886 Dickens left the force for health reasons and quickly died. The NWMP became the Royal Canadian Mounted Police in 1920.

Friedrich Nietzsche (1844-1900) was the philosopher who coined the oxymoron "God is dead" and the word Superman (German "Übermensch", meaning not a hero in Metropolis but a being evolved past today's human beings). He is considered an important precursor of existentialism and post-modernism. He has also been suggested as a prototype of Professor Moriarty, apparently out of a vague sense of evil about him. Born in Prussia, he was a professor for a decade at Switzerland's University of Basel, but resigned because of life-long health problems. A dramatic mental breakdown followed in 1889. His best-known published work is the four-part *Also Sprach Zarathustra* ("Thus Spake Zarathustra", 1883-1891).

Gerard Manley Hopkins (1844-1889) was, as the *Oxford Companion to English Literature* puts it, "a poet of much originality and a skilful innovator in rhythm". Educated at Oxford (where he studied under **Walter Pater**), he joined the Roman Catholic Church in 1866 and became a Jesuit priest as well as a teacher of classics. Often suffering from depression, he wrote poems privately and painfully. None of his verse (important works include "The Wreck of the Deutschland" and sonnets such as "Pied Beauty") was published during his lifetime. Owen Dudley Edwards in *The Quest for Sherlock Holmes* says repeatedly that Arthur Conan Doyle, while a pupil at the Jesuit-run Stonyhurst College, did not meet Hopkins, who was at that time at St. Mary's Seminary nearby; but oh, if only he had!

Jerome Caminada (1844-1914) was *The Real Sherlock Holmes*, according to a 2014 book under that title by Angela Buckley. More reliably, he was a police officer in Manchester, Britain's second-largest city, from 1868 to 1899, and head of the Criminal Investigation Division there for the last two years of his career. He was credited with solutions to hundreds of cases, including the notorious Manchester Cab Murder of 1889, which involved chloral hydrate poisoning. His style was said to depend heavily on informants and his willingness to move through the underworld in one of his many disguises. Buckley identifies Caminada's Moriarty as police killer **Bob Horridge**, arrested in 1887 at the Liverpool docks. In 1895, while still active on the force, Caminada wrote *Twenty-Five Years of Detective Life*; a second volume followed after his retirement.

John Sholto Douglas, 9th **Marquess of Queensberry** (1844-1900), is known as the creator of the modern rules for boxing, and as the man who brought down *Oscar Wilde*. The Queensberry Rules, promulgated in 1867, grew out of his love for sport, which also emphasized (fox) hunting and (horse) racing. It was said that he cared more for his horses and dogs than for his relatives. He was infuriated by the relationship of his third son, Lord *Alfred Douglas*, with Wilde, and in February 1895 he conspicuously called Wilde a "somdomite". Multiple legal actions followed, leading to Wilde's imprisonment. The Marquess was an  active atheist but was reported to have converted to Christianity on his deathbed.

Karl Benz (1844-1929) was one of the inventors of the automobile, receiving a patent in 1886 for a three-wheeled car powered by petroleum. Shortly afterwards, his wife and partner **Bertha Benz**, née **Ringer**, drove the car more than 120 miles cross-country to visit her mother, drawing public attention and making discoveries about maintenance and possible improvements (she invented brake linings). Benz had studied mechanical engineering at Karlsruhe Polytechnic University, operated an iron foundry and machine shop, began designing two-stroke engines in 1879, and had a working automobile with an internal combusion engine by 1885. The Benz company, based at Mannheim, was the world's largest automobile manufacturer in 1900 (it survives as the Mercedes-Benz division of Daimler). A "huge 100-horse-power Benz car" is mentioned in "His Last Bow", set in 1914.

Muhammad Ahmad (1844-1885), known as "the **Mahdi**", was a messianic Muslim leader in the Sudan region in the last four years of his life. A descendant of the prophet Muhammad, he came from a family of boat-builders, but became a religious teacher and reformer. Religious movements were in vogue, including the austere sect of Wahhabism, and a leader was anticipated who would free Muslim lands from European domination. In June 1881 Muhammad announced that he was the man. Religious and then military strife followed, bringing the Mahdi into conflict with Egyptian and then British forces. The capital, Khartoum, fell in January 1885 with the death of British general *George Gordon*. Muhammad died a few months later and was succeeded by *Abdallahi ibn Muhammad*.

Sarah Bernhardt, born **Rosine Bernardt** (1844-1923), was raised in a convent and sent to the Paris Conservatoire at 16 to be trained as an actress. Her life as actor and courtesan in the 1860s has been suggested as a source for Irene Adler's career. By 1870 Bernhardt, based at the Odéon Theatre, "had reached the heights of her acting career," says Biography.com, "propelled in part by her quirky behavior both on and off the stage." Famously, that included sleeping in a coffin, which she said helped her understand her tragic roles. She formed her own acting company for a world tour in 1880, and opened her own Paris theatre in 1899. She continued performing into old age, not deterred even by the amputation of her right leg after a 1905 injury. Famous for her performance as Hamlet, she put it on film in 1900; she has a star on Hollywood's Walk of Fame.

Nikolai Rimsky-Korsakov (1844-1908) was one of a cluster of Russian composers (he was almost an exact contemporary of **Modest**

Mussorgsky) whose music was distinctively Russian as distinguished from European. In this respect they differ from **Peter Tchaikovsky**, who more successfully and deliberately bridged the gap. Rimsky-Korsakov's style, says Wikipedia, "employed Russian folk song and lore along with exotic harmonic, melodic and rhythmic elements in a practice known as musical orientalism, and eschewed traditional Western compositional methods." For some time he maintained parallel careers in music and the navy; in 1873 the position Inspector of Naval Bands was created for him. Personal and political conflicts dogged his life, but he left behind such major works as the symphonic poem "Scheherazade", many operas (one of which includes the famous "Flight of the Bumblebee"), and arrangements or adaptations of folk songs.

Pablo de Sarasate (1844-1908) was a violinist; he played "at the St. James's Hall this afternoon", says Sherlock Holmes in "The Red-Headed League", set probably in 1890. He was also a composer, many of his works being light and flashy arrangements of Spanish dances or other composers' themes, designed to show off the performer's skill. Sarasate began performing in childhood in Pamplona, and made his Paris debut in 1860. He toured the world almost continuously for the next three decades, although by 1890 he had mostly retired to Biarritz. His violin was a Stradivarius, presumably not the same one Holmes claimed to have bought for a pittance in the Tottenham Court Road.

Sir **John Hare**, born **John Fairs** (1844-1921), is mentioned in "A Scandal in Bohemia", as Watson observes that Holmes's disguise and demeanour as an elderly nonconformist clergyman "were such as Mr. John Hare alone could have equalled". A Yorkshireman, he came to London at 21 to act at the Prince of Wales's Theatre and then the St. James's; later he became a theatre manager and producer. Hare was "the greatest character actor of his day", says the *Encyclopaedia Britannica*, specializing in roles as old men and other character and comic parts. At the end of his career, in 1916, he made two films.

Richard D'Oyly Carte (1844-1901) operated theatres, hotels and other enterprises in London from the 1870s onward. He was the impresario behind the partnership of Sir *W. S. Gilbert* and Sir *Arthur Sullivan* in the "Savoy operas", performed at his Savoy Theatre (built 1881) by the D'Oyly Carte Opera Company. He composed light opera himself as a young man, and was leasing a theatre and producing operas by the time he was 30. His enterprises included touring operatic companies, a Royal English Opera House, the Savoy Hotel, Claridge's, and Simpson's-in-the-Strand restaurant, which Sherlock Holmes and Dr. Watson are twice reported to have patronized.

Umberto I (1844-1900) was the second King of Italy, succeeding his father, **Victor Emmanuel II**, who had advanced from being King of Sardinia to leading a more or less united Italy in 1861. The kingdom included not just the island of Sardinia but the region of Piedmont in what is now northwest Italy, and Umberto was born in Piedmont's capital, Turin. He fought for Sardinia in the wars against Austria that led to national unification, saw his father become King of Italy, and succeeded to that title when Victor Emmanuel died in 1878. He took Italy into the Triple Alliance with Austria-Hungary and Germany, an arrangement mentioned in the story "The Naval Treaty", and into colonial power in Somalia and Eritrea, though his imperial ambitions were dashed when Italian troops were defeated by Ethiopia in 1896. Generally popular with the Italian people, he survived two assassination attempts but succumbed to a third, when an anarchist, **Gaetano Bresci**, shot him in Monza, a town near Milan.

Urban Napoleon Stanger (1844?-1881?) was a baker from Kreutznach in western Germany, who came to Britain in 1870 and bought a house in Lever Street in east London, where he ran a successful bakery, catering especially to other German emigrés. He gave a part-time job to **Felix Stumm**, whose own bakery had been less successful. They were friends, but Stumm formed a closer relationship with the boss's wife, **Elisabeth Stanger**. One evening in November 1881, the two men and a couple of friends spent an evening at the pub; Stanger came home, went into his house, and was never seen again. Stumm took over the business. Friends and creditors grew suspicious, and Stumm was eventually charged with forgery and served ten years in prison. Stanger, or his body, was never found. It has been suggested that this case helped to inspire the creation of Sherlock Holmes in *A Study in Scarlet*, which involves "Stangerson" rather than Stanger and takes place also in 1881.

William Clark Russell (1844-1911) was the author of dozens of novels about adventures at sea — including, apparently, the one Watson was reading when the events of "The Five Orange Pips" began. Russell also wrote drama, history, short stories, and a great deal of journalism, much of it also about life on the ocean blue. He was born in New York and educated in England and France, but left school when he was 13 to go to sea. The life of a midshipman, as he described it later, with bad food, endless toil, and sexual abuse, makes one wonder about Holmes's "prescription" for the erring Jacky in "The Sussex Vampire". Broken in health, he left the merchant navy eight years later, and soon threw himself into writing. His first salt-water novel was *John Holdsworth, Chief Mate* (1875), and he quickly became successful and influential. He is credited with drawing public attention to the working conditions of merchant seaman and helping to get reforms enacted into law.

William Spooner (1844-1930) offered a toast to "our queer old dean" (rather than "our dear old Queen") and told a lazy student that he had "tasted two whole worms" — in short, he was the man who gave spoonerisms their name. He was warden (1903-1924) of New College, Oxford, the institution where he had been a student, a lecturer, and a fellow, teaching history, divinity (he was, like most Oxford dons of the period, a Church of England clergyman) and philosophy. He is reported to have been an albino, with "a head too large for his body" and a genial, hospitable nature. He served for a time as examining chaplain for the Archbishop of Canterbury, assessing would-be clergy. Spoilsport historians maintain that most of the spoonerisms attributed to him are apocryphal. ("Elementary, my weird dachshund." — *Tiffany French.*)

Wynne Edwin Baxter (1844-1920) "was," according to Wikipedia, "an English lawyer, translator, antiquarian and botanist, but is best known as the Coroner who conducted the inquests on most of the victims of the Whitechapel Murders of 1888 to 1891 including three of the victims of Jack the Ripper in 1888, as well as on *Joseph Merrick*, the 'Elephant Man'." Originally from Lewes, Sussex, he held a series of municipal offices in Sussex and in London. As a coroner he presided over investigations of many suspicious deaths in east London and elsewhere, and during World War I he held inquests on air raid victims as well as executed German spies.

Alexander III (1845-1894) was Czar (emperor) of Russia from the death of his father *Alexander II* in 1881. "He was highly conservative," says Wikipedia, "and reversed some of the liberal reforms of his father." Though known as a peacemaker, he believed in military strength, and continued to assert Russia's presence in Asia without going so far as to provoke British sensitivities over India. During his reign Russia's existing alliance with Germany lapsed and an alliance with France replaced it, setting up the "double league which makes a fair balance of military power" referred to in "The Second Stain". Alexander was married to Princess **Dagmar of Denmark**.

Edgar, Freiherr **von Cramm** (1845-1909), was head of one of Germany's noble families, whose name the King in "A Scandal in Bohemia" borrowed as an alias. "You may address me as the Count Von Kramm, a Bohemian nobleman," he says, using a different spelling of the surname, and promoting the Freiherr (Baron) to a higher rank. At least Edgar's mother was a Countess, **Mechtilde**, Gräfin **von Veltheim**. His father was **Adalbert Hildemar von Cramm**, who died in 1861, passing the title along to Edgar. There is also the little matter of the 300-mile distance from Prague, capital of Bohemia, to Isernhagen in Lower Saxony, where the von Cramm family is based. The clan has financed the village church (now under Lutheran auspices) since the year 1329; Edgar and his brother **Burchard von Cramm** each donated a stained-glass window during renovations in 1898.

Eugène Grasset (1845-1917) was an important influence on artists such as *Alphonse Mucha* who developed what became known as Art Nouveau. Born in Switzerland, he ended up in Paris by 1872, and like *William Morris* and other members of Britain's Arts and Crafts Movement, he designed everything from fabrics to jewellery, as well as stained glass windows for the cathedral at Orléans. A few years later he turned to book illustration and graphic design, particularly posters; by the early 1890s he had commissions from publishers of *Harper's* and other magazines in the United States, and at several art schools in Paris he taught a generation of new creators.

Fred Enock (1845-1911) was an important figure in entomology, remembered for his detailed drawings of insects as seen under the microscope. He grew up in the family business of optical equipment and microscope slides, headed by his uncle **Edmund Wheeler**, who had originally been an ironmonger but was later a "naturalist" based in London, selling prepared slides and lecturing in schools. Enock assisted at the shop in Holloway, north London, and emulated his uncle by lecturing, writing and making slides. In the fall of 1892 it was Enock who reported an "extraordinary abundance" of the mustard beetle across England that summer. He "was possibly the most famous mounter ever of whole insects prepared in a lifelike manner without pressure," says a web site devoted to scientific curiosities. "They command premium prices to this day, as in his own time." There could be whimsy in his work: an 1895 drawing of two ants under a powerful magnifying lens is titled "A Confidential Conversation". Enock's cousin, **Edmund Wheeler Jr.**, became a noted portrait photographer.

Ludwig II (1845-1886) was King of Bavaria — "the only true king of this century", according to poet **Paul Verlaine**, who admired his impractical fairy-tale castle at Neuschwanstein and his patronage of the arts. He was an enthusiast of *Richard Wagner*, subsidizing some of his opera productions and falling into fantasies of himself being the

legendary knight Parsifal. King from the age of 18, when his father **Maximilian II** died in 1864, he spent all available revenue on construction projects and artistic performances, took no interest in government affairs, and endured Bavaria's subjection to Prussia in the warfare that led to the creation of the Empire in 1871. He spent little time in the capital, Munich, preferring the countryside and his castles. Darkly handsome and deeply introverted, he had no known love affairs and was probably homosexual. For much of his life he slept all day and was awake through the darkness. When his debts reached 14 million marks, his ministers had had enough; they enlisted reports from four psychiatrists, declared him insane, and deposed him; he died the next day.

George I, formerly Prince **Vilhelm** (1845-1913), was King of "the Hellenes" (Greece) from 1863 to his death, although he was not Greek: he was Danish, son of the prince who would later become King *Chris-*

tian IX of Denmark. After Greece deposed King **Otto** in 1862, king-makers scoured Europe's royalty for a replacement, and Vilhelm was chosen at the age of 17. He took the job seriously, learning the language, touring the country, and inducing the national assembly to write a constitution providing universal (male) suffrage. Over a long reign he presided over growth and modernization for Greece, and the 1896 revival of the Olympic Games. He kept in close touch with royal relatives across Europe, mustering their support against domination by the Ottoman Empire, and married Grand Duchess **Olga Constantinovna** of Russia.

Henry Petty-Fitzmaurice, 5th Marquess of **Lansdowne** (1845-1827), succeeded to the family title, estates and wealth at the age of 21 and quickly went into public life. By 1869 he held a minor government office, by 1883 he was Under-Secretary of State for India, and in 1883 he was named the 5th Governor General of Canada. In that role he helped the country get through the **Louis Riel** rebellion of 1885, the scandal surrounding government contracts for the Canadian Pacific Railway, and potential conflicts with the United States. He left his Canadian post in 1888 and was named Viceroy of India, a position he held for six years. Lord Lansdowne was Secretary of State for Foreign Affairs 1900-1905, no doubt as a successor to Trelawney Hope of "The Second Stain".

John Campbell, Marquess of Lorne, 9th Duke of Argyll (1845-1914), was the husband of Princess *Louise Caroline*, a daughter of Queen *Victoria*. Wikipedia observes that "The pair shared a common love of the arts, but tended to live apart and never had children. Further, Campbell formed close friendships with men who were rumoured to be homosexually inclined." He served in Parliament from 1868 until, ten years later, he was named Governor General of Canada, the Queen's representative in that country. He served 1878-1883 in that role, and the viceregal couple  were unexpectedly popular, especially when they proved to be generous and informal hosts. The marquess (he did not suceed to the dukedom until 1900) encouraged the founding of the Royal Society of Canada, collected Native artifacts, and travelled widely in Canada. He is remembered as the author of the psalm paraphrase "Unto the hills around", a staple of Canadian hymnody.

Joseph M. Stoddart (1845-1921) was managing editor of *Lippincott's Monthly Magazine*, published in Philadelphia from 1868 to 1915. In 1889, his principal, ***Craige Lippincott***, sent him to London to establish a British edition of the magazine and to sign up British authors. He invited three promising writers to dinner at the Langham Hotel: ***Oscar Wilde***; **Thomas Patrick Gill**, a young Irish journalist and Member of Parliament; and Arthur Conan Doyle. Wilde and ACD were persuaded to write short novels for the magazine, producing *The Picture of Dorian Gray* and *The Sign of the Four* respectively. The 1889 arrangement was standard practice: in 1886 Stoddart had commissioned a "sensational" novella from American writer **Julian Hawthorne**, price $1,000. It was a breakthrough for ACD, but Stoddart was already acquainted with Wilde. A frequent presence among American men of letters, he had been a guest when Wilde visited **Walt Whitman** at the latter's home in Camden, New Jersey, in 1882.

Thomas John Barnardo (1845-1905) was an Irish-born physician who began working with street children in London about 1870 and developed a network of more than 100 homes for them, the forerunner of today's agency Barnardo's. The intent was to feed and educate both boys and girls and eventually find work for them. Thousands of the youngsters were sent to live in Canada and Australia; Holmes's Baker Street Irregulars, who disappear from the stories after the very early years, may have left England in this way. Memoirs and historians have revealed that some "home children" from Barnardo's and other agencies were the victims of cruelty and overwork in Canada, although others found good homes.

Mary Ann (Polly) Nichols, née **Walker** (1845-1888), was the first of the five victims whose murders are generally attributed to Jack the Ripper. She was found dead, and mutilated with several stab wounds, in Buck's Row (now Durward Street) in the Whitechapel area of London's east end. She had married **William Nichols** in 1864, and they had five children; the marriage disintegrated about 1881, possibly because of Mary Ann's drinking, and William stopped making weekly support payments in 1882 when he learned that she had become a prostitute. For the remaining years of her life she chiefly lived in a series of workhouses, but just before her death was living in a lodging-house in Spitalfields, where she shared a room with one other woman. Her roommate, **Emily Holland**, told the inquest that Nichols was "very clean".

Sir **John Thompson** (1845-1894) was Prime Minister of Canada, sadly best remembered for having died at Windsor Castle — he suffered a massive heart attack during lunch with Queen *Victoria*. A lawyer from Halifax, and a convert from his Methodist upbringing to Roman Catholicism at a time when that was no small thing, he served as an alderman, a Conservative member of the Nova Scotia legislature, attorney-general and then premier of the province (1882), and a judge of the provincial Supreme Court. In 1885 he was persuaded to come to Ottawa as federal Minister of Justice, but he was soon involved in all the major issues, from copyright to fisheries. After the death of Sir *John A. Macdonald*, the Prime Ministership went briefly to Sir **John Abbott** and then to Thompson, from December 1892 until his death.

Wilhelm Röntgen (1845-1923) was the first winner of the Nobel Prize in Physics (1901) for his research into X-rays. Born in Germany but brought up in the Netherlands, he became a lecturer at the University of Strasbourg in 1875 — an institution which at that time was in Germany, thanks to the transfer of Alsace-Lorraine after the Franco-Prussian War. He shortly moved to Giessen, and then to the University of Würzburg, where his initial work on X-rays took place in 1895 as a by-product of studies of "cathode rays" that are produced when electricity is passed through gases at very low pressure. He noticed that certain minerals gave off invisible radiation that similarly lit up the cathode ray tube, and gave them a name from X, the symbol for the unknown. His wife, **Anna Ludwig**, placed her hand in the way of the rays, and a picture with bones and her ring clearly visible became the first "röntgenogram" or X-ray scan. Röntgen made his final move, to the University of Munich, in 1900.

William Worthen Appleton (1845-1924) was president of D. Appleton & Co., the publishing house founded by his grandfather, at the time Arthur Conan Doyle visited the United States in 1894. The company published ACD's book of medical stories, *Round the Red Lamp*, that autumn, and several other books would follow, including a 13-volume Author's Edition in 1902. William Worthen's father, **William Henry Appleton** (1814-1899), was still involved in the company, as were several other family members. The first book to be published by Appleton's dated from 1831, and the monumental *American Cyclopaedia* from 1857. By the 1890s the firm's stable of authors included **Charles Dickens**, *Benjamin Disraeli*, Jef-

ferson Davis, and many educators and scientists. William Henry was the first president of the American Publishers' Copyright League, and William Worthen followed in those footsteps, being influential in getting the International Copyright Act of 1891 passed, much to the pleasure of authors such as ACD.

Abdallahi ibn Muhammad (1846-1899) was probably the Khalifa, or "caliph", whom Sherlock Holmes visited according to his account in "The Empty House". Abdallahi was appointed by *Muhammad Ahmad*, leader of the Sudan region, to be Khalifa, commanding troops against a British and Egyptian army and taking part in the 1884-1885 siege of Khartoum at which *Charles George Gordon* was killed. After Ahmed, "the Mahdi", died in 1885, Abdallahi succeeded him, enforcing military government and Sharia law in the region. Arthur Conan Doyle's thriller about Islamic terrorism, *The Tragedy of the Korosko*, reflects attitudes and events of this period. Britain recaptured the Sudan in the late 1890s, notably under the leadership of General *Herbert Kitchener*, and Abdallahi was caught and killed.

Anna Katharine Green (1846-1935) was the author of *The Leaven-worth Case*, considered to be the first American detective novel. Published in 1878, after the author decided to give up poetry and try something new, it is the story of a murder in a New York mansion, and introduces police detective Ebenezer Gryce. "Familiar conventions [such] as the body in the library, the wealthy man about to change his will, the locked room, the use of ballistics evidence, a coroner's inquest, a sketch of the scene of the crime, and a partially burned letter all appeared in this novel," says WomenOfMystery.net. Green wrote more than 20 subsequent mystery novels, though none was as successful as her first. **Agatha Christie** credited Green's influence with leading her to write detective stories, and it is reported that Arthur Conan Doyle wrote to Green at her home in Buffalo asking to meet her when he was touring America in 1894 (there is no evidence that they did meet).

Auguste Escoffier (1846-1935) was a French chef, but he made most of his reputation in London, in the kitchens of the Savoy Hotel 1890-1899, having come to England along with hotel manager **César Ritz** and maitre d'hotel **Louis Echenard** at the invitation of entrepreneur *Richard D'Oyly Carte*. Dismissed in 1898 (along with the other two) for massive embezzlement, he stayed in London to spend a further two decades at the rival Carlton Hotel. "I am the emperor of Germany," *Wilhelm II* supposedly told him, "but you are the emperor of chefs." His work covered the full range of French or "haute" cuisine — for example, he defined the five basic sauces — and his invention of Peach Melba in honour of *Nellie Melba* is no more than an incident. He wrote several books on cookery himself, notably *Le Guide Culinaire* (1903).

Charles Stewart Parnell (1846-1891) might have changed the history of Ireland if he had just stayed away from *Katharine O'Shea*. Instead, the scandal around their adultery ended his political career. Parnell grew up with a resentment of British domi-nance in Ireland, which dated from the 17th century. Elected to Parliament in 1875, he advocated reform of land ownership and, eventually, "Home Rule" for Ireland, a policy shared by Liberal prime minister *William Ewart Gladstone*. By 1884 Parnell was leader of the Irish National League, and survived a smear campaign aimed at weakening him. But his party split following the 1889 O'Shea divorce scandal, and Parnell's strenuous efforts to push his cause led to his early death. Irish Home Rule was approved only in 1914; independence for much of the country followed in 1922.

Carrie Nation, née **Moore** (1846-1911), was arrested some 30 times between 1900 and 1910 because of her attacks on saloons in Kansas and elsewhere. She used an axe to smash bottles of liquor, denouncing alcohol as immoral and often illegal. She paid her fines from the fees she received for lecturing, and from the sale of souvenir hatchets. She spoke out on other vices as well, opposing erotic art, tobacco and indecent fashions. Nation, whose first husband had been an alcoholic, founded a local chapter of the Women's Christian Temperance Union in 1889, and campaigned for national prohibition (not introduced in the United States until 1920). The issue of temperance was lively across the Atlantic as well, as indicated by the "blue ribbon" of a total abstainer mentioned in "The Cardboard Box"; Nation visited Britain to speak in music halls, to a mixed reception.

Edward Collard (1846-1892) joined the City of London Police (not to be confused with the Metropolitan Police) in 1868 and was an inspector at the time of the 1888 Jack the Ripper murders. He personally investigated the killing of *Catherine Eddowes* in Mitre Square, and gave evidence at the inquest about the body (still warm) and blood (still liquid). "A piece of cloth was found in Goulston-street, corresponding with the apron worn by the deceased," he told the coroner. He was chief inspector for the Bishopsgate division at the time of his death.

Craige Lippincott (1846-1911) was president for 25 years (1886-1911) of one of the world's largest publishing companies, J. B. Lippincott & Co., based in the world's seventh largest city, Philadelphia. He was the son of **Joshua Ballinger Lippincott**, who had founded the company in 1836, but incorporated it only in 1885, a year before his death. Originally a publisher of Bibles, Lippincott's had

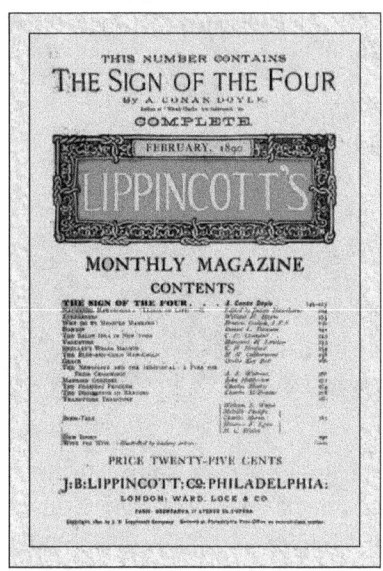

expanded into everything from textbooks to literature. *Lippincott's Magazine*, founded in 1868 and long edited by *J. M. Stoddart*, specialized in new fiction, including *The Sign of the Four* in February 1890. It was natural that when Arthur Conan Doyle visited Philadelphia in 1894, Lippincott should entertain him to dinner. "He was a man of great personal charm and youthful spirit, and had many friends," a biographer would write of Lippincott. "His favorite recreations were shooting and diving." Early one April morning in 1911, in his mansion in Rittenhouse Square, he shot himself dead.

Katharine O'Shea, née **Wood** (1846-1921) was the younger sister of Field-Marshal Sir *Evelyn Wood*, who won a Victoria Cross during the Indian Mutiny and was the commander 1889-1893 at the army base at Aldershot, which figures in "The Crooked Man". Katharine O'Shea married Captain **William O'Shea**, an Irish Member of Parliament, but began a long-running love affair with another MP, *Charles Stewart Parnell*, leader of the Irish Party, about 1880. William O'Shea challenged Parnell to a duel; scandal followed, and divorce in 1890. Katharine then married Parnell, whose career was already badly damaged, and Ireland's history significantly changed for lack of what he might have done. He died less than four months later. Unfriendly commentators called the lady "Kitty" for its improper connotation; she herself preferred "Katie".

Peter Carl (Karl Gustavovich) Fabergé (1846-1920) is best known as the maker of the "Fabergé eggs", jewelled creations commissioned for the ladies of the Russian Imperial family. A few such eggs, made between 1885 and the revolution of 1917, have disappeared, but 43 are still in existence. Before the sequence of eggs even began, however, the "House of Fabergé" had earned the title "Goldsmith by Special Appointment to the Imperial Crown" with impressive work in gold and gemstones, even including electric doorbells. The young Fabergé had been responsible for the family jewellery business since the age of 14, and took full charge in 1882 on the death of his father's master craftsman, **Hiskias Pendin**. Fabergé was particularly interested in the Tsar's collection of ancient and exotic objects at the Hermitage in St. Petersburg, and made some replicas as well as drawing inspiration for his original work.

Princess Helena Augusta, Princess Christian (1846-1923) was the fifth child of Queen *Victoria* and wife of a minor German royal, Prince **Christian of Schleswig-Holstein**. They married in 1866, and remained living in England, near Windsor Castle; the Prince was named an aide-de-camp to the Queen. Wikipedia sums up the Princess's public career: "Helena was the most active member of the royal family, carrying out an extensive programme of royal engagements at a time when royalty was not expected to appear often in public. She was also an active patron of charities, and was one of the founding members of the Red Cross. She was founding president of the Royal School of Needlework."

Samuel Dougal (1846-1903) was executed for what became known as the Moat Farm Murder — the climax of a career of seductions, forgeries, and two marriages that ended in the sudden deaths of his wives. The victim at Moat Farm, near Clavering, Essex, was Dougal's common-law wife, **Camille Holland**. She was shot in the head in May 1899, but her death did not come to public notice until 1903, after Dougal was accused of fraud in spending some of the considerable fortune Holland had brought to the relationship. Questions then arose about where Holland was, the police investigated, and in 1903 her body was found buried on the farm. Dougal was charged, convicted and hanged.

Sir **John Langman** (1846-1928) provided the funding for the field hospital that took Arthur Conan Doyle to South Africa for the first half of 1900. Langman had made a fortune in the jewellery business (some of it based on South African gems) and subsequent investments, and responded to public suggestions that private individuals should pay for services that were beyond the army medical corps. Langman, in partnership with **William Gibson**, had founded the Goldsmiths and Silversmiths Company (not a guild, in spite of its name) in Regent Street in 1880. ACD had met his son, **Archie Langman**, during his time enjoying the sporting life in Switzerland in 1894.

Whitcomb L. Judson (1846-1909) was the inventor of the zipper, or at least one of its inventors. An "automatic continuous clothing closure" had been patented as early as 1851 by **Elias Howe**, inventor of the sewing machine, and in 1893 Judson took the next step with his "clasp locker", essentially a chain of hooks and eyes to be used for buckling footwear. Judson, born in Chicago, had been a machinery salesman and inventor whose previous projects included a "pneumatic street railway" that never did work very well. To exploit his latest device he founded the Universal Fastener Company and showed off his invention at the 1893 World's Columbian Exposition. The next step was taken by **Gideon Sundback**, an engineer working for Judson's company, whose improved "separable fastener" with interlocking teeth was developed in 1913.

William "Buffalo Bill" Cody (1846-1917) was originally a frontiersman — soldier, scout during the Indian Wars, Pony Express rider, stagecoach driver, if his own stories were to be believed — and then a performer for sophisticated audiences in America and Europe. His career in the west reached a climax in 1868 with a bison hunting competition against another frontiersman, **Medicine Bill Comstock**, which Cody easily won. In 1872 he first joined a "wild west show" in Chicago; in 1883 he organized his own touring show. By 1893 it was Buffalo Bill's Wild West and Congress of Rough Riders of the World, which sometimes included celebrities such as *Annie Oakley* and *Sitting Bull*. The show toured Britain for several months in 1887 (with a command performance for Queen *Victoria*) and several times thereafter.

Alexander Graham Bell (1847-1922) was the principal inventor of the telephone, securing an American patent in 1876. It was in widespread use before the turn of the 20th century, and is mentioned in six Sherlock Holmes tales (including *The Sign of the Four*, set probably in 1888). Born in Scotland, working in England, Canada and the United

States on speech, hearing and electricity, he had hopes of developing technology to eradicate deafness. Research in Boston and Ontario led to an "acoustic telegraph". Bell and inventor **Elisha Gray** filed for patents on the same day. Historians still dispute their respective contributions to the modern telephone, but the Bell Telephone Company (represented by the modern AT&T and Bell Canada) brought telephones to market. In later years Bell did research in many fields, including aircraft and alternative fuels.

Annie Besant, née **Woods** (1847-1933), married a clergyman when she was 20, but they separated as she realized she did not believe in religion. Instead she joined the National Secular Society ("free thought") and later the Fabian Society (socialism). She and *Charles Bradlaugh* became editors of the weekly *National Reformer*, presenting many advanced views — they were charged with obscenity after it discussed contraception. Subsequently she moved on from social reform to Theosophy, the spiritual movement led by *Helena Blavatsky* and others. When she travelled to  India to explore the roots of Theosophy, she became involved in the Indian independence movement. In the 1920s she visited the United States with **Jiddu Krishnamurti**, a boy she had adopted and was presenting as the new World Teacher.

Archibald Primrose, 5th Earl of **Rosebery** (1847-1929), was one of the many noblemen who used their automatic membership in the House of Lords as an opportunity for serious involvement in politics and statesmanship. A graduate of Eton College and Christ Church, Oxford, he was twice a cabinet minister in the Liberal government of *William Ewart Gladstone*, and became the first chairman of the London County Council when it was created in 1889. When Gladstone retired in 1894, Queen *Victoria* chose Rosebery as the new Prime Minister, he being the least objectionable of the available Liberal leaders. His time in office was not a success, with the Conservative-dominated House of Lords unwilling to enact Liberal policies, and he resigned in little more than a year. A rare book collector and horse-racing enthusiast, he is thought to have been the wealthiest Prime Minister ever.

Arthur Kinnaird, 11th Baron **Kinnaird** (1847-1923), was a football player and a bank director, and a member of the House of Lords after his father's death in 1887. He graduated from Cambridge in 1869, and within a year was a director of the family bank; it merged with others in 1896 to become Barclays Bank, and he served as a director of that firm for the rest of his life. Meanwhile, he played football (soccer), mostly for the Old Etonians (alumni of Eton College, his school) but also for an elite amateur team, the Wanderers. Considered the greatest player of his era, he appeared in the Football Association Cup Final nine times. He was elected to the FA's governing committee before he left Cambridge, and was its president from 1890 to his death, standing up for football as an amateur sport even while professionalism took hold. He also served as national president of the YMCA and YWCA, served on boards of other non-profit organizations, and himself taught in the "ragged schools" organized by charitable groups in London's slums.

Bram Stoker (1847-1912) was the author of *Dracula*, the 1897 novel that defined most of what was common knowledge about vampires from that date until 2005. He may have based some of the novel on eastern European tales told by traveller and author ***Arminius Vámbéry***. The very title of "The Sussex Vampire" must have brought *Dracula* to mind for potential readers. Born in Dublin, Stoker worked as a civil servant and a theatre reviewer before going to work for actor and impresario ***Henry Irving*** as manager of the Lyceum Theatre (mentioned in *The Sign of the Four*) in 1878. His theatrical duties led him to help Irving buy the rights to Arthur Conan Doyle's one-act play "A Story of Waterloo" and produce it in 1894. While working for Irving until the latter's death in 1905, Stoker wrote and published short stories and nearly 20 novels including *The Lair of the White Worm* (1911). His wife was **Florence Balcombe**, whom ***Oscar Wilde*** had unsuccessfully wooed.

Charles Frederic Moberly Bell (1847-1911) was manager of *The Times* from 1890 to his death, bringing it up from a low ebb in its reputation to make it Britain's leading national paper. It is mentioned in half a dozen Sherlock Holmes stories. British, but born in Egypt, Bell was Alexandria correspondent for the paper when invited to return to London and take charge. He founded the *Times Literary Supplement* and brought the *Encyclopaedia Britannica* under the newspaper's auspices. Says the *EB* now: "His strong will, courage, and industry enabled him to keep the paper alive." By 1908 he had *The Times* in such condition that *Alfred Harmsworth*, Lord *Northcliffe*, was prepared to buy it.

Charlotte 'Lotta' Crabtree (1847-1924) was a hugely popular singer and actor, from her days as a child star in California, where was said to have been mentored by *Lola Montez*, to an adult career in which she was known as "the Nation's Darling". She was the highest paid performer in the United States in the 1880s, investing widely and also making large charitable donations, some of them for the building of community fountains. "While Lotta apparently had her share of romance," says Wikipedia, "her travel, lifestyle and mother made a long-term relationship difficult, and she never married."

Dame **Ellen Terry** (1847-1928) played Portia, Juliet, Lady Macbeth and the other great roles at London's Lyceum Theatre during a 24-year partnership with Sir *Henry Irving*. The relationship, close personally as well as on stage, stretched from 1878 to 1902. As a child she had acted in the company of **Charles Kean**; later she lived with architect and theatrical designer **Edward Godwin**, and performed for a season at the Court Theatre. After the years providing glamour for Irving's productions, both in London and on world tours, she acted with *Herbert Beerbohm Tree* and formed a close relationship with *George Bernard Shaw*. Shaw wrote parts in several of her plays specifically for her, and the two carried on a long intimate correspondence. Late in life she made several silent films, including "Pillars of Society" (1920), based on a play by *Henrik Ibsen*.

Edmund Gurney (1847-1888) "was the first 'full-time' psychical researcher in history," according to an article in the journal *Medical History*. "While he was primarily concerned with empirical evidence for telepathy, Gurney significantly contributed to the late nineteenth-century literature on hallucinations in the sane, and the psychology of hypnotism and dissociation." Originally his field of study had been music (his 1881 book *The Power of Sound* is still an important work in music theory), but in the last half-dozen years of his life he concentrated on hypnotism and related topics, including the phenomena that might explain the belief in witchcraft. He was a co-founder of the Society for Psychical Research (1883) along with *Frederic Myers* and **Henry Sidgwick**.

George Grossmith (1847-1912) was a funny man, the actor who played the comic leads in several **Gilbert** and **Sullivan** operettas including Major-General Stanley in "The Pirates of Penzance" and Ko-Ko in "The Mikado". He also performed privately, and wrote hundreds of comic songs as well as entertaining material for print. He and his brother **Weedon Grossmith** jointly created the 1892 novel *The Diary of a Nobody*, which brilliantly portrays middle-class suburban life. He was a life-long Londoner; his father, also **George Grossmith**, was a reporter for *The Times* at the Bow Street magistrates' court, and the younger George began his career doing similar work. He told an interviewer in 1888 that he had "experience of all classes of society, from the penny reading to the duchess's drawing room.... My entertainments last about an hour and a half, and my fee is fifteen guineas."

Hans Gross (1847-1915) was the leading expert on criminal investigation in Austria, and perhaps in Europe, though he is not mentioned anywhere in the Sherlock Holmes stories beside such continental figures as "Monsieur Dubugue of the Paris police, and Fritz von Waldbaum, the well-known specialist of Dantzig" ("The Naval Treaty"). Gross graduated as a lawyer in 1869 and worked as a magistrate and a professor of criminal law in a series of universities. His 1893 *Handbuch für Untersuchungsrichter* ("Handbook for Examining Magistrates") went through multiple editions and was published in English (1907) as *Criminal Investigation*. It coined the word "criminalistics" and deals with topics ranging from interrogation to crime scene photography — and can be seen as the prototype of Holmes's *The Whole Art of Detection*. Gross also founded and edited a journal of criminology, and established an institute of criminology at the University of Graz.

Henry Fitzalan-Howard, 15th Duke of **Norfolk** (1847-1917), was the highest-ranking duke in the British peerage, not to mention Earl Marshal of England, from his father's death in 1860 to his own death 57 years later. The title dates from 1483, and the family has traditionally been Roman Catholic, which led to bloodshed in the 16th century and some tension even in Victorian times. The 15th Duke served in government briefly (postmaster-general 1895-1900) but is better known as a philanthropist, especially supporting Catholic causes in an era when churches, colleges and other institutions were still being built up. He served as Lord Mayor of Sheffield, mayor of the Metropolitan Borough of Westminster when it was created in 1900, and Lord Lieutenant of Sussex. As Earl Marshal, he was responsible for organizing state ceremonies, though not Queen *Victoria*'s Golden and Diamond Jubilees.

Jesse James (1847-1882) was an outlaw who died at the hands of another outlaw, **Robert Ford**, labelled a coward by an enduring folk song. Tradition also makes James a hero, who somehow robbed the rich for the benefit of the poor. In fact he and his gang kept the money they stole from banks and trains from 1866 to 1882, though the gang was weakened after the loss of several members in a disastrous heist in Minnesota in 1876. "Scholars place him in the context of regional insurgencies of ex-Confederates following the American Civil War," says Wikipedia. Raised in Missouri, where his career of crime began, he made no secret of his Confederate loyalties, and often targeted banks and railroads associated with Republican (northern, anti-slavery) interests. In many of his robberies he was accompanied by his brother **Frank James**.

John Watson (1847-1939) was Canada's leading 19th-century philosopher, and a professor at Queen's University, Kingston, from 1872 to 1924. He came to Canada immediately after his graduation from the University of Glasgow to be professor of "logic, metaphysics, and ethics", and impressed students to the point that philosophy became the most popular major in the university. According to a biography on the Queen's web site, he was "the last of the great Christian idealists", and the first philosopher in Canada to achieve an international reputation. He wrote eight books and some 200 articles, and his liberal theology is said to have had a significant influence on the formation of the United Church of Canada in 1925. For 23 years he held the mostly honorary position of vice-principal of Queen's.

Millicent Fawcett, née **Garrett** (1847-1929), was president of the National Union of Women's Suffrage Societies, the largest organization pressing for women's right to vote in Britain, from 1890 until partial victory was achieved almost thirty years later. The NUWSS disavowed the sometimes violent tactics used by some suffragist groups, such as the movement led by *Emmeline Pankhurst*, and relied on political pressure, looking to the Liberal Party and then the new Labour Party. She and her husband, **Henry Fawcett**, himself a Member of Parliament until his death in 1884, also took an interest in other social issues; Millicent was the founder of Newnham College, Cambridge, and visited South Africa in 1901 to investigate British atrocities against civilians during the war there. The Representation of the People Act 1918 gave many women the right to vote, and the NUWSS dissolved after that success. Her sister was physician *Elizabeth Garrett Anderson*.

Paul von Hindenburg (1847-1934) was president of Germany in the era leading up to **Adolf Hitler**'s rule, but had previously been prominent as a military leader. The zeppelin *Hindenburg*, which exploded in 1937 on its 18th transAtlantic trip, was named in his memory. Born in a section of Prussia that is now in Poland, he attended military schools, entered the army in 1866, served in the Franco-Prussian War of 1870-1871, and retired in 1911 as a general. He was recalled to service when World War I began, and in 1916 was named chief of the general staff, a role in which he was in fact Germany's most powerful leader. He retired again at war's end, but was elected president of the country in 1925.

Sir **Ray Lankester** (1847-1929) was a zoologist and anthropologist whose important discoveries included traces of human settlement in Suffolk, on the east coast of England, 3 to 5 million years ago. He also identified parasites in blood — a major step towards explaining and treating such diseases as malaria — and did research in embryology that helped to confirm the theory of evolution by natural selection. He held a series of senior positions in the scientific world, including professorships at University College, London, and then at Oxford, and was superintendent of the Natural History Museum in London 1898-1907. Throughout his career he devoted atten-  tion to exposing fraudulent Spiritualist mediums, but Arthur Conan Doyle was grateful to him for scientific ideas that helped him develop his novel *The Lost World*.

Thomas Alva Edison (1847-1931) was, famously, the inventor of the light bulb (1879). His name finds its way into *The Hound of the Baskervilles* as Sir Henry promises to have Baskerville Hall wired for electricity, including "a thousand candle-power Swan and Edison right here in front of the hall door". The Edison and Swan United Electric Company was a court-ordered partnership of Edison, the American, with British inventor Sir *Joseph Swan*, who had patented essentially the same bulb in 1878. Edison can also be given credit for inventing the infrastructure of electrical distribution, such as plugs and switches; the phonograph (sound recording); the movie projector; and the stock ticker. An entrepreneur from childhood, he worked briefly as a telegraph operator, then in 1870 set up a laboratory in New Jersey and devoted himself full-time to inventing. The company he founded in 1880 became the General Electric Corporation, which maintained a rivalry with *Nikola Tesla* and his partner, **George Westinghouse**.

Annie Frost (1848-?) was a fraudster whose trial at the Old Bailey in October 1888 was a lively distraction from the Jack the Ripper murders. She was variously known as Mrs. **Gordon Baillie**, the Countess of **Moray** (a distinguished Scots title), and, to the police who tried to trace her, "Scotch Ellen". Apparently born in Peterhead, she had a record in all the cities of Scotland, in Rome and Paris, in Melbourne (where she spoke of acquiring a vast tract of land to help resettle Scotland's miserable displaced crofters), in Bristol and in London. **John Stuart Blackie**, professor at the University of Edinburgh, said she had tricked him out of a guinea; she lived for a time at the expense of Sir **Richard Duckworth-King**. In 1888 she appeared at the Old Bailey dressed in black silk, with a bouquet of roses on her lap, and accompanied by **Robert Percival Frost**, possibly her husband, as a tailor, a butcher, a bookseller, a dressmaker, a coal dealer and others testified about unpaid bills. Annie Frost was sentenced to five years in prison. By 1894 she was free again, defrauding a London picture dealer; as late as 1912 she served time in New York.

Arthur James Balfour, Earl of **Balfour** (1848-1930), was prime minister of Britain 1902-05, and so could be the original of the prime minister seen in "The Mazarin Stone". From a wealthy landowning family, and often characterised as aloof, he entered Parliament in 1874 as a Conservative, became private secretary to his uncle Lord *Salisbury*, and in 1886 entered the Cabinet. He took the premiership on Salisbury's resignation. Major issues during his term as prime minister included Irish Home Rule and the reform of tariffs, which weakened the Conservatives and drove Balfour from office. He was succeeded by Liberal *Henry Campbell-Bannerman.* During World War I he served a term as foreign secretary and was responsible for the Balfour Declaration promising a Jewish homeland in Palestine.

Louisa Parr, née **Taylor** (1848-1903), was the author of several novels, some of them published under the pseudonym Mrs. **Olinthus Lobb**. "Her books were written with style and humour that dealt pointedly with the oppression of women," says Wikipedia. Parr's most important book, *Adam and Eve* (1880), tells the story of a smuggler in

Cornwall and his cousin in London. The *English Dialect Dictionary*, compiled by **Joseph Wright** at the turn of the 20th century, apparently relied on this novel for examples of Cornish dialect — not to be confused with the Cornish language itself, which is entirely distinct from English and was, according to Sherlock Holmes, possibly akin to the Chaldean ("The Devil's Foot").

Grant Allen (1848-1899) was the Canadian-born author of articles and journalism on science and other subjects, as well as some thirty novels, the most famous being *The Woman Who Did* (1895). This book shocked many readers with its depiction of a woman who, protesting the unfairness of conventional marriage, had a child with her lover. In a series of detective tales, Allen created the amusing villain Colonel Clay. Allen was a friend of Arthur Conan Doyle, and persuaded him to move to the healthy climate of Hindhead, Surrey, in 1895. Later he asked ACD to write the final chapters of the novel *Hilda Wade*, then being serialized, when he realized he would not live to complete it.

Matthew Webb (1848-1883) was an accomplished sailor, becoming a Cunard Line officer, and a strong athlete. In 1875 he became the first person to swim the 21-mile width of the English Channel, from Dover to Calais, using the old-fashioned breast stroke and battling currents and jellyfish. As a national hero he made a fortune from allowing his picture to appear on souvenirs and matchboxes. He also received a gold medal from the Royal Humane Society for an incident in which he jumped from a steamer in mid-Atlantic attempting to rescue a sailor who had fallen overboard. In 1883, looking for a new stunt to build his reputation, "Captain Webb" declared that he would swim across the rapids below Niagara Falls. On the appointed afternoon, crowds watched as he walked from the Clifton House Hotel on the Canadian side of the river to a small boat and then, clad in a red swimsuit, stepped into the water. He could be seen for some time, but then spectators lost sight of him; his body was found four days later downstream at Lewiston.

Princess **Louise Caroline Alberta** (1848-1939), later Marchioness of **Lorne** and Duchess of **Argyll**, was the sixth child of Queen *Victoria* and the Prince Consort, *Albert*. She was artistically talented (and spent some time at the National Art Training School) and known for feminist and liberal ideas, and found herself bored at court despite her role for a time as the Queen's secretary. She was also acknowledged as a beauty, and was sometimes the subject of gossip. Eventually she fell in love with **John Campbell**, Marquess of **Lorne** and future Duke of **Argyll**, and they were married in 1871. The Marquess served as Governor General of Canada, 1878-1883, and the Marchioness was an energetic hostess as well as a patron of the arts. On her return to Britain she settled at Kensington Palace, living there the remaining 56 years of her life, only sometimes with her husband.

Melville E. **Stone** (1848-1929) was a Chicago newspaperman who became general manager of the Associated Press. He began as a reporter, founded the Chicago *Daily News* in 1876 and the *Morning News* in 1881, and headed the Associated Press from 1893 to 1921. The AP, as reorganized in that year, was the successor to the Western Associated Press, established in 1862 as a rival to a New York-based agency also called the Associated Press. Stone built its reputation for speed, accuracy and integrity and its central role in US news-gathering, and his name provided the nickname the AP enjoyed in the buccaneering days of American journalism: "Rocks". Tradition says that Stone invented the idea of having stores price items at 99 cents rather than $1, in the hope that the leftover penny would be used to purchase the *Daily News*, but as Wikipedia gently puts it, "there is some doubt as to its veracity." He was among local luminaries who entertained Arthur Conan Doyle when he visited Chicago in 1894.

Sir **Thomas Lipton**, 1st Baronet (1848-1931), was a rich man because of the tea trade, but his chief love was boats. As a teenager he held a series of jobs in Glasgow, New York and elsewhere, finally discovering the grocery business and bringing American get-up-and-go attitudes to Scotland. By 1882 he had shops in five cities and was known for brash advertising stunts, such as having pigs driven through the streets on their way to become bacon. He believed in buying direct from the farmers and producers, and extended this policy to tea, eventually owning plantations in Ceylon (Sri Lanka) to produce tea for his 300 shops and, soon, for other retailers — a trade that made him a multi-millionaire. In 1898 he turned his empire, including retailing, farming, baking, and Omaha stockyards, into a limited company. For recreation he sailed, often being seen in the Clyde near Glasgow, and entering the America's Cup race five times. He moved in high society, entertaining lavishly on his steam yacht *Erin*, and was known as a patron of sport and a philanthropist.

Sir **William Gordon-Cumming** (1848-1930), served as an officer in the Scots Guards in South Africa, Egypt and the Sudan, and hunted tigers in India. He was a friend of the Prince of Wales (later *Edward VII*) and did not lack for female company, often entertaining married women at his Harriet Street house in London's Belgravia. But his position in high society vanished after a scandal (not involving, as in "The Five Orange Pips", the Tankerville Club). In September 1890, Gordon-Cumming, the Prince, and others were guests at a house party at Tranby Croft, Yorkshire, and Gordon-Cumming was accused of cheating at baccarat. The matter was to be hushed up, but when rumours spread anyway, Gordon-Cumming filed suit for slander. He lost, was dismissed from the army, resigned from his clubs, and once commented that none of his friends had ever spoken to him again.

> *War Office, Pall Mall,*
> *12th June,* 1891.
>
> *Scots Guards,* Major and Lieutenant-Colonel Sir William G. Gordon-Cumming, Bart., is removed from the Army, Her Majesty having no further occasion for his services. Dated 10th June, 1891.

Wyatt Earp (1848-1929) was one of the stereotypical figures of the American west: gambler, deputy sheriff, buffalo hunter, pimp, and much more, and most famously participant in the "Shootout at the OK Corral" in Tombstone, Arizona, in 1881. As a young man he spent several years in Kansas frontier towns where cattle by the million were loaded onto railways on the way to slaughterhouses. Tombstone was a similarly bustling place in the middle of a silver boom; Earp's brother **Virgil Earp** was a United States marshal there, and he became a deputy sheriff. The notorious gunfight was a 30-second battle with a gang of thugs, in which three men died. Earp later followed the action to Idaho (gold), San Diego (real estate), Alaska (gold), and Nevada (more gold), with mining claims, race horses, and saloons marking his path. At the end of his life, living in Los Angeles, he was a consultant on cowboy movies.

William Wynn Westcott (1848-1925) was a physician, born in Warwickshire and educated at University College, London, who moved on from the Freemasons to become a leader of several occultist organizations. He joined the Societas Rosicruciana in Anglia (that is, the Rosicrucians) in 1880, later becoming its head; in 1887 he was one of the founders of the Hermetic Order of the Golden Dawn. He also founded a branch of the Theosophical Society. A decade later, he disavowed the Golden Dawn after suggestions that such involvement was not consistent with his day job as Coroner for the North-East district of London (1880-1910); however, he continued to head the Rosicrucians and to participate in other occult groups. He was the author of such books as *The Occult Power of Numbers* and *An Introduction to the Study of the Kabalah.*

W. G. (William Gilbert) Grace (1848-1915) was by general agreement the greatest cricket player of the 19th century, and remains a legend in the sport. For some time he held the record for the highest individual score in a match: 344 runs, achieved in 1876 when he played for the Marylebone Cricket Club. (The current record is 501.) Over his career, 1865-1908, he scored 124 "centuries" (100 runs in a match) in first-class cricket. A giant with a great black beard, he was a physician and nominally an amateur, but actually derived a fine income from playing the game, often in one-time guest appearances. He played at various positions, and was a successful bowler with a style that was old-fashioned even at the time. It was one of Arthur Conan Doyle's boasts that he had bowled Grace (struck him out) in a match in August 1900.

W. H. J. Boot (1848-1918) was an artist in oils and watercolours, who exhibited at the Royal Academy — a considerable distinction — from 1874 to 1884. He was also the author of the 1883 book *Trees and How to Paint Them in Watercolours*, and the art editor of the *Strand* magazine at the time (1891) when its success was just beginning. Russell Miller records in his biography of Arthur Conan Doyle that Boot, himself an experienced illustrator, "decided to commission **Walter Paget**, who had illustrated *Treasure Island* and *Robinson Crusoe*, to portray Holmes in pen and ink, but the project was passed in error to Walter's lesser known brother, **Sidney,** also a commercial artist. One story has it that Boot wrote to Sidney because he had forgotten Walter's first name;

another that Sidney opened Boot's letter because it was addressed to 'Mr Paget the illustrator'."

Ivan **Pavlov** (1849-1936) is best known for making dogs salivate, but his 1904 Nobel Prize was awarded "in recognition of his work on the physiology of digestion". By inserting what amounted to windows in the body, he was able to do research that explained the role of the nervous system in controlling the digestive process, including salivation. At a medical congress in 1903 he presented a landmark paper on conditioned reflexes as the producer of physical reactions. He spent most of his career at the Institute of Experimental Medicine in Leningrad (St. Petersburg), and was praised and funded by Russia's Communist government after the 1917 revolution, though he was openly contemptuous of its social policies.

James Whitcomb Riley (1849-1916) was already a highly successful poet when Arthur Conan Doyle, visiting his home town of Indianapolis in 1894, spent several hours talking, eating and perhaps drinking with him, some of it apparently in a rumpled hotel room. Riley's earliest poems were advertisements (he worked as a sign-painter for a time) and submissions to newspapers, but by about 1882 he was making money from selling poems and giving readings. Eventually his work made him wealthy, despite his widely recognized alcoholism. "Full of sentiment and traditional in form," says PoetryFoundation.org, "his work features rustic subjects who speak in a homely, countrified dialect." There is dispute about how authentic that dialect is, but he is recognized as "the Poet of Indiana".

Lord **Randolph Churchill** (1849-1895) was a younger son of the **7th Duke of Marlborough**, the husband of *Jennie Churchill*, and the father of Sir *Winston Churchill* — and, as well, an active figure in the politics of the 1880s. Elected to Parliament in 1874, he came to prominence within a few years as a leader of what were dubbed Independent Conservatives, calling the Conservative Party leadership (headed by *Benjamin Disraeli* and the *Marquess of Salisbury*) to account just as much as the ruling Liberals. Not temperate in his language, he called *William Ewart Gladstone* "the Moloch of Midlothian" at one point, and had no patience with the idea of Irish home rule. His "democratic Toryism" was in fashion by 1884, and he served successively as Secretary of State for India and Chancellor of the Exchequer.

Martha Tabram, née **White**, also called **Turner** (1849-1888), was stabbed to death late one night in August 1888, possibly a victim of the killer known as Jack the Ripper. She had been drinking with another prostitute, **'Pearly' Poll Connolly**, and a couple of soldiers in the White Swan in Whitechapel Road, and the two women had each gone off with one of the men. Her body was found, with 39 stab wounds, in the nearby George Yard Buildings early the following morning. Police, believing that she had been killed with a bayonet, held a series of identity parades to find the soldier who had been with her, but with no success. Martha White married **Henry Tabram**, a warehouse foreman, in 1869, and they had two sons; the couple separated in 1875, apparently because of Martha's drinking. She subsequently lived from time to time with **Henry Turner**, a carpenter, but was living on her own at a lodging-house in the weeks before her death.

William T. Stead (1849-1912) was a crusading journalist who considered newspapering a calling from God: "I felt the sacredness of the power placed in my hands," he once wrote about his first editorship, at the Darlington *Northern Echo* when he was just 22. He made that local paper a national voice, then brought his New Journalism to London as assistant editor of the *Pall Mall Gazette*, then its editor 1883-1889. Famously, in order to expose the evils of white slavery and child prostitution, he actually arranged the purchase of a thirteen-year-old girl, subsequently reporting on the events in a series titled "The  Maiden Tribute of Modern Babylon". He was the founder of the *Review of Reviews* (1890) and in later life he became an exponent of Spiritualism. He died in the sinking of RMS *Titanic*.

Peter F. Collier (1849-1909) was the founder of the Collier publishing house and *Collier's Weekly*, which was one of the leading titles during the American golden age of magazines. Born in Ireland, he came to Ohio as a youth, entered the printing business, and began publishing material first for Roman Catholic audiences and then for the general public. The magazine began in 1888 and took the *Collier's Weekly* name in 1895; the founder's son, **Robert J. Collier**, managed it after 1898. The stories of *The Return of Sherlock Holmes* (1903-05) and a few later Holmes tales made their first American appearance in *Collier's*, with classic illustrations by ***Frederic Dorr Steele***.

Sarat Chanda Das (1849-1917) was a teacher in Darjeeling, in the mountains of eastern India, who made two trips to Tibet for an apparent mixture of reasons. The first expedition lasted about six months (the latter half of 1879) and the second more than a year, from late 1881 to early 1883. Das brought back a sizeable collection of Tibetan and Sanskrit texts that were the basis for later research and writing, including *The Doctrine of Transmigration* (1893) and a Tibetan-English dictionary (1902). However, it became clear after the trips that he was also working as a British spy, collecting information about Tibet and the surrounding areas in a time when the "great game" pitted Britain against Russia for control of Tibet and India itself. He later had connections in the complex world of esoteric philosophies and new cults, and entertained visitors at Darjeeling including *Helena Blavatsky*.

Sir **Edmund Barton** (1849-1920) was the first Prime Minister of Australia when that colony became a self-governing, if not entirely independent, nation in 1901. (It thus acquired the same status, sometimes called "dominion", that Canada had had since 1867.) He was born in New South Wales, one of the six states that would federate to make up Australia, and served in its legislature from 1879, meanwhile working as a lawyer. He was involved in preparing a constitution for the new Commonwealth of Australia during the self-government campaign of the 1890s, and was asked to form a caretaker government leading up to the first federal election, held in March 1901. At that time he was elected to the new Parliament and his Protectionist Party formed a government. Barton resigned in 1903 to become a judge of Australia's new High Court.

Vera **Zassoulich** (1849-1919) was a young clerk in St. Petersburg when she got involved in radical politics as the Tsarist government of Russia tottered towards its end. "I could imagine no greater pleasure than serving the revolution," she said after being befriended by **Sergei Nechayev**, the co-author of *Catechism of a Revolutionist*. She was well-read, and threw herself into programs to educate workers, as well as herself working in a weaving collective. In 1877 the news broke that *Dmitri Feodorovich Trepoff*, the city's governor, had ordered a brutal flogging for one of his political prisoners, **Alexei Bogoliubov**. She went to Trepoff's office, shot him (not fatally, it turned out), and was arrested, but the jury was so impressed with her bearing, and what she had to say about police abuses, that it acquitted her. For the rest of her life she was involved in various political factions, notably the Mensheviks after the 1903 split between **Vladimir Lenin** and **Jules Martov**.

Sir **William Osler** (1849-1919) was a Canadian physician and pioneer of medical education, and is considered the founder of the internship system, under which young doctors learn by working directly with patients. He graduated from McGill University, taught at its medical school and then at the University of Pennsylvania, in 1889 became physician-in-chief of the new Johns Hopkins Hospital in Baltimore, and in 1905 went to Oxford as Regius professor of medicine. Osler was a keen collector of books, especially about the history of medicine. He received his baronetcy in the same honours list (1911) in which Arthur Conan Doyle was knighted.

Edward Smith (1850-1912) trained in the Royal Naval Reserve and then went to work as an officer for the White Star Line, which was noted for its fast (and, increasingly, luxurious) service on the North Atlantic route. He advanced to command a succession of ships, starting with SS *Republic* (1887). He was well known to passengers who expected the best, and was referred to as "the millionaires' captain". He was captain on the 1911 maiden voyage of RMS *Olympic* — the largest ship in the world, built as part of president ***Bruce Ismay***'s program to see White Star catch up with its rival, the Cunard Line. In April 1912 he was captain of RMS *Titanic* on its ill-fated voyage. As the ship took on water after striking an iceberg in the North Atlantic, Smith supervised the evacuation, released crew members from their duties, and was last seen entering the bridge alone, ten minutes before the sinking. His body was not recovered.

Aghornath Chattopadhyaya (1850-1915) was the first person from India to earn a doctorate in science. Born in a village in what is now Bangladesh, he was educated in Dacca and Calcutta, then went to the University of Edinburgh, where Arthur Conan Doyle would study a few years later. He graduated at the top of his class in chemistry, earned a DSc in 1876, and returned to India to a professorship at the University of Hyderabad. In 1887 he was founding principal of Nizam College. He and his wife, **Varada Devi**, were both poets and social reformers, and local rumour said he was an alchemist, turning base metal into gold that could be spent on building schools. His daughter **Sarojini Naidu**, one of eight children, was president of the Indian National Congress, of which Chattopadhyahya had been an early member.

Dmitri Feodorovich Trepoff (1850-1906) was a hard-line police chief and administrator in the Russian government in the last days before the 1905 "revolution" signalled the end of the Tsarist government. He was a son of General **Fyodor Trepoff**, who as governor of St. Petersburg was wounded in an 1878 assassination attempt carried out by *Vera Zassoulich*. At that date he was a military man himself, involved in the Russo-Turkish War; later he was brought into the police bureaucracy, and in 1896 became chief of police of Moscow. In 1905 he was appointed governor of St. Petersburg, the position his father had once held, and was soon instructing police to act "in the most drastic manner" to suppress strikes and control rebellious students. As conflict grew within the government, he was appointed by Tsar *Nicholas II* to be one of his personal staff. He survived several assassination attempts, but died of coronary artery disease within months.

Edgar W. (Bill) Nye (1850-1896) was a journalist with a quirky touch: when he founded a newspaper in Laramie, Wyoming, in 1881, he called it the *Boomerang*. "We can never be a nation of snobs so long as we are willing to poke fun at ourselves," he wrote about his sense of humour, which gained his paper subscribers all over the United States and beyond. His comic sketches were syndicated across the country and collected in such volumes as *Bill Nye's Comic History of the United States* (1894), and he later also wrote for such papers as **Joseph Pulitzer**'s New York *World*. Tall, thin, bald, he was a success on the lecture platform as well, and was the featured speaker at a New York dinner held for Arthur Conan Doyle at the end of his 1894 lecture tour.

George Bettany (1850-1891) had, like Dr. Mortimer in *The Hound of the Baskervilles*, a keen interest in skulls. He was co-author (with **William Parker**) of *The Morphology of the Skull*, published in 1877, the year he received his MA from Cambridge and became a lecturer at Guy's Hospital and elsewhere. Later he worked as an editor for Ward Lock, the firm that published *A Study in Scarlet*, and then for *Lippincott's Magazine* when it published *The Sign of the Four*. He also wrote for newspapers and magazines, and provided more than 200 entries for the *Dictionary of National Biography*. His books dealt with botany, geology, world religions, and (from Ward Lock in 1890) "The red, brown and black men of America and Australia, and their white supplanters".

Guy de Maupassant (1850-1893) was the great French master of short stories, and the author of novels, poetry and other works as well. His 1884 story "La Parure" (English: "The Necklace") is a heart-wringing tale, frequently anthologized. Maupassant was a protegé of **Gustave Flaubert**, who introduced him to prominent writers of the time and guided him in improving his work. He was also an energetic womanizer, and his life was overshadowed by syphilis, incurable at the time, acquired in his youth. His first significant story was published in 1880; about 300 more came within a decade, most of them dealing in various ways with the trials, appetites and tragedies of ordinary people. "Poor Guy de Maupassant has written 30 books since 1880, and has now gone mad," Arthur Conan Doyle wrote in a letter to his mother in 1892. The Frenchman had made a suicide attempt a few days earlier.

Herbert Kitchener, 1st Earl **Kitchener of Khartoum** (1850-1916), rose from being a young officer in the Royal Engineers, sent to Palestine in 1874 on a mapping expedition, to the rank of field-marshal and a position as a British icon. Recruiting posters showing Kitchener's face and pointing finger, with the slogan "Your country needs you", are still much imitated. In 1898 he was commander of the British forces that defeated the Khalifa, *Abdallahi ibn Muhammad*, in Sudan. The

following year he was chief of staff for the British commander-in-chief in the South African War, and in 1900 became commander himself, achieving victory but earning criticism (though not from Arthur Conan Doyle) for confining Boer civilians in concentration camps. He was commander-in-chief in India for a time, returned to Sudan, and when war broke out in 1914 was promoted to field marshal and appointed Secretary of State for War, a cabinet position. He was drowned when HMS *Hampshire* was sunk by a German mine off the Orkneys in June 1916.

Jean de Reszke (1850-1925) was a singer, a tenor, who appealed greatly to Sherlock Holmes. "Have you heard the De Reszkes?" he asks Watson at the end of *The Hound of the Baskervilles*. The plural suggests that Jean's brother **Édouard de Reszke**, a bass, was also to be performing. The two were often heard together; their sister, **Josephine**

de Reszke, was an operatic soprano. The performance Holmes was heading for was "Les Huguenots" and could also have featured *Lillian Nordica*. Jean de Reszke, born in Warsaw, made his operatic debut in Venice in 1874 as a baritone, and was heard in London for the first time later that year, at the Opera Royal in Drury Lane. He reinvented himself as a tenor in 1879, and became a star in Paris and London, now at the Royal Opera House, Covent Garden. His forte was French and German opera, and his performances did much to make opera a popular attraction for British audiences.

Joseph Whitaker (1850-1932) was a collector as enthusiastic as Nathan Garrideb of "The Three Garridebs". But whereas the latter never went out, Whitaker was out in nature as much as he could manage — enjoying his deer park (also stocked with sheep, emus and rheas), fishing, or observing and shooting birds. His home was Rainworth Lodge, near Mansfield, Nottinghamshire, a house with antecedents dating to the 12th century. There he accumulated not just bird specimens but deer horns, books, china, and the first known circular saw. Learning one day in 1883 that a gamekeeper had shot an Egyptian nightjar, a species almost unknown in Europe, he acquired the carcass and had it stuffed; he also had a stone erected to mark the spot. He was the author of eight books about nature, including one entitled *Nimrod, Ramrod, Fishing-Rod and Nature Tales*, and a contributor to scientific periodicals such as *British Birds* (established 1907, too late to be relevant to "The Empty House").

Kate Chopin, née **O'Flaherty** (1850-1904), was the author of two novels and about 100 short stories, mostly set in Louisiana, where she lived for a dozen years after her 1870 marriage to businessman **Oscar Chopin**. She had been born and grew up in St. Louis, and returned there after Oscar's death in 1882, beginning to write about 1889. "Most of her best-known work focuses on the lives of sensitive, intelligent women," says a web site devoted to her life and writings. "About a third of her stories are children's stories. By the late 1890s Kate Chopin was well known among American readers of magazine fiction." Her novel *The Awakening* (1899) was called vulgar and morbid, but is now considered an important work of American literature.

Lafcadio Hearn (1850-1904) was brought up in Ireland by relatives, his parents' marriage being an international disaster. He resisted the Roman Catholicism in which he was educated, and ended up at the age of 19 alone and impoverished in Cincinnati. He worked at odd jobs while educating himself, and wound up as a reporter for the *Cincinnati Daily Enquirer* with a reputation for colourful crime reporting. He married a black woman in 1874, but the marriage failed after three years. He subsequently spent a decade in New Orleans, again as a reporter; two years in Martinique; and 14 years, up to his death, in Japan, primarily as a teacher. His 15 books about Japan are his best-known writings.

Robert Barr (1850-1912) was an author born in Glasgow but raised in Canada. He taught in Windsor and published stories in the *Detroit Free Press* before returning to Britain. By 1892 he was well enough established in the English literary world to be co-founder (with **Jerome K. Jerome**) of the *Idler*. His parody "The Adventures of Sherlaw Kombs", published that year, may be the first Sherlockian pastiche. He also wrote more serious detective tales, such as *The Triumphs of Eugène Valmont* (1906). Barr became a friend of Arthur Conan Doyle, and wrote an interview profile in the *Idler* in 1894 which is an important source about ACD's literary opinions and style of life at that period.

Robert Louis Stevenson (1850-1894) was the Edinburgh-born author whose memorable works include *Treasure Island* (1883), *The Strange Case of Dr. Jekyll and Mr. Hyde* (1886), and *The Master of Ballantrae* (1889). He was a strong influence on Arthur Conan Doyle's early fiction, and Stevenson in turn admired ACD's work, famously retelling one of the Sherlock Holmes stories to a Samoan servant who understood nothing of British society or technology. His work with the closest affinity to Sherlock Holmes is the tales that make up the *New Arabian Nights* (1882) and *More New Arabian Nights: The Dynamiter* (1885), the latter written in collaboration with his wife, **Fanny Van De Grift Stevenson**. Stevenson, whose works also include poetry and travel books, dealt with illness all his life, and roamed the world seeking a salubrious place to live. He settled in the South Pacific in 1890, where he continued to write (and corresponded with ACD).

Sir **Edward Richard Henry** (1850-1931) introduced fingerprinting to Scotland Yard. He joined the Indian civil service in 1873, and by 1891 was Inspector-General of Police for the Bengal region. There he learned about the use of fingerprints and palm prints to identify individuals, a practice that had been in use for decades, and he developed a system of classifying existing prints. The Government of India published his book on the subject in 1897. In 1901 he was appointed Assistant Commissioner (Crime) of the Metropolitan Police, and established a fingerprint bureau there. He served as Commissioner from 1903 to 1918 and in that role was largely responsible for introducing police use of telephones and call-boxes.

Thomas Neill Cream (1850-1892) was a serial murderer, blamed for crimes in Canada, the United States and Britain, and eventually hanged at Newgate Prison for the killing of a London prostitute, **Matilda Clover**, in 1891. Cream was a physician, a graduate of McGill University, whose practice concentrated on abortion; he also sold his own formulation as a treatment for epilepsy. Medication provided a vehicle for him to administer strychnine to many of his victims, leading to muscular convulsions, asphyxia and painful death. He also had an intermittent sideline in blackmail, and had served a term in Joliet Prison, Illinois, for poisoning one of his patients.

William Melville (1850-1918) was the original 'M', or at least the original spymaster whose surname had that initial. Born in Ireland, he joined London's Metropolitan Police and was soon in charge of the "Special Irish Branch" set up to deal with Fenian terrorists working for the cause of Irish independence. The "Jubilee Plot" of 1887 against Queen *Victoria*'s life, which has been a staple of so many Sherlockian pastiches, was apparently a false flag operation aimed at discrediting the Irish nationalists, but Melville treated it as the real thing and neutralized the plotters. In 1903 Melville, by now a superintendent, retired from the Special Branch and became the first head of the War Office's Secret Service Bureau, the forerunner to what became the counterintelligence agency MI5.

Arthur Mackmurdo (1851-1942) was an architect and artist who was greatly influenced by *John Ruskin*. With colleague **Selwyn Image**, he founded the Century Guild of Artists in 1882, offering home furnishings and decoration with the direct involvement of individual artists — an important strain in the so-called Arts and Crafts Movement. His own work is considered among the earliest examples of Art Nouveau design. Mackmurdo was also interested in social reform issues and was active in the influential Society for the Preservation of Ancient Buildings.

Ferdinand Foch (1851-1929) was a Marshal of France and, for a time, the supreme commander of the allied forces that defeated Germany in World War I. He joined the army as a young man, just in time to take part in the Franco-Prussian War, and attended the war college, where he scored so high that he was asked to stay on as an instructor. A collection of his lectures was published as *De la Conduite de la Guerre* ("The Principles of War"). When the war began in 1914, Foch was given command of one of France's armies and fought at both the Marne (successfully) and the Somme (much less so). He was named chief of the general staff in 1917, promoted to the mystical rank of Marshal, and in March 1918 given command of the multinational force, a role that brought him into conflict particularly with the American and British commanders, **John Pershing** and *Douglas Haig*. Following the German surrender in November, he was elected unanimously to the Académie Française.

Llewellyn Atherley-Jones (1851-1929) was a barrister and politician who likely gave his name to Inspector Athelney Jones of *A Study in Scarlet* and *The Sign of the Four*. The son of **Ernest** Jones, a leader of the radical Chartist movement in the 1840s, he first came to prominence as the lawyer for the Miners' National Union during a mine safety inquiry in 1880. He soon became involved in left-wing Liberal politics, and was elected to Parliament in 1885 from a mining area in Durham. He was repeatedly re-elected, finally leaving Parliament in 1913 to become a judge in London. "He held a definite view that punishment is no cure for crime," said his obituary in the *Glasgow Herald*, "and favoured improved preventive methods."

Sir **John Murray IV** (1851-1928) was a great-grandson of the publishing pioneer who had established the firm of John Murray in London in 1768. He and his brother, **Hallam Murray**, took over the company on the death of their father, Sir **John Murray III**, in 1892. The firm had already published such notable authors as **Jane Austen** and Sir **Walter Scott**, and John IV added Queen *Victoria* herself, publishing her *Letters* beginning in 1907. Hallam left the business in 1908 after a quarrel, but John IV continued to build it up, acquiring the competing firm of Smith, Elder and Co. in 1916. In this way Arthur Conan Doyle became part of the John Murray stable of authors; the two-volume "John Murray edition" was the standard British edition of the Sherlock Holmes tales from 1928-1929 until the British copyrights expired in 1980. The firm was sold to a conglomerate by **John Murray VII** in 2002.

Sir **George Newnes** (1851-1910) was founder and publisher of the *Strand* magazine, where most of the Sherlock Holmes stories were first published. Originally a Manchester merchant, he entered publishing in 1881 with *Tit-Bits*, a weekly paper of entertainment and miscellaneous information for the lower middle class, which was becoming steadily more literate after the reforms of the 1870 Education Act. He introduced the *Strand* as a more respectable product, with a title taken from a fashionable west-end street just around the corner from the magazine's offices. It boasted modern typography and an illustration on every double page, and quickly became enormously successful, reaching a circulation of half a million. Not the least of Newnes's successful decisions was the hiring of ***Herbert Greenhough Smith*** as the *Strand*'s editor. George Newnes Ltd. went on to publish dozens of other periodicals, including boys' magazines, women's papers and sports news. Newnes also served as a Member of Parliament for the Liberal Party for twenty years.

Mary Augusta Ward, née **Arnold**, known as **Mrs. Humphry Ward** (1851-1920), was a granddaughter of **Thomas Arnold**, the almost legendary headmaster of Rugby School, and like him she applied religion to society in startling ways. Says the *Oxford Companion to English Literature*: "She embodied in her most famous novel, *Robert Elsmere* (1888), the view that Christianity could be revitalized by emphasizing its social mission and discarding its miraculous element." She wrote more than 20 other novels between 1881 and 1920, and was also involved in social work, particularly "educational settlements", though she opposed women's suffrage. Her husband, **Humphry Ward**, was an Oxford tutor and a writer of non-fiction; he edited *English Art in the Public Galleries of London* (1888).

Sir **Leslie Ward** (1851-1922) was an artist whose best-known work was a long series of caricature portraits published in *Vanity Fair* magazine under the nom de plume of "Spy". His portrait of ***William Gillette*** as Sherlock Holmes, published in February 1907, is a familiar image to Sherlockians, but Arthur Conan Doyle himself never made the list. He drew a total of 1,325 portraits for the magazine between 1873 and 1911 (about another 1,000 during the same period were done by other artists). Ward acknowledged that they grew more "sympathetic" to the prominent subjects as he advanced in social position himself. "Caricature should be a comic impression with a kindly touch," he said, "and always devoid of vulgarity." It was reported that he was paid "between £300 and £400" for each watercolour portrait.

Minna (Mabel) Collins (1851-1927) was a popular novelist and a stormy figure in Theosophist circles. Daughter of an unsuccessful poet, she supported herself at first by magazine writing and then also with romantic fiction (such as *An Innocent Sinner*, 1877). A husband, **Keningale Robert Cook**, introduced her to Spiritualism. Later she was interested in the mystical doctrines of Theosophy and involved with its often feuding leaders, including "Madame" *Helena Blavatsky*; her treatise of "Eastern wisdom", *Light on the Path*, appeared in 1888. Later novels also reflected Theosophical experiences. In 1889 she had a relationship with "magician" **Robert Stephenson** and believed that he had been Jack the Ripper.

Sir **Oliver Lodge** (1851-1940) was a prominent physicist and academic who became a believer in Spiritualism and explained it in scientific terms. Arthur Conan Doyle records in his autobiography that he talked with Lodge when they were both at Buckingham Palace one day in 1902 receiving their respective knighthoods, and that Lodge at that time was ahead of him in accepting Spiritualist beliefs. Lodge was at that time president of the Society for Psychical Research, and had just become principal of the new University of Birmingham. His book *The Survival of Man* was published in 1909. A graduate of the University of London, Lodge taught at Liverpool 1881-1900 before going to Birmingham. His research dealt with the properties of electromagnetic waves, lately discovered by *Heinrich Hertz*, and which he believed were transmitted through a pervasive medium called "ether" — which he also concluded was the way in which Spiritualist messages travelled. A number of Lodge's discoveries were important in the development of radio technology.

Alice Liddell, married name **Hargreaves** (1852-1934), was the original Alice in Wonderland, the little girl to whom *Lewis Carroll* (*Charles Dodgson*) told the story that became his 1865 book *Alice's Adventures in Wonderland*. She was the daughter of **Henry**

Liddell, dean of Christ Church, a college at Oxford where Dodgson was a lecturer in mathematics. Dodgson originally told the story in July 1862, and wrote it down for his young friend (as *Alice's Adventures Under Ground*) in 1864. Dates in that book, and an acrostic poem in its sequel *Through the Looking-Glass*, make the connection with Alice Liddell obvious. She also served as a model for some of Dodgson's amateur photography.

Archduke **Johann Salvator of Austria**, later known as **John Orth** (1852-1890?), was the son of **Leopold II**, Grand Duke of Tuscany, a friend of Austrian Crown Prince *Rudolf*, and an unsuccessful candidate for Prince of Bulgaria when that position was being created in 1879. (**Alexander of Battenberg** got the job.) He had, instead, a career in the Austrian army, and privately another interest: in 1883, under the pseudonym **Johann Traugott**, he wrote the ballet "Die Assassinen" for his inamorata, **Ludmilla (Milli) Stubel**, a dancer with the Vienna Court Opera. In 1889, determined to marry his Milli although she was a commoner, Johann renounced his titles, took the surname **Orth**, arranged for the marriage to be celebrated in London, and ran away with her to South America. They stopped at Montevideo in February 1890, and in Argentina in July, and were said to be heading for Chile, but their ship is thought to have been lost in a storm off Cape Horn.

Emperor **Meiji**, privately named **Mutsuhito** (1852-1912), was Emperor of Japan from 1867 until his death, and played a major role in bringing his country from obscurity and mediaeval conditions into the modern age and importance on the world stage. He bore little resemblance to the caricature emperor who appeared in the comic opera "The Mikado" in 1885. When he took office, Japan was largely ruled by a feudal official, the Shogun, but political conditions were unstable, and rule in the Emperor's name was largely restored in 1869, with a cabinet and parliament soon being established. Historians remain unclear on what the Emperor's role was in reform and modernization, or in Japan's victorious wars with China (1894) and Russia (1904-05).

Herbert Henry Asquith, Earl of **Oxford and Asquith** (1852-1928), was Prime Minister 1908-1916. He led a Liberal government after the retirement of Sir *Henry Campbell-Bannerman*, winning minority governments in two elections in 1910, and finally leaving office after a rift with *David Lloyd George*, who then succeeded him as Liberal prime minister. His time in office saw passage of the Parliament Act (reducing the power of the House of Lords); old age pension provisions, introduced by Lloyd George, who was serving as Chancellor of the Exchequer (finance minister); simmering controversy over women's suff-rage; and an agreement on Home Rule for Ireland, though implemen-tation was delayed by the beginning of World War I. First elected to Parliament in 1886, he had served as Home Secretary (the cabinet minister in charge of police and prisons) under two prime ministers and as Chancellor of the Exchequer under Campbell-Bannerman.

James Berry (1852-1913) was one of Britain's hangmen from 1884 to 1891. Previously a police officer and a shoe salesman, he applied to follow in the footsteps of innovator *William Marwood*, and in the course of his 131 hangings he further improved Marwood's "long drop" tech-nique, though not without errors, such as one execution in which the condemned man was actually beheaded by the rope. After retirement he wrote two books, *My Experiences as an Executioner* (1892) and *The Hangman's Thoughts Above the Gallows* (1905).

John French, 1st Earl of **Ypres** (1852-1925), was a Field Marshal when World War I began, having served eight years in the Royal Navy and then forty years in the army. His experience included action in the Sudan in 1884-1885 and in South Africa during the war of 1899-1901, and eventually he was Chief of the Imperial General Staff. He com-manded the British Expeditionary Force that went to France as World War I began in 1914. His mercurial temperament led to his replacement by Sir *Douglas Haig* late in 1915.

Lydia **Dingwell** (1852-1931) was acquitted of a dramatic homicide in rural Prince Edward Island in September 1894. "It happened in Souris," says the libretto of the 1968 opera "Johnny Belinda" (words by Mavor Moore, music by John Fenwick) based on the killing. "She shot her seducer for stealing her baby, but they let her go free 'cause she done it for love." Dingwell, like Belinda in the opera, could not hear or speak, but otherwise the dramatization — originally a play by Elmer Harris — is careless of the facts. The role of Belinda brought Jane Wyman an Academy Award for best actress in a 1948 film.

Martha Jane Cannary, known as **Calamity Jane** (1852-1903), was a cook, a nurse, a dance-hall girl, a Pony Express driver, a frontier scout, and from time to time a prostitute. "By the time we reached Virginia City, I was considered a remarkable good shot and a fearless rider for a girl of my age," she wrote in her somewhat dubious 1896 autobio-graphy. She had been 13 when she and her family arrived at Virginia City, Montana, from her Missouri birthplace. She claimed to have taken part in various skirmishes with Indian tribes on the American frontier, and told stories of such adventures in later years when she appeared in various wild west shows. In 1876 she was part of a wagon train that also included frontiersman **Wild Bill Hickok**; there is an unconfirmed tradition that she married him and bore him a daughter, and she was buried beside him at Deadwood, South Dakota.

Sir **Ernest Cassel** (1852-1921) was a German-born merchant banker who worked his way up from nothing in Liverpool and in France, went into business for himself, and became one of the richest figures of his generation. Industrial projects in his empire stretched from Turkey to South America. Retiring in 1910, he devoted his efforts to philanthropy (he gave £500,000, a vast sum, to education, as well as gifts for hospitals and the Red Cross) and to enjoying his British and foreign decorations and his friendships with King *Edward VII* and other prominent people.

Sir **Herbert Beerbohm Tree** (1852-1917) was one of the great British actors, and founder (1904) of the Royal Academy of Dramatic Arts. "He was above all a romantic actor with a genius for character parts and comedy," says the *Encyclopaedia Britannica*. From 1887 he was manager of the Haymarket Theatre in London, and from 1897 the owner-manager of Her Majesty's Theatre, where he lived in luxury and presented Shakespearean drama as well as modern plays and even an adaptation of *Charles Dickens*'s "The Mystery of Edwin Drood". In 1914 he starred as Henry Higgins in the first British production of *George Bernard Shaw*'s "Pygmalion", playing opposite *Mrs. Patrick Campbell*. His half-brother was caricaturist *Max Beerbohm*.

Tewfik Pasha (1852-1892) was Khedive, or ruler, of Egypt (and Sudan with it) from 1879, when his predecessor *Isma'il Pasha* was deposed, until his death. "Egypt and Sudan at that time was involved in financial and political troubles brought about by the policy of Ismail," said the *Encyclopaedia Britannica* in 1911, "and the situation was made worse by the inaction of Britain and France for some months following Tewfik's accession. Tewfik's people were dissatisfied, his army disaffected; his advisers were nearly all of the adventurer class, with their own ends to gain." British and French forces eventually moved in, and Tewfik became in effect a puppet ruler of Sir *Evelyn Baring* and his French counterpart. He was active in improving agriculture and education for the Egyptian people.

Alphonse Bertillon (1853-1914) was the pioneer of anthropometry whom Sherlock Holmes mentions in "The Naval Treaty" ("he expressed his enthusiastic admiration of the French savant"), though he is prickly when someone else brings up Bertillon's name in *The Hound of the Baskervilles.* As a clerk in the Paris police department, Bertillon devised a system of recording five body measurements, including height and the "cubit" (length from the elbow to the tip of the middle finger), to help in future identification of criminals. "Bertillonage" was officially adopted in 1883, in Paris and soon internationally, but gave way to the use of fingerprints, which Bertillon also studied. In addition he is credited with standardizing the "mug shot" or facial photograph, and with developing techniques for photographing murder scenes.

Bryan Charles Waller (1853-1932) was a friend of Arthur Conan Doyle's family who lectured in medicine at the University of Edinburgh and encouraged ACD to attend the medical school. He lodged with the family in Edinburgh in 1875, and by 1877 the family were living with him at 23 George Square. He inherited an estate at Masongill, in the Yorkshire Dales, moved there in 1882 to be the local squire (abandoning Edinburgh and medical practice), and induced ACD's mother, **Mary Foley Doyle**, to move there as well; she lived at Masongill until 1917. Scholars are divided about Waller's role in arranging to have ACD's father, **Charles Doyle**, institutionalized in 1876, and about the nature of his relationship with Mary. Waller's writings included poetry and *An Investigation Into the Microscopic Anatomy of Interstitial Nephritis*, based on his MD thesis.

Chulalongkorn, King Rama V of Siam (1853-1910), maintained the independence of his country — now called Thailand — at a time when Britain and France were colonizing most other parts of southeast Asia. "In the present state of Siam it is most awkward that I should be away from the office," Mycroft Holmes says in "The Bruce-Partington Plans". Chulalongkorn became king in 1868 after the death of his father, King **Mongkut**, and quickly embarked on reforms, visiting India among other places to see how western governments operated. He abolished slavery and torture, built railways, conducted a partly successful war against French incursions (1893), and signed a treaty with Britain (1909). He is the original of the Crown Prince who figures in "The King and I"; ***Anna Leonowens*** was the governess at his father's court, 1862-1867.

Cecil Rhodes (1853-1902) made a fortune in the diamond-mining regions of South Africa, and was the key figure in De Beers Consolidated Mines, formed in 1888. He used his money to advance his political plans, becoming premier of the Cape Colony at the tip of southern Africa, and forming the British South Africa Company to expand north-ward. After the unsuccessful 1895-1896 "raid" led by his right-hand man, ***Leander Starr Jameson***, Rhodes had to resign as premier, but kept his imperialist dreams of British Africa and the "Cape to Cairo" railway, which was never built. Matabeleland and the other territories occupied by British settlers in the 1890s were soon called "Rhodesia" in his honour (they are now Zambia and Zimbabwe). The disgraced Gilchrist in "The Three Students" planned to head off to obscurity in Rhodesia. Rhodes left his fortune to fund the Rhodes Scholarships for graduate study at Oxford.

Clementina Black (1853-1922) came from Brighton to London to write — the first of her seven novels appeared when she was 24 — and learn more about social problems, particularly those affecting working women. She worked to establish links between middle-class feminists and the male-dominated union movement. By 1888 she was a delegate to the annual Trades Union Congress, proposing a resolution that demanded equal pay for women. The following year she helped form

the Women's Trade Union Association, and in 1890 she was advocating a minimum wage of 4d per hour (about $1.75 in modern cur-
rency) for seamstresses. She was active in the socialist Fabian Society
and the suffragette movement, and was an advocate for cooperative
housing.

Grand Duchess **Maria Alex-androvna** (1853-1920) was one of
the best examples of how Europe's
19th century royal houses were one
big happy family. She was daughter
of *Alexander II* of Russia and his
empress, also named **Maria Alexan-drovna**, and married *Alfred, Duke of Edinburgh*, son of Queen *Victoria*
and Prince *Albert*, thereby becoming
both a British princess and, from
1893, Duchess of Saxe-Coburg and
Gotha. Her five children included
Princess Marie, who married
Ferdinand I of Roumania and
became the monarch, author, nurse
and (especially on her 1926 visit to
the United States) celebrity known
as "**Marie of Roumania**".

John Wesley Hardin (1853-1895)
was born and died in Texas, and he
loved his guns. Records are un-certain, but he shot at least 20
people dead, possibly 40 or more, mostly in quarrels over gambling,
cattle or women, though a few of his victims were lawmen who got on
his trail in Texas, Kansas or Florida. The Texas Rangers arrested him
and he served 17 years in prison, but the killings resumed when he got
out. He was finally shot dead in an El Paso saloon by constable **John
Selman Sr.** Hardin's name vaguely suggests "the peculiar persecution
to which John Vincent Harden, the well known tobacco millionaire, had
been subjected", mentioned in "The Solitary Cyclist", but really: what
tobacco? what millions?

Lillie Langtry, born **Emilie Charlotte Le Breton** (1853-1929), is one
of the chief candidates to be an original of Irene Adler, though she was
an actress rather than a contralto. Adler's birth in New Jersey slightly

suggests Langtry's birth in Jersey, Channel Islands; she was known as "the Jersey Lily". Her 1874 marriage to landowner **Edward Langtry** did not interfere with her theatrical career, 1881-1883 and intermittently after that, or her relationships with gentlemen ranging from American playboy **Frederick Gebhard** to the Prince of *Wales* (later *Edward VII*). She later managed the Imperial Theatre in London, owned race-horses, provided her endorsement to soaps and other products, and divorced and remarried, this time to aristocrat **Hugo de Bathe**.

Leopold, Duke of **Albany** (1853-1884), was the eighth child of Queen *Victoria* and Prince *Albert*, and was delivered with the help of chloroform, a recent invention that the Queen decided, not without criticism, to use. He was the first (but not the last) of Victoria's descendants to suffer from the haemophilia that also appeared in other, related European royal families. He also is thought to have suffered from epilepsy. Leopold was described as thoughtful and intellectual, and was a chess enthusiast. He spent four years studying at Christ Church, Oxford; while there, he became friendly with *Alice Liddell*, daughter of the dean of the college. In 1882 he married Princess **Helena** of Waldeck and Pyrmont, and they had two children. Early in 1884, while staying at a house in Cannes, France, he fell down a staircase, and died next day of a cerebral hemorrhage probably aggravated by the haemophilia.

Marie Elisabeth of Saxe-Meiningen (1853-1923) — not Clotilde as in "A Scandal in Bohemia" — was a member of minor German royalty who distinguished herself as a pianist, patron of the arts, and composer of music in several genres. The *Musical Standard* in 1880 called her "gifted and accomplished" and noted her recently completed "Willkommen" march and "a melodious cradle song, Leipzig". Her father, Duke **Georg II** of Saxe-Meiningen, was an enthusiast of the stage, but also of music; he was an important patron of **Johannes Brahms**, who gave piano lessons to the young Marie Elisabeth. In later life she entertained a circle of musicians and artists at her home in Berchtesgaden. She never married.

Sir **Flinders Petrie** (1853-1942) was the first professor of Egyptology in Britain (at University College, London), and pioneered scientific methods for archaeological excavation. His mother, **Anne Flinders**, was an Egyptologist, his father an electrical engineer, his grandfather the navigator and surveyor **Matthew Flinders**. Petrie's interest in archaeology, and especially precise surveying and careful excavating, started early with work in England. He first went to Egypt in 1880, and was galvanized by the rate at which ancient sites were deteriorating. He subsequently also pioneered scientific excavation in Palestine. An inscription found at Luxor in 1896, associated with the pharaoh Merenptah, is considered his greatest find.

Sir **Frederick Treves**, 1st Baronet (1853-1923), trained as a surgeon at the London Hospital in the Whitechapel Road, and became a specialist in abdominal surgery. In June 1888 he performed the first appendectomy done in England, and in June 1901 he was called on to treat the new King, *Edward VII*, for an attack of appendicitis, which he treated by draining the infection. Like Arthur Conan Doyle, he worked with a British field hospital during the South African War; his articles about the experience, published in the *British Medical Journal*, were later collected in book form. He was also author of *A Student's Handbook of Surgical Operations* (1892) and a number of other books. Treves is also remembered as the physician who looked after *Joseph Merrick*, the "Elephant Man", in the years leading up to his death in 1890.

Sir **Leander Starr Jameson,** 1st Baronet (1853-1917), was a physician and politician, but is chiefly remembered for his disastrous "raid" into the Transvaal state of South Africa in 1895. Jameson was a friend and adherent of *Cecil Rhodes*, whose colonial ambitions for Britain extended to all of South Africa and then the entire continent. Rhodes planned a raid aimed at overthrowing the Boer government of Transvaal, and although he tried at the last minute to postpone it, Jameson went ahead with 500 horsemen. His force was defeated and captured, Rhodes's political career and reputation were damaged, and Jameson, sent home to Britain, was sentenced to 15 months in prison. He later returned to Africa and served four years as prime minister of the Cape Colony, the core of what became (1910) the Union of South Africa.

Sir **Melville Macnaghten** (1853-1921) was a Scotland Yard (Metropolitan Police) official who wrote a major report on the Jack the Ripper case, six years after the murders took place. As a young man he managed his father's tea plantations in India, returning to England in 1888, the year of the Ripper murders. When Sir *Charles Warren* resigned as Commissioner of the police force, being succeeded by Macnaghten's friend *James Monro*, Macnaghten became assistant chief constable (1889) and then chief constable (1890). His 1894 report, which became public only in 1959, stated that there were five definite victims of the Ripper, and named as suspects **_Montague John Druitt_**, **_Aaron Kosminski_**, and Russian fraudster **Michael Ostrog**. Macnaghten became assistant commissioner in 1903 and retired in 1913.

Sir **Thomas Henry Hall Caine** (1853-1931) grew up partly in the Isle of Man, a land between England and Ireland where fogs, the Buggane, and the "little folk" prevail, and what he learned there figured in the background of much of his writing. Though he began adult life as an apprentice architect in Liverpool, he wrote for magazines when he could, and lectured about literature. Making his way to London, he lived for a time with the elderly **_Dante Gabriel Rossetti_**, who read Caine's first two novels and urged him to make use of his Manx knowledge. *The Deemster* (1887) and *The Manxman* (1894) were among his successes; his work in general can be classed as popular romance. Meanwhile the Isle of Man was becoming a tourist destination, and Caine made himself one of its attractions for a time, giving interviews and being photographed. He later returned to England, and visited the United States, to promote his work and supervise production of his plays.

Thomas (Tom) Dudley (1853-1900) was a sea-captain and the central figure in a legal case that spawned the "lifeboat problem", a staple of ethics classes ever since. He and a crew of three were taking the rickety yacht *Mignonette* from England to Australia in 1884 when the ship foundered in the South Atlantic, leaving the crew in a 13-foot lifeboat with almost no supplies. They grew desperate, and on the 20th day of the ordeal Dudley killed the youngest crew member, **Richard Parker**, with his pen-knife; he and the others ate Parker's flesh and drank his blood. Some days later, they were picked up by a steamship, and on their return to Falmouth, they were, apparently to their surprise, charged with murder. A court presided over by the Lord Chief Justice, **John Coleridge**, 1st Baron **Coleridge**, eventually found Dudley and another crew member guilty of murder; a death sentence was immediately commuted to six months' imprisonment.

Vincent van Gogh (1853-1890) was the Dutch artist who created "Starry Night", now a staple of popular culture, in June 1889, and more than 2,000 other artworks. He worked for a time as an art dealer, then considered theology, but at age 27 decided to study art instead, at an academy in Brussels. He painted his first major work in 1885, and soon afterwards fell among the Impressionist artists, including **_Henri de Toulouse-Lautrec_** and **Paul Gauguin**, who had a strong influence on his style. Mental and physical illness overtook him even as he was doing his greatest work (such as a large series of sunflower paintings). In 1888 he sliced off his own ear, in circumstances that are not well understood; the incident may have influenced "The Cardboard Box". He committed suicide in July 1890.

William Gillette (1853-1937) was a successful actor and playwright with a characteristic technique even before he first portrayed Sherlock Holmes in 1899. Afterwards he was a legend, of whom author ***Booth Tarkington*** famously said, "I would rather see you play Sherlock Holmes than be a child again on Christmas morning." Gillette played the lead in his own play "Sherlock Holmes", based on some of the original stories, some 1,300 times between 1899 and 1932, across the United States and Britain, and made a film of his play in 1916. He was noted for "the illusion of the first time", the very opposite of 19th century histrionic acting, and for capturing an audience's attention through stillness and silence. Other plays in his repertoire included "Secret Service" and "Too Much Johnson". His retirement home, Gillette Castle in Connecticut, is now a state park.

William 'Bat' Masterson (1853-1921) was a lawman in the legendary days of the American west, whose dapper figure and bowler hat have become familiar from media representations, particularly a 1958-1961 television series starring Gene Barry. Masterson was born in Canada and raised in various parts of the United States, becoming a buffalo hunter, gunfighter, and gambler. By 1878 he was a deputy sheriff in frontier Dodge City, Kansas, where he was associated with ***Wyatt Earp***, and also took part in rough-and-ready law enforcement in Colorado and Texas. In later years he was a sports writer and deputy United States marshal in New York.

Edward (Ned) Kelly (1854-1880) was an outlaw who has somehow become Australia's folk hero. He grew up with his mother's extended family on a large property in northern Victoria colony, where he was involved at an early age in the family business of cattle and horse thieving. At age 15 he spent seven weeks in jail as a "suspected accomplice" of a notorious bush-ranger. "The Kelly family saw themselves as victims of police persecution," says the *Australian Dictionary of Biography*. In April 1878 someone, possibly Ned, shot at a trooper who arrived at the family house to arrest his brother, **Dan Kelly**. Ned and Dan went into hiding, police went after them, and three troopers were killed in a skirmish. Two other men joined "the Kelly gang", which committed several robberies and ended up in a battle with police at a hotel in the village of Glenrowan in June 1880. Kelly, though wearing metal armour, was brought down by shots to the legs. He was arrested, tried, and hanged for murder at Melbourne.

Arthur Rimbaud (1854-1891) "was the enfant terrible of French poetry in the second half of the nineteenth century," says Poetry–Foundation.org, "and a major figure in symbolism." Born in a small town in northeastern France, he ran away from his domineering mother, spent a few weeks as part of the revolutionary Paris Commune of 1871, and embarked on a homosexual relationship with **Paul Verlaine**, who would later publish the iconoclastic, sometimes shocking poems he wrote during this period. (He would also spend two years in prison for shooting Rimbaud in the arm during a quarrel.) Rimbaud's writing continued to explore new directions for the poetic vocabulary, but he abandoned poetry by the time he was 21. He dabbled in various lines of work (including an enlistment in the Dutch army, followed by desertion while he was in Sumatra) and died following amputation of a cancerous leg.

Francis Marion Crawford (1854-1909) was an American author, though he lived most of his life in Italy and wrote dramatic stories of life in that country, many of them with occult or horror themes. His 1897 novel *Corleone* is said to be the first substantial treatment of the Mafia in literature. (Arthur Conan Doyle addressed it in "The Six Napoleons, 1904, and "The Red Circle", 1911.) His grandson **Howard**

Marion-Crawford (1914-1969) played Watson in 39 television plays in 1954-55, starring **Ronald Howard** as Holmes.

George Eastman (1854-1932) was the inventor who popularized photography with the introduction of his pre-loaded Kodak camera to the market in 1888. There were already many professional photographers, as well as hobbyists (although both the characters in the Sherlock Holmes tales who claim to have photography as a hobby are using it as an excuse to conceal what's really going on). Eastman, who was working as a bookkeeper, looked for ways to make the process less cumbersome, and developed a gelatin-based paper film and, in 1885, a device for holding rolls of film inside the camera. A more flexible type of film was developed for Eastman a few years later by chemist **Henry Reichenbach**. The Brownie camera came along in 1900, selling for $1 and originally intended for children. Eastman, who never married, is thought to have donated more than $100 million to philanthropic causes, particularly in Rochester, New York, where his company was based.

George H. Chirgwin (1854-1922) was "the White-Eyed Kaffir", a star of music halls and, as early as 1896, a few silent films. "Chirgwin had appeared as a black face minstrel from childhood," says the website Victorian-Cinema.net, "evolving an act that mixed sentimental songs, wisecracking comedy and a bizarre costume and make-up consisting of tight black body-suit, extravagantly tall hat and a white diamond painted over his right eye." He was especially known for the tear-jerker song "The Blind Boy", which provided the basis for a 1917 feature film.

Jennie Churchill, née **Jeanette Jerome**, formally **Lady Randolph Churchill** (1854-1921), was the daughter of a wealthy New York family. In 1874 she married Lord ***Randolph Churchill***, becoming one of "our fair cousins from across the Atlantic" to marry into British nobility, as "The Noble Bachelor" puts it. She became a star of British social and political circles: "Her American vivacity, her wit, and her beauty assured her of social success in London," says the *Encyclopaedia Britannica*. "She took no active part in her husband's political career, and his death in 1895 left her for some time at loose ends." But not  for long: she had two further marriages, both with much younger men.

She was also reported to have had many romantic affairs, possibly including one with the future King *Edward VII*. A son of her first marriage was the future prime minister *Winston Churchill*.

John Lane (1854-1925) was born into a farming family in Devon, but came to London as a teenager and, after working as a clerk for a time, went into the book business. He and **Charles Elkin Matthews** founded The Bodley Head in 1887, initially as a bookseller, then as a publisher. The firm — headed by Lane alone after 1894 — was noted for the *Yellow Book* with its scandalous *Aubrey Beardsley* illustrations. It also published the controversial novel *The Woman Who Did* by Arthur Conan Doyle's friend **Grant Allen** and **Arthur Machen**'s horror classic *The Great God Pan*, as well as work by **Ford Madox Ford**, **H. G. Wells**, and **Agatha Christie**.

Milan I (1854-1901) of Serbia is one of a number of eastern European princelings who can be roughly equated with the King who figures in "A Scandal in Bohemia". He was known for his extramarital affairs, including one with *Jennie Churchill*, although no contraltos are mentioned. Born in exile from Serbia, where his father had ruled, he was adopted by a cousin, Prince **Mihailo Obrenović III**, in time to be part of the dynasty's return to power. On Mihailo's assassination in 1868, Milan became the ruling prince, with a regency until he came of age four years later. In 1882 Serbia, throwing off the last traces of Ottoman Empire rule, was declared to be a kingdom and Milan became King. He abdicated in 1889, amid political and family turmoil.

Oscar Wilde (1854-1900) was a playwright, critic, and society wit in his own time, but in retrospect is best known as the victim of the s stigma that homosexuality carried in his time. Irish-born, he was a journalist, the editor of *The Lady's World* from 1887; author of *The Happy Prince and Other Tales* (1888); and playwright of *Salome* (French 1891, English 1894) and *Lady Windermere's Fan* (1892). His most enduring works are *The Picture of Dorian Gray*, commissioned by *J. M. Stoddart* in 1889 at the same time he induced Arthur Conan Doyle to write *The Sign of the Four*, and another play, *The Importance of Being Earnest* (1895). He was married (1884) to **Constance Lloyd**, and they had two sons, but he also had gay tastes, sometimes involving "rent-boys". A passionate affair with Lord *Alfred Douglas* led, thanks to the Marquess of *Queensberry*, to an 1895 prosecution under the Criminal Law Amendment Act 1885, which forbade "gross indecency" (male homosexual activity). He spent two years in prison, an experience that led to "The Ballad of Reading Gaol" and the essay "De Profundis", and died in exile in Paris.

Sir **Adolph Tuck**, 1st Baronet (1854-1926), was a prominent figure in Britain's Jewish community and a publisher of greeting cards, postcards, scrapbooks and other illustrated paper. He came to Britain as a child and grew up with the family business, originally a shop in Spitalfields selling German prints, later the publishing firm Raphael Tuck & Sons. He worked in the firm from 1869, and became managing director when his father retired in 1881, having already shaped the company's direction with its first manufacture of Christmas cards in 1871. A similar innovation came half a century later when Tuck began producing valentines. Arthur Conan Doyle became a director of the company and attended a dinner celebrating Tuck's 70th birthday in 1924. The baronet was deeply involved in Jewish organizations and their complex politics. A trust he created in 1912, designed to provide an income to future baronets so long as they were of "Jewish faith" and married to wives of "Jewish blood", resulted in litigation in 1969 about the meaning of those expressions under English law.

Sir **James Frazer** (1854-1941) was the author of *The Golden Bough*, a sprawling work of anthropology that sheds light from many angles on the human belief in resurrection. He spent most of his life at Trinity College, Cambridge, where he also wrote many other books about mythology and classical archaeology. "Frazer was not widely travelled," Wikipedia notes. "His prime sources of data were ancient histories and questionnaires mailed to missionaries and imperial officials all over the globe." The information he collected about beliefs and practices led him to see a pattern of dying and (often) reviving gods in many cultures, and to describe an evolution from primitive magic to religious belief and from there to scientific knowledge. A two-volume edition of *The Golden Bough* appeared in 1890, and a twelve-volume edition in 1915. "The symbolic cycle of  life, death and rebirth which Frazer divined behind myths of many peoples captivated a generation of artists and poets," says Wikipedia. Subsequent anthropologists have not all agreed.

Sir **Robert Borden** (1854-1937) was prime minister of Canada for the decade that spanned World War I, the period when the country's national identity was largely formed. A lawyer from Halifax, he was elected to Parliament in 1896 and led the national Conservative party for two decades starting in 1901. He became prime minister after campaigning in the 1911 election against a reciprocity (free trade) agreement with the United States that *Wilfrid Laurier*'s Liberals had negotiated. During the war he insisted on distinct identity for Canadian troops even under British command. He was returned to office in 1917, retiring in 1920. Borden's achievements include Canadian membership in the League of Nations (independent of Britain), the income tax, and women's suffrage.

William **Devery** (1854-1919) joined the New York City police in 1878, and within twenty years had its top job, superintendent of the police commission. His title became "chief of police" with a reorganization of the force in 1898. Less than a year earlier, he had been charged with bribery and extortion (having famously told his men, "If there's any grafting to be done, I'll do it"). His conviction was overturned by an appeals court. Reformers claimed that the grafting continued, and the force was reorganized again in 1901. Devery then served as an "assistant commissioner" for less than a year before reformist mayor **Seth Low** dismissed him.

George Turnavine Budd (1855-1889) was a friend of Arthur Conan Doyle at the University of Edinburgh medical school, who then offered him a job in his medical practice in a suburb of Plymouth. Budd saw a steady stream of patients at no charge, making his money from the sale of prescriptions. The relationship lasted less than two months, as ACD was stunned by Budd's wild and unorthodox methods; there were also money difficulties. ACD left, looking for another post, and eventually settled in Southsea, trying to eke out a living in practice by himself. A thinly disguised Budd appears as Dr. James Cullingworth in *The Stark Munro Letters*.

Herbert Greenhough Smith (1855-1935) was hired by *George Newnes* to edit his new *Strand Magazine* when it was founded in 1891. In that capacity he bought stories and articles from many writers, but none more important than Arthur Conan Doyle. "There was no mistaking the ingenuity of the plot, the limpid clearness of style, the perfect art of telling a story," Smith wrote about his first look at ACD's work. The "Adventures of Sherlock Holmes" made the magazine a success, and 58 of the 60 canonical stories were published there between 1891 and 1927. Born in Gloucestershire, and a graduate of St. John's College, Cambridge, Smith wrote half a dozen books in his own right, including *Castle Sombras: An Historical Romance* (1895). He retired from the magazine in 1930.

Homer Watson (1855-1936) was "the man who first saw Canada as Canada", in the words of one art historian, although the style of his landscapes, most set in south central Ontario, greatly resembles the work of the Hudson Valley school of painters in the United States, and also shows influences from British artists such as **John Constable**. Watson was born in Doon, a village that is now part of Kitchener, and spent much of his life there, although he travelled to New York and England to work on his art. His first major painting, "The Pioneer Mill", was bought in 1880 by the Marquess of *Lorne*, then Governor General of Canada, for Queen *Victoria*'s collection. International prominence followed; "The Flood Gate" (1900) is considered his masterpiece. Watson corresponded and exchanged visits with *Oscar Wilde*.

Marie Corelli, born **Mary Mackay** (1855-1924), was the author of some thirty novels, most of them best-sellers though not favourites with the literary critics. *Grant Allen* called Corelli "a woman of deplorable talent who imagined that she was a genius". *The Sorrows of Satan* (1895) is the story of a poverty-stricken artist who is tempted by the devil with vast riches. Like Corelli's other books, it is heavy with Christian doctrine and moralization as well as what would now be called new age thought and social commentary, all delivered with sentimentality. Its heroine is the first person ever to be named Mavis. Corelli never married, and lived for 40 years with her companion Bertha Vyver.

Houston Stewart Chamberlain (1855-1927) was British-born (in Southsea) but German by residence, marriage and disposition. He studied science in Geneva and the music and philosophy of **Richard Wagner** in Dresden, began to write about German culture and civilization, and in 1889 settled in Austria. He moved to Bayreuth, Germany, where Wagner had lived and where annual festivals of his operas are held, in 1909 with his second wife, Wagner's step-daughter **Eva von Bülow-Wagner**. His scientific and cultural works, notably *The Foundations of the Nineteenth Century* (German 1899, English 1911), provided an intellectual foundation for Nazism. He also associated with **Adolf Hitler** and other leaders of the Nazi movement in the 1920s.

John Lamond (1855-1932) was the author of *Arthur Conan Doyle: A Memoir*, which appeared in 1931 with the support of ACD's widow. Lamond was a clergyman, who had been minister of Greenside Church in Edinburgh, a Church of Scotland congregation. He was also a committed Spiritualist, and already the author of several books, including *The Eternal Christ*; a biography of Joan of Arc; and *Kathleen: A Study of the Supernormal* (1925), described as "a biography of, and an account of spiritualistic communications with, the author's daughter", who had died in 1922. His ACD book is as much about Spiritualism as it is about the man. Philip A. Shreffler writes that Lamond "views Conan Doyle's life as a series of causes — almost as a kind of knightly quest".

Mortimer Menpes (1855-1938) was an artist who was sent to South Africa in 1901 to draw scenes of the war there, and caught up with Arthur Conan Doyle at his Langman Hospital. He drew a sketch of ACD that has often been reproduced, and wrote about hospital conditions: "The only thing I can liken it to is a slaughter house." Australian-born, Menpes was trained in England and became a pupil and friend of *James McNeill Whistler*. His forte was etchings and "drypoint" intaglio prints, many of which became illustrations for travel books. Later in life he settled at Pangbourne, Berkshire, west of London, and operated an extensive fruit farming business.

Olive Schreiner, née **Lyndall** (1855-1920), was "the South African writer most famous in Britain", according to Paula M. Krebs in *Gender, Race, and the Writing of Empire*. "Schreiner used essays, allegory, polemic, and fiction to try to paint a portrait of South Africa.... *The Story of an African Farm* [1883], for all of its spirituality and experimentation, is at heart a Victorian realist novel." Arthur Conan Doyle praised it in lectures in 1894: "one of the greatest books ever written by a woman. She used her heart for an ink-pot." Schreiner was born to a missionary family in the Cape Colony (in an area now part of Lesotho) and lived most of her life in South Africa, with two intervals in Britain. She was interested in pacifism, socialism and the rights of women; her own sexual life is unclear but she corresponded with *Havelock Ellis* about sexual matters.

Sir **Patrick Quinn** (1855-1936) headed the so-called Special Branch of the Metropolitan Police (Scotland Yard) from 1903, when *William Melville* retired, to his own retirement in 1919. Responsibilities there included guarding the royal family, tracing and neutralizing anarchists or what would now be called terrorists, and, during World War I, battling German espionage. A memoir in an Australian newspaper in 1920 called him "the greatest detective the world has ever known.… A quiet and reserved man who never opens his lips about himself or his work, he is the custodian of all the secrets of the world's unrest.… He studies the methods of the Apaches, and knew the book of Anarchy from A to Z."

Bessie Bellwood, real name **Catherine Mahoney** (1856-1896), was a music-hall entertainer who was by no means invented for the film "The Adventure of Sherlock Holmes' Smarter Brother". Born in London to Irish parents, she worked in her teens at one of the many stinking leather processing plants in Bermondsey, just south of the Thames, then went on stage in the same neighbourhood at the age of 20. "She became a popular performer noted for her saucy stage manner and her ability to argue down even the toughest of hecklers," says Wikipedia. She moved a little upscale, became widely known for her impudent songs, drank enthusiastically, and gave away money generously, particularly to Roman Catholic charities.

Booker T. Washington (1856-1915) was a leader of Black people (then called Negroes) in the United States, emphasizing the role of education. Most notably he founded the Tuskegee Normal and Industrial Institute. Washington was born a slave in Franklin County, Virginia; his surname came from a stepfather. Eventually educated at Hampton Normal Agricultural Institute in Virginia, he became a teacher, and in 1881 was asked to head the new Tuskegee college in Alabama. "He reassured whites," says Biography.com, "that nothing in the Tuskegee program would threaten white supremacy or pose any economic competition to whites." In 1895 he went further with what was called the Atlanta Compromise: Blacks should accept disenfranchisement and social segregation as long as whites allowed them economic progress and an opportunity for education. His autobiography, *Up from Slavery*, was published in 1901.

Charles Frohman (1856-1915) was a producer, putting plays on the stage by 1886, owning six Broadway theatres, and extending his theatrical empire to London when he leased the Duke of York's Theatre near Trafalgar Square. As a teenager he sold theatre tickets in New York; he later toured the United States with a troupe billed as Haverly's

United Mastodon Minstrels. He managed the Madison Square Theatre for a time, had the Empire Theatre built to his specifications in 1892, and in 1896 formed the Theatrical Syndicate, a near-monopoly of stage production, with five partners. He scanned Arthur Conan Doyle's draft of a "Sherlock Holmes" play in 1898, contracted **William Gillette** to revise it, and eventually produced Gillette's play in the United States and Britain. It had its "copyright performance" at the Duke of York's in June 1899 before opening in Buffalo and then New York. Frohman died in the sinking of RMS *Lusitania* by the German navy in the early months of World War I.

E. Phillips Oppenheim (1856-1946) called himself "the prince of story-tellers" and demonstrated it with scores of novels and many short stories, particularly in the thriller genre. His books are, says the *Encyclopaedia Britannica*, "peopled with sophisticated heroes, adventurous spies, and dashing noblemen". Novels like his biggest hit, *The Great Impersonation* (1920), are said to have influenced the creation of James Bond. His writing brought him not only popularity but the sort of income that allowed a villa on the French Riviera, where he both lived the sybaritic life and wrote about it; he barely escaped when World War II closed in.

Frank Harris (1856-1931) was, in the words of a website devoted to his memory, "a man who idealised **Jesus**, **Goethe**, and **Shakespeare**, but played the role of rake and bounder so well that the role was almost universally mistaken for the man." Irish-born, he attended the University of Kansas, worked in the United States for a while, then went to Britain to be a journalist. He edited several periodicals in the year before World War I, then returned to the US to do more of the same. His four-volume autobiography, *My Life and Loves*, was published 1922-1927 in Berlin. It connects Harris with everything from the Great Fire of Chicago to the great thinkers of Europe, and describes many sexual encounters, with illustrations. The book is considered one of the classics of 20th century erotica.

Frank **Podmore** (1856-1910) wrote *Modern Spiritualism: A History and a Criticism* in 1902, 24 years before Arthur Conan Doyle's own *History of Spiritualism*. Podmore was a member of the Society for Psychical Research, as ACD was, but became a sceptic about Spiritualism (he did believe in extra-sensory perception). His greater interest was social reform, and in 1883 he was a founding member of a socialist debating society along with **Edith Nesbit** and **Havelock Ellis**. It was Podmore who suggested its name: the Fabian Society, honouring Q. Fabius Maximus, the inventor of guerrilla war. Podmore and **Sidney Webb** were the authors of the society's 1886 pamphlet *The Government Organisation of Unemployed Labour*. Podmore was obliged to resign from his post office job in 1907 because of rumours of homosexuality, and three years later was found drowned.

George Bernard Shaw (1856-1950) was Britain's greatest playwright after **William Shakespeare**, and winner of the 1925 Nobel Prize for Literature. Born in Dublin, he spent most of his life in London and Hertfordshire as a playwright, a critic, a reformer (he was a founder of the socialist Fabian Society), and a noted eccentric. His causes ranged from eugenics to vegetarianism and a new phonetic alphabet for spelling English words. Many of his plays, beginning with "Widowers' Houses" in 1892 and "Arms and the Man" in 1894, deal with social issues (housing and pacifism, respectively), and they became more urgent and pes-simistic as time went on. Shaw's best-known plays include "Caesar and Cleopatra" (1898), "Pygmalion" (1912), and "Saint Joan" (1923). Arthur Conan Doyle held very different views from Shaw's on most issues, and crossed swords with him in 1912 over whether Captain **Edward Smith** of RMS *Titanic* had been a hero.

James Keir Hardie (1856-1915) was the first Labour Member of Parliament. He grew up in poverty in Glasgow, employed from the age of 7, and became active in miners' unions in time for a major wave of strikes in 1880. Giving up on both Conservative and Liberal politicians, he set his eye on the House of Commons and was elected on his second try, 1892, from a district in suburban London. (Election placards pictured him wearing a deerstalker hat.) He helped form the Independent Labour Party in 1893; in 1900 he was first elected from the Welsh district of Merthyr Tydfil and Aberdare, which he represented until his death. He advocated pacifism, women's suffrage, and an end to segregation in South Africa. The Labour Party was formed in 1906 and Hardie was its leader for the first two years.

Nikola Tesla (1856-1943) is described with various superlatives as the greatest, most versatile and unluckiest engineer and inventor of the modern era. Born in a village in what is now Croatia, he came to the United States in 1884, already experienced in electrical engineering, and went to work for **Thomas Edison**. But they parted ways, and soon were in competition, with Tesla and **George Westinghouse** developing alternating current rather than Edison's preferred direct current system. By 1894 Tesla was experimenting with X-rays, by 1896 with radio, by 1898 with wireless telegraphy. Towards the end of his life he was interested in wireless transmission of electrical power. He collected more than 300 patents, but in a cut-throat business climate had trouble maintaining control of them, and lived in very modest circumstances in New York in his final years.

John Redmond (1856-1918) was leader of the Irish Parliamentary Party in Parliament, struggling without success to gain "home rule" — though not full independence — for Ireland. He was first elected to Parliament in 1881, as a follower of **Charles Stewart Parnell**, and stuck with Parnell's faction when his party broke apart in 1890. Ten years later he became party leader; in 1910 he found himself unexpectedly powerful when votes were so divided that **Herbert H. Asquith**'s Liberal government needed his support to stay in power. A home rule bill was introduced in 1912, and the dream might have been achieved by 1914, but Protestants in northern Ireland were clearly prepared to resist it by force of arms. World War I delayed action, and the 1916 Easter Rising, an armed rebellion among Catholics in the south, destroyed any hope of quick peaceful change.

Karl Peters (1856-1918) helped found the Society for German Colonisation in 1884 and then went to east Africa to make his ideas a reality. Fortified with several years' study of British colonial policy, he was confident he could found a German colony in the region even without official support. Chiefs in the region that is now Tanzania were persuaded, and early in 1885 so was the German government; the chancellor, **Otto von Bismarck**, announced the formation of a German protectorate, which expanded within a few years to be twice the size of Germany itself. A treaty in 1890 defined German and British "spheres of influence" in the region, and Peters became "commissioner" of the German protectorate. In 1895, following rumours of bloody abuses, he was fired, and turned his attention to exploration and writing.

Sigmund Freud (1856-1939) was the founder of psychoanalysis, a form of therapy now generally considered more art than science. The concepts he introduced to psychology include repression and the unconscious, the "Freudian" slip, infantile sexuality, the Oedipus and Electra complexes, hysteria, penis envy, phallic symbols, and the ego. His important books include *The Interpretation of Dreams* (1900), *Totem and Taboo* (1913), and *Moses and Monotheism* (1939). Freud received his medical degree from the University of Vienna in 1881 and practised in Vienna for most of his career, initially working with *Joseph Breuer* and using hypnosis. He gradually became more influential; an international psychoanalytic congress, though not officially under that name, was first held in Salzburg in 1908. Freud's interest in cocaine as an anaesthetic, stimulant, antidepressant, and cure for morphine addiction has led to imaginative connections between him and the early, self-injecting Sherlock Holmes.

Sir **Henry Rider Haggard** (1856-1925) was the creator of Allan Quatermain, who figures in a dozen adventure novels and has become a mainstay of pastiche and steampunk. Quatermain first appeared in *King Solomon's Mines* (1885), a melodramatic tale set in a lost African paradise; it may have influenced Arthur Conan Doyle's *The Lost World*. Haggard had spent some time in Africa before returning to England and entering law practice, but most of his time went to writing. The novel *She* (1887) has nothing to do with Quatermain, but does reveal Haggard's interest in occult matters as a

complement to physical adventure. His books are recognized for relatively sympathetic portrayals of Africans and other indigenous people with whom the British heroes come into contact.

Theobald von Bethmann-Hollweg (1856-1921) is mentioned in "His Last Bow", though not by name. "Unfortunately our good chancellor is a little heavy-handed," says Baron Von Herling, just before the German spies are unmasked. Von Bethmann-Hollweg was chancellor, or prime minister, of Germany from 1909 to 1917. A career in government made him president of the Brandenburg province in Prussia, then a cabinet minister, before he succeeded **Bernhard von Bülow** as chancellor. Historians argue about his role in the events leading to World War I, and in the conduct of the war, but he is generally seen as a moderate compared to increasingly powerful military leaders such as Admiral **Alfred von Tirpitz**.

Beatrice Mary, Princess **Henry of Battenberg** (1857-1944), was the youngest child of Queen **Victoria** and the first one her mother delivered with the help of chloroform. She became her mother's "baby" and companion after the death of Prince **Albert**, and the Queen allowed her to marry Prince **Henry of Battenberg** only on condition that the couple should live with the Queen. The Prince died of malaria while serving with British forces in South Africa in 1896. Beatrice acted as the Queen's companion and secretary, and after the Queen's death edited her journals, removing as much as two-thirds of the material, which is now lost.

George **Gissing** (1857-1903) had endless trouble with women, and re–flected it in 23 novels written between 1880 and his death — one a year, meant to stave off the poverty about which he also repeatedly wrote. His adulthood began with a month in prison (1876) after he was caught stealing from fellow-students in Manchester to support a prostitute, **Marianne (Nell) Harrison**. He later lived with her in London, endured a miserable marriage with another lower-class woman, suffered from illnesses real and imaginary, and made expensive bad decisions about the publication of his writings. He flirted with socialism, but ended as what one friend called a "despairing conservative", seeing little hope for social improvement. Still, some critics consider him one of the century's greatest writers, and *H. G. Wells* and *James Barrie* were his friends. His most important novels include *Workers in the Dawn* (1880) and *New Grub Street* (1891).

Heinrich Hertz (1857-1894) was one of the researchers who laid the foundations for modern science and engineering; his specific contribution was to prove the existence of electromagnetic waves, which carry radio and television signals. The measurement of wave frequency, sometimes called "cycles per second", was officially named "hertz" in his honour in 1930. Originally from Hamburg, Hertz earned his PhD at the University of Berlin in 1880, lecturing for a time at Kiel and then becoming a professor at Karlsruhe and finally, in 1889, at the University of Bonn. His experiments between 1886 and 1889 confirmed the theory presented in 1865 by *James Clerk Maxwell*.

Joseph Conrad, born **Józef Konrad Korzeniowski** (1857-1924), was the author of *Heart of Darkness* (1899), *Lord Jim*, and other novels that, as Biography.com puts it, "combined his experiences in remote places with an interest in moral conflict and the dark side of human nature....

Conrad was interested in showing 'psycho-political' situations that drew parallels between the inner lives of single characters and the broader sweep of human history." Born in Poland (actually in a town that is now in Ukraine), he spent time as a sailor before eventually settling in Britain. He always spoke English with an accent, and his books, which began with *Almayer's Folly* in 1895 and often touch on issue of colonialism, are said to recall his unstable boyhood in occupied Poland.

Lillian Nordica, born **Norton** (1857-1914), was an operatic soprano from Maine who could well have been the original, or one of the originals, of Irene Adler. She also sang in "Les Huguenots" with tenor *Jean de Reszke*, a performance that Sherlock Holmes probably refers to when he speaks in the last paragraph of *The Hound of the Baskervilles*. She trained at the New England Conservatory, made her operatic debut in Milan in 1879, and sang a variety of roles across Europe and in the United States, but came into her own with performances in Wagner's operas beginning in the early 1890s. Again, she was often paired with De Reszke, frequently at the Metropolitan Opera in New York. She died in Java following a shipwreck during her world tour. Several recordings of her voice survive, but they are rather disappointing.

Lewis Dyche (1857-1915) came west from West Virginia as an infant and grew up in Osage County, Kansas, where he worked on farms and met Kansa Indian tribes who lived nearby. As a University of Kansas student in 1881 he went on a field trip to what is now New Mexico and narrowly missed being attacked by a band of Apaches, the tribe whose fierce name had been borrowed by street gangs in Paris (as mentioned in "The Illustrious Client"). After graduation he trained as a taxidermist; his best-known job involved preserving the body of Comanche, the cavalry horse that was the only US Army survivor of the 1876 Battle of the Little Big Horn against the Lakota and other tribes. He also preserved dozens of animal specimens from Kansas and elsewhere in North America, which were displayed at the 1893 world's fair in Chicago and are now in the University of Kansas natural history museum.

Montague John Druitt (1857-1888) was found dead in the Thames, with stones weighting his pockets, a few weeks after the Whitechapel murders attributed to Jack the Ripper. He has been a prominent suspect ever since Inspector *Melville Macnaghten* famously nominated him as Jack in an 1894 memorandum. The son of a physician in Dorset, Druitt studied at Oxford, then became a schoolteacher and qualified as a barrister. By 1888, when the murders took place, he was practising law on the Western Circuit and had "chambers" in the Inner Temple, one of the legal precincts in the City of London. He also had a teaching position in Blackheath in southeast London, and played cricket for Blackheath (not rugby, as Watson had done according to "The Sussex Vampire"). In July 1888 Druitt's mother suffered a mental illness and was institutionalized; sometime that autumn, he lost his teaching job, for reasons that are not clear. His suicide followed.

Robert Baden-Powell, 1st Baron **Baden-Powell** (1857-1941), was the founder of Scouting. He served in the British army in India and South Africa, and was impressed by the talents of young soldiers during the 1899-1900 siege of Mafeking. (Arthur Conan Doyle was serving at a field hospital in South Africa during the same time.) A handbook Baden-Powell had written for soldiers was soon being used by youth leaders in Britain to teach observation and woodcraft. His revised version, *Scouting for Boys*, was published in 1908, and the formation of Scout troops followed, soon joined by Guide groups for girls, as well as Wolf Cubs and Brownies. "B-P" was given the title Chief Scout of the World in 1920.

Samuel S. McClure (1857-1949) was the Irish-born publisher of *McClure's Magazine*, which was founded in 1893 but struggling when Arthur Conan Doyle visited the United States the following year. ACD promptly invested $5,000 — essentially all the proceeds of his American lecture tour — into the business, and waited twenty years for his profit. McClure believed in giving writers time and scope for investigative articles, and developed a newspaper syndicate to spread the costs. Financial reorganization forced him out of the business in 1911, but the monthly magazine, which sold for 15 cents, lasted until 1929. The publisher's younger brother, **Robert McClure**, was the magazine's agent in London, and a friend of ACD.

Sir **Edward Elgar** (1857-1934) grew up in a musical environment — his father owned a music shop in Worcester — and became one of Britain's great composers. His best-known work a century later is the 1901 "Pomp and Circumstance" march in D major that provided the tune for the triumphal anthem "Land of Hope and Glory". He also wrote cantatas, symphonies and other works, including "The Dream of Gerontius" (1900) based on a poem by *John Henry Newman*. "His long struggle to establish himself as a pre-eminent composer of international repute was hard and often bitter," says a website devoted to his work. "For many years he had to contend with apathy, with the prejudices of the entrenched musical establishment, with religious bigotry (he was a member of the Roman Catholic minority in a Protestant majority England) and with a late Victorian provincial society where class consciousness pervaded everything." His knighthood came in 1904 and a further order of chivalry in 1928.

William Howard Taft (1857-1930) was President of the United States 1909-1913, and later chief justice of the Supreme Court. A lawyer and then a local judge in Ohio, he served as solicitor-general of the United States, a federal judge, governor-general of the Philippines (an American possession after the Spanish-American War of 1898), and finally secretary of war. In that possession, president *Theodore Roosevelt* thought, Taft would be well prepared to be his successor as a "progressive" Republican president, and it worked, as he defeated *William Jennings Bryan*. A major part of his work as president was, in the Roosevelt tradition, working to demolish industrial monopolies known as trusts. However, he lost Roosevelt's support, and Taft was defeated by Democrat **Woodrow Wilson** when he tried for re-election in 1912.

Antoine Marfan (1858-1942) was a French physician whose research and clinical work was largely concerned with immunity to tuberculosis and with children's diseases generally, but who gave his name to a congenital syndrome affecting connective tissue. Marfan's syndrome, which has been identified in Jefferson Hope of *A Study in Scarlet*, commonly causes long fingers and long bones generally, subluxation of the lens of the eye, and deterioration of the aorta, among other symptoms. The name dates from an 1896 case that Marfan presented to a Paris medical society, although his specific patient is now thought to have suffered from a different malady, arachnodactyly. Marfan's career was largely spent at the Hôpital des Enfants Malades in Paris.

Beatrice Webb, Lady **Passfield**, née **Potter** (1858-1943), was an early member of the socialist Fabian Society and a founder (1895) of the London School of Economics. Her contributions as an economist, reformer and writer included creation of the term "collective bargaining". Her initial career was in social work, and she assisted with a study of the London slums being carried out by her cousin **Charles Booth**. In 1890 she met **Charles Webb**, later Baron **Passfield**, who was already involved in social research; they married in 1892 and worked together for the ensuing 51 years. Beatrice Webb's writings include *The Co-operative Movement in Great Britain* (1891). She served on a royal commission on poverty (1905-1909) and presented a minority report calling for the creation of a welfare state, someting that began to happen in Britain 40 years later. With Sidney, Beatrice co-founded the *New Statesman Magazine* (1913), joined the Labour Party (1914), and wrote a massive history of British local government as well as an uncritically admiring book about the Communism of Soviet Russia (1935).

John L. Sullivan (1858-1918) was the last unofficial heavyweight champion of bare-knuckle boxing, and the first champion of gloved boxing after new rules were introduced. Championships were unofficial in the bare-knuckle era (a sport about which Arthur Conan Doyle wrote admiringly in *The Croxley Master* and other works) but in 1887, in his home town of Boston, Sullivan was presented with a belt hailing him as "the Champion of Champions". In 1889, at Richburg, Mississippi, Sullivan knocked out **Jake Kilrain** in the 75th round. Under the new Marquess of *Queensberry* rules, Sullivan faced *'Gentleman Jim' Corbett* in New Orleans, considered the centre of boxing, in September 1892 and was defeated in the 21st round.

E. [Edith] Nesbit (1858-1924), was, says the *New York Review of Books*, "able to create a world of magic and inverted logic that was entirely her own. Yet Nesbit's books are relatively unknown in the United States." Her more than 40 books (about children, and mostly read by children) "combined realistic, contemporary children in real-world settings with magical objects and adventures and sometimes travel to fantastic worlds," says Wikipedia. The best known is *The Railway Children* (1906); others are *The Wouldbegoods* (1899) and *Five Children and It* (1902). Nesbit also wrote several adult novels as well as poetry. She and her husband, **Hubert Bland**, had a stormy relationship, and were among the founders of the socialist Fabian Society.

Eleonora Duse (1858-1924) was recognized as Italy's greatest actress by the middle of the 1880s, and soon afterwards was performing in New York and London as well. Says the famous 11th edition of the *Encyclopaedia Britannica*, published in 1911: "Madame Duse's reputation as an actress was founded less on her 'creations' than on her magnificent individuality. In contrast to [*Sarah Bernhardt*] she avoided all 'make-up'; her art depended on intense naturalness rather than on stage effect, sympathetic force or poignant intellectuality rather than the theatrical emotionalism of the French tradition." She was best known for her performances in plays by Italy's **Gabriele D'Annunzio** (one of several artists with whom she had romantic relationships), Norway's *Henrik Ibsen*, and France's *Alexandre Dumas*.

Emmeline Pankhurst, née **Goulden** (1858-1928), grew up in a family of political activists, and in 1879 married another one, **Richard Pankhurst**, a lawyer who had written the Married Women's Property Act of 1870. Ten years later she founded the Women's Franchise League to advocate for women's right to vote, and in 1903 the more radical Women's Social and Political Union, whose members were the first "suffragettes" (described as "furies" in the tale "His Last Bow"). Over the next decade she was involved in many demonstrations — joined by her daughters, notably **Christabel** — and was arrested, went on hunger strikes and endured force-feeding. The suffragette movement paused during World War I; the Representation of the People Act 1918 gave women over 30 the right to vote (that was lowered to 21, the same age as for men, in 1928).

Émile Durkheim (1858-1917) was one of the founders of sociology, along with *Karl Marx* and *Max Weber*. "Chief among his claims," says the Internet Encyclopedia of Philosophy, "is that society is a *sui generis* reality, or a reality unique to itself and irreducible to its composing parts. This reality can only be understood in sociological terms, and cannot be reduced to biological or psychological explanations." He was born in France's Lorraine region and taught philosophy and social sciences the University of Bordeaux and, later, at the Sorbonne in Paris. His major works include *The Division of Labour in Society* (1893) and *Suicide* (1897). "He hoped to use his sociology as a way to help a

French society suffering under the strains of modernity," the Encyclopedia says, "and during World War I he took up a position writing anti-German propaganda pamphlets."

Harry Gordon Selfridge (1858-1947) was, as viewers of the ITV television series "Mr. Selfridge" know, the founder of Selfridges department store in London's fashionable shopping district. Selfridge was born in Wisconsin and had worked 25 years at Marshall Field's department store in Chicago before deciding to open a store himself in London, which he thought was lagging behind American cities, and also Paris, in the quality of its retailing. "Selfridge promoted the radical notion of shopping for pleasure rather than necessity," says Wikipedia. That and other innovations made the store a fashionable success for a quarter of a century, and it remains a landmark at 400 Oxford Street, along with its competitor Harrods, a mile and a half away in the Brompton Road. Selfridge was a lavish spender; he lost most of his fortune in the 1930s and died in poverty.

John Theodore Tussaud (1858-1943) was the great-grandson of **Marie (Grostholtz) Tussaud**, the sculptor who came to fame making effigies of the victims of the guillotine during the French Revolution, and subsequently founded her wax museum in Baker Street in 1831. The museum's new site in the nearby Marylebone Road opened in 1884, and in 1889 the founder's descendants sold it to a consortium of new owners. John Theodore, however, remained as manager and chief artist, and played host to a celebrated dinner in 1903 marking the centenary of his great-grandmother's first arrival in Britin. He also wrote a book about the family business, *The Romance of Madame Tussaud's* (1920). He was himself a sculptor who exhibited his work at the Royal Academy.

Max Planck (1858-1947) was the winner of the 1918 Nobel Prize in Physics for his pioneering work in quantum theory. He studied at Munich and Berlin, spent several years in private research on thermodynamics and particularly entropy, and in 1885 was given a position at the University of Kiel; four years later he moved to the University of Berlin. As a dean at Berlin in 1914 he was able to create a position for *Albert Einstein*. His key discovery, dating to 1900 and now known as the Planck postulate, is the idea that energy can be emitted only in "quantized" form — in effect, tiny pellets of radiation. Planck's constant, used in calculations for such quanta, is a tiny number conventionally expressed by the letter h. Planck himself thought his idea merely a useful mathematical trick.

Prince **Henry of Battenberg** (1858-1896) was a member of minor German royalty, and an officer in the Prussian army, who married Princess *Beatrice*, daughter of Queen *Victoria*, in 1885. He was appointed honorary colonel of a battalion in the Hampshire Regiment, and there were rumours that he would take an active commission in the Life Guards. The latter did not happen at that time, but he later received a colonelcy, and died aboard ship on his way to take part in the Fourth Ashanti War, one of five conflicts that pitted Britain against an empire in the Gold Coast region of west Africa (now Ghana).

Rudolf, Crown Prince of Austria-Hungary (1858-1889), was the son of Emperor *Franz Joseph I* and Empress *Elisabeth*, and heir to the empire. He was married (1881) to Princess **Stéphanie**, daughter of King *Léopold II* of Belgium. He had strong interests in science, notably geology, and is thought to have had more liberal political views than his father, but his interests in women and drink were even stronger. His best-known mistress was Baroness **Marie Vetsera**, daughter of an Austrian diplomat, who took up with the Crown Prince when she was about 17. In January 1889 he and she were found together, shot to death, at the Crown Prince's hunting lodge at Mayerling in the Vienna woods. The assumption has always been that the deaths were a murder-suicide, although more complex plots have also been suggested. The death left the Emperor's brother, Archduke **Karl Ludwig**, as the heir, to be followed by his son, Archduke *Franz Ferdinand*, assassinated in 1914.

Sir **Edward Marshall Hall** (1858-1927) was the most celebrated barrister of his era, defending in one important or spectacular criminal trial after another. He had thought of entering the church, and then considered the stage, but he chose law, and was called to the bar (that is, became a barrister) in 1888. Critics said his knowledge of the law

was weak, but he brought his acting ability with him and used it effectively to sway juries and judges. In the 1894 case of a prostitute, **Marie
Hermann**, charged with killing a client, he famously appealed to the
jury: "Look at her, gentlemen. God never gave her a chance. Won't
you?" Hall served in Parliament starting in 1900, and was knighted in
1917.

Sir **Harry Johnston** (1858-1927) was a naturalist, author (especially of
travel books), and painter, but chiefly an imperialist. Sent in 1884 to
lead a scientific expedition to Mount Kilimanjaro, the highest mountain
in Africa, he turned the trip to political advantage as well, negotiating
treaties with local chiefs (in what is now Tanzania) on behalf of the
British East Africa Company. Every such agreement was a move in
Britain's competition with Germany for control of eastern and central
Africa. A far bigger move would be a British railway from Cairo in the
north to Cape Town in the south; Johnston and *Cecil Rhodes* were
among those who formulated such a plan, never executed. Johnston's
career on behalf of British colonialism also took him to Nyasaland (Mala-
wi), Mozambique, Rhodesia (Zambia), Katanga (part of Congo) and
Uganda. His writings include *The Backward Peoples and Our Relations
with Them* (1920).

Sir **Havelock Charles** (1858-1934) was an army doctor in India with a
career longer and more successful than Watson's. Born and educated in
Ireland, he went through the prescribed course at Netley in 1882 (just
four years behind Watson, according to *A Study in Scarlet*) and was
quickly sent to India. He served with the Afghan Boundary Commission, was assigned to teach anatomy at Lahore and then at Calcutta,
stayed unwounded, and eventually retired as a lieutenant-colonel. He
was then named to the honorary post of "serjeant surgeon" to King
George V, served as a member and then president of the Medical Board
of the India Office, and was promoted to major-general. Along the way
he was president of the Society of Tropical Medicine and Hygiene.

Theodore Roosevelt (1858-1919) was President of the United States
and a Nobel Peace Prize winner, but those achievements were in the
20th century. In the 19th, he grew up in New York City, attended Harvard, and in 1882 became the youngest member of the New York State
Assembly. He took a two-year break from politics to sample frontier
life in the Dakota Territory, then served in a series of public offices
including chairman of the New York City Police Commission, where
he did his best to make reforms effective. He took another break from
government work to serve with a cavalry unit dubbed the "Rough Ri-

ders" in the Spanish-American War, 1898. He was elected Governor of New York the same year, became Vice-President of the United States in 1901, and suddenly became President on the assassination of *William McKinley*. Highlights of his presidency (1901-1909) include the Sherman Anti-Trust Act, the Panama Canal, the National Monuments Act, and work to end the Russo-Japanese War, the achievement that earned him his Nobel.

Tobias Branger (1858-1939) was a shopkeeper in Davos, Switzerland, who taught Arthur Conan Doyle to ski, effectively creating the sport of recreational skiing. A 1999 article in the *Telegraph* recalls that Branger and his brother, **Johann Branger**, "had the foresight to realise that this skiing business could be as big as cheese, chocolate and watches. They imported skis from Norway and improved the leather-and-metal bindings." In March 1894 they guided ACD, who was spending the season in Switzerland for the sake of his wife's health, across the Mayenfelder Furka Pass from Davos to Arosa, about 13 miles.

Wilhelm Fliess (1858-1928) was a physician, a specialist in the ear and throat, who became a friend of *Sigmund Freud*, contributed to his theories, and promoted the belief that there is a significant connection between the nose and the genitals. His theory of "nasal reflex neurosis" was presented in an 1892 book, and Freud sometimes referred patients to Fliess for nasal surgery, or anaethesis of the nasal mucosa with cocaine, to treat psychological symptoms. Fliess also developed a theory of "vital periodicity", later known as biorhythm. He was born and practised in Berlin, but was introduced to Freud by *Joseph Breuer* and met with him regularly in Vienna starting in 1887. Their partnership ended with a quarrel in 1904.

Fergus Hume (1859-1932) wrote the best-selling detective novel of the nineteenth century, *The Mystery of a Hansom Cab*. The author, a barristers' clerk in Melbourne, self-published the first edition in 1886, but it caught on quickly, selling 100,000 copies in Australia and an estimated 500,000 worldwide. That figure outstrips *A Study in Scarlet*, which appeared a year later (but was written in 1886 and cannot have been influenced by Hume). *A Hansom Cab* juxtaposes the investigations of Detective Gorby with social conditions in Melbourne, which had been a gold rush town just a century earlier and was now one of the world's largest cities. Hume, born in England and educated in New Zealand, returned to England in 1888 and in his remaining years wrote dozens of other books, none of them so successful.

Alfred Dreyfus (1859-1935) was an officer in the French army who became the victim of a miscarriage of justice and subsequent international scandal. In 1894, when information about artillery hardware was making its way to Germany — France's traditional enemy — Dreyfus was blamed, convicted, and sent to the hideous penal colony at Devil's Island (Cayenne, French Guiana), where he spent four years. Supporters, most prominently the writer *Émile Zola*, charged that Dreyfus was the victim of anti-Jewish prejudice. He was eventually pardoned, exonerated and returned to a military command, and fought in World War I. The actual traitor was another officer, **Ferdinand Esterhazy**, who fled France to avoid consequences.

Fanny Adams (1859-1867) was the eight-year-old victim of a notorious murder in Alton, Hampshire. Her mutilated and dismembered body was found in a field. **Frederick Baker**, a solicitors' clerk, was convicted and hanged. *Brewer's Dictionary of Phrase and Fable*: "The Royal Navy, with grim humour, adopted her name as a synonym for tinned mutton, which was first issued at this time. Sweet Fanny Adams became, as a consequence, a phrase for anything worthless and then for 'nothing at all'. The 'F' of the initials is often taken as the 'F-word'."

George Curzon, Marquess Curzon (1859-1925), was Viceroy of India and later Foreign Secretary. He was educated at Oxford and served briefly in Parliament, then travelled for several years in Asia, coming home with a keen sense of the "great game" pitting Britain against Russia for control of India. After holding minor government positions, he was named Viceroy in 1899; in that role he sent *Francis Younghusband* on his 1903 expedition to Tibet. Thanks to interpersonal conflicts that were the constant theme of his career, he resigned in 1905 and was not back in the cabinet until 1915. When **Andrew Bonar Law** retired as prime minister in 1923, Curzon hoped for the position, but was passed over. He was twice married, both times to American women, and had a protracted affair with novelist *Elinor Glyn*.

Havelock Ellis (1859-1939) was a physician, trained at St. Thomas's Hospital in London, and one of the early researchers into sexual behaviour and psychology. His 1897 book *Sexual Inversion*, written jointly with **John Addington Symonds**, was the first in six volumes collected under the title *Studies in the Psychology of Sex*. It was sufficiently scandalous, a year after the trial of **Oscar Wilde**, to lead to charges against one bookseller. Its ideas, and Ellis's writings on autoeroticism, are thought to have influenced everyone from **Sigmund Freud** to lesbian novelist **Radclyff Hall**. He also developed theories on transgender identity, and was interested in eugenics. The word "homosexual" is attributed to him, although he said he disliked it because it combines Greek and Latin roots. His wife was lesbian and women's activist **Edith Lees**.

Jerome K. Jerome (1859-1927) met Arthur Conan Doyle at a dinner hosted by the *Idler* magazine in 1892, when both were young authors, and they were friends for years, though Jerome was somewhat critical of his Spiritualist passions in the 1920s. He was an actor for a time, claiming "I have played every part in *Hamlet* except Ophelia," and his first book was *On the Stage and Off* (1885). Many books, articles and plays followed, the most famous being *Idle Thoughts of an Idle Fellow* (1886) and the comic classic *Three Men in a Boat* (1889). He also edited the *Idler*, and in that role commissioned some of ACD's work including several of the medical short stories that were collected in the anthology *Round the Red Lamp*. Largely self-educated (he had left school at 14), Jerome also became a lecturer and world traveller; during World War I he volunteered as an ambulance driver for the French army.

Henri Bergson (1859-1941) received the 1927 Nobel Prize in literature "in recognition of his rich and vitalizing ideas and the brilliant skill with which they have been presented". A teacher of philosophy at various institutions and, from 1901, a professor at the elite Collège de France, he emphasized the influence of mind on matter and "l'élan vital", the life force, on the progress of evolution. His first significant work, titled in English *Time and Free Will*, was based on his thesis and appeared in 1889; *Matter and Memory* followed in 1896, and other essays later. He was a friend of **William James**, although they did not agree on many points. In 1913 he was president of the Society for Psychical Research, of which Arthur Conan Doyle was a member.

James **Leslie Stephen** (1859-1892) was the son of *James Fitzjames Stephen* and, according to *Rudyard Kipling*, a "genius" at poetry; two books of his work, both with Latin titles, were published in 1891. Earlier, shortly after his graduation from Cambridge, he spent a few months as tutor to Prince *Albert Victor*, Duke of *Clarence*, the heir presumptive to the throne, then 19 and preparing for university himself. He also did some journalism, clerked for his father, and lectured at Cambridge. Stephen is thought to have suffered from bipolar disorder, aggravated by a head injury, and spent some time in a mental institution. The Prince, his former charge, died early in 1892, aged 28; when Stephen heard the news he stopped eating, and died within days. He has been proposed as a candidate to be Jack the Ripper, but there is no evidence.

Joseph-Alexandre Lestrade (1859-1926) was born in Saint Lucia, and studied medicine at the University of Edinburgh, where he was two years behind Arthur Conan Doyle. Like ACD, he had previously studied at Stonyhurst College, a Jesuit boarding school. After receiving his degrees of Bachelor of Medicine and Master of Surgery in 1883, Lestrade returned to take up government work in Saint Lucia, a British colony although largely French-speaking. In 1904 he was residing in the town of Soufriere and serving as Colonial Assistant Surgeon, a position with duties that included giving vaccinations, inspecting food safety, and coping with occasional yellow fever outbreaks. (A report in the *British Medical Journal* in 1901 noted that malaria was endemic in the low-lying areas.) A document from the Public Record Office in London indicates that in 1905 Lestrade was facing "charges", their nature not specified. Scholars speculate that ACD borrowed his fellow-student's surname, which is French rather than English, for Inspector G. Lestrade.

Kenneth Grahame (1859-1932) had a difficult childhood and a troubled family life, and had little opportunity himself of messing about in boats, but the book he wrote about the river lives on. He first went to work in the Bank of England, and by 1899 — still a young man — had reached the weighty position of corporate secretary there. At the same time he entered London's literary circles and began to write for publication. His first widely successful work was a set of stories about a family of orphaned children, but he is now remembered chiefly for *The Wind in the Willows*, based in part on bedtime stories he would tell his young son. The book describes the personalities and adventures of Rat, Mole, Toad and Badger up and down the Thames. It was published in 1908 and not initially well reviewed, but sales were high and it has become a classic for children and former children.

Thomas James Wise (1859-1937) was a forger, a very sophisticated one. He was first of all a critic, writing in the *Bookman*, and a rare-book collector, whose Ashley Library attracted scholarly visitors to London (it is now part of the British Library). From studying books and producing bibliographies, he moved to stealing pages from books in the British Museum to improve his own copies; from printing limited facsimile editions of old poems and pamphlets, he advanced to creating new and spurious first editions of works by such authors as **Robert Louis Stevenson** and **Elizabeth Barrett Browning**, which of course brought high prices. Suspicions arose in the 1890s, notably in the 1894 book *Early Editions* by **J. Herbert Slater**, but extensive proof of the racket came in a 1934 publication by two scholars, *An Enquiry Into the Nature of Certain Nineteenth Century Pamphlets*, which identified some 50 of Wise's supposed rare finds as counterfeits. Later scholarship raised the number of fakes to approximately 200.

Wilhelm II (1859-1941) was the Kaiser — the Emperor of Germany — who is referred to in the story "His Last Bow". He was the son of **Frederick III**, who was Emperor for a few weeks before dying of cancer, and **Victoria**, Britain's Princess Royal. His parents tried with little success to raise him with liberal values, instead watching him become an impetuous and chauvinistic Prussian. (The hot-headed monarch who wrote a dangerous letter in the story "The Second Stain" is often identified as being Wilhelm.) He succeeded to the throne (and subsidiary offices including King of Prussia) in 1888, at the age of 29, and quickly clashed with the aging, incrementalist Chancellor, **Otto von Bismarck**, forcing his resignation in 1890. Over the next two decades he steered German foreign policy in a direction that left his country largely isolated and made it easy for World War I to begin; a particular enthusiasm was building up a massive German navy. As the war unfolded, the Emperor's power dwindled, largely moving to generals such as **Paul von Hindenburg**. In November 1918, when defeat was imminent, the army mutinied and Wilhelm abdicated.

Alphonse Mucha (1860-1939) designed posters for beer, biscuits and bicycles, and pretty much founded the school of design known as Art Nouveau. He was born in Moravia, a region of what is now the Czech Republic, and moved to Paris in 1887 to continue his art studies and earn a living making advertising illustrations. By chance in 1894 he got a commission to do a poster for actress *Sarah Bernhardt*; that led to more work for Bernhardt and for other clients, in the form of posters, product designs, wallpaper and book illustrations. "Mucha's works frequently featured beautiful young women in flowing, vaguely Neo-classical-looking robes, often surrounded by lush flowers which sometimes formed halos behind their heads," says Wikipedia. "In contrast with contemporary poster makers he used pale pastel colors." Work by Mucha, as well as other Art Nouveau designs, enjoyed a renaissance during the psychedelic 1960s.

Annie Oakley, born **Phoebe Ann Mosey** (1860-1926), was a brilliant sharpshooter from her childhood in western Ohio, where she made money hunting game. In her teens she married a noted show business marksman, **Frank E. Butler**, and they joined *Buffalo Bill Cody*'s Wild West Show in 1885, with five-foot-tall Oakley (a stage name) the acknowledged star. "She would shoot holes through cards thrown into the air before they landed," the website Biography.com says, "inspiring the practice of punching holes in a free event ticket being referred to as an 'Annie Oakley'." She recovered from a 1901 railway accident to perform for another two decades. The musical "Annie Get Your Gun" is based on her life.

Florence Farr, married name **Emery** (1860-1917) was a notable West End actress, apparently a mistress of *George Bernard Shaw*, a leader of the Hermetic Order of the Golden Dawn, and a vocal advocate of women's rights. A classmate at Cheltenham Ladies' College introduced her to London's artistic circles, and she was soon living in London's bohemian Bedford Park neighbourhood. She was a model for at least one painting by Sir *Edward Burne-Jones*. Farr performed on stage as an amateur and then a professional, and soon caught Shaw's eye as well as that of *William Butler Yeats*, who cast her in their plays. She was also the first woman in England to perform in works by *Henrik Ibsen*. It was Yeats who introduced her to the Golden Dawn in 1890; she rose to a powerful position in its hierarchy, but resigned as the society crumbled in 1902. She took up Theosophy, and spent her last years as a teacher in Ceylon.

Edward W. Barton-Wright (1860-1951) was influential in introducing Japanese martial arts into Europe. He worked as a civil engineer in Egypt and Malaya, and in the late 1890s spent three years in Japan. During this time he learned multiple forms of jujitsu, which he combined with boxing, singlestick fighting and other arts to form his own urban self-defence system, named Bartitsu. It is generally thought that this system was the "baritsu" which Sherlock Holmes claims to have used against Professor Moriarty at the Reichenbach Falls. Barton-Wright opened a popular "School of Arms and Physical Culture" in London in 1900; it closed in 1903, the year "The Empty House" was published.

Frederick Rolfe, alias **Baron Corvo** (1860-1913), was the eccentric, if not delusional, author of the 1904 novel *Hadrian VII*, in which a young English priest (himself, as he imagined things) accidentally becomes Pope. He also wrote several other novels, some of them more or less autobiographical. Some of his fiction features idealized relationships between older and younger men of the kind that apparently made up Rolfe's own sexual life. Born in London, he converted to Roman Catholicism, felt a calling to become a priest, and studied for that purpose at Birmingham and in Rome, but did not live up to the church's expectations or get along well with others, and supported himself by painting as well as writing. He was a constant letter-writer, often focusing on his many grievances; **W. H. Auden** called him "one of the great masters of vituperation".

Hamlin Garland (1860-1940) was a young American writer, becoming recognized for his realistic portrayals of rural life, when Arthur Conan Doyle first met him during ACD's North American tour in 1894. They crossed paths several times, and ACD autographed a copy of *The Memoirs of Sherlock Holmes* for Garland. They would meet again in Britain in 1899 and 1906, and when ACD lectured on Spiritualism in New York in 1922, Garland chaired the meeting. His short stories of pioneer life on the Great Plains (his own family had lived in Wisconsin and Iowa) were collected in *Main-Travelled Roads* (1891) and succeeding volumes. He also wrote a number of novels, including *A Son of the Middle Border* (1917). He had a life-long interest in psychic phenomena, and towards the end of his life became an outspoken believer.

Ignacy Paderewski (1860-1941) was an internationally famous pianist, and a Polish patriot so energetic that he was briefly prime minister of his country. His concerts in Europe and the United States in the 1890s, along with his histrionic personality and wild hair, were the focus of acclaim and excitement. He also edited piano works, particularly those of **Frédéric Chopin**, and composed music of his own. Based in the United States during World War I, he pressed Poland's cause, and in January 1919 the provisional president of the newly independent country asked him to form a non-partisan government. He represented Poland at the Paris Peace Conference that led to the Treaty of Versailles.

Lizzie Borden (1860-1927) was acquitted of charges that she killed her stepmother, **Abby Durfee Gray Borden**, and father, banker **Andrew Borden**, in their home in Fall River, Massachusetts, on a hot summer day in 1892. No one else was ever charged, despite suggestions that other family members or the housemaid might have wielded the fatal axe, and most historians now believe Borden was guilty. So does folklore, which still declares that "Lizzie Borden took an axe and gave her mother forty whacks." There had been family tension over money and other issues, and descriptions of the household suggest a claustrophobic life for Lizzie and her sister **Emma Borden**. She lived in prosperity in Fall River the rest of her life and enjoyed a relationship with fast-living actress **Nance O'Neil**.

Nicholas II (1860-1918) was Tsar ("Emperor of All the Russias") from 1894 until he was forced to abdicate, and then executed, in the Bolshevik revolution. He was the oldest son of *Alexander III*, and succeeded to the throne when his father died of nephritis in 1894. "Reeling from the loss, and poorly trained in affairs of state, Nicholas II hardly felt up to the task of assuming his father's role," Biography.com notes. A defeat in the Russo-Japanese War of 1905 was followed by "Bloody Sunday" in St. Petersburg, in which troops killed more than 1,000 people demonstrating for better working conditions and democratization. Strikes swept across Russia. Although Nicholas agreed to recognize an elected assembly, the Duma, his resistance to reforms in general, and poor decisions including the ascendance of peasant holy man *Grigori Rasputin*, led to the end of his reign as the last Tsar.

Owen Wister (1860-1938) was the inventor of the "western" with his 1902 novel *The Virginian: A Horseman of the Plains*, unless indeed the second half of *A Study in Scarlet* deserves the title of the first western novel. Wister was himself an easterner, born in Philadelphia, and practised law there before devoting hismself full-time to writing. Howver, he spent his summers in Wyoming starting in 1885 and used that setting for some of his early writing. *The Virginian* includes such tropes as the schoolteacher in love with the cowboy, and the gunfight showdown. Wister's other work includes several more novels, many short stories, and volumes of history and biography, among them a 1930 book about his life-long friendship with **Theodore Roosevelt**, who had been a classmate at Harvard. Arthur Conan Doyle dined with Wister in Philadelphia during his American tour in 1894.

Sidney Paget (1860-1908) was a young painter and newspaper artist when he was chosen to illustrate the Sherlock Holmes stories in the *Strand* magazine. He drew a total of 356 illustrations, done in black-and-white watercolour, from the first *Adventures* in 1891 to the last of the *Return* in 1904. His drawing for "Silver Blaze" of Holmes and Watson in a railway carriage has become a virtual icon. The artist's brother **Walter Paget** was the model for Holmes, and Paget's own deerstalker became the detective's "travelling cap". He went on to produce drawings for many other stories by Arthur Conan Doyle, and for other authors' works in the *Strand* and elsewhere. In 1897, it is reported, he painted Doyle's portrait.

Sir **James M. Barrie** (1860-1937) was a British author best known as the creator of Peter Pan. Some of his books deal with the village life he knew as a child in Scotland, notably *Auld Licht Idylls* and *The Little Minister*. He and Arthur Conan Doyle were contemporaries at the University of Edinburgh, but met in London as fellow-writers. ACD joined Barrie's less-than-serious cricket team, the Allahakbarries, and the two collaborated on the comic opera "Jane Annie" (1893), which was not a success. Barrie was a small man and has been suspected of odd tendencies, largely because of his friendships with boys, as reflected in *Peter Pan*. Says the *Encyclopaedia Britannica*: "Barrie idealized childhood and desexualized femininity but took a disenchanted view of adult life."

Sir **Robert Donald** (1860-1933) was a newspaperman from Edinburgh who eventually served on a number of the London-based national newspapers, becoming editor of the *Daily Chronicle*. "The Cardboard

Box" and "Silver Blaze" make it clear that Watson, if not Holmes, read the *Chronicle*, which was generally known as Liberal in its editorial policy. Donald was tapped by prime minister **David Lloyd George** to advise on government communication and propaganda during World War I, and when Lloyd George founded United Newspapers (later United Business Media and now UBM) in 1918, Donald became the holding company's managing director.

Sir William Robertson, 1st Baronet (1860-1933), was the only British soldier ever to begin a military career as a private and end as a field marshal. After working briefly as a footman in an aristocratic house, he enlisted in 1877, aged 17, in the Queen's Lancers. In 1888 he made the jump to an officer's commission, serving in India and being wounded in action in 1895. Skilled at languages, he worked in intelligence and taught at the Staff College at Camberley, Surrey. In World War I he was quartermaster-general, chief of staff, and finally Chief of the Imperial General Staff, with **Douglas Haig** as Commander-in-Chief and Lord **Kitchener** in the post of Secretary of State for War.

Theodor Herzl (1860-1904) was one of the founders of Zionism, the movement that eventually led to the independence of Israel in 1947. For a time, however, Herzl did not consider a Jewish homeland in Palestine, as it was then called, to be practical without the support of world leaders and particularly Sultan **Abdul Hamid II**, and instead considered a British proposal to create a homeland in "Uganda" (actually Kenya), or a possible alternative in Argentina. Herzl was born in what is now Budapest, worked as an international journalist, and in 1896 published an influential book, *The Jewish State*, which led to a growing Zionist movement. In 1897 he became the first president of the World Zionist Organization.

Théodule Meunier (1860-1907) was one of a trio of anarchists (the other two were **Emile Henry** and **Auguste Vaillant**) who carried out a series of bombings in Paris in 1892. One of his contemporaries said he was "as passionate for the search for the ideal society as Saint-Just, and as merciless", putting the anarchist struggle in the context of French revolutionary ideals from a century earlier. Meunier fled to London and lived as a refugee for a time, but Scotland Yard arrested him in 1894, evidently exactly as the events of "The Empty House" were unfolding. He was extradited after a Queen's Bench ruling that set a precedent about whether terrorists are "political" offenders, and spent the rest of his life at the Devil's Island penal colony.

Walter Richard Sickert (1860-1942) was, as a critic wrote in the *Guardian* in 2013, "a bold painter who was not afraid to put sex and sleaze into his art at a time when most British artists were timid and repressed". His work includes nudes and scenes from the demi-monde of London, and has been compared to that of ***Henri de Toulouse-Lautrec*** and **Edgar Degas** from Paris. Born in Germany, Sickert came to Britain as a child, developed his artistic style as an apprentice to ***James McNeill Whistler***, and in the early 20th century became a member of the Camden Town Group, recognized as pioneers of British modernist art. Several modern writers have suggested Sickert as a candidate for the murderer Jack the Ripper, although no one with direct knowledge of the case ever put his name forward.

William Jennings Bryan (1860-1925) ran for president of the United States on the Democratic ticket three times, being defeated twice (1896 and 1900) by ***William McKinley*** and once (1908) by **William Howard Taft**. He was known as a mighty orator and a champion of prohibition and populism — and particularly an advocate of "free silver", the policy of recognizing silver, not just gold, as the backing for currency. This issue, known as "the bimetallic question" or simply bimetallism, is mentioned in "The Bruce-Partington Plans" and was fiercely debated in the US in the 1890s. Days before his death, Bryan battled **Clarence Darrow** in the "Scopes Trial", in which he supported Tennessee's 1925 Butler Act forbidding the teaching of human evolution.

Douglas Haig, Earl **Haig** (1861-1928), was "among the handsomest men I have ever known", but utterly without humour, according to Arthur Conan Doyle in his autobiography. ACD met Haig, a principal British commander in World War I, during a tour of battle areas in France in 1915. Haig had been a soldier since 1885 and served in India, in Sudan during the campaign of 1898, and in South Africa during the Boer War; by 1906 he was on the general staff in London. He landed in France with the British Expeditionary Force in 1914 and was placed in command at the end of 1915. Though much admired in his day, Haig  was "the model of class-based incompetent commanders unable to grasp modern tactics and technology", Wikipedia says today.

Alfred North Whitehead (1861-1947) was a mathematician, logician and philosopher "best known," says the *Stanford Encyclopedia of Philosophy*, "for his work in mathematical logic and the philosophy of science. In collaboration with **Bertrand Russell**, he co-authored the landmark three-volume *Principia Mathematica* (1910, 1912, 1913). Later he was instrumental in pioneering the approach to metaphysics now known as process philosophy." He studied at Cambridge and was then a fellow at Trinity College there, 1884-1910; a lecturer at the University of London, 1911-1924; and finally a professor at Harvard, where he worked largely on the philosophy of education.

Dame **Nellie Melba**, born **Helen Porter Mitchell** (1861-1931), was a star at the Royal Opera House, Covent Garden, in the last decade of the 19th century and the first decade of the 20th, and became an international celebrity. She had sung a little as a young woman in Australia, but trained in Paris in the 1880s and began singing prima donna (soprano) roles in 1887. World tours, and invitations to sing for kings and queens, followed. She was not self-effacing: "There are lots of duchesses, but only one Melba," she once said. "For newly federated Australia, Melba represented glamour, success, and international acceptance," says the *Australian Dictionary of Biography*. She began making recordings in 1904, and a series of farewell concerts began in 1926.

Eille Norwood, born **Anthony Edward Brett** (1861-1948), was one of the early and great Sherlock Holmeses on the movie screen. Arthur Conan Doyle called his performance "masterly". Working with **Hubert Willis** as Watson, he made 47 silent films, all but two of them 20-minute shorts, within three years, 1921-1923. The detective's milieu, as presented by Stoll Pictures, was London of the 1920s, not the Victorian era. Norwood was particularly hailed for his brilliant presentation of Holmes's disguises, and there were stories of him fooling fellow actors and director **Maurice Elvey** and once almost being tossed off the set because no one recognized him. He was a veteran stage actor, and acted Holmes in Cardiff and London in "The Return of Sherlock Holmes" in 1923.

Ferdinand I (1861-1948) was Prince Regnant of Bulgaria for 21 years and then King for another decade. He can easily be seen as one of the originals of the eastern European king who figures in "A Scandal in Bohemia", although many of his indiscretions appear to have been with men rather than women. A scion of the House of Saxe-Coburg and Gotha, which was related by blood or marriage to all of

Europe's royalty, he was elected Knyaz (reigning prince) in 1887. Bulgaria pulled away from its traditional patron, Russia, for some years, but they were reconciled after the 1895 assassination of liberal prime minister **Stefan Stambolov**. In 1908 Ferdinand declared Bulgaria officially free of the Ottoman Empire, and made himself Tsar (king). He supported Germany and Austria-Hungary during World War I and was obliged to abdicate (1918) after their defeat.

Frank Shacklock (1861-1937) played first-class cricket between 1883 and 1905, although the standard of "first-class" was not officially defined in Britain until 1895. He batted and bowled right-handed, and scored 2,438 runs in his career although he never made a century (100 runs in one innings). At various times he played for Nottinghamshire, Derbyshire, Marylebone (the team whose home field is Lord's Cricket Ground in London), and sides in New Zealand. It has been suggested that Arthur Conan Doyle, who was certainly a cricket enthusiast, borrowed Shacklock's name for his great detective, and teammate **William Mycroft**'s name for the detective's corpulent brother.

Fridtjof Nansen (1861-1930) received the Nobel Peace Prize in 1922 for his work on behalf of the League of Nations, in saving prisoners of war, refugees, and victims of the Armenian famine. He had also been involved in negotiating the 1905 independence of Norway, his homeland, which had previously been united with Sweden. And he had done research in oceanography and zoology as a professor at the University of Oslo. But he is best remembered for his journeys of exploration, including the first crossing of Greenland (1888) and the nearest approach to the North Pole that had ever been achieved (1895). It was the Greenland expedition, in which a party of six spent two months crossing ice and mountains on skis, that inspired Arthur Conan Doyle to take up cross-country skiing in Switzerland, and ACD met Nansen at a reception and lecture in London in 1897.

H. H. Holmes, real name **Herman Webster Mudgett** (1861-1896), was a serial killer now best known as the central figure in *The Devil in the White City* by Erik Larson (2003). A medical graduate, he went into the pharmacy business in Chicago and built a hotel in time for the Columbian Exposition, or world's fair, of 1893. In that building, equipped with gas chambers, secret passages and other conveniences, he killed dozens of people (the number is unknown), particularly young women. He would prepare the bodies and sell skeletons or organs for medical teaching. After the fair Holmes carried on a career of insurance fraud and killing across the United States and Canada; he was hanged in Philadelphia for the murder of an accomplice.

Jane **Beadmore** (1861-1888) was the 27-year-old victim of a murder in Birtley, County Durham, that was associated with the Jack the Ripper killings in London because of knife wounds to the neck and abdomen. Two Scotland Yard officials travelled north and quickly concluded that the similarities were not great. Before long an arrest was made: **William Waddell**, a jilted suitor. He confessed, attributing the crime to liquor. "He also stated that he had been reading the accounts of the Whitechapel murders in London, and his mind must have been deranged," the *Durham Chronicle* reported. Waddell was hanged at Durham Gaol.

William J. Burns (1861-1932) preceded **J. Edgar Hoover** as director of the FBI, then simply the Bureau of Investigation, serving 1921-1924. He had begun his career as a Secret Service agent, gaining attention for an undercover investigation of corruption in the San Francisco city

government. He then formed his own firm, the William J. Burns International Detective Agency. Says the FBI's website: "A combination of good casework and an instinct for publicity made Mr. Burns a national figure. His exploits made national news, the gossip columns of New York newspapers, and the pages of detective magazines." After retirement, Burns wrote "true crime" stories based on his work. Arthur Conan Doyle spent time with Burns during his 1914 visit to New York, and wrote about him in *Western Wanderings*, especially noting the 1915 **Leo Frank** murder case.

Henry Croft (1861-1930) was the founder, while still in his early teens, of the Cockney (east London working class) tradition of Pearly Kings and Queens, now an attraction for tourists and an organization that raises funds for hospitals and other charities. As a street-sweeper, Croft came to know the habits of street traders, known as costermongers — "their generosity and their fashion of smoke pearl buttons sewn on the piped seams of their trousers, jackets, waistcoats and caps", says the Pearly Society website. With an eye to publicity so he could raise money to help the less fortunate he began to collect pearl buttons, sewing them on a hat and then a suit. An early beneficiary (1880) was the London Temperance Hospital. "Many of the Costermongers became the first Pearly Families," the website says.

Joseph Henry Ball (1861-1931) was a friend of Arthur Conan Doyle during the Portsmouth years. An architect who had studied under **Alfred Waterhouse**, a major figure in the Gothic Revival movement, Ball was responsible for such buildings as St. Agatha's Church (1895) in the Landport district of Portsmouth. Simultaneously he designed Undershaw, the Doyle house at Hindhead, Surrey. He had also helped to trace Charles Doyle's artless drawings for reproduction in the first edition of *A Study in Scarlet*. Andrew Lycett's biography *The Man Who Created Sherlock Holmes*: "Arthur looked upon Ball as a restless seeker after truth made in his own mould. At one stage he considered him as a prospective match for his sister Connie, telling his mother that his friend was both handsome and spiritual."

Rabindranath Tagore (1861-1941) was the winner of the Nobel Prize in Literature for 1913, and two years later received a knighthood, but afterwards resigned it as a protest against British policies in his home-land of India. "Although Tagore wrote successfully in all literary genres, he was first of all a poet," says a biography on the Nobel web site. "For the world he became the voice of India's spiritual heritage; and for India, especially for Bengal, he became a great living insti-tution." His fifty books of poetry began with *Manasi* (1890) and *Sonar Tari* (1894), translated into English as *The Golden Boat*. He also wrote plays, short stories, novels, travel diaries and other works, and was influential in Bengali music and art.

Annie **Crook** (1862-1920) was a London shopgirl who has entered the folklore of the 1888 Jack the Ripper murders despite the lack of any significant evidence for her involve-ment. Her grandson, **Joseph Gorman**, apparently developed a theory — first set out in a 1976 book, *Jack the Ripper: The Final Solution*, by Stephen Knight — that Crook had been secretly married to Prince *Albert Victor*, the Duke of **Clarence**, and that the Ripper victims were killed by the prince's associates because they knew the truth, which would have caused political scandal. The theory implicates Sir *William Gull* and *Walter Sickert*. It figures in the plot of the 1979 film "Murder by Decree", in which Sherlock Holmes (Christopher Plummer) locates Crook (Geneviève Bujold) and learns the story.

Bruce Ismay (1862-1937) went to work as a young man with the White Star line of transAtlantic steamships, headed since 1868 by his father, **Thomas Ismay**. He became a partner in 1891 and president on his father's death in 1899. In 1902 Ismay and *J. Pierpont Morgan* conducted negotiations that led to White Star becoming a unit of the International Mercantile Marine Company, and for a time Ismay was president of IMM. In 1907, spurred by the Cunard Line's recent launch of the *Lusitania* and *Mauretania*, White Star decided to build its own huge, luxurious liner. RMS *Titanic* was launched in May 1911 and sank on its maiden voyage from Southampton to New York in April 1912. Ismay, travelling on that voyage with his valet and his secretary, stepped into one of the half-filled lifeboats and was rescued by RMS *Carpathia*. It is said that his hair turned white overnight.

Carolyn Wells (1862-1942) was an early and prolific author of American mystery novels, as well as children's stories and one of the first books about detective fiction, *The Technique of the Mystery Story* (1913). Her first book was published in 1896; it was about 1909 that she discovered the work of *Anna Katherine Green* and decided she could do it too. Her dozens of mystery novels (such as *A Chain of Evidence*, 1912) have the reputation of being entertaining but trivial. Her verse had the same qualities; it included some well-known limericks as well as an early Sherlockian poem, "Ballade of Baker Street", published in *Collier's* magazine in 1908. A librarian in New Jersey, who was barely slowed down by deafness resulting from scarlet fever, she married **Hadwin Houghton**, whose father had founded the publishing firm Houghton Mifflin, in 1918, but he died the following year.

Edith Wharton, née **Jones** (1862-1937), was the author of more than forty novels, including *The Age of Innocence* (1920). She grew up in the wealthy social circles of New York City (with summers in Newport), and much of her writing is set in that world, and among Americans travelling in Europe. She eventually made her own home in Paris; the love of her life was not her husband but British journalist **Morton Fullerton**, whom she met there. Says a website from the Smithsonian Institution: "She was a born storyteller, whose novels are justly celebrated for their vivid settings, satiric wit, ironic style, and moral seriousness." But her writing career actually began with *The Decoration of Houses* (1897), calling for an end to Victorian clutter; she did not publish her first novel until she was 40.

Connie Mack, born **Cornelius McGillicuddy** (1862-1956), was manager and owner of the Philadelphia Athletics baseball team 1901-1950. Considered one of the great managers in major league history, he was notable for his gentlemanly style. Arthur Conan Doyle saw him May 30, 1914, when the A's, with Hall of Fame third-baseman **John "Home Run" Baker**, played a doubleheader against the Yankees at New York's Polo Grounds. (He probably watched the second game: the Yankees won 10-5.) ACD tried the sport himself soon afterwards at Jasper, Alberta. "I have all the prejudices of an old cricketer," he wrote in *Our Second American Adventure*, "and yet I cannot get away from the fact that baseball is the better game."

Florence Maybrick, née **Chandler** (1862-1941), was an Alabama girl who married a much older man, cotton broker **James Maybrick**. They met on board ship, married in London and settled in Liverpool, where they lived a high-society life and both had numerous extramarital affairs. When James, who was in the habit of dosing himself with strychnine and other nostrums, died in May 1889, Florence was charged with murder. She was convicted, but her death sentence commuted in the midst of a dispute over whether the poisons she administered could actually have caused her husband's death. She served 14 years in prison.

Harry Baskerville (1862-1960) was a coachman employed by *Bertram Fletcher Robinson*, a friend of Arthur Conan Doyle who lived at Ipplepen, Devon. Robinson and ACD explored Dartmoor in 1901 and worked out plans for a novel to be set there. It seems likely that ACD borrowed the driver's name for the cursed family in *The Hound of the Baskervilles*. Several sources report that Robinson gave a copy of the novel to Baskerville, with an inscription including "apologies for using the name".

Hawley Harvey Crippen (1862-1910) was hanged at Pentonville Prison for the murder of his wife, music-hall artiste **Belle Elmore** (also known as **Cora Turner** and **Kunigunde Mackamotski**). Born in Michigan, Crippen had been trained in medicine, but from 1900 worked in England at a series of jobs. He and his wife both had outside romantic interests, and to prevent Cora running off with his savings, Crippen poisoned her with hyoscin hydrobromide and let it be known that she had returned to the United States. When suspicion grew, he fled to Europe and then the US with his mistress, **Ethel le Neve**. Chief Inspector *Walter Dew* pursued and arrested them; Cora's body was found in the cellar of Crippen's London house, and identified by **Bernard Spilsbury** in his first major case as a pathologist.

Ida B. Wells (1862-1931), was born a slave and became a pioneer leader in the struggle for Black civil rights in the United States. In 1884 she resisted being moved from the first-class car to a crowded smoking car on the Memphis and Charleston Railroad, and won compensation in court, though the Tennessee Supreme Court later reversed the victory. In 1889, following a lynching of three men, she organized a campaign to have Blacks move out of Memphis, then took up the campaign against lynching generally, speaking across the United States and (in 1893 and 1894) in Britain. Her 1892 pamphlet *Southern Horrors: Lynch Law in All Its Phases* was reprinted several times. She helped organize a boycott of the 1893 Columbian Exposition in Chicago because she felt American Blacks were not being adequately represented. Wells married **Ferdinand Barnett** but did not usually use his surname.

John Kendrick Bangs (1862-1922) was an American humourist and author of some of the earliest Sherlockian pastiche writing, including *A House-Boat on the Styx* (1895), *The Pursuit of the House-Boat* (1897), and *R. Holmes & Co.* (1906). He was working as an editor for Harper & Brothers when Arthur Conan Doyle visited him in Yonkers, New York, during his 1894 North American tour, and they became friends, sharing experiences as the fathers of young children. Bangs returned the visit in England years later. His career included editorship of magazines including *Puck* and *Harper's Weekly*, and freelance writing and lecturing.

Joseph Merrick (1862-1890) was the so-called Elephant Man, whose physical deformities made him a sideshow attraction and led to his early death. His story is told in the 1980 film "The Elephant Man", starring John Hurt. The cause of Merrick's lumpy skin, distorted limbs and huge head is unclear; one theory is that he suffered from neurofibromatosis (von Recklinghausen disease). Abandoned by his family as a teenager, he spent four years in the workhouse at Leicester before offering himself to a show promoter. Sir **Frederick Treves**, a surgeon at the London Hospital, took an interest in Merrick, and rescued him when he was abandoned by dishonest promoters.

Mary Kingsley (1862-1900) was an explorer who wrote about her time in west Africa and pressed for changes in the way Britain and other European powers viewed their colonies. Her father, **George Kingsley**, had also been a traveller, and from 1886 to his death in 1892 the family lived in Cambridge and Mary helped organize her father's notes and

prepare his definitive book, intended to be a comparative study of sacri-
ficial rites around the world. After his death she decided to travel to
Africa to continue his investigations, despite a total lack of experience,
language skills, equipment, or sensible advice. On two journeys (1893
and 1894) she visited territory stretching from the modern Sierra Leone
east and south to the Congo Republic, up rivers and into forests not previously seen by Europeans. In Gabon she saw gorillas, a species almost
unknown at the time, and reacted with "horrible disgust". Settling in
London, she wrote *Travels in West Africa* (published 1895) and a
sequel. She died of typhoid while nursing Boer prisoners at a camp near
Cape Town during the South African War.

Montague Rhodes (M. R.) James (1862-1936) wrote ghost stories,
collected in four volumes that are considered the finest of their kind.
"It's no simple sentimentality," a James website says about the appeal
of his work, "nor a cheap roller-coaster thrill. It has something to do
with an off-kilter Englishness, a certain respectability besieged but also
defined by the bizarre, the chaotic and the arcane. In part at least, it's
tied up with that unique, brave and terrible period of European history
in which these stories were written." James was a life-long academic, a
specialist in mediaeval studies, at King's College, Cambridge, and wrote
many of his tales to be read to colleagues at Christmas. His first
collection, *Ghost Stories of an Antiquary*, was published in 1904, and
his final book in 1925.

O. Henry, real name **William Sidney Porter** (1862-1910),
was an American writer of short stories, famous especially
for "The Gift of the Magi" and "The Ransom of Red Chief".
He grew up in North Carolina, and worked for a time in Texas, but lost
his job as a bank teller when funds were found to be missing.
Eventually convicted of embezzlement, he served three years in prison.
Meanwhile, he was writing stories for *McClure's Magazine* and other
outlets under his pseudonym, many of them with his characteristic
surprise plot twists. On his release, he moved to New York and began
an energetic period of writing. Several collections of short stories were
published beginning in 1904. The story "The Adventures of Shamrock
Jolnes" dates from 1911.

R. Austin Freeman (1862-1943) was the creator of Dr. Thorndyke,
the fictional detective who denied being "an irregular practitioner" but
was instead a barrister, a physician and a polymath. In almost two dozen
novels (beginning with *The Red Thumb Mark*, 1907) and five collections of short stories, Thorndyke examines physical evidence and brings

an improbable range of specialized knowledge to bear in solving mysteries. Freeman is said to have been the inventor of the "inverted" detective story, in which the identity of the criminal is clear and the narrative tells how he or she is unmasked. Freeman himself was a physician (graduating from Middlesex Hospital in 1887) and worked for a time in the Gold Coast, now Ghana. After returning to England in 1891 he concentrated on writing rather than medicine, although he served in the Royal Army Medical Corps during World War I.

Théophile van Rysselberghe (1862-1926) was an Impressionist painter, and could well have been one of the "modern Belgian masters" whose work Sherlock Holmes admires in *The Hound of the Baskervilles*. He was born in Ghent and studied art in Brussels, but was fascinated by the orientalism in fashion in the 1880s, and made several long trips to Morocco to observe and paint. His work was an instant success when he began to exhibit in Brussels in 1883. Originally in the traditional realist style, his work moved quickly toward Impressionism under the influence of *Pierre-Auguste Renoir* and **Claude Monet**, and he discovered the pointilliste technique at a Paris exhibition in 1886. Along with portraits and landscapes, he was commissioned to do a series of tourist posters for the Compagnie des Wagons-lits, travelling across Europe in 1895 in the process.

Sir **Edward Grey**, 3rd Baronet, later 1st Viscount **Grey of Fallodon** (1862-1933), was an experienced and weary statesman by the time of his supposed remark as World War I began: "The lamps are going out all over Europe; we shall not see them lit again in our lifetime." He had begun life as a rich and indolent young man, serving as unpaid secretary to Sir *Evelyn Baring* and somehow catching an interest in politics. A Liberal Member of Parliament from 1892, he served as Foreign Secretary in the late days of *William Ewart Gladstone*'s government and again 1905-1916 under *Henry Campbell-Bannerman* and *H. H. Asquith*. He was a diplomat of the old school, believing in closed-door negotiations and agreements, the sort of thing that figures in the story "The Naval Treaty". Thus the mutual defence agreement Britain reached with France and Russia in 1907 was not well enough understood to deter Germany from doing exactly the things it did that led to war in August 1914.

Sir **Arthur Vicars** (1862-1921) was Ulster King of Arms, the official responsible for heraldry and ceremonial matters in Ireland, from 1893 to 1908. English-born, he had an affinity for Ireland and lived there most of his life, becoming an authority on its genealogy. As king of arms, Vicars was responsible for the so-called Irish Crown Jewels, actually the insignia of the Order of St. Patrick, which were stolen from Dublin Castle in 1907. The jewels were never recovered, but many allegations were made; the incident has been suggested as a source for the events of "The  Bruce-Partington Plans". Vicars accused one of his subordinates, **Francis Shackleton**, and resented being himself under suspicion and being removed from his post as king of arms. He was shot dead by armed men in an incident during the Irish War of Independence.

Abdul Karim (1863-1909) was the "Indian secretary" and intimate friend of Queen *Victoria* in the last decade of her life. Sent to Britain in 1887 as a servant, he advanced from waiting at table to teaching the Queen Urdu and, apparently, advising her on Indian affairs (but probably not, despite accusations, spying on behalf of Muslim leaders). He roused resentment among both servants and members of the royal household for his arrogant bearing and privileged position, comparable to that of *John Brown* earlier; racial dislike was also a factor. On the Queen's death he was sent back to live on a property near Agra that she had insisted be made over to him.

Archduke **Franz Ferdinand** of Austria (1863-1914) was heir to the throne of the Austro-Hungarian empire, and would have succeeded his uncle, Emperor *Franz Joseph I*, in due course had he not been assassinated in Sarajevo in June 1914 — the incident that precipitated World War I. He was the son of the Emperor's younger brother, Archduke **Karl Ludwig**, and the Archduchess, Princess **Maria Annunciata** of the Italian state known as Bourbon and the Two Sicilies. Karl Ludwig became the heir following the 1889 suicide of the Emperor's son Crown Prince *Rudolf*, and himself died in 1896. Franz Ferdinand was described as a violent man who did not get along with the Emperor; he held a military position from the age of 14, and was an enthusiastic hunter who travelled the world shooting at things. His wife **Sophie Chotek** (who was not of royal blood, so that the marriage had to be morganatic) died with him in Sarajevo, shot by young assassin **Gavrilo Princip**.

Ambrose Small (1863-1919?) was in the process of selling his chain of theatres, across and beyond Ontario, when he disappeared one day in December 1919. He ordered a Cadillac for his wife that morning, the first fruit of the $1.7 million the theatre deal was bringing him; had a meeting with his lawyer at the Grand Opera House in Toronto in the afternoon; and was not seen again. There were murmurs that the wife, **Theresa Kormann**, might have a lover who might have put a body in the furnace at another Grand, the opera house in London, Ontario, which Small also owned. Certainly Small, a self-made millionaire, had women in his life; he loved to buy them chocolates and entertain them in his private suite in the theatre. There was also talk of gambling debts and sharp business dealings. But no trace of Small was ever found; he was declared legally dead in 1923. An ambitious reporter asked Arthur Conan Doyle about the case when he visited New York in 1922, and he said he was willing to look into it, but nothing came of the idea.

Arthur Morrison (1863-1945) was the creator of detective Martin Hewitt, whose adventures were so like the adventures of Sherlock Holmes that an enthusiastic editor recently republished them substituting Holmes's name for Hewitt's. In their original apparances in the pages of the *Strand* and other magazines, during the years of Holmes's great hiatus, they were illustrated by *Sidney Paget*. In book form, *Martin Hewitt, Investigator* appeared in 1894, *The Chronicles* in 1895, *The Adventures* in 1896, and *The Red Triangle* in 1904. "Of Doyle's contemporary imitators," Ellery Queen has written, "the most durable (indeed, the only important one to survive over the ages) is [Hewitt], a man of awe-inspiring technical and statistical knowledge." Morrison, who grew up in London's east end, also wrote more realistic fiction about life in the impoverished quarters of London, most notably *A Child of the Jago* (1896), as well as journalistic work and articles about Japanese art.

David Lloyd George, 1st Earl **Lloyd-George of Dwyfor** (1863-1945), was Britain's Prime Minister 1916-1922, and the architect of the 20th century welfare state. Born in Wales, with Welsh as his first language and Nonconformism as his religious preference, he worked as a solicitor, served on the Carnarvonshire county council, and in 1890 was elected to Parliament as a Liberal. He worked largely on Welsh issues at first, but became better known following his opposition to the South

African War. Given a cabinet position in the government of Sir *Henry Campbell-Bannerman* in 1906, he served for eight years as Chancellor of the Exchequer, and in 1909 presented the "People's Budget" raising taxes to pay for new social benefits (and outraging the House of Lords). An unemployment insurance system followed in 1911. His time as Prime Minister was largely taken up with the management of World War I, but further social reforms followed the war. Lloyd George was the last Liberal to head the government, as his Liberals were largely eclipsed by the growing Labour Party.

Francis Younghusband (1863-1942) was a lively figure in the "Great Game" pitting Britain against Russia for influence. As a young officer in the 1st King's Dragoon Guards, he explored Manchuria with a couple of colleagues, then went on without them, crossing the Gobi Desert and finding a new route back into India (the Mustagh Pass). Two years later, probing the frontier to the north of India, he and a small contingent of Gurkhas were entertained by a Russian officer in the latter's camp. A subsequent trip took Younghusband to Chinese Turkestan (Uighur territory). As the Great Game went on, he was asked in 1902 to lead a British expedition to Tibet — in effect an invasion — and con-  cluded a treaty with officials at Lhasa, but killed so many Tibetans en route that the agreement had to be repudiated. Home in England, he served as president of the Royal Geographical Society; he also wrote a number of mystical books expressing thoughts he said had come to him during his visit to Tibet.

Ewan George Fitzroy Macpherson (1863-1926) was a Church of England clergyman who spent most of his career as a chaplain to the Forces. He served 1892-1894 at Portsmouth, the home of the Royal Navy, where Arthur Conan Doyle still had social connections. ACD must also have known about his activity during the South African War, where he received multiple medals and other honours and was at Lady-smith during the dramatic 1899-1900 siege. When World War I began, he served for a time with the British Expeditionary Force in France, then became Assistant Chaplain General, the senior C of E position in the Royal Army Chaplains' Department. He retired from the Army in 1922. Shortly after Macpherson's death, ACD wrote "The Lion's Mane" and gave his name to the man killed by *Cyanea capillata*, Fitzroy McPherson.

Sir **Anthony Hope Hawkins**, sometimes just called **Anthony Hope** (1863-1933), was the novelist who created one of the classics of Victorian corn, *The Prisoner of Zenda* (1894). Its Ruritanian tropes — the English adventurer, the Balkan prince (not unlike the King in "A Scandal in Bohemia"), the coincidences and hair-raising escapes — have been widely used by subsequent authors. Hawkins was a barrister with much free time, and decided to fill it with writing; he was first published in 1890. In the end there were 32 novels, including a Ruritanian sequel, *Rupert of Hentzau*, as well as plays and other writing.

George Safford Parker (1863-1937) was the founder of the Parker Pen Company, which began operations in 1888 in Janesville, Wisconsin. As a teacher and a part-time seller and repairer of fountain pens, he was dismayed by the way they leaked ink and soon wore out, and he experimented with better designs; he received his first patent in 1889. The "Lucky Curve" capillary feed system followed in 1894. A series of innovations led to the Parker Duofold pen, widely known as "Big Red", in 1921. Sales in Britain began in 1924, and Arthur Conan Doyle provided an endorsement for the Duofold, allowing the manufacturer to say in its advertising that some of the Sherlock Holmes stories were written with it. Other inventors were addressing the same problem in the same period: **Lewis Waterman**, an insurance agent in New York, had his first fountain pen patent in 1884.

Henry Ford (1863-1947) was the inventor and industrialist who brought automobiles to a mass consumer market through automated production. He stuck close to his birthplace of Dearborn, Michigan, making Detroit the world centre of the car industry for decades. Ford apprenticed as a machinist and also studied bookkeeping; in 1881 he went to work as an engineer for *Thomas Edison*, meanwhile working away on his ideas for a motor vehicle. (*Karl Benz*, *Gottlieb Daimler* and others had been doing the same thing.) He established the Ford Motor Co. in 1903, and by 1914 introduced the moving assembly line as the key technology of mass production. The "little Ford" mentioned in "His Last Bow" (set in 1914) must be a Model T, manufactured in America from 1908 to 1927 and in Trafford Park, near Manchester, starting in 1911. Ford was known for treating employees well, with generous wages and profit-sharing, but also for antiSemitism and opposition to American involvement in World War I.

Mary Jane Kelly (1863?-1888) was blonde and blue-eyed and good-looking, and considerably younger than the other known victims of the Jack the Ripper murderer. She was the last of the five "canonical" victims, killed early on a Saturday morning in November 1888, in her room in Miller's Court, off Dorset Street (not the same as the Dorset Street four miles away that intersects Baker Street). Kelly was born in Ireland and lived in Wales, where she had a brief marriage with a coal-miner (killed in an explosion) and worked as a prostitute in Cardiff. She claimed to have come to London in 1884 and worked in a high-class brothel. She was attached to two or three other men before meeting **Joseph Barnett**, a fish porter, in 1886; the two lived together at various addresses until a few days before the murder. At that time she was supporting herself through street prostitution and had a reputation for being rowdy when drunk.

Pierre **de Frédy**, Baron **de Coubertin** (1863-1937), was the founder of the modern Olympic Games, which also drew on ideas developed by British physician and fitness advocate **William Penny Brookes**. A member of an aristocratic French family, de Coubertin credited the presence of games in British boys' schools, especially as organized by headmaster **Thomas Arnold** of Rugby School, for much of Britain's international might; he looked also to the role of athletics in ancient Athens. A Congress in Paris in 1894 established the Olympics, with the first games held in Athens in 1896. De Coubertin was president of the International Olympic Committee at the time of the 1908 Games in London, at which Arthur Conan Doyle was conspicuous.

Sir **Arthur Quiller-Couch** (1863-1944) is supposed to have been the inspiration for Rat in **Kenneth Grahame**'s 1908 children's novel *The Wind in the Willows*. Born to a family of writers and folklore collectors, he published his first novel while still at Oxford, and went on to write many other novels as well as verse and literary criticism, including edited editions of several Shakespeare plays. He spent the last three decades of his life as a professor at Cambridge; his first series of lectures became the book *On the Art of Writing* (1916). He is particularly known as the editor of the *Oxford Book of English Verse* (1900). Born in Cornwall, which has linguistic and political traditions quite different from those of England, Quiller-Couch remained connected to that region all his life and was recognized as a Bard by the cultural organization Gorsedh Kernow.

Sir **Max Pemberton** (1863-1950) was a friend of Arthur Conan Doyle and the author of adventure stories such as *The Iron Pirate* (1893) and *I Crown Thee King* (1902). The latter book is actually set in the time of a queen, **Mary I**. A review in the *Spectator* when it was published observed that "The manner of the story is that of the older convention of romances — language, dresses, attitudes, and situations are all eminently picturesque, but not quite eminently convincing." Readers liked Pemberton's work, though. He was briefly editor of the boys' magazine *Chums*, and was founder of the London School of Journalism.

Walter Dew (1863-1947) joined the Metropolitan Police in 1882, and by 1906 was a Chief Inspector. Four years later, he was the police officer who managed to arrest the celebrated murderer ***Harvey Crippen***; when he published his memoirs in 1938, he titled them *I Caught Crippen*. A chapter in that book was "The Hunt for Jack the Ripper". At the time of the 1888 Ripper murderers, Dew was a detective with the Criminal Investigation Department: "Whitechapel, Spitalfields and Shoreditch were now my hunting-ground, with hundreds of criminals of the worst type as my quarry…. Marie *[Mary Jane] Kelly* was the most horribly mutilated of all Jack the Ripper's victims. I know because I was the first police officer on the scene of that ghastly crime in Miller's Court, a cul-de-sac off Dorset Street."

William Randolph Hearst (1863-1951) was born with money and made enormously more through his publishing empire. He began with the *San Francisco Examiner* and added newspapers in other American cities, including the New York *Journal*, as well as the magazines *Cosmopolitan* and *Harper's Bazaar*. He hired the finest journalists available, but did not hesitate to make up the news, generally with a right-wing jingoistic stance (he is largely credited with making the Spanish-American War a success). At his ranch and castle at San Simeon, California, Hearst entertained the likes of actress **Marion Davies** and ***Charlie Chaplin***. He is the thinly disguised central figure of the 1941 film "Citizen Kane".

Charles Dawson (1864-1916) was the discoverer of Piltdown Man, and is now thought by many to have been the hoaxer who created the spurious fossils. (In any case, it was not Arthur Conan Doyle who created the spurious skull and jawbone, despite his known interest in anthropological finds and his proximity to the Piltdown site in Sussex.) Dawson was a lawyer, for whom archaeology was a hobby that he hoped would lead to academic acceptance. As early as 1893 he reported finding prehistoric, Roman and mediaeval artifacts in a disused mine near Lavant, Sussex, and produced a Roman statuette oddly made of cast iron. The Piltdown artifacts were initially accepted by most scientists as an evolutionary "missing link" and dubbed *Eoanthropus dawsoni* in Dawson's honour after he and Sir **Arthur Smith Woodward** reported on them in the *Quarterly Journal of the Geological Society*. They were finally proven in 1953 to be a fake, based on a modern human skull and an orangutan jaw, with chimpanzee teeth.

Albert Victor Christian, Duke of Clarence (1864-1892), was the first son of Albert, Prince of Wales (later *Edward VII*) and thus heir presumptive to the throne. "Eddy" was inconclusively linked to the Cleveland Street scandal of 1889 involving a male brothel. "Albert Victor's intellect, sexuality and mental health have been the subject of much speculation," says Wikipedia. Some writers have attributed the 1888 Jack the Ripper murders to him, though official records make clear that he was not even in London at the time. Shortly after becoming engaged to *Mary of Teck*, and when he was about to be appointed Viceroy of Ireland, he died in an influenza epidemic.

Dame **Marie Tempest**, born **Marie Susan Etherington** (1864-1942), entertained theatre-goers for more than half a century as the star of comedy and light opera. "She debuted in 1885 as Fiametta in the operetta *Boccaccio*," says the *Encyclopaedia Britannica*, "but it was the title role in *Dorothy* (1887), which ran for 931 performances, that established her reputation." In 1895 she was touring North America when George Edwardes' Company summoned her back to London to star in the racy musical "An Artist's Model", which ran for more than a year at Daly's Theatre, just off Leicester Square. In later years she performed in work by **Somerset Maugham**, **Noel Coward** and **St. John Ervine**.

Elinor Glyn, née **Sutherland** (1864-1943), coined the slang term "It", meaning charisma or sex appeal, and heated up her romantic novels with sentences like this one: "She purred as a tiger might have done, while she undulated like a snake." Born in Jersey, though she spent some of her childhood in Ontario, she grew up an exotic redhead, with romantic aspirations for herself and for the women in her writing. In 1892 she married land-owner **Clayton Glyn**, but she was less than faithful to him. Her scandalous novel *Three Weeks* (1907) was said to be based on one of her own love affairs, though not the one with *Lord Curzon*, Viceroy of India. Other books, some of them run-away best-sellers, included *The Visits of Elizabeth* (1900). In the 1920s she made her way into the Hollywood in-crowd and wrote many screenplays. Her sister was **Lucy, Lady Duff-Gordon**, the fashion designer "Lucile", whose dressmaking shop opened in 1893 in London's west end.

Henri de Toulouse-Lautrec (1864-1901) was, as the Metropolitan Museum web site puts it, "an aristocratic, alcoholic dwarf known for his louche lifestyle". He was also, through a brief career, a significant post-Impressionist artist in Paris: "Lautrec's posters promoted Montmartre entertainers as celebrities, and elevated the popular medium of the advertising lithograph to the realm of high art. His paintings of dancehall performers and prostitutes are personal and humanistic, revealing the sadness and humor hidden beneath rice powder and gaslights." He arrived in the city in 1882, studied with the portrait painter **Léon Bonnat**, and came to prominence creating posters for the newly opened Moulin Rouge cabaret. His work often portrays such performers as **Jane Avril** (born **Jeanne Beaudon**), **Louise Weber** ("La Goulue"), and the exuberant red-headed **Loie Fuller**. Absinthe, syphilis and pycnodysostosis were his downfall.

Israel Zangwill (1864-1926) "was probably the best known Jew in the English-speaking world at the start of the twentieth century", says the Jewish Virtual Library website. A friend of Arthur Conan Doyle, he was a journalist, a comic writer, a social critic, and an outstanding voice on Jewish issues, known for his 1892 novel *Children of the Ghetto*, and later for his play "The Melting Pot", which made that phrase popular as a description of American society. Other works included *The Big Bow Mystery* (1892), said to be the first locked-room mystery novel. He was involved in issues ranging from women's suffrage to pacifism, but particularly Zionism (he worked for a time with **Theodor Herzl**). In 1905 he formed the Jewish Territorial Organization, which looked at possibilities for a Jewish home from Africa to Canada. Despite the 1917 Balfour Declaration promising a homeland in Palestine, he maintained that resettling the existing Arab population would be impossible.

John George Spenzer (1864-1932) was studying chemistry and toxicology at Cleveland's Western Reserve University at the same time Sherlock Holmes was reportedly doing his researches in the laboratory of St. Bartholomew's Hospital. He received a medical degree in 1884, did graduate study at WRU and in Strasburg and Paris, and came home to teach, initially at the College of Pharmacy. By 1910 he was on the faculty of WRU teaching legal chemistry and medical jurisprudence. "He became a regional expert on blood and poison analysis and was often called upon for blood identification," says the *Encyclopedia of Cleveland History*. His case notes and specimen samples, as well as some clippings he collected about Sherlock Holmes, are preserved in the library of what is now Case Western Reserve University.

Maurice Leblanc (1864-1941) was a prolific author of fiction, and the creator of Arséne Lupin, the French nemesis of Sherlock Holmes. Lupin, who in the Parisian tradition is somewhere on the borderline between burglar and detective, appeared initially in magazine short stories from 1905 onwards. Three of them are overtly Sherlockian: "Sherlock Holmes arrive trop tard" (1906), "Arsène Lupin contre Herlock Sholmès" (1907), and "L'aiguille creuse" (1908). All three have been variously translated, and the name of Sherlock Holmes variously altered; the 1907 story, for example, has been published in English as *The Blonde Lady*. A bibliography of Leblanc's fiction includes more than two dozen novels and collections.

Max Weber (1864-1920) was one of the founder of modern sociology, known most of all for his 1905 book *The Protestant Ethic and the Spirit of Capitalism*, which described "the disenchantment of the world" as an important factor in the creation of a modern, "rational" society, and introduced the concept of the "work ethic". In contrast to **Karl Marx**'s approach, he attached great importance to the reasons individuals attribute to their behaviour, not merely to describing that behaviour. Weber studied at several German universities, earning both a law degree and a PhD, and taught at Freiburg for a year before settling into a job at the ancient University of Heidelberg in 1896. A mental breakdown kept him from work for several years, but he returned to lecturing and to

writing; he produced books on Chinese and Japanese religion and Judaism, but did not complete books on Islam and Christianity to finish the
series.

Nellie Bly, real name **Elizabeth Cochrane** (1864-1922), was a reporter
known for dramatic stunts and exposés, including an 1889-90 trip around
the world in 72 days. She began her career with the Pittsburgh *Dispatch*, covering women's issues both frivolous and serious, but in 1887
got a job at the New York *World*, where she accepted an assignment to
spend a few days in a mental institution. Her exposé of the dreadful
conditions produced sensational stories for the *World* and, later, a book,
Ten Days in a Mad-House. At 31 she retired from journalism, married
an older man, and successfully managed his business after his death,
though she later returned to reporting, covering World War I and the
suffragette movement.

Richard Harding Davis (1864-1916) was a
journalist, first in his native Philadelphia and
then in New York, and did not shy away from
exciting topics. His reporting on the 1889 flood
that devastated Johnstown, Pennsylvania, helped
bring him to national attention. Later he reported on the Spanish-American War, the South
African War of 1899-1900, the Russo-Japanese
War, and eventually World War I, for a series
of magazines and newspapers. A list of his
books includes some three dozen titles, including memoirs of his experiences and also
romantic novels. With his square, clean-shaven
chin, Davis was reportedly the model for many
of the men drawn by illustrator **Charles Dana Gibson** as the escorts for
his popular Gibson Girls at the turn of the century.

Robert Cecil, Viscount **Cecil** (1864-1958), was a barrister for almost
two decades before embarking on political and international work that
brought him the 1937 Nobel Peace Prize. A son of Lord *Salisbury*, he
served briefly as Salisbury's secretary during his early years as Prime
Minister. In 1887 he was called to the bar (recognized as a lawyer), and
he continued in civil law practice until 1906. He was co-author, with
Joseph Hurst, of *The Principles of Commercial Law* (1891, 1906). Entering Parliament and serving in various government posts during World War
I, he developed *Proposals for Maintenance of Future Peace*. After the
war he was involved in drafting a charter for the League of Nations,

representing Britain at international conferences, and advocating "collective security".

Sir **Roger Casement** (1864-1916) was a British diplomat whose reports brought attention to the abuses perpetrated in the Congo by the administration of King *Léopold II* of the Belgians. He became a friend of Arthur Conan Doyle as ACD prepared to write *The Crime of the Congo* (1908), in cooperation with **Edmund Morel** of the Congo Reform Association. Casement, more and more interested in the issue of independence for his native Ireland, left the diplomatic service, soon helped form the Irish National Volunteers, and with the outbreak of World War I looked for German help. He was arrested, and his "black diaries", detailing homosexual liaisons, were used in an attempt to discredit him. Casement was convicted of treason and, despite a campaign for clemency in which ACD joined, was hanged at Pentonville Prison.

Aaron Kosminski (1865-1919) was a suspect in the 1888 Jack the Ripper murders, first known to have been suggested in an 1894 memorandum by Sir *Melville Macnaghten*. He was born in Russia (present-day Poland or Ukraine) and came to Britain about 1881 along with other family members as part of the massive exodus of Russian Jews to western Europe and north America. As Macnaghten described him, "This man became insane owing to many years indulgence in solitary vices. He had a great hatred of women, especially of the prostitute class, & had strong homicidal tendencies." Kosminski, who worked as a barber in Whitechapel, was twice went to a workhouse because of odd behaviour such as a refusal to eat normal food or to wash, as well as auditory hallucinations. He was committed to Colney Hatch lunatic asylum in 1891. Direct evidence linking him to the Ripper case is scant, and the story is further complicated by the records of another asylum inmate, **David Cohen**, whose real name may have been **Nathan Kaminsky**.

Alfred Harmsworth, Lord **Northcliffe** (1865-1922), was a powerful influence on British public opinion through his media empire, Amalgamated Press. Beginning as a freelance journalist, he founded newspapers and magazines, and later bought them; eventually he had control of the *Daily Mail*, *Daily Mirror*, *Sunday Dispatch*,

Observer, *Times*, and *Sunday Times*. One historian summarizes his power: he "controlled half the London press, at a time, before radio or television, when publications were the only media of mass communication." In particular he is given credit for bringing down the government of **Herbert Henry Asquith** in 1916 and making **David Lloyd George** prime minister in his place.

Baroness **Emma Orczy** (1865-1947) was born of a Hungarian noble family that settled in England in 1880. In 1894 she married **Montague MacLean Barstow**, and it fell to her to earn much of their keep through writing novels. Her great success dates from the play, and then the novel, *The Scarlet Pimpernel*, written in 1903. It tells the swashbuckling story of an English aristocrat who gets embroiled in politics and adventure in France during the Reign of Terror of the 1790s. Sequels about the Pimpernel and his supporters followed until 1940, as well as many other books, and brought Orczy wealth as well as fame.

Edith Cavell (1865-1915) was a British nurse working in Belgium during World War I, who was executed for treason by a German firing squad. The daughter of a Church of England vicar, she worked first as a governess (including five years in Brussels, 1890-1895) and then as a nurse, returning to Brussels in 1910. When the war began, she found herself involved in sheltering British and other allied soldiers and helping them escape the German authorities. Cavell became a major figure in British propaganda and national mythology. Her statement that "Patriotism is not enough. I must have no hatred or bitterness towards anyone" was widely quoted.

George Samuel Dougherty (1865-1931) was an operative with the Pinkerton Detective Agency for 23 years starting in 1888, rising to be head of its New York office. He then served 1911-1913 as deputy commissioner of the New York Police Department, where he headed the investigation of the *Charlie Becker* case. Leaving the NYPD, he became a partner with his brother, **Harry V. Dougherty**, in a private detective agency, wrote several books about crime, including *A Word about Criminals* (1916), and became an instructor at the NYPD's training school.

George V, previously **Duke of York** (1865-1936), became King on the death of his father, *Edward VII*, in 1910. He had not at first expected to reach the throne, but became the heir when his older brother, Prince *Albert Victor*, Duke of *Clarence*, died in 1892. The following year, George married Princess *Mary of Teck*, who had been engaged to his late brother. George served in the Royal Navy for 15 years starting when he was 12, acquiring a tattoo on a visit to Japan. As Prince of Wales (from 1901) and then as King, he toured the Empire, but also liked to retreat into quiet times with the royal stamp collection. His reign saw constitutional changes in Britain to increase democracy, full legal independence for Canada and other dominions, Home Rule and then independence for Ireland, the General Strike of 1926, and the transforming horrors of World War I.

Rudyard Kipling (1865-1936) was the poet, short story writer, and novelist of empire, and winner of the 1907 Nobel Prize for literature. His reputation remains controversial, as some critics consider the author who wrote of "the white man's burden" racist and jingoistic. He was born in Bombay son of a British art teacher, and his best-known works draw on the Anglo-Indian experience: *The Jungle Book* (1894) and its 1895 sequel, *Kim* (1901), and the *Just So Stories* (1902). Two of his poems, "If —" and "Recessional" (the latter written for Queen *Victoria*'s Diamond Jubilee) are sentimental classics. Kipling and his American wife, **Caroline Balestier**, settled in 1891 in Brattleboro, Vermont. Arthur Conan Doyle visited their house, Naulakha, in 1894, and played golf over a nearby pasture with his brother-in-law, **Beatty Balestier**. The Kiplings returned to England in 1896, settling in Devon and then Sussex.

Mrs. **Patrick Campbell**, born **Beatrice Rose Tanner** (1865-1940), was the actress who reportedly said, "It doesn't matter what you do in the bedroom as long as you don't do it in the street and frighten the horses." She had a successful stage career from 1888 to 1928, appearing both in London and on Broadway. A highlight was her 1914 performance as Eliza Doolittle in the first production of "Pygmalion" by *George Bernard Shaw*, with whom she had a passionate relationship by correspondence. With the advent of sound films she went to Hollywood and worked as a voice coach, as well as appearing in several films between 1920 and 1935. Her first husband was, as her preferred name might suggest, **Patrick Campbell**, who was killed in the South African War; her second, **George Cornwallis-West**, a former husband of *Jennie Churchill*.

William Butler Yeats (1865-1939) was an Irish poet and playwright, not just by chance of birth but by choice of raw material. Legends, folklore and songs found their way into his writing, even though he lived in England for much of his life. Several of his plays dealt with the exploits of the legendary Irish warrior Cuchulainn. He favoured, however, the elite Anglo-Irish class from which he had come, and was disappointed when Irish history went in other directions with independence and civil wars. His work also reflected his occult interests (he was a long-time member of the Order of the Golden Dawn). Yeats had a prolonged, passionate relationship with **Maud Gonne**, an outspoken advocate of Irish nationalism, though both of them were married to others.

Beatrix Potter (1866-1943) was the author and illustrator of *The Tale of Peter Rabbit* (1902) and 22 other "little tales" for children. She lived with her parents in London until she was 40, and kept much of her life secret, including a coded diary and, for a long time, her romance with **Norman Warne**, the editor at Frederick Warne & Co. who handled her books. Eventually she accepted his proposal, but he died of leukemia before they could marry. In 1905 Potter, now wealthy on the proceeds of her books, bought Hill Top, a farm at Sawrey in the Lake District, where she threw herself into country life. "Dressed in clogs, shawl and an old tweed skirt," says PeterRabbit.com, "she helped with the hay-making, waded through mud to unblock drains and searched the fells for lost sheep." She worked to preserve country properties and traditional country life, and left "a large body of remarkable scientific illustrations of fossils, archaeological finds, mosses and lichens, wild flowers, microscope drawings and, most importantly, fungi".

Ernest **William Hornung** (1866-1921) created Raffles, the "amateur cracksman", and his sidekick Bunny Manders, and dedicated his stories to his brother-in-law: "To A.C.D. This form of flattery." Hornung had married **Constance Doyle** (1868-1924), a younger sister of Arthur Conan Doyle, in 1893. He grew up in Yorkshire, spent three years in Australia as a tutor, and took up writing; some of his work uses Australian backgrounds and, arguably, betrays Australian attitudes. Stingaree, a bushranger who is also a gentleman, was a step toward the creation of Raffles. *The Amateur Cracksman*

(1899) was followed by *The Black Mask* (1901), *A Thief in the Night* (1905), and *Mr. Justice Raffles* (1909). As burglars residing in the fashionable Albany, rather than detectives in Baker Street, Raffles and Bunny are inevitably seen as mirrors of Holmes and Watson, and the same-sex affection is far more overt.

Fred Karno, born **Frederick John Westcott** (1866-1941), was a star performer in British music halls, the pioneer of smacking people in the face with pies, the father of slapstick comedy in general. He owned and managed theatres as well as performing, and in the 1920s, with music halls in decline because of the movie industry, worked briefly in Hollywood. Stars including *Charlie Chaplin* and **Stan Laurel** began their careers working with Karno. But he is often best remembered for sarcastic lyrics sung (to a hymn tune) by British troops in World War I: "We are Fred Karno's army, the ragtime infantry. We cannot fight, we cannot shoot, what bleeding use are we?"

Herbert George (H.G.) Wells (1866-1946) was the author of *The Time Machine*, an 1895 novel that was instantly popular and has been imitated (and used in crossovers) ever since. He followed that with *The Invisible Man* (1897) and *The War of the Worlds* (1898), as well as dozens of other novels not so well remembered. Wells also published short story collections and much non-fiction. He was a member of the socialist Fabian Society and had a keen interest in how society would evolve, expressing some of the possibilities through his science fiction, to the point that he has been called "the father of futurism". His 1920 *The Outline of History* included observations on where he thought the events of the past and present were leading, and a call for the creation of world government. Born into a shopkeeping family in Kent, Wells was twice married, and also had a series of love affairs; he had a son with novelist **Rebecca West**.

James 'Gentleman Jim' Corbett (1866-1933) defeated the world heavyweight boxing champion, *John L. Sullivan*, in 1892 and held the title for five years. From his early years in San Francisco he was known as a "scientific" boxer, a term suggestive of what Holmes says about his own boxing technique in "The Solitary Cyclist": "a straight left against a slogging ruffian". Between boxing bouts, and after giving up the sport in 1903 following a defeat by **James Jeffries**, he worked as an actor and even appeared in a dozen films.

Mary Pearcey, née **Wheeler** (1866-1890), has been unconvincingly suggested as a candidate for the title of Jack the Ripper. What is more definite is that she was hanged for the bloody murder of a romantic rival, which took place in the Camden Town neighbourhood at about the same time that the events of "The Red-Headed League" may have been unfolding elsewhere in London, in October 1890. Pearcey's boyfriend, **Frank Hogg**, had married another woman, **Phoebe Styles**, after getting her pregnant. A baby, also named Phoebe, was born. Pearcey invited the new Mrs. Hogg to call on her; neighbours heard screams; the woman's body was found on a rubbish-heap in Hampstead, bloody and mutilated, and the baby's body in Finchley. The trial was a national sensation.

Frederick Ponsonby, 1st Baron **Sysonby** (1867-1935) was the son and grandson of generals, and had a military career himself: he served in the South African War and World War I, but only reached the rank of lieutenant-colonel. In 1920 he wrote a book about his regiment, *The Grenadier Guards in the Great War of 1914-1918*. Following in the footsteps of his father, Sir **Henry Ponsonby** (1825-1895), who had been private secretary to Queen *Victoria*, he held various offices for the royal family, including assistant private secretary to the same Queen for the last four years of her life and then to King *Edward VII*. He was Keeper of the Privy Purse, in charge of royal finances, from 1914 to his death. These experiences, and a reputation as a wit and social lion, formed the background for his anecdote-filled autobiography, *Recollections of Three Reigns*, which was not published until 1952.

Marie Curie, born **Maria Sklodowska** (1867-1934), was the first woman to win a Nobel Prize, and the only woman who has won Nobels in two fields (physics 1903, chemistry 1911). She was, along with her husband **Pierre Curie** up to his death in 1906, the pioneer of research into radiation, and it was radiation that killed her — she died of aplastic anemia as the result of exposure to radium. Her research into radioactivity (a word she coined) began with uranium and led to the discovery of polonium (1898) and radium (1902), the development of X-ray technology, and the first hint of radiation as a therapy for cancer. Born in Warsaw, she lived most of her life in Paris, where she studied at the Sorbonne and became its first female professor. Marie and Pierre's daughter, **Irène Joliot-Curie**, was the Nobel winner for chemistry in 1935.

Mary of Teck, later **Queen Mary** (1867-1953), was the wife of King *George V,* and thus Queen from the time he came to the throne in 1910. Her father was **Francis, Duke of Teck**, a minor German royal, but Mary was born and brought up in England. Before becoming engaged to George, she had been engaged to Prince *Albert Victor*, Duke of *Clarence*, but he died before their planned wedding. Mary and George married in 1893, and had six children, two of whom reigned as King, **Edward VIII** and **George VI**. She was Queen during World War I and the difficult period of social change in Britain which followed, and lived to see her granddaughter become Queen **Elizabeth**

II. The luxury liner RMS *Queen Mary*, launched in 1936, was named in her honour.

Pearl Craigie, née **Richards** (1867-1906), was a Boston-born writer who lived most of her life in England and produced novels and plays under the pseudonym **John Oliver Hobbes**. Her work is described as characteristically "bohemian", with the best-known book, *Some Emotions and a Moral,* clearly based on her own brief unsuccessful marriage. Though a devout Roman Catholic, she moved in fin-de-siècle circles with the likes of *Aubrey Beardsley*. Her 1894 play "Journeys End in Lovers' Meeting" (a phrase from Shakespeare that was also quoted by Sherlock Holmes) was written for *Ellen Terry*.

Sir **Casimir van Straubenzee** (1867-1956) was the very model of a modern major-general, who as Inspector-General of the Royal Artillery at the end of World War I certainly knew a chassepot rifle from a javelin. He came from a military family and was born at Kingston, Ontario, home of the Royal Military College of Canada, which he attended and where he taught for several years (with a break to serve in the Fourth Ashanti War in west Africa, 1895-1896). After his service in World War I he was promoted to major-general and served as commander of British forces at Singapore and then Malaya. He was the author of *Recollections of Sportsmen and Sport in Days of Yore* (1900?) and, in view of his expertise about firearms, is thought to have been the original of "old Straubenzee", the maker of air-guns mentioned in "The Mazarin Stone".

Alfred Herbert Wood (1868-1941) was Arthur Conan Doyle's secretary for thirty years, and by many accounts an important model for the character of Dr. Watson, stocky and mustached. Wood was an Oxford graduate, and a mathematics teacher at Portsmouth Grammar School (which he himself had attended) when he first met ACD, apparently through the latter's interest in school and amateur sports. They became friends, and Wood sometimes visited Undershaw once the Doyle family settled there in 1896. In January 1901 a letter from ACD to his mother called Wood "very useful and cheery"; soon afterwards he was officially the author's secretary, dealing with correspondence and arrangements. He sometimes copied out ACD's manuscripts for the printers, and his handwriting has been mistaken for ACD's on occasion. During World War I he fought with the Sussex Regiment, reaching the rank of major. ACD left him an annual pension in his will.

Alice Keppel, née **Edmonstone** (1868-1947), grew up in her family's ancestral home, Duntreath Castle near Scotland's Loch Lomond, the daughter of a retired admiral and baronet, Sir **William Edmonstone**. In 1891 she married **George Keppel**, son of an earl but far from wealthy. Says an admiring web page: "Since Alice was strikingly beautiful (with an hourglass figure, alabaster skin and thick chestnut hair) the two of them soon hit upon a simple plan: she would take on wealthy lovers whose income would finance their lifestyle and provide George with business connections." Her career of such relationships, and her reputation as a society hostess, reached a climax when she met the Prince of Wales (soon to be *Edward VII*) in 1898. "Within weeks," says the same web page, "she had replaced his previous mistress (the indiscreet **Daisy Greville**, Countess of **Warwick**), and she remained with him until his death in 1910." Her daughter, **Violet Keppel**, later **Trefusis**, was the lover of poet **Vita Sackville-West**.

Charles Rennie Mackintosh (1868-1928) was an architect and artist who lived most of his life in Glasgow, in a period when that bustling city was a natural place to be designing both manufactured objects and buildings. The Glasgow School of Art building is his most prominent work, and a building he designed in Mitchell Street, originally the Glasgow *Herald* offices, is now an art and design centre. Mackintosh was influenced by Japanese design, popular beginning in the 1870s, and he in turn was an influence on European art nouveau. Working in furniture, textiles, metal and painting, he collaborated with his wife, **Mar-**

garet MacDonald; the two were prominent members of what came to be called the Glasgow School.

Caroline Otero, born **Agustina Otero Iglesias** (1868-1965), was by all accounts one of the sexiest women who ever lived. Born in Spain, she had enjoyed affairs, a marriage and a singing and dancing career by the time she was 20. Soon afterwards she created the character of "La Belle Otero", presenting herself as an Andalusian gypsy and coming to star in Paris's Folies Bergère. She also wound up as a courtesan associated with the wealthy and noble, reportedly including **Edward VII**. There were rumours of duels and suicides, and from her gentlemen she acquired a vast fortune, which she gradually gambled away, dying in poverty in Nice.

Frederick Lanchester (1868-1946) was a pioneer of automotive engineering, a field in which Britain was a world leader until the 1950s. After working briefly in the patent office, Lanchester took a job in 1888 as assistant factory manager for an engine manufacturer in Birmingham; within a couple of years he had several patents for improvements and had designed a more powerful engine than any the company had previously made. In 1893 he left the firm to do full-time research, which led to more patents and, in 1898, the Gold Medal Phaeton automobile. Lanchester and his brothers started their own manufacturing company, which produced a steady series of innovations, including the invention of the accelerator pedal. Calculations that he developed to predict the performance of aircraft in warfare led to what is now the discipline of operations research.

Emily Murphy, née **Ferguson** (1868-1933), was the first woman in the British Empire to serve as a magistrate. She was appointed to the bench in Edmonton, Alberta, in 1916 after persuading the provincial attorney-general that if the evidence in prostitution cases was "not fit for mixed company", then there should be courts where women would preside and hear all the facts. Murphy, born into a family of lawyers, was self-taught in the law and had already run a successful campaign for improved laws protecting married women's property. Once she took office as a magistrate, there were protests that women were not entitled to hold government positions because they were not legally "persons". A legal action brought by five women, including former suffrage activist **Nellie McClung**, took 12 years to move through the courts, finally leading to a 1929 ruling in their favour, in what has become known as the Persons Case.

Mwanga II (1868-1903) was Kabaka of Buganda — that is, king of a region of east Africa, within the modern nation of Uganda, that was particularly powerful during colonial times. Its line of kings stretches back to the 14th century. Mwanga succeeded to the kingship in 1884 on the death of his father, **Muteesa I**, was deposed in 1888 in a British-supported rebellion, became king again in 1889, ceded some powers to the British East India Company, but was deposed again in 1897 following military conflict with Britain. His chief policy was resistance to the advances of colonial powers in Africa, represented by Christian missionaries,  both Protestant and Roman Catholic, as well as Muslim proselytizers. He had a number of Christian and Muslim converts executed, including the 22 Roman Catholic men, burned alive in 1886, who were elevated to sainthood in 1964 as the "Uganda Martyrs".

Gaston Leroux (1868-1927) was the author of *Le Fantôme de l'Opéra* ("The Phantom of the Opera"), which has somewhat eclipsed his other work, including novels of mystery, horror, fantasy, romance and adventure. Seven of them, including *The Mystery of the Yellow Room* (1908), a classic locked-room puzzle, feature reporter Joseph Rouletabille. Leroux, brought up in a ship-building village in Normandy, worked as a journalist and critic in Paris and abroad, and reported on the 1896 incident in which a man was killed when two counterweights fell from a chandelier into the audience at the Paris Opera — the seed for *The*

Phantom of the Opera. The website OnlineLiterature.com notes that *The Phantom*, "written in gripping journalistic style, was first serialised in the French newspaper *Le Gaulois* in 1909 and other newspapers in Europe and North America. It was first translated to English in 1911 by **Alexander Teixeira de Mattos**," and became popular after the 1925 film starring **Lon Chaney**.

Gertrude Bell (1868-1926) studied history at Oxford University and became a writer, archaeologist, and political negotiator in the Middle East beginning in 1899. "Her writings on her experiences across the globe informed British audiences about the distant parts of their empire," says the website Biography.com. "Bell became involved in the political reinvention of Mesopotamia, where she helped colonial authorities install ruler **Faisal I** as monarch of Iraq. She pioneered the idea of retaining antiquities in their country of origin rather than transporting them to European centers of learning. The result of Bell's efforts was the National Museum of Iraq."

Maxim Gorky, real name **Aleksey Maksimovich Peshkov** (1868-1936), was bitter ("gorki") about mistreatment by a series of employers in his youth in the Russian city of Nizhny Novgorod, and wrote feelingly about working-class life in the stories that he published from 1895 onwards. He went on to write plays and novels, less successful than the early work, and eventually an autobiographical trilogy. As his writing brought in generous royalties in the years before the Russian revolution, his contributions to the Bolshevik party were an important source of its funding. He was exiled for several years following the 1905 uprising, and again after the 1917 revolution when he fell out with Bolshevik dictator **Vladimir Lenin**, but eventually returned to be a hero of the Soviet Union.

Tappan Adney (1868-1950) was there with his camera when tens of thousands of miners and would-be miners raced to the Yukon in 1897-1898 — the so-called Klondike gold rush. His reports and photos from the northern frontier, done on assignment for *Harper's Weekly*, were turned into a book, *The Klondike Stampede*, which went through many editions. In 1900 he was on hand for a subsequent gold rush, in Nome, Alaska. Other products of his many talents include 110 illustrations for the 1897 *Handbook of Birds of Eastern North America*; murals in the Hudson's Bay store in downtown Winnipeg; a revival of the craft of birchbark canoe building (more than 100 of his models survive); and a collection of photos of rural Ontario circa 1930.

Booth Tarkington (1869-1946) was an American author now best remembered for his funny and poignant book about boyhood, *Penrod* (1914, with a sequel in 1916). He was born in Indianapolis, lived in Indiana much of his life (though settling on the Maine coast in retirement), and set much of his fiction in Indiana. "Much of Tarkington's work consists of satirical and closely observed studies of the American class system and its foibles," says Wikipedia. "He himself came from a patrician Midwestern family that lost much of its wealth after the Panic of 1873."

Cecil **Foster Seymour Vandeleur** (1869-1901) came from an English family based in County Clare, Ireland, which had a military tradition (a cousin, **Robert Seymour Vandeleur**, 1869-1940, rose to be a brigadier-general). C. S. F. Vandeleur joined the Irish Guards, won the Distinguished Service Order in Egypt, and was a lieutenant-colonel at the time of his death in an ambush near Waterval during the South African War. "Colonel Vandeleur refused to surrender, and was shot through the heart," a newspaper report said. *The Hound of the Baskervilles*, in which a character's alias is Vandeleur, had been published a few months earlier. Arthur Conan Doyle, who had worked at a South African field hospital in 1900, probably met Vandeleur, and mentions him in *The Great Boer War*.

Emma Goldman (1869-1940) joined the anarchist movement in New York in 1889, and was in trouble many times thereafter for "inciting to riot", disseminating information about contraception, interfering with the military draft, and a (failed) assassination attempt against industrialist **Henry Clay Frick**. In 1919 she and her lover, **Alexander Berkman**, were deported to Russia, the country from which she had come in 1885. Even as a teenager she had been interested in the Russian anarchist, or Nihilist, movement after the 1881 assassination of *Alexander II*; she arrived in America in time to be caught up in excitement after the 1886 Haymarket riot in Chicago. For the next two decades she was involved in labour agitation, free speech and anarchist publications, prison reform, birth control and conscription. Sent back to Russia during the Bolshevik revolution, she was first enthusiastic, later disillusioned.

Grigori Yefimovich Rasputin (1869-1916) was born to a Siberian peasant family and remained illiterate. Feeling spiritual or mystic leanings, he considered becoming a monk but instead travelled to Greece and Palestine and wandered through Russia. In 1906 he arrived at the country's capital, Saint Petersburg. Two years later he was introduced to Czar *Nicholas II* and Czarina **Alexandra**, and persuaded them that he could heal their sickly son, the Czarevich **Alexis**, one of several members of European royalty who suffered from haemophilia. He gained a strong influence over the Czar, and became the target of competing political factions seeking to make use of him. He developed a reputation as a "mad monk" and a libertine, and a group of conspirators eventually managed to assassinate him; it took poison, a beating, gunshots and finally drowning to finish him off.

Howard Thurston (1869-1936) is regarded by many as the greatest stage magician of his time. His career began when he ran away from home to join a circus, where he learned the business along with fellow magician **Harry Kellar**, with whom he formed a longstanding partnership. Thurston was known initially as "the King of Cards" for his "rising card" illusion and exceptional skills with a pack. Later he toured America and Europe and, as a magician, rivaled *Harry Houdini* as the most famous miracle performer of his day. "He produced lavish shows, adding pretty women and humor where Kellar had more formal presentations," according to one website on magical history. "While his original fame rested on card manipulations, Thurston's later reputation was built with large stage illusions. One of his popular tricks was to make a Whippet automobile filled with beautiful ladies disappear." It was recorded that Thurston's traveling show used eight rail cars' worth of props and equipment.

Mohandas K. Gandhi, known as **Mahatma** (1869-1948), is remembered as an iconic figure of pacifism who used non-violent resistance ("satyagraha") to press for independence for his native India. Seeking qualifications that would let him succeed his father as a colonial administrator, Gandhi travelled to London in 1888, studying at University College for three years, trying out dandyish western ways and qualifying as a barrister at the Inner Temple. He practised briefly in Bombay, then spent 21 years in South Africa as a lawyer and activist battling discrimination against Indian residents. Returning to India, he joined the Indian National Congress and advocated independence; by 1920 he was the Congress's leader. His campaigns of "non-cooperation" and passive resistance to taxes and other policies eventually led him to prison time during World War II. Independence came in 1947, with the bloody "partition" separating Pakistan from India.

Valdemar Poulsen (1869-1942) was an assistant engineer for the Copenhagen Telephone Company when he began experimenting with techniques for recording sound magnetically. Earlier work had been done by British engineer **Oberlin Smith**, but it was Poulsen who, in

1898, received a patent for a device that used magnetized steel piano wire running between spools. At 84 inches per second, it could record for 30 minutes. He thought of the device as a basis for a phone answering machine, and it was shown off at the Paris Exhibition of 1900, but commercial success eluded him. Poulsen later developed paper and plastic tape coated with magnetic powder, the technology that was used for later generations of recording machines.

Katherine Florence, née **Rogers**, married name **Williams** (1869-1952), was a Broadway actor who played Alice Faulkner in the original New York production of "Sherlock Holmes" by *William Gillette*. Born in England in a small town outside Birmingham, she began appearing on American stages as a child with her mother, actor **Katherine Rogers**. At the age of 18 she had a role with **Lillie Langtry** on one of her repeated American tours. From then on she was on stage just about every season. "Sherlock Holmes" ran at the Garrick Theater on West 35 Street, managed by *Charles Frohman*, for 235 performances from November 1899 to June 1900, with Gillette as Holmes and **Bruce McRae** as Watson. Florence married actor **Fritz Williams** in 1896; they appeared together in "On and Off" at the Madison Square Theater in 1898.

Adolf Loos (1870-1933) was a pioneer of "modern" architecture. He actually built few buildings, but those were "rigorous examples of austere beauty", says a website about architecture based in Slovakia. Loos was born in what is now the Czech Republic and worked in his father's masonry shop before being trained in Germany and the United States. He went into architectural practice in Vienna, and in 1897 began publishing essays that soon gave him an international reputation, crowned with the appearance of "Ornament and Crime" in 1908. Excess ornamentation, he wrote, was criminal — "not for abstract moral reasons," as the website puts it, "but because of the economics of labor and wasted materials in modern industrial civilization."

Alfred Adler (1870-1937) was one of the pioneers of psychology, particularly responsible for developing "individual psychology" and the idea of the inferiority complex. Educated at the University of Vienna, he began medical practice as an ophthalmologist in that city, where Arthur Conan Doyle had studied ophthalmology in 1891. Adler later joined *Sigmund Freud*'s psychoanalytic circle, from which he split in 1911, continuing to develop his own ideas and practice psychiatry. He came to the United States as Nazi influence rose in Austria in the 1930s.

Annie Londonderry, real name **Annie Cohen Kopchovsky** (1870-1947), was the real solitary cyclist, who made her way around the world 1894-1895 on a 21-pound men's Sterling bicycle. She took steamers as well as riding her bike, but did pedal long distances in the United States, France, Egypt, the Holy Land and Yemen in the course of 15 months of travel. The trip was prompted partly by a craze for round-the-world adventure (*Jules Verne*'s *Around the World in Eighty Days* had appeared in English in 1873) and partly by advertising initiative on the part of the Londonderry Lithia Spring Water Company, which persuaded Kopchovsky (a mother of four) to change her name and carry its banner. After the trip she wrote in the New York *World* that "I am a 'new woman', if that term means that I believe I can do anything that any man can do."

Bertram Fletcher Robinson (1870-1907) was a friend of Arthur Conan Doyle, whose contribution to the genesis of *The Hound of the Baskervilles* is acknowledged, with various wording, in all the early editions of that book. Having met on a ship returning from the South African War, they took a golf holiday together in Norfolk in March 1901, when the idea was born. A trip together to Dartmoor followed, to look at locations and encounter *Harry Baskerville*. In the end ACD wrote the book alone, giving Robinson credit for his "account of a West Country legend" and "help in the details". A scandal hit the news about 2005 with claims that ACD had then murdered Robinson to hide his theft of the Hound story. In fact Robinson died of typhoid at age 36. His brief life had included time spent in Uruguay with *Giuseppe Garibaldi* and a lively career as a sportsman; he also wrote dozens of short stories.

Charlie Becker (1870-1915) was a New York police officer in an era of pervasive corruption and attempts by reform politicians to root it out. His connection to Sherlock Holmes's friend, Wilson Hargreave, of the New York Police Bureau ("The Dancing Men"), is unclear. A policeman from 1893, he took part in a corruption investigation in 1906, then was named to head a vice squad. A few years later he was being accused of taking enormous kickbacks from brothels and gambling halls. In July 1912, bookmaker **Herman Rosenthal** was shot dead when he went public with his grievances about the shakedown. District attorney **Charles S. Whitman** had Becker charged with Rosenthal's murder; he was found guilty and electrocuted at Sing Sing.

Cyril Angell (1870-1937) was the husband of Arthur Conan Doyle's youngest sister, **Bryan Mary Doyle** (1877-1927). He was a Church of England priest from Westmorland in northwest England. Angell and "Dodo", as she was called, became engaged in 1897 and married in 1899. ACD was called on to help them financially, notably in 1900 when Angell became a partner in a private school. It was not a success, and he returned to active church work at a parish in London. Angell performed ACD's wedding to **Jean Leckie** in 1907. He is immortalized in a passage in "The Solitary Cyclist" in which Holmes teases Violet Smith: "Oh, Cyril is his name!"

Erskine Childers (1870-1922) was, like so many young men of his background, caught between Britain and Ireland; in his case the path led to a firing squad during the Irish Civil War. Childers was born in London, grew up in County Wicklow, attended Cambridge, took a government job, served in the South African War and World War I, and considered running for Parliament as a Liberal. But about 1914 he got involved in supplying arms to Irish nationalist groups, and after the war he played complicated roles in the negotiations that led to the Irish Free State in December 1922. Thought to be a republican insurrectionist, he was arrested by the Free State and executed. He is also remembered for his 1903 novel *The Riddle of the Sands*, about amateur yachtsmen (like himself) caught up in espionage in the Frisian Islands along the Dutch, German and Danish coast.

Jan Smuts (1870-1950) studied law at Cambridge, read law in London, and went home to South Africa in 1895 only to be drawn immediately into the complex politics of the region. He was based at first in the Cape Colony, which was British, and then in the Transvaal, which was predominantly occupied by Boers (settlers of Dutch origin, like himself). He was an officer in the South African War of 1899-1901, developing effective guerrilla tactics against over-stretched British armies. When peace came, he played a significant role in the negotiation of responsible (democratic) government for Transvaal and then, when the Union of South Africa was formed in 1910, for all of the new nation. During World War I he was a member of the Imperial War Cabinet in London; he later served as Prime Minister of South Africa 1919-1924 and again 1939-1948.

Lady **Maud Warrender**, née **Ashley-Cooper** (1870-1945), was a talented amateur musician, and a friend of Sir *Edward Elgar*, who wrote the song "Pleading" for her in 1908. The daughter of *Anthony Ashley-Cooper*, Earl of **Shaftesbury**, she married a naval officer, Sir **George Warrender**, who became an admiral; she accompanied him to the Kiel regatta in June 1914 in which British and German officers socialized and admired one another's ships, weeks before the outbreak of World War I. After his death in 1917 she lived in a relationship with American soprano **Marcia van Dresser**. She was notable for her work in organizing charity concerts and her support of women's suffrage; photographs of her in elegant stage costume appeared in magazines frequently at the turn of the century. She also served as a lady-in-waiting to Queen *Mary*, and was involved with the creation of the Queen's Dolls' House, for which Arthur Conan Doyle contributed an original story, "How Watson Learned the Trick". Her name may have been borrowed for Miss Minnie Warrender, mentioned in "The Mazarin Stone".

Lord **Alfred Douglas** (1870-1945), known to his friends as "Bosie", was a significant lyric poet and author, not merely the boy-toy who led to the downfall of *Oscar Wilde*. "Within his chosen framework of the

'Italian' or Petrarchan sonnet, he was a master," says his great-nephew, Lord Gawain Douglas, on a website devoted to his memory. Wilde himself wrote to his young lover: "It is a marvel□that those rose-leaf lips of yours should have been made□no less for music of song than for madness of kisses." Douglas was the son of the 9th Marquess of **Queensberry**. His homosexual affair with Wilde began in 1891; Douglas remained loyal to Wilde after the 1895 scandal, and was chief mourner at his funeral.

Marie Lloyd, real name **Matilda Wood** (1870-1922), was the Queen of the Music Hall. "She first appeared at the Eagle Tavern in London aged 15 as Bella Delmare, singing 'My Soldier Laddie'," says the website of the Victoria and Albert Museum. "By 1885 she had become Marie Lloyd with her hit song 'The Boy I Love is Up in the Gallery'. She was a huge success and topped the bill at the West End music halls." Three times (1891-1893) she starred in Christmas pantomimes at the Theatre Royal, Drury Lane, a London theatrical tradition; later she made several American tours. Lloyd was famous for ad libs, high-kicking dances, showing off her underthings, double en-

tendres (in songs like "She'd Never Had Her Ticket Punched Before" and "She Sits Among the Cabbages and Peas"), and a dirty wink at her audience. As the V&A website also notes, "she had three unsuccessful and very public marriages." The Sherlock Holmes tales contain no mention of London's music halls, but one (in "The Stock-Broker's Clerk") of Day's Music Hall in Birmingham, where Lloyd might well have performed during a tour.

Ernest Rutherford, 1st Baron **Rutherford** (1871-1937), was born and educated in New Zealand, and taught at Canada's McGill University for a decade (1898-1907), but was working in Britain by the time he received the 1908 Nobel Prize in physics. He held professorships at the University of Manchester (1907-1919) and then at Cambridge, working with such scientists as **Hans Geiger**, **Niels Bohr**, and **H. G. Moseley**. Described as "the father of nuclear physics", he was the author of several books, starting with *Radioactivity* (1904). His Nobel Prize was awarded for "investigations into the disintegration of the elements", that is, radioactive decay. His later work produced the 20th century understanding of atoms, with a nucleus, orbiting electrons, and much space in between.

Guangxu, personal name **Zaitian** (1871-1908), was the ninth Qing emperor of China. He was named Emperor as a four-year-old, becoming successor to his cousin, **Tongzhi**, and was dominated for most of his life by two dowager empresses. The 1894 Sino-Japanese War, a disaster for China, came before he began to rule directly without the regency of his aunt, Dowager Empress **Cixi**, in 1889. The Emperor was interested in the changes being introduced in Japan under Emperor *Meiji*, and in 1898 instituted a spectacular "Hundred Days Reform" program that included a budget process, the founding of a university, railway construction, and imperial protection for Christian missionaries. Probably as a result, he was removed from direct rule by a coup organized by Cixi. Unrest grew over foreign influence in China, leading to the Boxer Rebellion by a nativist faction in 1899-1901. Troops arrived from a coalition of foreign nations, and the Emperor had to leave the capital, Beijing, for a year and a half. In his last years he was essentially a prisoner of the Dowager Empress, and he is thought to have died from arsenic poisoning, possibly by her doing.

Emily **Davison** (1872-1913) was an activist in the women's suffrage movement, jailed many times for arson and other forms of violent demonstration, and finally killed in a dramatic incident during the Epsom Derby horse race. She studied at Oxford (but as a woman was not eligible, at that time, to receive a degree) and worked as a governess. She joined the Women's Social and Political Union, headed by *Emmeline Pankhurst*, in 1906, but carried out protests well beyond what the WSPU had endorsed. During a term in Holloway Prison in 1912 she seriously injured herself by throwing herself down a staircase. In June 1913 she went to the Derby (a major annual sporting event, featured in "Shoscombe Old Place") and ran onto the track during the race. Historians have examined newsreel footage and other evidence but are not certain what her intentions were. She was trampled by a horse owned by King *George V*, and died four days later; the jockey was injured but survived.

George Joseph Smith (1872-1915) was the perpetrator of the "brides in the bath" murders, a case that helped establish the technique of showing the similarity among crimes as evidence that the same person had committed them. Smith, who grew up in London, had been involved with the criminal justice system since the age of 9. Through his adult life he was involved also with a series of women, going through a form of marriage a total of eleven times from 1898 to 1914 under various names. Often he made off with the women's assets and disappeared, but he drowned three of his supposed wives in the bathtub to acquire both their savings and the proceeds of insurance policies. The case was investigated by Inspector **Arthur Neil** of Scotland Yard with the assistance of Home Office pathologist ***Bernard Spilsbury***. Despite a defence by Sir ***Edward Marshall Hall***, Smith was found guilty of murder and hanged.

Aubrey Beardsley (1872-1898) is the best-known of the "fin-de-siècle" or "decadent" artists associated with the Art Nouveau movement in Britain in the 1890s. Influenced by the French artist **Henri de Toulouse-Lautrec** and by the fashion for Japanese art, he specialized in book illustrations done in black ink with strong contrast between black and white areas. Many of his drawings, famously those for ***Oscar Wilde***'s *Salome* and for an edition of *Lysistrata*, were strongly erotic, tending toward the grotesque and perverse. Beardsley was a founder of the art quarterly *The Yellow Book*, but left its editorial staff after the Wilde scandal of 1895.

Ivan Bloch (1872-1922) was the first scientist to specialize in sex, and the man who gave the world a lost book of the **Marquis de Sade**. Born in the Oldenburg region of Germany, Bloch was a physician — a skin specialist — but became interested in the science and social science of sex, and in 1906 his definitive book was published (English title, *The Sexual Life of Our Time*). Using the alias **Eugène Dühren**, Bloch published the *Life and Works* of de Sade in 1899, and the newly discovered text of *The 120 Days of Sodom* in 1904. The editor commented that he thought de Sade's extensive catalogue of sexual fetishes, written while he was in prison in 1785, would have ""scientific importance to doctors, jurists, and anthropologists".

Oscar Slater, born **Leschziner** (1872-1948), was a petty criminal who found himself imprisoned in 1909 for a murder in Glasgow. **Marion Gilchrist**, a wealthy elderly woman, was bludgeoned to death in her flat, and a diamond brooch stolen, though other jewellery was untouched. Circumstantial evidence pointed to Slater (in particular, he had recently pawned a diamond brooch) and he was sentenced to death, though the sentence was quickly commuted to life imprisonment. A public outcry about miscarriage of justice came to the ears of Arthur Conan Doyle, who investigated the case and in 1912 published *The Case of Oscar Slater*, demanding an inquiry and Slater's release. As evidence of police corruption emerged, ACD continued to be involved in the case; Slater was finally released, with a cash payment by way of compensation, in 1927.

Sir **Maximilian Beerbohm** (1872-1956) — "the incomparable Max", according to *George Bernard Shaw* — was a caricaturist, dramatist, reviewer and novelist. His most enduring work is the satirical novel *Zuleika Dobson* (1911), about a femme fatale who cuts a swath through the young men of Oxford University. A half-brother of *Herbert Beerbohm Tree*, he spent much of his life in Rapallo, Italy, with his wife, **Florence Kahn**. Says the *Encyclopaedia Britannica*: "He attracted to Rapallo a constant stream of distinguished visitors, who were charmed by his conversation and found in him a living archive of amusing anecdotes of the literary, artistic, and social circles of late Victorian and Edwardian England."

Edmund Dene Morel, born **Georges Morel de Ville** (1873-1924), was a French-born journalist who has been suggested as the original of Edward Malone, the narrator of Arthur Conan Doyle's 1912 novel *The Lost World*. He worked with ACD as they campaigned for an end to atrocities in the Congo, ACD as the author of *The Crime of the Congo* and Morel as founder of the Congo Reform Association. Initially an employee of a Liverpool shipping firm, Morel became aware of the issue about 1893, and in 1903 founded a weekly journal, the *West African Mail*, to publicize the abuses. By 1908 the Belgian king, *Léopold II*, had been compelled to give up direct rule of the Congo, but the campaign continued with ACD's pamphlet in 1909 and a speaking tour during which Morel and ACD appeared together in cities across Britain. Morel campaigned against British involvement in World War I (he spent six months in prison) but served briefly in Parliament, 1922-1924.

Frederic Dorr Steele (1873-1944) was the leading American illustrator of the Sherlock Holmes tales, or at least the final 32 short stories, mostly creating black-and-white illustrations and colour covers for *Collier's Weekly*. "These portraits were the finest of Holmes done up to that time, perhaps the finest that ever were or ever will be done of him," says Walter Klinefelter in his book on illustration. The model Steele used for Holmes was actor *William Gillette*. Steele was primarily a book illustrator, having worked with texts by such authors as *Richard Harding Davis* and *Rudyard Kipling*. He spent his working life in New York, where he was a member of the elite Players Club, and was a friend of such early Sherlockians as **Vincent Starrett** and **Gray Chandler Briggs**. Shortly before his death he had been working on illustrations for a projected Limited Editions Club version of the stories.

Leon Czolgosz (1873-1901) was electrocuted in October 1901 for the murder of United States president *William McKinley* the previous month. Czolgosz grew up in poverty in Detroit and other cities, and as a workman was prompted by the bitter labour conflicts of the late 19th century to explore socialism and anarchism. He is also thought to have suffered a nervous breakdown, and finally to have been inspired by the 1900 assassination of King *Umberto I* of Italy. His opportunity came when McKinley visited Buffalo for the Pan-American Exposition, a world's fair which ran May through October, and stood to shake hands with a line of visitors. When Czolgosz reached the head of the line he pulled out a revolver and shot McKinley twice; the president died eight days later.

Harry Houdini (1873-1926), real name **Ehrich Weiss**, was an escape artist, conjurer and showman who was born in Budapest and grew up in Wisconsin. He adopted his pseudonym in 1894 as a tribute to a French magician of an earlier generation, **Jean Eugène Robert-Houdin**. His wife **Wilhelmina Beatrice Rahner** ("Bess") soon became his assistant in handcuff escapes and other performances as his flamboyance, and his ability to escape jail cells and other dramatic situations, made him world-famous. His escape from a water-filled, locked metal "milk can" was a staple. Houdini flirted with Spiritualism, but soon turned to exposing fraudulent mediums, of whom there were many. His friendship with Arthur Conan Doyle dissolved in 1922 because ACD could not endure Houdini's scepticism.

Thomas Glendenning Hamilton (1873-1935) was a prominent physician and politician in Winnipeg, and from about 1918 a devotee of

Spiritualism — or, as he preferred to call it in view of his strong Christian beliefs, psychic research. "Hamilton conducted séances," scholar Barbara Rusch writes, "and investigated mental telepathy, table rapping, bell-box ringing, automatic writing, deep-trance drawings, communications from deceased persons and ectoplasm constructions." Some of his work was done with the help of a neighbour who was a medium, **Elizabeth Poole**. Arthur Conan Doyle sat in séances at the Hamilton home during his 1923 visit to Winnipeg.

Emma Shrivell (1874-1892) was one of four prostitutes for whose murders *Thomas Neill Cream* was hanged. She had been born in Brighton and had an older brother; records do not name the father, but their mother, **Elizabeth Shrivell**, married when Emma was 3, and had other children. Emma apparently made her way to London and became one of its thousands of prostitutes. Estimates of their number vary widely, and Shrivell clearly was not on the lowest rung of the profession since she had a room of her own. Cream met her along with **Alice Marsh**, who at 21 was three years older than Shrivell, one night in April 1892 in St. George's Circus, a landmark intersection in Southwark. He went home with them to **Charlotte Vogt**'s rooming-house in nearby Lambeth. There they drank Guinness and presumably engaged in sexual activity, after which Cream gave the women what were later described in evidence as "long pills". The pills contained strychnine. Both women were still alive when police arrived, summoned by the landlady when she heard their screams. Marsh died on the way to St. Thomas's Hospital; Shrivell lived long enough to describe the poisoner.

Gilbert Keith Chesterton (1874-1936) is best remembered for his 61 stories featuring priest and detective Father Brown, published between 1911 and 1936. However, he wrote millions of words in other genres, including theology, criticism and drama, and the 1908 thriller *The Man Who Was Thursday*. Most of his work carries a more or less explicit Christian message; he was a high-church Anglican much of his life, converting to Roman Catholicism in 1922. Father Brown is as unassuming as Sherlock Holmes is eccentric, his method being to place himself inside the heart and soul of the criminal and so to understand the deed, the sin and the hope. Chesterton's writing is rich in parable and paradox; he was known as a stout, rumpled, disorganized, genial man who enjoyed debates with the likes of *George Bernard Shaw*. Dr. Gideon Fell in the novels of **John Dickson Carr** is thought to have been based on him.

Guglielmo Marconi (1874-1937) is remembered as the leading inventor in the development of radio, or "wireless", the technology behind the "naval signals" mentioned in "His Last Bow", and which would eventually lead to television as well. Marconi began his experiments in 1895, as a young man in Italy; he received a patent for "a system of wireless telegraphy" in 1896. He sent messages between England and France in 1899, and between Cornwall and Newfoundland two years later, with commercial service following shortly. Marconi shared the 1909 Nobel Prize for Physics with **Karl Ferdinand Braun** (1850-1918), who also made advances in radio technology and invented the cathode ray tube.

Sir **Winston Churchill** (1874-1965) was Prime Minister during World War II, and by some polls the greatest Briton of all time, but he had had other careers long before that. The son of Lord *Randolph Churchill* and *Jennie Churchill*, he was an indifferent student, attended the Royal Military Academy Sandhurst, and served in India and Sudan, seeing action several times. In his spare time he sent reports home to newspapers, and afterwards he wrote two books. Leaving the army, he worked as a correspondent for the *Morning Post* during the South African War. He entered Parliament in 1900, and soon held the office of President of the Board of Trade; in that role he introduced Britain's first minimum wage in 1908. Among other offices, he was First Lord of the Admiralty 1911-1915 and again 1939-1940, Chancellor of the Exchequer 1924-1929, and finally Prime Minister 1940-1945 and 1951-1955.

Alternately a Conservative and a Liberal through his political career, he headed a coalition government during most of World War II. Churchill's writings include the four-volume *History of the English-Speaking Peoples* and the six-volume *The Second World War*; he received the 1953 Nobel Prize for Literature.

Aleister Crowley, born **Edward Alexander Crowley** (1875-1947), liked to be called "the wickedest man in the world" and "the Beast". After studies at Cambridge he settled in London and in 1898 joined the Hermetic Order of the Golden Dawn. In 1904 he founded a philosophy, or religion, called Thelema. Its website now describes Crowley thus: "He is best known as being an infamous occultist and the scribe of *The Book of the Law*, which introduced Thelema to the world. Crowley was an influential member in several occult organizations, including the Golden Dawn, the A.'A.', and Ordo Templi Orientis. He was a prolific writer and poet, a world traveler, mountaineer, chess master, artist, yogi, social provocateur, drug addict and sexual libertine." A central principle of his teaching: "Do what thou wilt."

Edgar Wallace (1875-1932) wrote more than 170 novels and close to 1,000 short stories, most of them thrillers, with much action and little social perception. He was the first author whose detectives were regularly police officers rather than amateurs. Raised in an impoverished family in east London, Wallace left school at age 12, sold newspapers and worked at other jobs, and by 1898, inspired by **Rudyard Kipling**, was writing poetry, newspaper dispatches from the South African War, and then mysteries. He published his first book, *The Four Just Men* (1905), himself. Stories followed based on his experiences as a newspaper correspondent in the Congo. By the 1920s he was writing prolifically, reportedly producing a book within three days by dictating onto wax cylinders for later transcription. He was also earning a high income, and spending everything he earned, much of it on racehorses. Wallace wrote the first draft of the screenplay for the 1933 film "King Kong".

Jacques Futrelle (1875-1912) was the author of "The Problem of Cell 13" and other stories featuring "The Thinking Machine", more formally known as Prof. Dr. Dr. Dr. S. F. X. Van Dusen. He was born in Georgia, and began his writing career as a teenage reporter for the Atlanta *Journal*, later moving to jobs in Boston and New York. "Cell 13", his first Van Dusen story, was a forerunner of the "locked room" genre of mystery, in which the central character uses logic to escape from a prison cell. It was published in the Boston *American* in 1905. The brilliant, relentlessly logical professor appeared in several novels as well as short stories over the next few years. Futrelle was fond of technology and novelty; in one story, "The Problem of the Lost Radium", Van Dusen assists Nobel-winning scientist **Marie Curie**. Futrelle died in the sinking of RMS *Titanic*.

James J. Jeffries (1875-1953) was, according to some experts, the greatest heavyweight boxer in history. Born in Carroll, Ohio, he worked as a boilermaker — experience that gave him upper body strength as well as his enduring nickname — and gained boxing experience as a sparring partner for the then heavyweight champion, **Gentleman Jim Corbett**. In 1899 he defeated the new title-holder, **Bob Fitzsimmons**, for the championship, and after a series of successful defences he retired undefeated in 1905. The next champion, **Jack Johnson**, was the first Black man to hold the title, and Jeffries agreed to face him in hopes of recovering the title for a White man. Arthur Conan Doyle was invited to referee the fight, but was unable to travel to Reno for the event in July 1910. Johnson defeated Jeffries in 15 rounds.

John Buchan, Lord Tweedsmuir (1875-1940), was a star student at Oxford University (and president of the Oxford Union for a term in 1900), a young administrator in Britain's South African colonies, a war correspondent and propagandist, a Member of Parliament representing Scotland's universities, and eventually Governor General of Canada 1935-1940. In that role he promoted Canadian nationalism, multiculturalism and cultural institutions. At the same time, Buchan was author of nearly 30 novels, as well as other books. His best known work is the spy thriller *The Thirty-Nine Steps* (1915), and several of his other novels present further adventures of his hero Richard Hannay, including *Greenmantle*, which deals with Muslim agitation during World War I.

George Edalji (1876-1953) was the central figure in a protracted miscarriage of justice that Arthur Conan Doyle called "an appalling tragedy". Edalji was a young solicitor from a mixed-race family (author of *Railway Law for the Man in the Train*) who was accused in 1903 of wounding a pony and other animals near his home in Great Wyrley, Staffordshire. He went to prison, but attacks on animals in the area continued, as did abusive letters to the family, some of which had come as early as 1888. He was released from prison in 1906, but not exonerated. ACD joined in the campaign to have him pardoned, and investigated  in person, testifying from his medical expertise that Edalji, with "myopia of eight dioptres", could not have negotiated fields at night as was claimed. ACD's exposition in the *Daily Telegraph* was published as *The Story of Mr. George Edalji* (1907). A pardon was eventually granted, but there was no compensation for Edalji. ACD identified the man who did commit the mutilations and write the letters, but he was never prosecuted.

Jack London, born **John Griffith Chaney** (1876-1916), was the author of *The Call of the Wild* (1903) and other novels and short stories of adventure. Born in San Francisco, he "rode trains, pirated oysters, sho-veled coal, worked on a sealing ship on the Pacific and found employ-ment in a cannery", all in his teenage years, according to the website Biography.com. He wrote his first story in 1893, but interrupted the writing life to join the Yukon gold rush. From 1899, when magazines started publishing his stories, he "made it a practice to write at least a thousand words a day", the site says, and became prosperous in contrast with the poverty of his earlier years. Eventually he produced more than 50 books, as well as journalism, including his coverage of the Russo-Japanese War in 1904. He maintained a keen interest in social justice and the rights of workers, themes that appear both in his journalism and in such fiction as his 1908 dystopian novel *The Iron Heel*.

Mata Hari, otherwise **Margaretha MacLeod**, née **Zelle** (1876-1917), was an exotic dancer and seductress who was executed for spying on behalf of Germany during World War I. She grew up in the Nether-lands and lived for a time with her husband in the East Indies, where she studied eastern dance. By 1905 she was a notable exotic dancer in Paris using her adopted name, Mata Hari, or "the sun", and posing as Javanese. Her specialty was performances and photographs in which she was nude except for a jewelled bra and headgear. She kept com-pany with wealthy and influential men and, as World War I ap-proached, politicians and military leaders. She was arrested in Paris in February 1917, convicted of espionage, and executed by firing squad.

Thubten Gyatso (1876-1933) was the 13th Dalai Lama, described by a Buddhism web site as "a true temporal and spiritual leader who guided his people through a firestorm of challenges to the survival of Tibet". He was taken to Lhasa as a toddler, having been recognized as the suc-cessor of the 12th Dalai Lama, **Trinle Gyatso**, who died in April 1875. He would thus have been front and centre when Sherlock Holmes made his alleged visit to "the head lama" in 1892, though he did not receive authority as the ruler until 1895. Tibet at that period was independent, but under some influence from China and much attention from Britain and Russia, competing for power in what was dubbed "the grand game". Maintaining Tibet's independence, in the context of tumultuous events in China, was the life's work of the 13th Dalai Lama.

Isadora Duncan (1877-1927) was a dancer whose performances, according to a critic in 1905, gave "the sense of a glorious nakedness". She is considered the pioneer of modern dance. "Her style of dancing eschewed the rigidity of ballet," says the website of the foundation that bears her name, noting her "free-flowing costumes, bare feet, and loose hair". Her style of living was also ostentatiously free, and she bore two children out of wedlock, one of them to theatrical designer **Edward Gordon Craig**. Her unusual first name is shared by Isadora Klein of "The Three Gables", whose life was also unconventional. Duncan was born in San Francisco, left home at 18, and was dancing in Europe when she was 22; her breakthrough came in Budapest in 1902. She established schools of dance in Berlin, Paris and Moscow. Her death was as flamboyant as her life: her flowing scarf was caught by the wheel of a sports car in which she was riding in Nice.

Frank Westwood (1877-1894) was the victim of a dramatic murder in Toronto in October 1894. Someone came to the door of the family mansion and, when he came to the door, shot him through the chest. He lived long enough to describe the assailant as a slim young man with a mustache. Weeks later, **Clara Ford**, described in the fashion of the time as "a mulatto tailoress", was arrested and, after gruelling interrogation, confessed: she had disguised herself in male costume and shot Westwood because he had teased her about her colour and tried to take liberties with her. Arthur Conan Doyle, on his way to Toronto during his North American lecture tour, was asked for an opinion. "Strangely absorbing," he called the mystery. When the case came to trial, Ford denied every-

thing, and was acquitted in short order. Historians' consensus is that Ford, who was acquitted, did shoot the young man, out of sexual jealousy or revenge.

Karl Baedeker (1877-1914) was a chemistry researcher and professor at Germany's University of Jena, where he did pioneering studies of semiconductors, in particular cuprous iodide. He was killed in action at Liège, Belgium, in the opening days of World War I. He was a grandson of **Karl Baedeker** (1801-1859), founder of the publishing house that bears his name and is best known for tourist guidebooks. The English-language guide to Switzerland, including the Reichenbach Falls, was first published in 1863.

Maurice Costello (1877-1950) played the title role in a 1905 film, "Adventures of Sherlock Holmes; or, Held for Ransom", which is considered the first serious moving picture of Holmes's adventures. Publication of the *Return* stories had just been completed, and the stories of *His Last Bow* were still in the future. **H. Kyrle Bellew** played Watson in the eight-minute film, which was directed by **J. Stuart Blackton** and released by Vitagraph Studios. Born in Pittsburgh, Costello acted on the vaudeville stage in the 1890s before launching his film career, which included dozens of films up to the 1940s, though his success was primarily in the silent-movie era.

Sir **Bernard Spilsbury** (1877-1947) performed an estimated 20,000 autopsies during his years as pathologist for the Home Office. (Index cards noting his findings in some 7,000 of those examinations survive.) Educated at Oxford and at St. Mary's Hospital, London, he started work as a pathologist at St. Mary's in 1905, and after the *Harvey Crippen* murder prosecution in 1910 he was called into one high-profile investigation after another. He appeared in court, a widely-recognized dapper figure testifying for the prosecution, in dozens of front-page cases including the *George Joseph Smith* "brides in the bath" murders. He was popularly considered to be infallible, although judges began to express some doubt in later years; modern researchers have identified a number of cases in which he contributed to miscarriages of justice. Spilsbury committed suicide by gas in his laboratory at University College, London.

William Hope Hodgson (1877-1918) was the creator of "Carnacki, the Ghost-Finder", who first appeared in a book of stories under that title published in 1913. He wrote much other fantasy, horror and science fiction as well between 1904 and his death, and was praised by **H. P. Lovecraft** for his "serious treatment of unreality". Horror on the water was his specialty, as he drew atmosphere and stories from his years as a cabin boy and a sailor. "The theme of bullying of an apprentice by older seamen, and revenge taken, appeared frequently in his sea stories," Wikipedia notes. Hodgson was killed in World War I, during the Battle of Ypres in April 1918.

Edward Plunkett, 18th Baron **Dunsany** (1878-1957), was a soldier (wounded during Ireland's 1916 Easter Rising), chess and pistol champion of Ireland, a cricketer, a campaigner for animal rights, and the author of more than 60 books, as well as plays and poems, under the name of "Lord Dunsany". His best known works are fantasy short stories, mostly published from 1905 to 1919, notably the collection *The Gods of Pegana*, which introduced his own imaginary world. (He is thought to have been a major influence on **H. P. Lovecraft** and, more recently,

Neil Gaiman.) Half a dozen books beginning in the 1930s are made up of stories told by "Jorkens", a clubman who has travelled the world and seen many strange things.

Albert Einstein (1879-1955) was a high school graduate in 1896, having dropped out of one school in his native Germany, become an accomplished violinist, written a scientific paper on "the ether in a magnetic field", renounced his German citizenship to avoid the draft, and been persuaded to give formal education another try in Switzerland. He received a science teaching diploma in 1900 from the Zurich Polytechnic, went to work in the Swiss patent office (having failed to find a teaching job), and married in 1903. In 1905 he completed doctoral work at the University of Zurich, and published four major scientific papers including one on "special relativity" and one on the relationship between mass and energy. In 1908 he joined the University of Bern as a lecturer. Still ahead were his reputation as the world's greatest scientist, his fully formed theory of relativity, the popularity of his equation involving the speed of light squared, his move to the United States, and the 1921 Nobel Prize in physics.

James Branch Cabell (1879-1958) came from the Virginia aristocracy and was the author of some 52 books including 18 that make up the *Biography of the Life of Manuel* in novels, poetry and essays. His best-known book waas *Jurgen, a Comedy of Justice* (1919), which was the subject of a two-year obscenity lawsuit. Cabell seemed to attract scandals, including rumours (all disproved) about homosexual orgies and a family murder. In the 1934 essay collection *Ladies and Gentlemen*, he drew attention to his 18th-century ancestor **Richard Cabell** of Buckfastleigh, Devon, whose tomb is the centre of legends about a spectral hound. He asserted that the historic Cabell was the original of Sir Hugo Baskerville, and that Arthur Conan Doyle had "made out of your legend a striking book" in the form of *The Hound of the Baskervilles*.

Lily Loder-Symonds (1879-1916) was a close friend of Arthur Conan Doyle's second wife, **Jean Leckie**, and bridesmaid at their wedding in 1907. By 1914 she was living at Windlesham, the Doyles' house in Sussex, and looked after the three children while ACD and his wife toured North America. Always frail, she was almost bedridden with lung troubles by 1915, and suffered a major blow with the death of three brothers in the battles around Ypres that spring. She began to receive messages from her brothers through "automatic writing", a recognized technique of Spiritualist communication; late in 1915 she also reported a message from Jean's brother, ***Malcolm Leckie***, who had died the previous year, including details that ACD was confident only he and Malcolm could have known. The incident was a major impulse behind ACD's public profession of faith in Spiritualism late in 1916, after Loder-Symonds's death.

Nancy Astor, formerly **Shaw**, née **Langhorne**, Viscountess **Astor** (1879-1965), came to Britain from Virginia in 1897, newly divorced and bringing along her young son. Like the American beauties referred to in "The Noble Bachelor", she soon married into the aristocracy, with a wedding to **William Waldorf Astor** in 1906. They had five children by the time Astor's father died in 1919 and he became the 2nd Viscount Astor, and thus had to leave his seat in the House of Commons to enter the House of Lords. Nancy won the election to succeed him as the Conservative member for Plymouth Sutton, becoming the first woman ever to take a seat in Parliament. She remained an MP until 1945, with policies that included temperance, women's rights, and the determination (represented by prime minister **Neville Chamberlain**) to prevent a second world war by appeasing German aggression. The Astors entertained lavishly at Cliveden, their house in Buckinghamshire.

Charles 'Bert' Massey (1880-1915) was a wealthy Toronto ne'er-do-well, a grandson of businessman and philanthropist **Hart Massey** (1823-1896), and the victim in a notorious homicide. Massey, who worked as a motor-car salesman, was shot to death at his own front door by a maidservant he had attempted to rape. The maid, **Carrie Davies**, was found not guilty of murder. Charlotte Gray's 2013 book about the case, *The Massey Murder: A Maid, Her Master and the Trial That Shocked a Country*, was a best-seller. Other grandsons of Hart Massey, whose fortune largely came from the Massey-Harris (Massey-Ferguson) farm equipment company, included **Vincent Massey**, a Governor-General of Canada, and actor **Raymond Masssey**, who played Sherlock Holmes on screen in "The Speckled Band" (1931).

Malcolm Leckie (1880-1914) was a physician (a graduate of Guy's Hospital, near the Southwark end of London Bridge) who joined the Royal Army Medical Corps shortly after he finished his training in 1908. He served for several years with the army in Egypt and Sudan, and when World War I began he was assigned to the 1st Northumberland Fusiliers. The regiment was sent to France in mid-August 1914 and was in action within ten days. As the soldiers retreated, a number of wounded men were left behind and were taken prisoner by German forces. Among them was Leckie, who died five days later in the convent hospital at Frameries. He was the first of 903 medical officers to be killed during the four-year war. His older sister, **Jean Leckie**, had married Arthur Conan Doyle in 1907, and the brothers-in-law had become friends. His death was one of the incidents that led ACD to become a public advocate of Spiritualism after the war, and he maintained that Leckie's spirit had sent him unmistakable messages from beyond the grave.

Wilhelmina (1880-1962) was Queen of the Netherlands for 58 years, from the death of her father, King *William III*, in 1890 to her abdication in 1948 in favour of her daughter, who became Queen **Juliana**. She was thus the head of "the reigning family of Holland", for whom Sherlock Holmes supposedly provided a service ("A Scandal in Bohemia"). Britain's Queen *Victoria*, whom she visited in 1895, described Wilhelmina as "very intelligent and very cute". Her mother, the dowager Queen **Emma**, served as regent until Wilhelmina reached the age of 18, when she was enthroned, with celebrations that emphasized the role of women and involved women from the country's Indonesian possessions as well as the strictly Dutch. In 1901 she married Duke **Henry of Mecklenburg-Schwerin**. At the time of the South African War she was hostile to Britain, and she kept the Netherlands neutral in World War I despite concern about Germany's intentions.

Vincenzo Peruggia (1881-1925) stole the Mona Lisa one August day in 1911 — a crime worthy, some authors of fiction have thought, of Professor Moriarty. He had formerly worked in the Louvre, the Paris museum where the Leonardo da Vinci painting resides, and knew the routine: he hid overnight, emerged wearing a staff uniform, lifted the painting off its pegs, and walked out with it. Some two years later he tried to sell it to a gallery in Florence, apparently believing that *La Gioconda* should be returned to her homeland. Police were notified; Peruggia was arrested and served seven months in prison.

Douglas Fairbanks, born **Ullman** (1883-1939), was the host for the first Academy Awards ceremony (1929), reflecting his status as one of Hollywood's top stars of all time. That was in the days of silent films, when Fairbanks played the swashbuckling, athletic hero in "The Mark of Zorro" (1920), "Robin Hood" (1922), and "The Thief of Bagdad" (1924). With *Mary Pickford*, *Charlie Chaplin*, and director **D. W. Griffith**, he formed United Artists in 1919. Fairbanks and Pickford were married in 1920, and were well known for entertaining at their mansion Pickfair. Arthur Conan Doyle met the couple, the greatest celebrities of their day, in Los Angeles in 1923. Fairbanks did not make a successful transition to the era of sound films, with "The Taming of the Shrew" (1929), starring him opposite Pickford, being a notable flop. They were divorced in 1936.

Maude Fealy, born **Maude Mary Hawk** (1883-1971), was a stage and film actress whose career included a year playing Alice Faulkner, the heroine of *William Gillette*'s play "Sherlock Holmes". She was 18 when she first played the role during Gillette's 1901-1902 tour of Britain; Gillette, playing Holmes, was 48. Her Broadway debut had been the previous year, in "Quo Vadis", based on the successful 1896 novel by **Henryk Sienkiewicz**; her mother, **Margaret Fealy**, was also in the cast. Maude Fealy stayed in England for several years after the Gillette tour, performing with *Henry Irving*'s company. She made nearly 20 silent films between 1911 and 1917, and later was a playwright and acting coach.

Marjorie Bowen, real name **Gabrielle Long**, née **Campbell** (1885-1952) was a prolific author of horror and suspense novels as well as books in other genres. Her first novel, *The Viper of Milan*, was written at the turn of the century, when she was 16 years old, but was not published until 1906, allegedly because publishers did not think a teenage girl ought to be encouraged to write about hideously cruel nobles in mediaeval Italy. (The book, with its dark fatalistic outlook, is said to have been a major influence on **Graham Greene**.) She continued writing, in a clear and practised style, without interruption for half a century. For years she was the only support of an impoverished, dysfunctional family, and happiness came late in her life, with her second marriage and two children.

Lily **Elsie**, birth name **Elsie Hodder**, formerly **Cotton** (1886-1962), was an actress, a little too late to be one of "the celebrities and beauties of the day" whose photographs Holmes and Watson see in a window at the end of the story "Charles Augustus Milverton". Hundreds of pictures of her were for sale, showing off that "perfect Grecian profile, enormous blue eyes, and hauntingly sad smile", as a website in her honour now says. Born in Leeds, she had a step-father who worked in theatre, and as a child she appeared in the music halls as "Little Elsie". She became a chorus girl, then an instant star as Sonia in "The Merry Widow" at Daly's Theatre in London in 1907, for impresario **George Edwardes**. "Her face adorned chocolate boxes, biscuit tins, and advertisements for cosmetics," the website notes, and *David Lloyd George* was among her fans. "I'm always rude to men," she once said, "and the ruder I am the more they like me." She married the wealthy **Ian Bullough** in 1911, and returned to the stage only briefly a few years later.

Alfonso XIII (1886-1941) was King of Spain from his birth, his father **Alfonso XII** having died during his mother's pregnancy. Early in his reign, Spain lost many colonial possessions through the Spanish-American War. He was able to keep his country neutral during World War I, but he became unpopular following a colonial war in Morocco. After a left-wing republic was proclaimed in 1931, Alfonso went into exile, although he did not formally abdicate until 1941, following the bloody Spanish Civil War. Alfonso was an enthusiastic booster of Spanish tourism, and a patron of sports teams including Real ("royal") Madrid FC. He married **Victoria Eugenie of Battenberg**, a daughter of Britain's Princess *Beatrice Mary*.

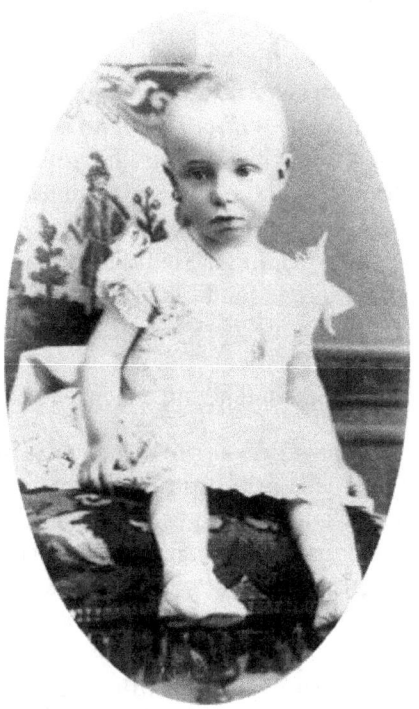

Charlie Chaplin, later **Sir Charles Chaplin** (1889-1977), was British-born, the son of music hall artiste **Hannah Chaplin** (**Lily Harley**), and began his long entertainment career with stage appearances in London. In the fall of 1905 he took the role of Billy the pageboy in *William Gillette*'s curtain-raiser "The Painful Predicament of Sherlock Holmes" and his full-length "Sherlock Holmes". Coming to the United States, in a company headed by comedian *Fred Karno*, he began making films in 1914, first for Keystone Studios and other companies, then as a co-owner of United Artists. He is an icon of the silent film era as "the Little Tramp", notably in "The Gold Rush" (1925), "Modern Times" (1936), and "The Great Dictator" (1940). Expressing political views through his films led to charges during and after World War II that he was a Communist, and when he went to Britain for the premiere of "Limelight" in 1952 he was not allowed to return to the United States for some 20 years.

Gilbert John Cubitt (1891-1977) was the young son of the proprietress at the Hill House hotel in Happisburgh, Norfolk, **Emma Cubitt** née **Elden**, when Arthur Conan Doyle stayed there in 1903. ACD signed his name in an autograph book in which young Cubitt had already drawn a series of stick figures representing letters of the alphabet, and his sister **Edith Alice Cubitt** had drawn similar figures on a musical staff. Those drawings are likely the source of the cipher in the story "The Dancing Men", though other stick-figure alphabets have also existed, including one in *St. Nicholas* magazine in 1874. The hero of the story is named Hilton Cubitt, presumably for the boy and his family. Gilbert Cubitt spent much of his life as a Royal Air Force instructor, and served in both world wars. The autograph album is now owned by the Toronto Public Library.

Mary Pickford, born **Gladys Smith** (1892-1979), was a leading lady in the glamorous age of silent films, though her most successful roles were as little girls. Born in Toronto, she acted on stage from the age of 7, and in 1909 began acting for film director **D. W. Griffith** of Biograph. She then moved to Famous Players, making features such as "Rebecca of Sunnybrook Farm" (1917). Along with Griffith, *Charlie Chaplin*, and **Douglas Fairbanks**, she formed United Artists in 1919; she married Fairbanks the next year. Arthur Conan Doyle met the couple, the greatest celebrities of their day, in Los Angeles in 1923 and described Pickford as "intensely psychic, with many gifts of the spirit". She did not adapt well to the advent of sound in film, or the need to play more adult roles; her last major screen appearance was in 1933.

Marjorie Kay (1898-1949) was the actress who played Alice Faulkner — the heroine, modelled in part on Irene Adler — in the 1916 film "Sherlock Holmes". At the very end of the film, and of the 1899 play by *William Gillette* on which it is based, Alice has a romantic moment with Holmes, played by Gillette himself. A daughter of Detroit society, and still a teenager when she acted with Gillette, Kay joined the US Naval Nurse Corps shortly after making the film. She served at a hospital at Neuilly-sur-Seine and possibly other hospitals, and drove an ambulance. (Supervising the American nurses was **Anne Harriman Sands Rutherford Vanderbilt**, a pillar of New York society.) Kay returned to the United States with a souvenir belt to which were attached 154 military buttons, collar ornaments, shoulder badges, hat badges and belt buckles from Allied armies and even those of Germany and Austria. She posed for a Red Cross fund-raising poster, performed on Broadway in 1920, and reportedly sang with **Enrico Caruso** at the Metropolitan Opera. In later years she ran an entertainment bureau and dance studio in Hartford, Connecticut. Her final husband was **William L. Anderson**.

Index

Page numbers in **bold type** indicate a full biography; page numbers in light type indicate a mention in someone else's biography. Names connected by an ampersand (&) are spouses, siblings, or parent and child.

Also from MX Publishing

MX Publishing is the world's largest specialist Sherlock Holmes publisher, with over a hundred titles and fifty authors creating the latest in Sherlock Holmes fiction and non-fiction.

From traditional short stories and novels to travel guides and quiz books, MX Publishing caters for all Holmes fans.

The collection includes leading titles such as Benedict Cumberbatch In Transition and The Norwood Author which won the 2011 Howlett Award (Sherlock Holmes Book of the Year).

MX Publishing also has one of the largest communities of Holmes fans on Facebook with regular contributions from dozens of authors.

www.mxpublishing.com

Also from MX Publishing

Our bestselling short story collections 'Lost Stories of Sherlock Holmes', 'The Outstanding Mysteries of Sherlock Holmes', 'Untold Adventures of Sherlock Holmes' (and the sequel 'Studies in Legacy') and 'Sherlock Holmes in Pursuit'.

Also from MX Publishing

Sherlock Holmes and The Adventure of The Grinning Cat

"Joseph Svec, III is brilliant in entwining two endearing and enduring classics of literature, blending the factual with the fantastical; the playful with the pensive; and the mischievous with the mysterious. We shall, all of us young and old, benefit with a cup of tea, a tranquil afternoon, and a copy of Sherlock Holmes, The Adventure of the Grinning Cat."

Linda Hein, Hein & Co Used Books, and founding officer of the Amador County Holmes Hounds Sherlockian Society